The Outside Lomcovak Club presents:

Lady Caine

by
Steve Mansfield-Devine

For the original Delicious Tricia

International Edition, first published 2009
Copyright © Steve Mansfield-Devine 2009

The right of Steve Mansfield-Devine to be identified as the author has been asserted in accordance with the UK Copyright, Design and Patents Act 1988.

All rights reserved: no part of this publication may be reproduced, stored in a retrieval system, or transmitted in any form or by any means, electronic, mechanical, photocopying, recording, or otherwise without the prior written permission of the Author. This book may not be lent, resold, hired out or otherwise disposed of by way of trade in any form of binding or cover other than that in which it is published without the prior written consent of the Author.

This novel is a work of fiction. Names, characters, places, and incidents are either the products of the author's imagination or are used fictitiously, and any resemblance to actual persons, living or dead, business establishments, events or locales, is entirely coincidental.

Published by WebVivant Press, Normandy, France
www.webvivant.com/books/

The Outside Lomcovak Club
www.lomcovak.com

ISBN: 978-0-9561514-0-7

Somewhere in the Americas ...

... some time around 1995

1: Unplanned ground encounter

Maybe it's concussion, thought Walkaway. He touched the bruise on his forehead, fell to his knees and threw up. He spat out the last chunks of his lunch and thought, Does concussion feel like this?

He sat on the ground, his back to a palm tree, his eyes narrowed against the glare of his burning aircraft. He wiped vomit from his chin and used his sleeve to sponge the sweat from his brow. He was very pleased with himself.

The wrecked plane crackled and spat but no longer roared the way it had when Walkaway had first stumbled from the broken fuselage. The flames waved lazily now, and the shadows they cast around the darkening airstrip seemed to lack enthusiasm. He watched the smoke lift into the air, rising straight at first, in the shelter of the trees. Then it twisted in the breeze that blew it west.

Apart from the shadows, he was alone. The short dark strip had no buildings, nothing man-made other than the reddish gash of the runway cut through the palms, the sea glittering at one end, the beckoning darkness of the trees at the other.

The horizon also burned red where the sun had gone down. Its glow was feeble now and quickly yielded to ink blue and then the cool black of the arriving night.

Walkaway noticed a rip in his America West captain's jacket and wondered how long it had been there. His pants were from a Delta uniform and appeared to be fine, as were the Nikes. These he'd found in a locker that he believed to be his but which, on later reflection, he realized had been merely unlocked. He was wearing odd socks and spent a moment trying to work out which one was correct.

Walkaway stroked the briefcase on the ground next to him. A charge ran through his fingertips from the stippled texture of the case. He knew it contained answers if he could only formulate the right questions. He hadn't opened it yet: he was sure that its contents wouldn't make any sense to him now, and he couldn't bear to look at a puzzle until all the pieces were in place. And for that to happen he needed help.

The Piper Seneca blazing on the runway was his first step in summoning that help. As far as his employers were concerned, it was in the wrong place at the wrong time. But they wouldn't be worrying about the plane. They'd be thinking of the briefcase too.

Something moved to his right. He turned and stared and could just discern the outline of a small animal — maybe a chipmunk, he thought, or a rabbit, or perhaps something previously undiscovered or something thought extinct. He wanted to touch it, but it was too far away. The breeze caught the edges of the shape and lifted it gently, and Walkaway saw that it was a collection of leaves and litter. He spoke to it anyway.

"I've never done anything," he confessed to the litter creature, "nothing that meant a damned thing because how do you know what you should do? I push at the world and it pushes back harder. But maybe," and here he tapped the briefcase, "maybe because of me, something will happen now." He stroked the case, and examined the numbers set in the combination locks, trying to read them as a code. This is my lever, he thought. I guess it could have been a bomb or a play or an assassination or two terms as president, but this is it.

Walkaway wasn't sure if he'd spoken aloud. He nodded to the litter creature. "I guess it doesn't make much difference to you, does it? Thoughts or words. Pretty much the same."

He sighed and his head swam. He leaned back, rested his head against the tree, basked in the heat of the fire.

Something made his forehead tickle. He removed his TWA crew cap and rubbed the skin. When he pulled his hand away he found his fingertips covered with what he thought might be blood. It looked, smelled, tasted and felt like blood. He put his hand to his ear and rubbed his fingers together. There was no noise, but then he wasn't sure what sound blood should make. Ah well, four out of five ain't bad, he thought. I must be bleeding.

Walkaway worried for a few moments about the possibility of a scar. He had lasted for forty years without picking up a single distinguishing feature. He liked to describe himself as average. Medium height, medium build, brown hair and a characterless face were part of his professional equipment. In a job where descriptions are dangerous, Walkaway had mastered the art of being forgettable.

He closed his eyes and breathed deeply, clearing his mind. As he relaxed he felt himself washed by warm air, the crackle of the fire and the distant sound of the surf. In the dying minutes of daylight, as he'd made his final approach, he'd got a good view of this tiny island, with its dirt strip on one side and fishing hamlet on the other. Walkway didn't know its name and wasn't even sure of its exact location. But he was certain it was far enough away from where he was meant to be.

He was sticky with drying sweat and felt the urge to wash. He looked up at the sky to see if it might rain, but it was cloudless.

To kill time, he flipped open his logbook and began to record the details of the flight. He hesitated over the 'Number of Landings' column and then wrote *1*. In the 'Remarks' section he put *Unplanned ground encounter. Non-fatal*. Looking at the completed entry, he had a twinge of unease. Filling in the log always felt like a confession.

It was a large logbook and contained the dates, times, hows and wheres of every flight Walkaway had made as a pilot, at least in the nineties. Other logbooks covered previous decades, but they were lost now. Most of the entries meant nothing to him anyway. Some evoked flashbacks of varying degrees of detail, though he was unwilling to make any connection between the images in his head and the data on the page. The entries were in his own spidery, haphazard hand and so he accepted the information as fact. The images, however, were spontaneous and uncontrollable, and he was reluctant to grant them anything more than circumstantial status.

He put the logbook away and relaxed, gazing up at the sky which was filled with stars now that the sun was down and the light from the wreck was ebbing. Walkaway tried to put together some of the pieces of the past few weeks, but it just made the dizziness worse. There was no clear path to this moment, to his being lost in the Caribbean. Even Walkaway's flight planning had contained an element of chance. Deliberately, he had failed to account for winds aloft, so that he had drifted where the breeze took him. He thought that would give him a big enough margin of error. If I don't know where I am, he thought, how can they?

He always drew comfort from being lost. He knew it was a problem he could fix if the need arose. This time, he knew the shape of the island, and with a good map and a few hours' effort he could probably pin down the location precisely: at least as precisely as the map would allow, if the map's information was good and not just the hallucinatory doodlings of a demented cartographer, or liar, or someone labouring under a misplaced trust in the categorical precision of geography, or a madman. Or he could ask someone, perhaps. Someone in the nearby village. If they said the same thing as the map, perhaps they could be trusted. Or he could use what they said as a working proposition until he encountered some contradictory information.

Walkaway smiled. It was a plan, of sorts.

Still confused, but a little rested, he rose and went looking for a boat to steal.

2:
You want him dead, right?

José shifted the Uzi to a more comfortable position. He rested the folded-out stock on his hip. He had to place it carefully so as not to put a crimp in his suit. With his other hand he ran a finger around the sodden collar of his shirt. Fuck this jungle, he thought.

For the past couple of minutes he'd watched a strange, long-nosed animal that had emerged from the jungle and now snuffled around the edges of the clearing. The sun was still low and the clearing a place of dank, simmering shadows. José had trouble following the movements of the animal.

"Hey, man," he yelled to Jesus. "Take a look at the bear."

Jesus ignored him and pretty soon José went back to brooding about his suit. It hadn't made him nearly as happy as he'd thought it would.

Jesus had got his first, in Nassau, on their latest run to the Keys. They had stopped in the Bahamas to pick up gas for the boats before making the tricky part of the trip into US territory. While José pumped fuel, he saw Jesus make off towards the port exit.

"What the fuck you think you doin'?"

"Going shopping."

As soon as the tank was full, José went after him. He found Jesus coming out of an outlet store. He wore a dark blue, double-breasted suit with a chalk stripe, high-buttoned with lapels that reached almost to his shoulders. The pants were baggy and had large cuffs.

"You look like a fucking gangster," said José. Jesus flushed with pride.

Then they hit Miami, offloaded the consignment and laid low, waiting to get paid. The boss took them to a part of the city José had never seen before. "No-one knows us here," the boss explained. José knew better than to ask why that was important.

Their hide-out was a flea-bitten motel attached to a half-derelict strip mall. One of the few remaining stores was Fancy Joe's Designer Boutique and Sporting Goods and in the window, next to the shotguns, pup tents and survival gear were several suits of a lustre José had never previously experienced. He knew at once that he must have the blue one. Jesus would covet the blue one.

He was in the store for no more than twenty minutes. He came out with a box of .44 magnum shells, a clasp knife with a built-in flashlight, an overdue change of underwear . . . and the suit. The next day he went back for a set of Armani labels. He was planning to sew them into the jacket as soon as he worked out how.

It was the best suit he'd ever owned, though it sometimes threw off sparks. Now it was ruined, creased beyond repair and spattered with mud.

Fuck this fucking jungle, he thought.

His hand moved to his throat to loosen his tie, but then he noticed that Jesus still had his knotted tight. He let his hand drop. Jesus stood under a tree near the river's edge, staring morosely into the dark, sluggish water, his own Uzi hanging limp by his side. His suit was uncreased. In the dappled light filtering through the overhead camouflage netting, the fabric shimmered as though shot through with silver, or maybe chrome, and hundreds of tiny points of light flared and glittered from the silver jewellery around his wrists and neck.

Fuck Jesus, thought José. He looked back at the clearing that ran fifty yards inland from the river. It had been dynamited out of the jungle and was now occupied mostly by four large huts, several piles of oil drums and assorted construction litter. There was a faint chemical smell that had given José a sore throat on his first day and a weird hum that got on his nerves. Stripped tree trunks held up the camouflage netting that made the clearing relatively cool. Occasionally a person would walk from hut to hut, and every few days a floatplane used the river to land or take off. But the clearing was many miles further upstream than any tourist was likely to venture, and most of the time it gave every impression of desertion.

José had no idea where they were. Jesus said he reckoned they were still in South America, maybe still in Colombia. Neither one of them was sure if Colombia even had jungles like this, as they'd spent their entire adult lives commuting directly between Bogotá and Miami. But Jesus felt sure that if the country did have a jungle, this was it.

José disagreed. Their journey to the clearing had been a seemingly endless nightmare of boats, planes and helicopters that had left José in a near-coma for several hours. He hated the jungle more than anything, but flying ran it a close second. He couldn't bear to think that he'd gone through all that and still not got out of the country.

Jesus turned towards José and spat. "I tell ya man," he said, "when I get the money from this deal, I'm setting up on my own."

"You said that last time. You always say that. I can't remember a time you didn't say that."

"I —"

"— Don't say you mean it this time."

"Well I do."

José mulled this over. "Can I come with you?"

Jesus scowled. "Fuck, I'm bored," he said.

"How about playing a game?" said José.

"Game? What sort of game?"

José looked at his gun, stroked its stubby barrel and pouted. "I don't know. Don't you know any games?"

A huge butterfly staggered past a couple of yards away. José made a pretend pistol out of his fingers and jabbed it at the creature. "Pah! Pah! Pah!" he puffed. As he tracked the butterfly his attention was caught by a movement in the undergrowth. He brought the Uzi to a firing position, but then realized it was the same animal he'd seen before.

"That bear's still there, man," he shouted to Jesus. "Weird."

Jesus turned round slowly and focused on the animal.

"No way, asshole. Ain't no bears 'round here. That's a wolf, man."

"A what?"

"Wolf. Baby wolf."

"Baby nothing. That's a full-grown animal."

"Bullshit."

"Bullshit yourself."

José scowled at Jesus and took an inventory of all the things he hated about the man — his thick curly hair, the body hair peeking from collar and cuffs, the chronic beard stubble, above all his height. José was stocky and just made five foot seven — "average height," he'd boast, "in Colombia". His own hair was thinning: what was left he'd grown long and tied back in an unconvincing pony tail. It took him a week to grow a five o'clock shadow.

Hating Jesus gave José a sense of purpose, and had done for many years. They had grown up together in Florida, among Colombians and Cubans, and their one notable achievement in childhood was that, in spite of their environment and pronounced Latino accents, they both spoke lousy Spanish, pretty much limited to the words for gun, drink, money, drugs and VD clinic. It had built a strong bond between them.

José searched for something to say. His free hand patted his pockets and pulled a book out of his jacket. It was The French Lieutenant's Woman. "You wanna read something?" he said.

"You showed me that already," scowled Jesus.

"It's a war book."

"You said that." Jesus stared off at the jungle.

"It's good shit," said José. "Real literature an' all."

"It'll be bullshit like all the others. What was that gangster book?"

"Crime and Punishment."

"Right. Full o' fucking commies. And that porno book?"

"Lady Chatterley's Lover."

"Did it have any sex in it?"

"I don't know."

"Right. Man, that woman really fucked with your head."

José's love of literature was new. It had started at a party a few weeks before. He was watching his boss's back when a woman he didn't know walked up to him and started talking. That had never happened to José before and, momentarily stunned, he found himself simply listening to her. She kept calling him André, which was okay. She was saying something about literature. About how great writing turned her on. Later, she slipped away without him noticing. But that night left him with a desire to know more. He managed to find a bookstore in Miami and said to the clerk, "I need those books that turn on chicks. What are the good books? I want the best."

The French Lieutenant's Woman fell from his hand. Its pages fluttered and a small piece of card was carried a few feet by a rare and sudden breeze. "Dammit!" spat José. "Now I've lost my place." He made no move to retrieve the book.

"Now this is good shit," said Jesus. He pulled a magazine from his pocket and held it aloft. It was Truck Pull Babes. "It's the swimsuit issue," he beamed.

José edged closer, but Jesus stuffed the magazine back into his jacket, patted his pockets, pulled out a cigarette pack and put a cigarette to his lips. He patted his pockets again then turned to José. "You got a light?"

José felt a tiny tingle of pleasure, as he always did when Jesus needed him. He sensed the cool weight of the Zippo in his trouser pocket against his hot thigh. "No," he said. "Given up."

Suddenly Jesus tilted his head back, his features alert. "You hear that?" he asked.

"What?"

"Someone's coming."

José listened hard. Then his eyebrows rose in recognition. "It's a boat," he said.

"Boat bullshit," said Jesus. "It's a plane."

"Bullshit yourself, that's a boat."

"Plane."

"Boat."

They both listened in silence for a while, until the noise resolved itself unmistakably as a boat.

"Plane," said Jesus.

José gave him what he hoped was a pitying look. At that moment, at the edge of the clearing, the tamandua had finally found what it was looking for — a nice juicy termite mound. Its strong furry tail wrapped around a nearby bush to keep it stable while its forelegs ripped open the nest and its long snout sucked up the insects.

The sound caught José's attention. "It's that fucking bear," he said.

"Wolf."

"For fuck's sake, it's a bear."

"Go screw yourself. It's a wolf."

José levelled his Uzi, pulled the trigger and blew the tamandua into small pieces. "Now it's a nuthin'."

* * *

Rotsky picked a piece of tobacco from his blonde moustache and spent a few happy seconds speculating how long it had been there. His supply of Cubans had run out two days before. Or was it a week? Anyway, he'd definitely been out of cigars for a while. He made a note to look for a moustache brush.

He was in the flying school office, resting on a steamer chair, his feet hanging over the end. Laid out straight, he ran to six foot three. He was wearing mirror shades, and a tie-dyed flying suit, now faded but whose colours retained the ability to dazzle given the right light. As protection against the chill of the air conditioning, he wore a leather A2 flying jacket. In his right hand was a half-full bottle of rum, capped, which he'd been holding on to since the previous evening, unable to pick a moment when he was sure he wouldn't need it anymore. In his left hand was a bill from an aircraft maintenance company. Rotsky kept staring at the numbers but couldn't make any sense of them.

The bill was for work carried out on Rotsky's P-51 Mustang, a World War Two fighter that was being slowly overhauled up at Stead Airfield, north of Reno. It was slow work because Rotsky had an idiosyncratic approach to paying bills.

They can't need this much money, he thought. No-one needs this much money all at once. Rotsky looked at the top of the bill. Sure enough, there was his name and the address of his post office box in Las Vegas. He flipped it over. The other side was blank and Rotsky found this vaguely disturbing, as though something was being kept from him. He flipped it back again and rechecked the figures. They hadn't changed. He examined the arrangement of the words, rather than the words themselves, to see if there might be some meaning in the form of the bill, some message he had missed. There was nothing. He scanned the columns of figures as though reading instruments, as though they might rise and fall as they registered his dissatisfaction with them. The numbers remained resolutely insensitive. Hell then, he thought, that's the way it is.

Rotsky had been getting a lot of bills lately, bills from people he knew had more money than him, had thriving businesses and places to live. It had been many years since Rotsky had lived anywhere, though he stayed lots of places. Mostly he just threw the bills away. Without the money to pay them, holding on to the bills would have been pointless.

There was a rattle as someone opened the main door and let the screen door clap shut behind him. It was the flying school owner, a small, crumpled man in oil-stained overalls, oil-stained baseball cap and a dark, permanent scowl.

"You got visitors," he said. "Men in suits. I hope you're sober, gaddammit."

Rotsky raised an eyebrow. He noticed the owner's blackened hands and smeared face.

"You get that oil filter changed?" he asked.

The owner growled.

"There's a lot needs doing to that plane," said Rotsky. "At least, there's a lot that could be done. We need a proper mechanic around here."

"Oh sure. And are you gonna pay him? I sure as shit can't."

"Did you say 'suits'?"

The owner looked disoriented for a second.

"Oh ... yeah, yeah. They're right outside. Don't look much like customers. Are you in trouble?"

"Do they have dogs?"

"Dogs? Why the fuck would they have dogs? I didn't see no gaddamned dogs."

Rotsky smiled. It might have been disarming if it hadn't been for the previous night's rum still in his veins. It made the left side of his face collapse and his smile twist into a sneer. He stood and immediately realized he needed to piss. But the restroom was a shack the other side of the airfield. He figured he'd better talk to the suits first.

He walked outside into the scorching Nevada sun. It was still early, but already hot and bright. Even with his shades he was dazzled for a second. Rotsky stopped and waited for his eyes to accommodate to the light, though there was little to see. The featureless airfield eventually gave way to barely undulating scrub. There were no trees, and only a couple of buildings, including the one Rotsky had just left. Rotsky loved this landscape — its lack of complication, where nothing was hidden and nothing had to be guessed or assumed.

When his eyes recovered he spotted the two men, dressed in identical dark suits and carrying leather briefcases. They stood in the shade of a Cessna 150's wing.

From a distance, both men were well-built and square-jawed, with cropped hair and new, pink tans. Out-of-towners who had been around for a few days looking for him, Rotsky assumed. If the suits hadn't been so cheap he would have said they were gangsters. As it was, his best guess was feds, maybe FAA.

There was a cough to Rotsky's left. An Elvis impersonator sat under a sun umbrella, sipping an iced tea. Maybe I've forgotten a lesson, thought Rotsky. I'll check later.

Rotsky walked to the aircraft and joined the two men under the wing. It was just high enough for the men to stand beneath it, but too low to be comfortable. They stood facing each other, their heads bowed and their knees slightly bent.

For Rotsky it was a doubly-strange sensation. As he'd approached the men he had found their suits exerting a peculiar effect on him. There was a nervous current in his gut and by the time he joined them he felt three feet tall and six years old. When he tried to look at the men his vision blurred. It was like in his dreams when there would be something of immense significance before him but he couldn't turn his eyes to look at it.

He stared at the men's feet. One of them wore new black Oxfords so shiny that Rotsky could have shaved in them. The other man wore old All Star sneakers, one blue the other green.

"Are you Rotsky?" asked Shiny Shoes with a two-packs-a-day voice.

"Yessir," mumbled Rotsky.

"Excuse me?"

Rotsky tried to look directly at Shiny Shoes, but his head swam, so he peered at the ground again.

"It's possible," he said. "Depends. Who's asking?"

Rotsky realized he was pouting and pulled his lips back in.

Shiny Shoes cleared his throat. "We believe —"

"—believe," interrupted Sneakers. Shiny Shoes rose slightly on the balls of his feet and Rotsky thought he heard him sigh.

"We believe —"

"— just a minute," interrupted Rotsky. "You haven't told me who you are." He made a quick survey of the local area, just to be sure the old man had been right about the dogs. He didn't see any.

"Is that important?" asked Shiny Shoes.

"Well it would help," said Rotsky. He was more confident now that he had something definite to discuss. "Names matter, don't you think? They do to me. Sometimes. Depends on the names, I guess, but anyway it would help me decide if I want my lawyer present."

This was a bluff. Rotsky hadn't had access to a regular lawyer for years. He managed to look up and found Shiny Shoes smiling indulgently. "There's no need for that, really. We are simply working on behalf of our employer who is trying to recover some mislaid property."

"— property," said Sneakers.

"Haven't got it."

"What?"

"— what?" muttered Sneakers.

"Whatever it is that —" started Rotsky, then turned to look at Sneakers. The man's face was blank and his eyes dull. Rotsky turned back to Shiny Shoes. "What's wrong with *him*?" he asked.

"He's on beta blockers," said Shiny Shoes, then seeing the incomprehension on Rotsky's face, added: "They inhibit the effects of adrenaline, help with the stress —"

"— stress," said Sneakers.

Shiny Shoes frowned and pulled a file from his briefcase. He leafed idly through the pages, not really looking at them.

"What do you do?" asked Shiny Shoes.

"When?"

"Well . . . you know . . . most of the time."

"Whatever needs doing."

Shiny Shoes frowned and bit his lower lip. "What do you do for a living?"

"For a living? Fly, mostly. Eat. Drink. Dance when I'm drunk. Sleep. Breathe. Look, listen and smell. Taste and touch whatever needs tasting and touching. Drive or walk. Read and write. Fuck, if I can and it seems the right thing to do. And when it doesn't. But mostly I fly. That's how I live."

"I mean, what exactly is it you do here?" he asked.

"Chief flying instructor."

Shiny Shoes looked around. It was a small airfield — a hut for the office, a small hangar, a gas pump and one other Cessna 150.

"Bit of a come-down, isn't it?" asked Shiny Shoes. "I mean, for a smuggling legend like you?"

"—come down," said Sneakers.

"Smuggling?" said Rotsky. "Who said anything about smuggling?" He felt the ground slip beneath him. Rotsky relied on inertia to keep his world stable, and he sensed these men were a dangerous force.

"I just did."

Rotsky paused. "Yes," he said. "That's right." He noticed how, each time he said something, Shiny Shoes glanced at the documents in his hand, as if to verify what had been said. Yet it was obvious he wasn't reading anything written there. The pointlessness of this act worried Rotsky. He felt that he should have something to do himself. Rotsky flipped open the door of the Cessna, leaned inside and flicked on the master switch. He checked the fuel gauges. One read zero but had an 'INOP' sticker across it, so that meant nothing.

"There's no need to be modest," said Shiny Shoes. "We've done a lot of research into you. You're an interesting guy. No criminal record to speak of. According to our sources at the FBI, CIA and DEA, there isn't a single file with your name on it, though you sure do turn up in a lot of footnotes. You've led a charmed life."

"I get by," said Rotsky over his shoulder. He hit the beacon switch and peered through the rear window to check that the red light atop the tail fin was flashing. It wasn't. Rotsky pulled an INOP sticker from a map pocket and slapped it on the switch. It joined similar stickers on the VOR, ADF, second radio and cigarette lighter. Rotsky turned off the master switch. He removed the control lock and backed out leaving the door open. "All in order," he muttered to himself.

"Maybe so," said Shiny Shoes. "But I've seen your Air Force record, too. You were promising there for a while. Your fitness report says you're well above average intelligence but with a tendency to . . . ah . . ." Shiny Shoes glanced down and shuffled some papers, " . . . 'see the world in an oblique way'. How'd you get so fucked up?"

"Attitude problem, I guess." Rotsky moved towards the tail, running his hand along the skin of the empennage. Shiny Shoes followed him and Sneakers shuffled along behind. They both winced as they moved from the shade of the wing.

"You were busted out for 'incompatibility'," said Shiny Shoes. "What does that mean?"

"I was a pacifist." Rotsky rocked the elevator up and down. He noticed that the hinges were a little rusty and the ground wire was frayed. He walked around to the right side of the aircraft.

"You were a fighter pilot," insisted Shiny Shoes.

"I was a pilot who flew fighters. Does that make me a fighter pilot?"

"Well . . . yes."

"Well, maybe." Rotsky was at the wing now. He peered at the aileron hinges and ran his eye along the underside skin of the wing. It undulated gently, but nothing that might suggest a damaged spar. "You sure do know a lot about me. That means you're feds, right?"

"Anyone can get that stuff if they want it bad enough." Shiny Shoes paused for a moment. "You know, the information we have on you makes for interesting reading. I think there are some connections that the authorities haven't noticed. If they ever put it all together, you could be in real trouble."

"— trouble," said Sneakers.

"Wow, that's scary." Rotsky kicked the right tyre, moved to the nose, unhooked the Dzus fasteners and opened the engine cover. He checked for loose or worn wires, cracked engine mounts and bird nests, then unscrewed and lifted the dip stick. Four quarts. "Is that a threat?"

"No sir. Merely apprising you of the situation. My friend here has the threat, but before that, let me ask you a question. We understand you know a certain Guy Renouf."

"Maybe." Rotsky was a little unnerved. There were names that, when introduced into a conversation by a man in a suit, probably meant trouble, maybe even a long prison sentence.

There was a silence during which Rotsky felt the power of the suits reassert their hold. To break it, he turned back to the aircraft. He kicked the nosewheel tyre and ran his hand along the leading edges of the prop. There were several small nicks that might have to be filed out soon. Rotsky counted four screws missing from the engine cowlings.

"Walkaway Renouf? Yeah I know him. Well I knew *a* Walkaway Renouf, if it's the same guy. Haven't seen him in a while, though. Not since . . . well, not in a while."

"That's a shame. The organization we represent —"

"So you're not feds?"

"We never said we were."

Rotsky checked the static port and kicked the left wheel. He moved out to the left wingtip. He pulled a dead wasp from the pitot tube and the aileron hinges showed signs of rust. "She's a beaut," he pronounced.

Shiny Shoes cocked his head to one side and gave Rotsky a quizzical look.

"Can you tell me why you're hopping around like that?"

Rotsky realized he was rocking from foot to foot.

"I need to piss," he said.

"Oh yeah, that's right. Some kind of medical problem, yes?"

"Shrapnel," said Rotsky. "Caught a SAM over Vietnam. Lost half my bladder."

Shiny Shoes shuffled some of the papers in the file.

"Well, that's weird," he said. "According to your medical insurance claim you had an entire bladder up until a year ago, when the doctors took that varicose vein out of it."

"— varicose," muttered Sneakers.

Rotsky glared in reply.

"Let's get down to business," said Shiny Shoes. "We know that—"

"Did you say 'organization'?"

Shiny Shoes mentally backtracked.

"Yes, that's right. Mr Renouf worked for us for a while as a . . . company pilot. We thought you might know where we could find him."

In spite of his dizziness, Rotsky smiled. "Walkaway? Your company pilot? You still got any aircraft?"

Neither of the suits smiled.

"So what'd he do? Heist the company Lear?"

"We didn't say that Mr Renouf had taken anything, simply that we wished to talk to him."

"Can't help you."

"Oh we think you can. Maybe you don't know where he is right now, but we think you can find him. And when you do, I want you to call us."

Shiny Shoes handed Rotsky a business card. It was blank except for a hand-written, out-of-town phone number. Rotsky glanced at it then stuck it in one of the pockets of his flying suit.

"Any reason why I should?" he asked.

"You may remember I mentioned a threat," said Shiny Shoes. "I'll hand you over to my colleague."

Sneakers now looked directly at Rotsky. His face cleared slightly, as though he'd just remembered something pleasant. He stepped forward, pulled some papers from his briefcase and smiled like a man who enjoys his job.

* * *

Another tiny wave rolled across the river and slapped gently against the small boat. Enrico Díaz tightened his grip on the sides and closed his eyes. Behind him, a stinking peasant fiddled with the stalled outboard motor.

Díaz was aware of the pitted aluminium under his fingers. He hated boats — any boats. He especially hated metal boats because he couldn't see how anything made of metal could float. The fact that they did just terrified him all the more. He had almost turned back when he first stepped into it and felt it give beneath his weight. But it was the only transport to where he needed to go. That's why he was travelling upstream in, what seemed to him, a foolishly small vessel, not much more than a row boat with an asthmatic engine, driven by a half-mad *pastuso* up a . . . well, *something*-infested river.

It was early morning, the sun not fully risen, and the jungle squatted ragged black along the edges of the river, swaddled in mist, harbouring god knows what malevolent beasts. Díaz cautiously opened his eyes and glowered at it accusingly, head turning from side to side as if in unwilling disbelief at the jungle's treachery in offering no refuge from the boat. The tormented screech of unseen animals wafted unceasingly from the darkness.

The peasant noticed Díaz's discomfort. "Never get out of the boat," he cackled.

Díaz had tried to hire a floatplane and found that his credit was no longer good. The pilot threw copies of unpaid bills at Díaz and screamed about how hauling his huge ass around the skies had played hell with the plane's fuel consumption. "If my men were here, you would not be so disrespectful," Díaz had yelled as he retreated through the door.

Díaz thought he detected the work of other, faceless agents at work in the matter of his cancelled credit. Any other time he would have brooded over this. Right now he couldn't get the words "huge ass" out of his mind.

Bearing Díaz's two hundred and seventy pounds left the boat with only a few inches of freeboard. Now and then the cold water splashed his fingers, carrying with it, he imagined, vile prehistoric diseases from the jungle.

"*Jodido!*" cursed the peasant. Díaz heard bangs and rattles and then a tubercular grumble as the engine came back to life. The boat eased forward and Díaz couldn't resist a sigh of relief. The river terrified him, but it was better than what he'd just left.

It had started out as an ordinary Corporation board meeting, a chance for the tough guys to hang out and admire the size of each other's egos. All the big shots were there, from the Medellín, Cali and Bogotá cartels and the major Miami distributors. Díaz was feeling pleased with himself. This was his first major Corporation convention. He'd earned his place at the table with a daring, large-scale smuggling scam involving dolphins, condoms and a travelling aquatic animal show. It had ended in disaster, like most of his schemes, but he knew that his colleagues appreciated the genius of the concept. It felt like he was finally starting to move up in the world.

Only a day into the convention, the boss had called the meeting to order. He slapped his fat hand on a table and bellowed, "Let's get down to business."

As the conventioneers settled themselves into armchairs and bean bags, the boss surveyed the room with an air of patrician menace. Finally, as silence fell, he started.

"You all know me."

This was a bad start for Díaz. No-one knew the boss's name. Most of the men just called him *El Jefe*. But Díaz, who was from Polk County, had always called him Jeff.

"This is a time of war," beamed Jeff. "We are the generals in the War on Drugs. And as you all know, when there's a war, people get rich." He patted the stomach that was threatening to burst from his Tommy Hilfiger jacket. "Many of you have done great things." He scanned the room without his gaze ever alighting on Díaz. "Some of you have performed less well." Now he looked straight at Díaz. "But we forgive those whose heart is in the right place." The smile he now adopted made Díaz wonder in which place his heart would end up.

The smile disappeared. "But not all is well. Remember our history. When Nixon talked about the War on Drugs, more than twenty years ago, we all smiled. We knew how strong we were. We knew we had a popular product. We were not afraid of the DEA or the CIA."

Some among the audience chuckled at the memory.

"Then came Ford and Carter and we heard little more about it. Until . . ." Jeff paused for effect. "Reagan."

A low murmur of dissatisfaction rumbled around the room.

"Now our drugs were not just for fun anymore. Now they were political. They were currency. Yes, yes, the *Americanos* became our best customers. But it was like feeding a beast. Even our language was debased. Contra no longer meant *contrabandista*. And as the CIA cornered the market, our faithful customers, our distribution networks, withered on the vine. Even while we made friends with those who had once been our enemies, we were being suckered, weakened, our values were being compromised. Under Bush it was no better. And what do we have now?"

The audience shrugged their shoulders. They had no idea.

"Clinton."

Another round of chuckles, less certain this time.

"A pussy-whipped president who plays sax and wants to be liked. And while he is being everybody's friend, the agents of his government are helping themselves to our business. You all know how our planes stand idle while the US Air Force ships the product to America. You know how much the CIA controls distribution and marketing. And while they squeeze us at the delivery end, guerillas in our own country, our own compatriots, are taking charge of production and cornering the market on hostages."

He turned and took a few paces, head bowed, then turned to face them with an expression that had darkened.

"As if that isn't enough, we must contend with ineptitude among our own number." Once more his gaze settled on Díaz. "Tell me, Enrico. When may we expect the return of the two tonnes of product we loaned you?"

Díaz wiped his forehead. "I . . ." The word came out as a squeak. How could he tell him? What was left of the drugs, as well as small traces of rubber, were now thinly distributed among thousands of cans euphemistically labelled 'tuna'. Díaz briefly considered telling them to take a trip to the canned fish section of their local supermarket, but he thought better of it. "Soon," he said. He fought for breath. "Very soon."

Jeff approached and stopped before Díaz, who sank further into his dangerously flattened bean bag. The looming bulk of the boss appeared to vibrate with some interior turmoil. Díaz thought he might erupt in a very literal way.

"Tell me about your little factory in the jungle," rumbled Jeff. Before Díaz could answer, the boss continued. "You know we don't like junior executives running their own operations."

The room was silent. Díaz searched for support in the faces of the other Board members. They were cautiously sombre. The room now had the atmosphere of an unpopular relative's funeral.

The door burst open. Two gangsters with red eyes, loosened ties and machine-pistols slung casually across their backs carried between them a huge silver platter piled high with white powder. "The new vintage has arrived!" they announced. Behind them, came a procession of near-beautiful women, cheaply but enthusiastically dressed, chattering with excitement. These, Díaz knew, would be the town's finest whores. The meeting was over.

Only two days later, Díaz managed to slip away unnoticed. But the Board would remember his factory soon enough. They would make all kinds of assumptions, none of them healthy for Díaz. Sooner or later the Board would pay him a visit. The question was whether he'd be alive to greet them.

Díaz caught the edge of a strange smell. He wanted to blame it on the peasant at the back of the boat, but he'd been catching hints of it for days. He looked morosely at his feet. His new shoes were still glossy, as he expected. He'd paid a fortune for them the week before, and the salesman in Cali had insisted they were top of the range. But now the leather looked suspiciously like plastic. He thought his feet might be rotting.

Díaz looked nervously over his shoulder, as if expecting to see the Board members hurrying after him. Instead, all he saw was the creased face and blackened teeth of the idiot at the tiller.

"Nice morning, huh?" said the peasant.

Normally Díaz wouldn't even have acknowledged the existence of such a low-life. The emaciated body, shabby oil-stained clothes and bare feet were common enough in this part of the world, and Díaz couldn't explain the expensive Breitling chronometer on the man's wrist, but even in such a poor region the man managed to exude an air of extreme deprivation. And he was short, something the six-foot Díaz could never tolerate. So it was a measure of Díaz's discomfort that he engaged the man in conversation.

"Yes," he said.

* * *

Rotsky pushed in the cigarette lighter and looked around the aircraft. Gah! he thought, a spam can. He leaned forward and tapped the air speed indicator. The needle remained doggedly at the 100 knot mark, the plane's maximum cruise speed. Rotsky frowned and tapped again. The needle didn't move. He sighed.

His hand went to the control yoke, fingers tracing lightly along the smooth plastic, unconsciously seeking a weapons selector switch or a fire button. They halted instead at the strap-on press-to-talk button.

Rotsky frowned. He drummed his fingers on the yoke and then reached into one of the pockets of his flying suit. The fingers returned empty of the Havana they'd been seeking. Rotsky's frown turned to a scowl as the cigarette lighter popped.

For a Cessna 150, the aircraft was especially well-equipped. Rotsky had done a lot of work on it himself, installing an autopilot, cassette/radio system, racing seats and sun roof, and taking out unnecessary items like duplicated navigation instruments: if what you have goes wrong, you weren't meant to get there was his philosophy. But even after all that, it was still just a Cessna 150.

Something else was bothering him too, something he didn't want to think about right now.

"You okay, dude?"

Rotsky realized he was squirming in his seat and somehow his companion had picked up on it. He was sharing the cockpit with a skinny, five-foot-five teenager called Vinnie.

"You okay, man?" repeated Vinnie. "You seem kinda restless." He lifted a video camera and aimed it just above Rotsky's head, as though he somehow wanted to record his thoughts.

"War wound," snapped Rotsky, shifting in his seat. "Got it that time in Venezuela. Shot up by a SWAT team, or something. Anyway, whoever they were, those vicious bastards followed me right into the goddamn jungle."

"I heard it was the booze," said Vinnie.

"Well you heard wrong, dammit!" snapped Rotsky. He sucked in a deep breath. Don't blame the kid, he thought. It's not his fault I'm stuck with this weekend-pilot's plane. "Sorry, man. Bad day."

"What's wrong." Vinnie switched off the camera and dropped it in his lap. "What did those guys want?"

"They've got Tricia," said Rotsky. "They're gonna tear her apart unless I find someone for them."

"Shit," said Vinnie. "Sorry." A blank expression came over his face. "Who's Tricia?"

"My P-51 Mustang. The one I rent out to movie companies and airshows and stuff. Those sons of bitches have foreclosed, or factored the debt or some kind of shit. And they said they're gonna lift my ticket—"

"—Ticket?"

"Pilot's licence. And the weird one said something about an unfortunate accident, though I couldn't work out if he meant something that *might* happen to me or something that *has* happened to him."

"So where are we going?" asked Vinnie.

"Reno. I need to make some phone calls."

"Couldn't we have done that back at the field?"

"That old bastard would've made me pay for the calls."

Vinnie thought that over for a second.

"Isn't this his plane?"

"Sure. Why do you ask?"

"Won't he make you pay for the flying time?"

Rotsky considered this. "Not if we don't take it back," he said.

"Isn't that stealing?"

"Hell no. Rule one-ninety-nine. Airplanes want to be free. All airplanes belong to all pilots. We're not going to keep it. Whoever takes it next, they'll be stealing." He waited a moment. "Unless they don't keep it either."

Vinnie ran his fingers around the camcorder, as though reaffirming the positions of its controls. "Who are you going to call?"

Rotsky knew the answer to this, but seeing as Vinnie had asked the question he thought it over again.

"Friends," he said. "People who might have an idea why two guys in suits want to find Walkaway. It's a question of uncertainty, Vinnie. Dangerous gaps in your knowledge. At times like this, it's important to be with people you trust, people with whom you have no gaps."

"Does that mean we're moving on again?"

"I guess so."

"You didn't really think this through, did you Rotsky?"

"Sure I did. Lots of times." He was silent for a second. "Never came out this way though."

Rotsky already had other things on his mind. The lower part of his body was sending out urgent signals. He needed something to take his mind off the discomfort. Maybe some instructing will do it, he thought.

"Hey Vinnie, you wanna fly?"

Being blind, Vinnie didn't get many breaks. Being called Vinnie in a town like Las Vegas is hard enough, thought Rotsky. But he loved flying and Rotsky took him up whenever he could. He liked to take the controls and there was no way he could notice that the autopilot was on.

"No sweat dude," chimed Vinnie. The boy's English upper-class accent was smooth and naturally patronizing, but he was trying hard to fit in and Rotsky was doing his best not to notice.

Vinnie lightly gripped the control yoke with his left hand: the right one fluttered around indecisively while he figured out what to do with it. In the end, he let it fall on to his knee. The Cessna droned on regardless.

Rotsky scanned the instruments, and as usual found himself puzzling over their significance. He could read what they said with no trouble, and he knew how to act on what they told him. But he couldn't help feeling that their meaning must go deeper than just his current speed, height, climb rate and fuel state. The juxtaposition of the needles and figures had to be a kind of semaphore broadcasting a more vital and profound message about his predicament. He'd once found himself discussing this subject with his wingman, back in the Air Force. "For instance," he'd asked, "what does it mean when all the needles point at zero?"

"It means you're *parked*, Rotsky," scoffed the pilot.

"Well okay, what about when all the needles are at maximum?"

"That means you're *dead*, any second now."

Rotsky wasn't sure the guy was getting his point, and had let it drop, but it was an idea that had never gone away and wherever Rotsky went, he would sound people out, testing them with the idea, gauging their reactions, hoping to pick up some clues or a different angle on the problem.

Rotsky noticed that Vinnie was holding back the yoke. The pressure he was exerting was slight but noticeable to someone of Rotsky's experience.

"Hey, Vinnie, trim it out a little, will ya?"

Vinnie had no idea what Rotsky meant by trimming it out and the best he could do was to adopt a purposeful expression and tighten his hold on the yoke. Rotsky leaned forward and nudged the trim wheel up a fraction to counter Vinnie's grip.

This kind of point-to-point flying bored Rotsky, but he was soon busy selecting frequencies, talking with air traffic control, setting squawk codes and maintaining heading. When they were close to the airport, Rotsky took control back from Vinnie, snapped off the autopilot and ran through the pre-landing checklist. Brakes off, gear down, mixture rich, pitch fine, fuel on, harness tight, weapon safeties on, cocktails secured, evidence stashed. Only three of the items were relevant to this aircraft and flight but the practice was useful.

Rotsky turned on to base leg, but made no move to reduce power or select flaps.

"What's happening, dude?" asked Vinnie. He always knew when the flight entered a new phase.

"Turning finals," said Rotsky.

"Cool. Height?"

"One thousand."

"Isn't that a little high?"

"You bet. OLC rule . . . I told you about the OLC, right?"

"OLC?"

"Outside Lomcovak Club."

"No, I don't —"

"—OLC rule nine-thirty-two. Always maintain height until the last moment. Never know when you're gonna take ground fire. A shoulder-launched SAM can really fuck up your approach."

"This is Nevada, Rotsky."

"Exactly." Rotsky threw Vinnie a triumphant beam. Then he noticed the boy's confused expression and dark glasses. He carried on grinning anyway.

"*Cessna Two Five Zero, do you intend to land?*" said the voice on the radio.

Rotsky picked up the mic and hit the talk button. "I guess I'm gonna have to, sometime," he said.

"Is that Rotsky?"

"Yup."

"Okay, Rotsky, you're number one for landing."

By now he was over the runway threshold, still at a thousand feet. He chopped the power, trimmed, selected full flaps, trimmed again and put the Cessna into a side slip. The aircraft went downhill like a wounded duck until at the last moment Rotsky kicked off the yaw, hauled back on the yoke and put the tyres on the runway with a kiss that brought a smile to his lips.

* * *

Raúl Escobar had also slipped unnoticed from the Corporation convention. He had seen an opportunity and didn't want to waste time. As he stepped from the borrowed Corporation Learjet at Bogotá airport he was met by a huge man whose expensive couture suit and hundred-dollar haircut failed to disguise his dangerous physique. This was the only man that Escobar trusted and he needed him now more than ever.

The big man took Escobar's bag and stood expressionless, awaiting an order. Escobar frowned at him unhappily, then raised an eyebrow. The big man appeared to remember something, scanned the area to check there were no witnesses and executed a tiny bow.

Nothing was said until they were safely inside the rented limo and heading for Escobar's ranch. The excitement that had driven Escobar home had ebbed into frustration and fatigue, and he needed a moment to calm down and gather his thoughts. He gazed out of the window and noticed how the warm morning light painted a thin veneer of charm on the city's sprawling slums. They should put darker tinted glass in these cars, he thought.

Escobar caressed the leather of the limo's seats and then pressed a button to raise the bullet-proof window between them and the chauffeur. He picked a remote control unit from the seat and aimed it at a small TV set. He wanted to check the news programme for coverage of his return. He pressed a button. Nothing happened. He pressed all the buttons. The TV set remained blank and mute. Escobar wound down a window and threw out the remote.

His right-hand man, Hipólito, gazed out of the window. He was a man of great natural menace and profound ugliness, tall, wide and built like a tank, his face heavily scarred, who prided himself on being able to handle just about every weapon ever built, though his preference was for the bolas. Escobar was glad they were sitting now. Out on the airport tarmac Hipólito had towered over him. Escobar was just five foot seven, on a good day.

As befitted his station, Escobar was the first to break the silence.

"Give me a fucking drink," he said.

Hipólito popped open the drinks cabinet, pulled out a chilled bottle of Dom Perignon and half-filled a crystal glass. He handed it to his boss. Escobar drained it. A hint of a smile appeared on his lips.

"We've got work to do," he said. "Did you bring my appointments diary?"

"No, boss."

"Why not?" As soon as he'd asked the question, Escobar knew the answer. He wanted to put his fingers in his ears, but knew it wouldn't look appropriately dignified.

"Because you don't have any appointments."

Escobar watched the adobe slums turn into ragged shanty shacks. "What about the pool hall project?"

"Cancelled."

"The basketball team?"

"Disbanded. Half of them were killed last week in a freak machine-gunning accident."

"Shit!" Escobar thought ruefully about the new team shirts, now wasted. "What about the interview with the newspaper?"

"Which one?"

"Whaddya mean, 'which one'? *Del Mundo Escobar*, for fucksakes."

Hipólito refilled Escobar's glass, then very carefully replaced the bottle in the drinks cabinet. "It's kind of on hold. The printer won't print any more issues until we pay his bill."

"Did you talk to him?"

"I had a real good talk to him."

"And?"

"Too soon to tell. He hasn't regained consciousness." Hipólito let loose an encouraging smile. "What's the work?"

Escobar nearly missed the question. His head was crowded with fragmented dreams. "What?"

"You said we have work to do."

"Ah yes." Escobar brightened at the prospect of the new project. "That fuckwit Díaz is being stupid again. But I think it could be to our advantage."

"You want him dead, right?" asked Hipólito. He enjoyed his work and hadn't much liked Díaz.

"I want what he's got. If he gets hurt in the process . . . well, that's a tragedy."

Hipólito looked puzzled. "So . . . dead or not dead?"

"Dead is fine."

The two men smiled and the car swished on in contented silence for a few miles, its suspension at first making light of the progressively deteriorating road surface. Escobar's ranch was hidden away in the Cordillera mountains, partly for security, partly because he loved the isolation. Up there he could forget about the Corporation and about what he did for a living. The price he paid was convenience. There was not enough flat ground for a proper airfield and he hated the small, noisy prop planes that used the short dirt strip at the edge of the ranch. So Escobar was forced to tolerate the rough roads, though he got through a lot of cars that way. He was thinking of buying a helicopter.

About five miles out of town, where the shanty-like suburbs finally succumbed to jungle, they passed a construction site. A twelve-foot high portrait of Escobar stared back at the passing men. He was smiling, gazing beatifically across a green and sunny landscape, his head ringed by a sunburst halo. Behind him a crowd of clean peasants with joyous expressions were engaged in a variety of pursuits — playing basketball, typing on computers, talking into mobile phones. Behind the portrait, rusting bars poked untidily from dissolving grey concrete. The Raúl Escobar Leisure and Careers Complex had looked that way for the best part of two years. Escobar himself had put it down to union trouble and had got his staff to bust a few heads, but the truth was that he'd run out of money. Escobar's funds were always limited and he'd been dismayed to discover that the bill for the poster, the promotional video and the inaugural press party had soaked up three-quarters of the total budget. The DEA took up the slack for a while. From time to time they delivered a packet of cash so long as Escobar used it for social projects unrelated to drugs. "Sure," said Escobar each time, and meant it when he said it. The packets stopped coming anyway. Hipólito had paid a visit to the PR company in charge of the project and two days later the firm's owner had sent a letter from his hospital bed offering a five per cent discount. Escobar took it.

The car hit a bad rut with a spine-jangling bump. Escobar lowered the partition window.

"Hey! Slow down," he told the driver. "You're using too much gas. Fifty-five is the best speed. Am I made of money?"

Hipólito topped up Escobar's glass, which he'd drained several times. Escobar's mellowed mind turned to more pleasant things, to those he loved and cherished. Suddenly his eyes flashed open as he remembered something important.

"Hey! Did you get my present?"

Hipólito smiled indulgently and nodded to a pile of coats on the seat next to Escobar.

"I wanted to surprise you," he beamed.

Escobar rummaged in the coats and pulled out a large, shallow package. He dropped it on his lap, enjoying the weight and savouring the moment. In a flash he'd ripped off the covering paper and had flipped open the lid. From the box he pulled one of the crudest looking guns he'd ever seen, seemingly little more than a pipe with a wooden stock. Reaching into the box again he brought out a long, straight clip for the gun.

"It's full," warned Hipólito.

Escobar's face was lit up like a child at Christmas. "It's perfect," he gasped. "It's just what I wanted."

He fondled the gun for a while, itching to insert the magazine, though his respect for weapons wouldn't let him.

"A Sten Mark 2(S)," Escobar breathed. "Integral silencer, nine millimetre parabellum, thirty-two round box magazine, cyclic rate of four hundred and fifty rounds per minute, muzzle velocity one thousand feet per second. It still has the leather sleeve around the silencer casing. Perfect."

"I checked out the suppressor," said Hipólito. "It's in good condition. Doesn't seem to have been used much. I think it's Korean war vintage."

"Yes, yes, almost certainly. Thank you."

It was Escobar's dream to own the world's finest collection of machine guns. This one completed his collection of Stens and he couldn't have been happier. Of course, he'd paid for it and had told Hipólito where to look for it, but he liked to think of the gun as a present.

Escobar's face reappeared at the window. They passed a long row of faded election posters, all identical, showing a younger Escobar, smiling but with a hint of seriousness as befits a potential leader of his country.

It had been a couple of years since Escobar had last sought office — any office. The job didn't matter, it was the fact of being elected that was important to him. He refused to buy a position: he needed to put himself above the wholesale corruption of his opponents. Escobar knew that if he was elected fairly, that would make him a true man of the people, while putting him in his rightful place above them.

Escobar had some major drawbacks as a politician, though. The first was his hatred of children. His decision to delegate the job of kissing babies to Hipólito wasn't popular with the children or their mothers. Escobar's other problem was that he never won a single vote. It took him years to realize that even his own men were voting against him, not out of hatred but out of honour. They had accepted the bribes of his opponents — a process that was older than democracy itself — and felt duty-bound to vote for them.

Like many politically ambitious but thwarted men before him, Escobar abandoned democracy for terrorism. He created his own band of freedom fighters. The *Escobaristas* were raised from his own men, some local villagers with nothing better to do and a rag-bag of down-on-their-luck *contrabandistas*, *banditos* and bums. They blew up a few minor government buildings, robbed a bank and kidnapped a group of American tourists who thought it was part of their *Colombia Experience* package tour. One of them threatened to sue when the *Escobaristas* had let them go without having first bound and gagged them. Seeing that it was leading nowhere, Escobar cut off the terrorists' supply of drink and drugs and they soon drifted away.

The bumpiness of the road intruded into Escobar's reverie. The suspension was now having trouble coping and that meant they were getting near the ranch. Escobar wanted to get his plan into action before they arrived. This needed to stay confidential and he wasn't happy about discussing something so sensitive in a house infested with servants. As drug barons went, Escobar felt he wasn't especially paranoid, but he did like to be careful. He raised the partition window again.

"Okay, let's get down to business. Díaz has a factory and I want it. I want it working for us or I want it destroyed, but either way we need to find out what he's doing there, how long he's been doing it and who his clients are."

"Do you know where this place is?" asked Hipólito.

"Not yet, but I have someone working on that. We should know in a day or two. I want to move fast, hit him before he knows we're coming."

* * *

Vinnie realized the family fortune was disappearing when he stopped bumping into it. He'd been blind just a short while and hadn't quite got used to it. Even in the vast spaces of the family mansion, deep in the spoiled luxury of the English countryside, Vinnie had trouble moving more than a few feet without hitting something old and valuable. Then it suddenly got easier and the rooms began to echo in a cold, penurious way.

There was tension in the air, too. Vinnie's parents never spoke much about their work but it was obvious things weren't going well. Vinnie's father, Lord Haversack, described himself as a 'financial consultant and agent for overseas business concerns'. His mother called herself his 'personal assistant', which meant hiring a secretary to do most of the work. They didn't like to answer the phone.

They had taken Vinnie out of school as soon as his eyesight failed, and he wanted for little and had little to do. He mostly just hung around the house, trying to map its ever-changing geography. He got to overhear a lot of conversations in the echoing chambers, which was how he knew the house was mortgaged to the hilt and in danger of being lost. It would be the first time in fourteen generations that a Haversack hadn't owned the estate.

One day, his father tapped Vinnie on the shoulder to get his attention.

"You listening, boy?"

"Sure pop." Vinnie had been listening to a lot of US TV programmes. He liked the way the language sounded.

"We're thinking of making a business trip to America," his father said. There was an odd, distant tone in his voice, as though his mind was on something else. "Thought you might like to come along. Make a nice break for you and so forth. Add a family atmosphere to the proceedings, so to speak. Does that sound agreeable?"

"Sure, dude," Vinnie said. His parents took this to mean yes.

They flew to Chicago where Vinnie's father had arranged a meeting with a business associate to "discuss financing". The meeting took place in a night club: at least, Vinnie thought it probably was a night club, judging by the noise and atmosphere. He was overwhelmed by the racket and the density of the atmosphere.

He slumped in a seat, and from time to time an anonymous benefactor pressed a drink into his hands. Vinnie thought it might have been a woman, judging from the hands holding the glass.

Vinnie would never forget Rotsky's first words to him.

"Who are you staring at, *dogface*?" he'd asked.

It hadn't occurred to Vinnie that he might be staring at anyone. In his tired state he found the idea mildly amusing, and his only reply was a lopsided grin.

"You okay bud?" asked the voice.

"It's my birthday," said Vinnie. It had only just occurred to him. He wasn't precisely sure of the date, but it had to be roughly right. "Eighteen today."

"Oh man, that's a crying shame. Alone on your birthday."

Vinnie found this funny. When he'd finished laughing he said loudly: "I'm not alone, am I pop? Pop?" As he listened to the thumping music and tinkling glasses, an icy wave rolled up his spine. "Father?"

All hell broke loose. Vinnie tried to stay calm, concentrated hard to filter and identify the individual noises in the cacophony. There were voices, lots of them, distorted by drink, volume and physical deformity. There was the din of everything breaking — glass, wood, metal and bones. There was a strange animal screeching noise that Vinnie never did work out, but hoped he'd never hear again. And there was the stranger's voice close to his ear saying: "Time to leave, I think."

It took a few days for Vinnie to calm down and sober up, during which Rotsky quizzed him about his parents.

"What line of business were they in?"

"Insurance, I think. Financial investments." Vinnie thought hard about it. "I don't know, really."

Vinnie described his parents, and Rotsky had a vague recollection of seeing them in the night club, talking to a huge man with a deep tan. Vinnie explained that his father was supposed to meet someone who called himself 'King Zipa'.

"Either it's a code name or the guy's a wrestler," said Rotsky. "Could be, from the size of him."

"I don't think the king himself turned up," said Vinnie. "Not from what my father said."

"Oh yeah? What was that?"

"It was 'oh shit, it's that bastard'. Wasn't so much what he said as how he said it. I wonder if it was the big guy who stole my video camera."

"Video camera?"

"Yeah, You know, my loss of sight was pretty sudden. It could come back the same way. I want a record of everything I might've seen. I want to know what I've been through."

Rotsky asked around, talked to the people he knew who conducted financial business in night clubs, but he came up with nothing.

"Don't worry, man," he said, "we'll find them." Neither one of them thought that going to the police would be a good idea.

Rotsky bought Vinnie a new camcorder, "Top model," he said. "Autofocus, all that shit. I got you ten spare batteries and the Deluxe Turbo charger. Takes five batteries at a time."

"Tapes?"

"What tapes?"

"Blank tapes. For the camcorder."

"Uh, next week, I promise."

Vinnie stayed at Rotsky's office, in reality not much more than a prefabricated shack alongside a hangar at a small suburban airfield, but it had a bunk, a bathroom and an endless supply of fascinating sounds. It was during this time that he developed his love of aero engines. He had never heard anything so raw, so powerful, so utterly *erotic*.

Several times Vinnie heard voices discussing the riot at the club in tones of awe and wonder, and he realized what a favour Rotsky had done him, pulling him out of there when he had. When Rotsky went away for a while, to make some enquiries, Vinnie was happy to guard the office. For three weeks the linemen at the airfield brought him food and kept him company. Vinnie learned to navigate his way around the airfield; his acute hearing helped him avoid whirling propellers better than most sighted people. And for the first time in his life Vinnie felt he belonged somewhere.

Then Rotsky returned, harried and unhappy. For two hours he railed against the horrors of a strange dark world that Vinnie didn't know, a world populated by spooks, feds, junkies, pimps, whores, niggers, spics, greaseballs, wasps, wops, kikes, Catholics, dogs and — Vinnie wasn't sure he'd heard this correctly — varicose veins.

"People are scum, Vinnie, even people you don't know and haven't met. Even people you *will* never meet."

From the way his voice kept fading back and forth it sounded to Vinnie like Rotsky was constantly looking over his shoulder. Then, at last, there came a break in the torrent. Vinnie listened to the sound of an AT-6 taking off, and as the radial engine blared he felt a slight tingling in his groin. Then Rotsky's voice came back, subdued and eerily distant.

"Hey Vinnie. How'd ya like to live in Las Vegas?"

Vinnie thought about it.

"Rotsky, I need money," he said. "If I can't put some serious cash together, someone is going to get my home. I don't know who, but I do know the only way to hold on to my home is to have enough money to pay off the family debts. I want my home, Rotsky."

"And your folks?"

"Folks? Oh, my parents. We can't rely on them."

"But you want to find them, right?"

"Oh, I'm sure they'll turn up."

"Okay, son. We'll find this King Zipa and get your money. We'll make a start in Vegas."

* * *

"What the fuck did you do that for?" Jesus whined. He dragged himself from the river.

José's rapid dispatch of the tamandua had caught Jesus off-guard and off-balance. José was actually quite impressed by how far Jesus had jumped into the river. Now he was back on the bank, pulling weeds and unnameable bits of river detritus from his clothes and not looking happy.

"Holy mother! Look at this. Damn suit's ruined, man. It's my best fucking Zegna. That's fifty bucks you owe me."

"Hey, Jesus. It ain't my fault. I forgot, okay? It's tough to work with a guy who's scared of guns."

"I ain't scared of guns," Jesus snapped. "I just don' like loud noises, that's all."

They were seconds away from a major squabble, but just then the faint putt-putt of the approaching boat became suddenly louder. The two men knew it was either Díaz or trouble. José wasn't about to take chances and loaded a new clip into the Uzi, while Jesus eyed the gun malevolently.

Within a few minutes they could make out the shape of the boat, and when it got close enough to recognize its occupants, José relaxed his guard. No sooner had the boat bumped the river bank than Díaz was ashore, palpably relieved.

"Four hours! Four goddamn hours I've been in that fuckin' thing," he explained to his unimpressed colleagues.

"What happened to the cruiser, man? You lose it?" asked José.

"Sunk."

"Sunk?"

"What did I just say?"

"But you can't *mean* 'sunk'," insisted José, his voice a little higher. He'd liked the cruiser. Boats were the only form of transport he could really tolerate, apart from Porsches. "You've gotta made a mistake."

"Hey!" Díaz was red-faced. "Who's the fucking boss here?"

José and Jesus looked at each other and shrugged.

"How?" asked José.

Díaz sighed. "It was a party, okay? At parties ... well, shit happens. Now listen, we got more important things to worry about than sunk cruisers. Unless we get a few things sorted out around here, and I mean like right now, we're all dog meat."

"Sorted out?" José didn't like this kind of talk. It usually meant work. "Whaddya mean, sorted out?"

Díaz turned to the boatman. "You can leave now."

The boatman arched his eyebrows and held out his hand, flat and palm upwards. Díaz grumbled and fished out his wallet. He dropped a few bank notes into the waiting hand. It didn't move. He dropped a few more and within seconds the boatman had restarted the engine and was pulling away.

"You in some kind of hurry?" yelled Díaz.

"Got a plane to catch," shouted the boatman over his shoulder. "I like to check in early, make sure I get a window seat."

Díaz watched the boat putter down the river for a while, the turned to his accomplices.

"Whaddya mean, sorted out?" asked José.

"We've got to get out of here. Get the stuff moved down to Santa Marta. Pay off everyone and start packing."

"Most of them have gone already," said Jesus.

"Why the rush?" asked José.

Díaz looked at José with an expression he'd developed that was meant to look stern and authoritative. José thought he looked constipated.

"I think we're going to have trouble with Escobar," said Díaz. "I didn't like the way he was looking at me at the meeting. That sonofabitch is going to give us trouble."

"*Pablo* Escobar?" gasped José. "Cool!"

"Not Pablo, you dipshit," scoffed Jesus. "He's dead."

"Bullshit he's dead. He's the boss man. The chief."

"The fucking stiff," snorted Jesus. He turned to Díaz. "He's dead, am I right?"

Díaz sighed loudly. "Pablo Escobar *is* dead," he said. "Long time. I'm talking about Raúl Escobar, and he's alive. Too fucking alive."

* * *

For Vinnie, the first few days in Las Vegas had been a dizzying cacophony of machine noise. He was submerged by it, totally lost. Rotsky had reacquainted himself with people who didn't always sound happy to see him, and he asked around about King Zipa. No-one had heard of him.

Vinnie didn't pay much attention though. As they went from casino to bar to casino, he moved in a captivated daze, drunk on the constant crashing din of coins. Within hours he'd learned to distinguish one type of slot machine from another, and could gauge the size of a person's win to within a couple of dollars.

Once he'd acquired the basic grammar of the crashes, taps and rattles, he found himself enjoying the strange disharmonies and stuttering rhythms. There was an oiled erotic charge to the sound of money moving.

"When someone gets a big win, I see these weird, amazing images," he confessed to Rotsky one day in Circus Circus.

"Oh yeah? What kind of images?"

Vinnie shifted on his bar stool. "Well, at school, I used to have these magazines under my bed . . ."

Just then bells rang and lights flashed and a slot machine poured hundreds of quarters into the lifted skirt of a crying, middle-aged woman.

"Rotsky," gasped Vinnie. "Where's the nearest men's room?"

The next day, Rotsky relocated them to the small airfield outside the city that was to become their home. He was reluctant to venture downtown but he could see that Vinnie was missing the sound of small change. As compensation, Rotsky frequently took him to bars, sometimes in Vegas, sometimes as far as Reno. Rotsky's favourite haunt was the Green Parrot, a topless, bottomless, godless bar lost in one of Reno's industrial zones. That's where they'd gone after the visit from the Feds.

It was known unofficially as the Walking Clusterfuck Bar. It was so far off the beaten tourist track, so far down the back alley of civilization, that any holidaymaker or conventioneer walking into the place had to be lost beyond redemption already. Inevitably, the Clusterfuck became the focus for a weird and unsavoury band of no-hopers, the ones who were banned from every other bar in town, the ones who were walking the ragged edge of physical and nervous breakdown, the ones who were wanted in every state except Nevada.

For the dancers it was the last stop before hell or jail. The occasional lucky one would find god and get shipped out to the local asylum. The unlucky ones were there every night, bumping and grinding to music so loud and distorted that you couldn't tell which era it was from. The girls didn't have any clothes on but nobody minded very much.

"Believe me, Vinnie," said Rotsky, "you're better off not seeing this shit."

For Vinnie, the main attraction was the inevitable row of slot machines beside the bar. Sometimes Rotsky would give him a handful of quarters which Vinnie would make last all night. Most of the time, though, he simply waited nearby for someone else to play. He would amble up to the machine and lean intimately against the side, ear to the metal, a smile on his face. Anywhere else, this might have been regarded as eccentric. In the Green Parrot, it seemed oddly innocent.

The bar opened at ten in the morning and closed at six the next morning. The intervening four hours were for the owner to repair the previous night's damage and find new staff.

It was an hour past opening time and Rotsky was having trouble getting credit.

"No fucking way, man. Do I look like Santa Claus?"

"Well . . ." said Rotsky. He was talking to Doug Sauvé, the barkeeper. He was a big guy, not quite as tall as Rotsky but twice as wide, with a florid complexion, long straggly grey hair and a white beard.

Vinnie groped his way to a chair. He sat, then felt for the table. It was a stretch so he tried to shuffle the chair forwards. It wouldn't budge. Like all the furniture in the Green Parrot, the chair was nailed to the floor.

They were in a relatively peaceful section of the establishment, which meant that Rotsky and Doug could hear each other talking at distances of almost two feet.

Rotsky leaned on the bar. He noticed for the first time that it was made of Kevlar. Pressed into the surface at regular intervals was the manufacturer's name, BarArmor. "Look. Doug. What's the big deal? All I want is a tab. You'll get paid. I'm just a tad short of cash today, that's all."

An old man sitting next to Rotsky cackled loudly. He seemed to be doing a bad Walter Brennan impression. "Hee hee. Short of cash. That's rich."

Doug stared coldly at the old man. "Why the fuck don't you go home?"

"Can't."

"Why not?"

"Elvis is there."

"Elvis is at your house? What's Elvis doing at your house?"

Walter Brennan leaned back and gave Doug a pitying look. "What the hell you *think* he's doing there? Fumigating it, of course."

"Fumigating?"

"Yeah. Place is full of bees. They dead now, but I still ain't going back." Doug grinned and handed him a beer. "Thanks," said Walter Brennan. "Don't mind if I do." He shuffled away into the darkness of the bar.

Doug turned his attention back to Rotsky and the grin disappeared.

"So. Short of cash, huh? I hear you've got your P-51 up at Stead. What's it called?"

"*Delicious Tricia*," said Rotsky, sullenly.

"Yeah, that's right. That's, what . . . a half-million dollar airplane? Must be costing you a packet to get it overhauled."

"I get a special deal," Rotsky mumbled. "Besides—"

"Hell, when didn't you get a special deal? You can afford to run that airplane but you can't afford a round of drinks. When was the last time you used money in this place?"

"I like to barter. You look after me, I look after you."

"And how do you do that exactly?"

"I cut you a piece of the action."

"Action!" Doug was nearly apoplectic. "Oh yeah. Like that Mexican scam?"

"Hey, that was just a routine import/export operation. It's not my fault people have suspicious minds."

"Those people were paid to have suspicious minds, Rotsky. They were immigration officials. When they're faced with two hundred half-crazed Mexicans jogging up to the border claiming to be part of a charity marathon race, they're entitled to ask a few questions. Like how come none of them are wearing running shoes? Or any shoes? And how come most of them are in boxer shorts? And the speed was not a wise move."

"Are you kidding? They were the laziest sons of bitches I ever met. OLC rule two four nine — you gotta have a reason. If it hadn't've been for the speed I'd never have got the bastards running."

A small, wiry man wobbled to the bar. His long thin hair was sweat-pasted to his head in wild swirls that showed plenty of piebald scalp. The top three buttons of his cheap pink shirt were undone, and it had worked its way loose of his mauve trousers. "Did Jerry come through here?" he asked. "You seen my jacket? Has Marge called?" He raised his left hand and stared at his bare wrist. "I gotta get home," he said and tottered out of the bar.

Doug turned his attention back to Rotsky. "Yeah, well maybe a little less speed would have done the trick. Some of those poor motherfuckers were still running round their cells a week later. And one other thing —"

"What?"

"You should have taken their money *before* you aimed them at the border."

"Yeah, well, maybe —"

There was an explosion from the dark interior of the bar that didn't sound like it was part of the stage act.

"Probably the owner," yelled Doug. "Don't worry, it's just a thunderflash. If things were really getting out of hand he'd let off a grenade."

Rotsky walked into the darkness. It was filled with a pungent smoke. When his eyes had adapted to the dark, he saw a smoking hole at the edge of a small patch of floor that had no furniture nailed to it. In the centre was a small, cross-eyed, grey-haired man, who swayed wildly and yelled unintelligible epithets in a thick accent that Rotsky couldn't identify. These outbursts were aimed directly at customers, most of whom were slumped senseless over their tables. Rotsky walked back to the bar.

"That the owner?"

Doug nodded.

"Where the hell's he from? New Jersey?"

"He's Bucharest-Glaswegian," said Doug. "His mother was Rumanian and his father was Scottish. No-one can understand a fucking word he says. That's what he does most of the time — stands in the middle of the dance floor insulting people. Most people think he's some kind of deranged floor show. Some days he gets better tips than me."

"You work for a guy like that but you won't give me a tab?"

Doug closed his eyes, inhaled slowly, then opened his eyes with a sigh. He reached under the bar and pulled out two cold Buds and handed them to Rotsky.

"On the house," he said. "Now go away."

Rotsky took hold of the bottles. At exactly the same time, cutting through the din of the music, he heard what sounded like a fire bell. The coincidence confused him, and he spent a few seconds trying to work out if the two could be connected.

"What the fuck's that?" he yelled to Doug.

"It's the fire bell," Doug yelled back. "I've got it rigged to the phone. Never hear it otherwise. Back in a moment. Don't steal anything."

Rotsky did his best to look hurt and made a point of having his hands in plain view, harmlessly resting on the bar when Doug came back a few seconds later.

"It's for you," he said.

* * *

Billy Cook rolled over in his bunk, fell out, hit the floor hard and bounced. He sprang back onto his hands and knees then reared up holding his hands in front of his face as though to ward off an attacker. Nothing happened. There was silence. "Shit," muttered Billy. He eased himself to his feet and stretched his bruised limbs, then looked around the room afraid he might find an audience. Billy's situation was precarious enough without people seeing him do stupid things like this.

He was alone, which Billy celebrated with a more ebullient "Shit!" before looking for his clothes. It took him about a minute to realize he was wearing them.

Dappled light on his window told him it was daytime, though he had no way of telling what time of day. Billy had never been able to grasp whether the sun rose in the west or the east. And he had no idea which way his window faced. He contemplated this double jeopardy, as he did most times he woke. His lack of conclusions was a comfort to him. It also allowed him to put off, for a minute or two, the next big decision: whether to leave the room. If he waited long enough, if he simply refused to go out, they would come and get him eventually. But by that time they'd be mad as hell, and the abuse would start again. On the other hand, if Billy went out of his own accord, that would simply remind them of his existence, and might goad them into abuse. Worse, they might make him . . .

An engine spluttered into anger nearby. An outboard, Billy thought, and then realized he'd been hearing such engines during the past few hours of fitful sleep. Something must be happening, he thought, and tried to think what that might be. It was difficult because Billy had no idea what had happened during the past few weeks, hadn't a clue as to the nature of the activity around him, and so had little information on which to base an informed judgment.

The engine noise dropped and receded. Soon it was quiet — as quiet as it ever gets in the jungle. Billy cast a cautious glance out of the window. He saw trees and leaves. That was all he ever saw. Trees and leaves. It was the best view he'd ever owned. Through the thin wood and glass, Billy could now make out the constant chattering sounds of the jungle and nothing else. The absence of evidence of his fellow jungle-dwellers brought him a moment's comfort, but he couldn't shake the faint unease at the thought that the situation was changing in ways unknown to him.

Billy had a drifter's instinct about when to move on. A signal would fire inside him and he would pack his things, ready to take the first opportunity to get out. He'd been packed for two weeks now. It was getting to the point where he was thinking of unpacking again. He decided to check his things, just in case.

There was a faded and worn ex-army backpack hanging from the foot of his bunk. Billy emptied it on to the bed and ran a fast inventory: lucky bear, mess tin and utensils, change of clothes, lucky wombat, spare sneakers, rain cape, tin of spam, lucky elephant, compass (broken), Swiss Army knife, prophylactics, half a bar of chocolate, personal stereo, five cassette tapes in boxes, an empty tape box and a Rolling Stones tape without its box. Billy looked around for his lucky panda and found it under the pillow with a Mini-Maglite and a copy of *The Dharma Bums*. The flashlight was switched on, its batteries flat.

Billy packed carefully. That took two or three minutes. He looked around the room for something else to do. It was bare, nothing even for his eye to settle on. Nothing except the door. Billy fiddled with a strap of the pack and tried not to look at the door, but it drew his gaze. Billy shuffled alongside the bed, picked up the pack again and read the badges sewn to it, several of them now hanging loose. Mexico, Nicaragua, India, Sri Lanka, London, Paris, Brazil, Peru, Disneyland they read. There was another, Colombia, in a side pocket that Billy had resolved to sew on as soon as he came across a needle and thread.

Billy sighed. There was nothing for it. He dropped the pack on the floor, kicked it under the bed for safety and left the room. A short, bare corridor took him to the other end of the pre-fabricated building. The wood beneath his feet was springy, already rotten.

He made it to the kitchen without meeting anyone, which wasn't uncommon. He looked around in dismay at the machines and utensils. He still hadn't worked out what most of them were for. When he'd taken the job, Billy had been dizzy with the *soroche*, the Andean altitude sickness, and faint with hunger, and he wasn't too sure where the confusion arose, but he soon found himself installed as the camp cook. "My *name*'s Cook," he told them many times. "We know," they'd said slowly.

The fact that he couldn't cook wasn't discovered until they were deep in the jungle. Billy was still sick. He'd tried treating the *soroche* with the Indians' traditional method of chewing coca leaves, but it didn't work for him. He tried cocaine which still left him sick, though he didn't mind so much and found he could get a lot more work done. Finally he found the solution was just to up the dose. He was lucky that his new boss was happy to pay him in coke.

His new boss was less happy with the food Billy prepared. When the tinned food ran out, fresh produce started arriving from downriver and Billy had little idea what to do with it. There were things that Billy had never seen before. Sometimes he would be presented with a frond-covered artefact and not know if it was vegetable or fruit or part of the strange chemical processes that seemed to be going on all around him.

He saw little of the other workers: they mostly stayed inside their own huts, from which came unnerving hums and acrid smells. Even when he met the people delegated to collect the food from him they wouldn't talk. They would stare glumly at the food then turn a look of hatred and loathing on to Billy. When he'd finished, Billy would go to his room and drink himself into an *aguardiente* coma. When the drink ran out, he just stayed in his room.

Billy picked up a plate and thought about washing it. There was definitely something wrong. From the kitchen window he could see two of the other huts. Nothing moved. Absolutely, noth—

"Oh shit!" gasped Billy. His chest tightened and he couldn't breathe, but when he did finally force a deep gasp, it was clean jungle air that ran into his lungs. The smell's gone, he thought. No humming. It's too damn quiet.

Billy burst from the hut and ran into the next one. It was a jumble of pipes and glass tubes and bottles, but no people. The next hut was the same. He ran to a third which was bare. "They've left me behind," he cursed. "The rotten bastards have left me here to . . . um, rot." Billy suddenly felt very small and alone, as though the jungle was already closing over him. "The sons of . . ."

A noise filtered through Billy's anger. The sound of an outboard engine, maybe two engines, maybe more. Billy smiled. They're coming back for me, he thought. Then the smile disappeared. Oh shit. Oh sweet fucking jesus.

They're coming back for me!

Billy ran deeper into the hut as though to hide, before realizing that it was empty. He ran to the door, but stopped before going outside. The engines were close now, and throttling down as the boats approached the riverbank. What if they see me leave? he thought. He looked back at the bare room to see if there was a place he'd missed. There wasn't. Fuck! He bolted from the hut, head down, not looking toward the sound of the engines. There were shouts now, and gun shots. He speeded up, crashed through the kitchen door and stopped. His head spun back and forth looking for a hiding place, his gaze too frantic to focus. Shit shit shit! The shouts and gun shots were closer. A bullet smashed the window, shattered plates and ripped away the door jamb. The fridge, thought Billy. It was a big fridge, big enough to store enough food for the whole team for a month. And he knew it was empty. Billy yanked open the door, yanked out shelves and climbed inside. He grabbed the egg tray and pulled. The door banged shut and the light clicked out. Billy was in total darkness. Safe at last, he thought.

* * *

Vinnie was nervous. Rotsky had been gone for a little while, and the crashing din of the Walking Clusterfuck bar made him feel unusually isolated. He fondled the video camera, but denied his normal sound clues he had no idea where to point it. He was glad when the bartender spoke.

"So, what's your story kid?" asked Doug.

"Say what?"

"What?"

"Did you say story?"

"Yeah, story. How'd you end up in a sorry place like this? You're from England, right?"

"Yeah, right on dude." Vinnie sensed Doug's unease but was unsure what to say next. Rotsky had warned him about the need to keep everything on a need-to-know basis. Of course, Vinnie had no way of telling who needed to know what, and Doug was his sole point of reference at the moment. "I came over here with my parents," he said. "They were on a business trip, but I'm beginning to think that the business wasn't something my forebears would have approved of."

"How so?"

"I think it was something illegal."

"Your family rich?"

"They used to be. But the family house is mortgaged now and we're heavily in debt."

"But your family used to be wealthy?"

"Fabulously."

"Then your forebears would understand. How'd you think they got their money? Where are your parents now?"

"They disappeared. In Chicago. In a bar. They were meeting with this huge man — Rotsky tells me he was huge — then there was a fight and ... that was that."

"Rotsky was there?"

"That's how we met."

"Uh-huh."

Above the cacophony of the music system, Vinnie thought he could make out the squeak of someone cleaning a glass. "How long have you known Rotsky?" he asked the barman.

There was a pause. Vinnie thought he heard Doug sigh, but it was hard to tell.

"Jeez, I don't know. On and off I think I've had the pleasure of Philip Z Rotsky's acquaintance for fifteen years, give or take. And you know, I don't think there's been a single minute of that time that the sonofabitch hasn't owed me money."

"Zee? Oh, you mean zed. What's the zee stand for?"

Doug chuckled. "Why don't you ask him? No, no, just kidding. It's safer not to." Doug paused for a second. Vinnie got the impression he was checking they were alone. "He doesn't like to talk about it much, says it brings back bad memories."

"Of what?"

"Well, the way I heard it was this. Rotsky was down in Louisiana, in a major league poker game on Lulu's flying whorehouse —"

"— Lulu?"

"Look, if you keep asking questions you ain't gonna get to hear this. Anyway, seems Rotsky was winning and the other guys weren't too happy about it. There was a judge and a couple of big shots from the Chamber of Commerce and they were used to winning. Rotsky was a wild child then. He was just drunk at the game but he wasn't in what you'd call a stable state of mind. There were some accusations and an argument and it all got out of hand. Then Rotsky snapped, started howling and stomping around the airplane yelling all kinds of weird stuff the big shots couldn't understand. The judge said Rotsky sounded like some kind of blood-crazed Zulu, and that was just too much."

"How so?"

"Well Rotsky took it to be some kind of redneck racist crap. Don't get me wrong: Rotsky's no saint, but a racist he ain't. He went for the judge. Tried to strangle him with one of Lulu's garter belts. Would have done it too, if he hadn't had to take it off her first. Then he set Benny loose."

"Benny?"

"Lulu's pet gator. The judge saw him coming and left — pretty damn fast. Escaping with his life wasn't enough, though. When he sobered up the next day he got to thinking about all the money he'd left on that plane, so he had Rotsky arrested on a charge of alligator molestation. They got laws like that down there. He couldn't make it stick, of course, but it meant they could hold him for a few days. The judge made sure Rotsky was locked up with the perverts and the loony toons. It wasn't the best few days of his life. They hauled him up in court but had to let him go because of lack of evidence."

"So the Z stands for Zulu?"

"That's right. The name stuck. Rotsky didn't like it much and people who use it around him don't tend to stay healthy for too long, but Rotsky never did have a middle name, so he's always used Z as his initial ever since."

"Sheeit!" mused Vinnie. "I hope I never run into that judge."

"Not very likely," said Doug. "A few days later he woke up to find himself surrounded by DEA agents. They'd had a tip-off that he was dealing smack and sure enough there was a kilo of the stuff in his refrigerator which he said he'd never seen before. Not that the cops needed the drugs bust. You see, they found him in bed with an alligator. And what's worse, the alligator was drugged. That's a mandatory life sentence in those parts."

Vinnie was impressed and was about to ask a few more questions when Rotsky's voice boomed from somewhere nearby.

"Looks like these people are serious about finding Walkaway," he said.

"Oh yeah?"

"Uh-huh. That was my friend in Florida calling back. She's just had a visit from some guys in suits."

"Her too, huh?"

"Yep. Rounding up the usual suspects, I guess. Thing is, she thought they were feds at first, like I did, but they didn't show her any ID. She thought there was something weird about them. They didn't say anything about any company, though."

"So are they good guys or bad guys?"

Rotsky grinned. "I hadn't thought of it like that."

* * *

Quinn wasn't getting any prettier. The face staring back at him from the rear view mirror was like a tree trunk, he decided, with a line for every one of his sixty-three years. Except that one of them wasn't from age.

Quinn traced the long scar with a fingertip. He resented the way it was disappearing among the wrinkles. He thought of it as a kind of decoration, a badge, if not of honour then at least of dedication to his trade. Now it was fading behind these other lines that were just as hard-earned, but unwanted. Quinn's stomach gave an uneasy flip. He wondered what it might mean if the scar vanished completely. What then?

Deep behind his eyes, Quinn felt the warning shot of a headache. He rubbed his eyes, collapsed back in the seat and glared dolefully out of the side window of his rental car. For several hours he'd been doing exactly that, staring at a DC-3 parked on the edge of Tico airport. Quinn's car was on a back road that ran outside the perimeter fence, parked inconspicuously alongside some trailers. Next to him, on the passenger seat, was a camera with a 300mm lens, loaded and ready to take snaps of anybody who got into or out of the aircraft. But all the time he'd been there nobody had been near the plane, and Quinn was starting to think it was empty, maybe even abandoned. It was certainly decrepit enough for him to believe that it hadn't been touched in years. Once a bordello red, the paintwork was now so scuffed, chipped and covered in oil that it was hard to make out the markings. Only the nose art remained clearly visible — a scantily-clad woman with angel's wings holding a thick wad of dollar bills in one hand, a large calibre pistol in the other and surrounded by the words '*Divine Providence*'. Quinn never considered himself a religious man, but he thought there might be some blasphemy involved and that caused a faint squirming sensation deep inside what he imagined was his soul.

Along the road he saw two young men with long hair, earrings in ears and noses, tattered t-shirts and cut-off jeans, gliding on rollerblades, arms held out like children emulating aircraft. They were laughing. "Fucking low-lifes," Quinn muttered. Briefly he considered starting the engine, putting the pedal to the metal and running them down. After all, he had full collision damage waiver. But in the end he had to concede that it might compromise the stake-out. "Namby-pamby fucking faggots," mumbled Quinn. One skater executed a graceful pirouette. "Hippie-fucking-dippies. Uh . . ." Quinn struggled for another deprecating epithet, but his list came up short.

"Goddamn this job," Quinn muttered. He flipped open the glove compartment and rummaged around the assorted litter with increasing agitation until finally he slammed the door shut. "Goddamn!"

It had been just eighteen hours since Quinn had picked up the Buick from the Miami airport car rental pound, but already the floor and seats were covered in sweet wrappers, pizza boxes, empty beer and Dr Pepper cans, the rental documents and — somewhere — Quinn's last pack of cigarettes. Last, because he was under orders to give up, or else. He wasn't taking it well.

"*Goddamn!*" he yelled, and smacked the steering wheel with his fists.

Age wasn't being kind to Quinn. Every time he looked at the pizza boxes he could feel the weight of his stomach. Once, he'd had the body of an athlete which, coupled with a rifle, had proved an awesome killing machine. Born in Australia, Quinn had always considered himself a patriot, but he'd still felt compelled to leave the army. After Vietnam, Australia just wasn't getting into any decent wars. After years of aimlessly trekking from one petty skirmish to the next, Quinn set himself up in the US as a freelance personal security consultant, and for a while he had done well. But he found it difficult to maintain the necessary discipline and had turned to food for comfort. Soon the high-paying personal protection jobs drifted away. People with a thousand dollars a day to spend tend to have high standards about presentation.

In a few years Quinn was going to have to think about retirement, and what did he have to take him into his twilight years? His own hair and most of his own teeth and that was about it. Pension plans had never been part of any job Quinn had ever had: indeed, in his line of work, planning for the future had always seemed a tad optimistic.

Sitting all day at the edge of an airfield watching a piece of aerial junk wasn't his idea of a good time. It wasn't even his idea of a good job, but it was the only one he'd had in the past six months. He took a deep breath, held it and let it out slowly. Unconsciously, his hand moved into the inside pocket of his suit jacket and drew out the flip-top pack of Marlboros.

"Yeah! Fucking-A," he beamed. He opened the pack. It was empty.

3:
This is Cocoa Beach, for god's sake

Sally Doigt knew that someone was watching her. She could feel the gaze, like cold fingers on her skin.

She was used to attention, but there was something different about this. This was more than gut reaction. It was a finely honed professional response. Somewhere out there was a real problem.

She stood, hitched up the hem of her micro-bikini pants and adjusted the straps of the top. As she ran a hand over her skin, to brush off the sand, Sally took a surreptitious look along the beach. Her eyes met those of a fat, pink man rubbing oil into his fat, pink wife.

Who is he? thought Sally. *Why is he smiling like that?*

She scanned across the beach and every time her eyes settled on a man, she found he was looking straight back at her.

What the hell are they looking at? she thought. *What do they want?*

Sally looked at her own body, as if following their gaze. There wasn't an ounce of spare flesh on her. Every muscle was toned to perfection. Her body was a powerful machine, designed for hard work and swift action. She ran a hand through her bobbed blonde hair, kept short enough that it never got in her eyes. Dry sand tickled down her back.

It had been a strange week, one of those times when business was slow but there was money in the bank. In the past five years there had been plenty of times like this, and Sally's boss would cut her free for a while, to find some little project of her own. This time, however, the message had been clear: "Stay close and be ready. I don't know when you'll be needed and we may have to move fast."

Sally had developed a well-tuned antenna for trouble and it was telling her that whatever her boss had feared had now manifested itself on this beach. She repacked her beach bag and folded her towel, all the time taking quick glances around her.

As she walked off the beach towards the parking lot, Sally carefully scanned the people around her. Some of the men smiled at her. *Bastards!* she thought. *What is it they know?*

By distributing her beach kit around the BMW convertible, she was able to walk a full circle without making it obvious. All she could see was the usual collection of bleached, burnt and bustling holidaymakers. Reluctant to return to her motel with the problem in tow, she decided to hang around for a while, to see if the observer showed his hand.

On the opposite side of the parking lot to the beach was a restaurant with a rooftop bar. Sally threw on a sun dress, grabbed her purse and walked up the stairs. An old couple came the other way and Sally scrutinized them intently. "It doesn't just fall off, does it?" said the old woman to her husband as they passed. "Surely it goes black first."

In the bar, Sally ordered a club soda and took a seat with a clear view of her car and most of the rest of the parking lot. For the next hour or so she studied everyone who came into her field of vision. Her eyesight was eagle-sharp, and years of practice had given her the ability to spot even the tiniest movement, so she was confident that she had missed no-one. Every man she saw looked like he had something to hide, but she noticed nothing surprising, no behaviour she couldn't put down to holiday high spirits or late afternoon bad humour.

Eventually her attention waned. *You've been working too hard, kid,* she told herself. *This is Cocoa Beach for god's sake. Take a break. Relax.* She started to think about lunch. Piped music stuttered from the bar's PA system — a steam organ version of *Oh, Susannah* — and Sally knew she couldn't stick around much longer.

And then she saw him. Or rather, she saw him and then she didn't. The first glimpse had been out of the corner of her eye, but it had caught her attention immediately. He was at the edge of the parking lot, about four spaces along from her car and doing nothing in particular. She turned her head for a better look, but just then about thirty old women, in terry-towelling shorts, cashmere t-shirts and cardigans, rolled into the parking lot on tricycles, yelling like kids, right in front of her man. When they moved on, he was gone.

Sally had no doubt about what she'd seen. Something had registered. Nothing she could name, but her instincts had helped keep her alive and healthy these past five years and she wasn't about to go against them now. She ordered another club soda.

This time she didn't have quite so long to wait. Just as she was draining the glass she saw him again, much closer this time, leaning against the side of a Jeep. He looked like a bum, wearing a yellow Hawaiian shirt, cut-offs and Reeboks, all of which were well-worn and unwashed. His hair was wildly disarrayed and his open mouth revealed blackened teeth. And then Sally saw what had triggered her attention in the first place. It was something she recognized immediately. On his right wrist was a Breitling pilot's chronograph.

But that wasn't what drew her attention now. It was the fact that the bum was looking straight at her and grinning.

* * *

Rotsky was silent. He hadn't been able to smoke for a couple of hours, and though he and Vinnie were flying, Rotsky was ten yards from the controls. It had taken all of Rotsky's persuasive powers, and a stubborn refusal to leave the bar, before he had managed to talk Doug into cashing in his frequent flyer points. "Put it on the tab," he'd told Doug. "It won't fit," the barkeeper had said. Yet even the free flight hadn't cheered up Rotsky. The fate of *Delicious Tricia* was much on his mind.

The silence lasted until the 767 touched down in Orlando. They collected their luggage and walked into the concourse. Rotsky pulled a Brazilian cigar from his pocket, lit up, exhaled with a sigh, grimaced at the sharp cloud of smoke and finally spoke.

"Oh shit! Just my luck."

"Yo man! What is it?" asked Vinnie. And then, less ebulliently: "Who is it?"

"It's goddamn Shiny Shoes."

"Shiny Shoes? Who's Shiny Shoes?"

"Remember . . . oh no, I guess you don't. He's one of the guys from Las Vegas, the ones looking for Walkaway. At least, the ones who *said* they're looking for Walkaway. I wonder what he's doing here."

"Looking for Walkaway?"

Rotsky took a moment to think about it. Shiny Shoes hadn't seen him yet. The airport was busy but Rotsky's flying suit made him conspicuous. "The best form of attack is attack," he muttered and took Vinnie by the hand.

Shiny Shoes didn't see Rotsky until they were close, and then his face seemed to register shock more than recognition. What happened next completely threw Rotsky. Under the circumstances, he couldn't see that it was anything but desperately sinister. Shiny Shoes smiled.

"Well, well. Mr Rotsky. What brings you to Florida?" He held out his hand. Rotsky stared at it for a second, decided it looked safe enough and shook it.

"Whatever. Stuff. Life. Same thing as you, I guess."

"Ah, I see." Shiny Shoes' expression was a little more cautious now. "You think Mr Renouf might be here."

"As good a place as any."

"Indeed. You know, we are really quite concerned for him. We'd hate to think he'd had an accident while working for the company. There could be all sorts of compensation complications, if you see what I mean."

"Sure. You never did say who your company is."

"Didn't I? Oh, excuse me. Here's my colleague —"

Shiny Shoes nodded to the arrivals gate, where Rotsky could see his partner from Las Vegas staggering under the weight of two large suitcases.

"You'll excuse me if I give him a hand, won't you? But just before I go, there's something I meant to ask you back in Vegas."

"Shoot," said Rotsky.

"What do you know about Lady Caine?"

"Never met her," said Rotsky.

"That's right," chimed Vinnie. "None of the women Rotsky knows are ladies."

"Yeah, very funny, you're a real comedian," said Shiny Shoes.

Rotsky had opened his mouth to say the same thing, but stayed silent for a moment. Finally, he said: "So, who is she?"

"Huh! Two comedians." Shiny Shoes turned away and walked off to join his partner.

* * *

Sally shook her head. Were her eyes playing tricks? From her vantage point in the rooftop bar she had a good view of the parking lot and the entrances to the beach. Having spotted the bum who, she was now convinced, was tailing her, she should have been able to keep tabs on him. And yet he kept disappearing, vanishing as if at a magician's command behind sudden distractions — a babbling posse of over-sixty beach volleyball players, a busload of phosphate miners in beachwear and hard hats heading for the sand, and coming from the beach, a small group of emaciated, under-dressed young girls, one wearing a 'Cocoa Beach Teeny Bikini Queen' sash, followed by a larger group of disturbingly solemn young boys. Sally wondered if the bum might have orchestrated these diversions simply to unnerve her. Each time, just as Sally thought she might be in the clear, that the bum had got fed up of waiting, he reappeared just as magically, sitting on the hood of a car in the middle of the lot, or leaning against a lamp post, or pulling something from a trash bin. And every time the same questions flashed through Sally's mind: *Who is he? What does he want? Why me?*

She had to take control. She paid for her drinks and, careful to give no acknowledgement of the bum's existence, collected her things and strolled to her car. She flopped into the driver's seat, casually fussed with a few things in the glove compartment, fixed her lipstick, fired up and reversed out of the lot at around fifty miles an hour. A handbrake turn got her facing the right way and she accelerated away, turning frequently, ignoring red lights and stop signs. She didn't look back, didn't want to know who or what was behind her.

A few minutes later, she pulled a screaming, waggling turn on to Highway One, heading north, her foot flat on the floor. There was another squeal of tyres behind her, as if an echo of her own. Her natural reactions made her check the rear view mirror, but she saw only normal traffic behind her. Then she glanced left. She stared straight at the bum, sitting in his own convertible, grinning insanely. His car veered closer. It hit hers with a muffled bang and squeal of folding metal. Sally felt a grinding vibration through the wheel. Her car lurched to the right, ran off the road into the parking lot of a McDonalds and headed straight for a parked police cruiser.

Sally never knew whether what happened next took seconds or hours. Certainly there was a sudden contortion of time as she approached the rear of the police vehicle. She pumped the brake rapidly, without apparent effect, and she knew that the collision was inevitable, yet she had time to read the notices on the rear of the cruiser: *To protect and serve, Dial 911,* a bumper sticker: *Stop those litters, Spay your critters,* and in the rear window was a yellow diamond with the words *.357 magnum on board.* Later she would remember all of that, but not the crash itself. The world became a cocktail of blurred pictures and distorted sounds as she dropped in and out of consciousness. Every now and then she'd pick out something she could recognize — a strip light, the squeal of a gurney wheel, the smell of hamburger. For a few seconds she could see clearly, but was deaf. Then her world went black, though she could hear with a clarity that bordered on pain.

"You hear about that cop down the hall?" said a voice. Sally struggled to answer, but couldn't speak. She tried to raise her hand, to signal her distress, but her entire body felt encased in ice.

"You mean the one with the quarterpounder in his windpipe?" said another voice.

"Yeah. He's real lucky to be alive."

"How's that?"

"You try breathing with a quarter-pound of prime beef and a sesame bun in your throat. He'd be dead right now if it hadn't been for his partner."

"What'd he do?"

"Gave the guy a tracheotomy, even though he was wounded himself. Way I hear it, he lost an eye to a Chicken McNugget, but didn't think twice. Cut open his partner's throat with a pocketknife. Lucky, really, that he had a straw handy."

The voices continued, but indistinct now. Words stretched and distorted. Finally, everything went away, and Sally drifted into sleep or death, she didn't care which.

* * *

Escobar wasn't sure that the man from the pet food company was paying attention. He kept looking over his shoulder and his hands fumbled nervously in his pockets or scratched obliviously at his ass. He'd been like this ever since Escobar had introduced him to Hipólito and explained that the big man took care of all payments to tradesmen. Escobar prodded him and they continued their walk through the garden.

"You see," insisted Escobar, "this has been a wealthy land for many centuries." Escobar carried a small trowel which he waved at the mountains. "More than two thousand years ago, a great and proud people prospered on the fertility and mineral wealth of Colombia." He ran his gaze around the mountains, as if able to discern the ghosts of these people. "They were the Muisca, a cultured people with sophisticated religious and political systems. They were renowned for their exquisite gold work and for their export trade in salt and emeralds." He spat into a vegetable patch. "Then the Spanish *conquistadors*, obsessed by the myth of El Dorado, tore out the heart of the

Muisca culture. They murdered the Indians and stole their gold."

He sighed and gazed mournfully at the ground. "And the Indians fought each other. The Zipa from Bacatá — you would call it Bogotá — fought the Zacque from Hunza while the Spaniards looked on."

The pet food man tripped on a garden rake and only just remained upright. He stopped, pulled a handkerchief from his pocket and wiped his brow.

"Now the blood of the Muisca has been diluted," droned Escobar. "But there are those—" he cast a meaningful look at his visitor "—who can trace a direct line back to the king of the Zipa. There are those—" he added emphasis here because he wasn't sure the pet food man was getting the point, "—who comprehend the true meaning of our country's history."

Escobar dropped to his knees, his head bowed, and examined a wilted cauliflower. There were tears in his eyes. Maybe it's the altitude, he thought. This was his diagnosis when any plant in his kitchen garden died, as most of them did, sooner or later.

The country estate had not been a great success. Escobar saw his huge, sprawling *finca* as his kingdom, a microcosm of Colombia itself. It had been bought with the proceeds of his smuggling activities, first from sneaking goods into Colombia and then smuggling cocaine out. In the early days it had been a crusade. With huge import duties, the common people of Colombia simply couldn't afford goods that weren't local. And so it had become Escobar's mission to give them what they needed at prices they could manage — TVs, watches, perfumes and designer clothes. At one time, Escobar was known throughout his village as King Levi.

It was Escobar's dream that his country estate, and ultimately Colombia herself, should become self-sufficient — wealthy enough to afford imports and rich with local produce that the world would clamour to buy. He foresaw himself as a national hero, above the triviality of law. Though he looked European, Escobar was a *mestizo*, the only child of an Indian mother and a Creole father, both killed during *La Violencia* of fifty-five. He knew he had a direct line to the desires and hearts of the people.

He'd even given some of them work on his mountain estate. The *finca* was Escobar's haven. He felt safe there. Yet that same remoteness made it impossible to run as a business, and insupportable as a stronghold. The farm had been part of a plan to change that. If they could grow the food they needed, he and his team would be invulnerable, Escobar thought. And besides, it would save a lot of money on the food bill.

Escobar owned everything he could see from his house — the valley, the hills. Once, much of it had been fertile farmland. Now the land ran wild, and Escobar's dream of reclaiming it for coffee had faded. He lost the money he needed for the ranch when he tried to launder it through Europe. His accountant had set it up — something to do with insurance, Escobar was vague on the details. "Impeccable credentials," the accountant had said about the European agents. "Actual nobility." Escobar liked the sound of that, but the money disappeared anyway. Two million dollars.

Hipólito arranged a meeting with the agents to request a refund. He came back empty-handed with a 'don't ask' expression that Escobar had learned to respect. Until he remembered he was the boss.

"They won't be no more trouble," was Hipólito's only comment. He punctuated it with a snarl that made Escobar's guts churn. He gave Hipólito a small pay rise.

Desperate for success, Escobar had put his remaining cash and all his cocaine into Díaz's dolphin scam. He poked the dead cauliflower.

A listless growl came from the other side of a high fence. This seemed to remind the pet food man why he was there and he cleared his throat. "About . . . about this bill. It *is* very large."

Escobar looked up, his eyes dry now. He reached into a pocket and pulled out a tiny gold object, shaped like a teardrop. It looked like an earring. "You see this? This is part of our heritage. Your heritage."

"It— it is?"

"Of course. This is a ceremonial . . . object of the Tayronas, which I personally rescued from a burial site in the Sierras."

"You robbed a grave?" The pet food man's opened wide as though his reply had both surprised and terrified him.

Escobar trembled with indignation. "*Robbed!* I—"

"—hey, boss!"

Hipólito strode towards them. The pet food man backed off, wringing his hands. "We'll be in touch," he squawked, then turned and ran for his car. Escobar stayed on his knees. He pointed to the cauliflower.

"Look at this," he said. "It's a disgrace. Where's the head gardener?"

Hipólito stared at the plant.

"You shot him."

"Shot him? Why would I shoot a gardener?"

"Well, you had him shot, anyway. The plants all died. You said he should join them."

"Oh." Escobar's memory of events before the Corporation meeting was already a little hazy. "Yes, well, see he gets replaced." Escobar regarded Hipólito cagily. "Did you get this week's FBI list?"

"The Ten Most Wanted? Yeah, pulled it off the web this morning."

"Am I —"

"No boss."

Escobar plunged the trowel deep into the soil. He did it again and again. Finally he paused, trowel in mid-air. "What about Hernandez?"

Hernandez was a former business partner of Escobar. He'd moved over to the Cali cartel just in time and had recently bought most of Colombia's Atlantic seaboard.

"Yes boss," said Hipólito. "He's still at number seven."

The trowel headed back into the soil. Escobar lifted it and prepared to plunge again.

"But there is a warrant out for you," said Hipólito. He managed to produce a half-smile.

"There is?" Escobar stood, a grin emerging slowly. "What for?"

Hipólito shifted his weight repeatedly from one foot to the other. He looked at the ground, then at everything in the vicinity except Escobar. Finally, with downcast eyes and a hushed voice, he said: "Not sure. The satellite link went down before I could check. I think it was something to do with parking tickets."

Escobar threw the trowel like a knife at the soil. It bounced off a stone and landed on his foot. He pretended not to notice.

"The connection is working okay?"

Hipólito nodded.

The satellite system had cost Escobar the last of his CIA money. And it was the CIA that had taken the cash. They left him with their old communications system which gave him a low-speed Internet connection. It still had 'Property of the CIA' etched in the hardware. And everyday few hours, for no apparent reason, it just stopped working.

"Who's that?" snapped Escobar and pointed to a pale, thin young man who shuffled nervously just beyond the garden gate. Either side of him stood two grim-faced men with guns. Escobar had hired them to lead the raid on Díaz's jungle factory and their presence made him nervous. "I was expecting a report, not a gift."

Hipólito smiled at what he assumed was a joke.

"It's just a little something the boys picked up in the jungle," he explained. "I thought you might find it interesting."

Escobar brushed the soil off his knees and motioned to the house. "Let's discuss this over coffee," he said.

Just then several rapid booms rolled over the landscape from the surrounding hills.

Escobar and Hipólito squinted into the distance. They watched brown clouds burble into the sky. Around them buzzed black insects, moving improbably fast.

"They're bombing the Zipa Terraces," said Hipólito. "Dumb fucks. There hasn't been a dope crop there for two years. Did you forget to pay off the air force again, boss?"

"Maybe," grumbled Escobar. He thought of the Navy and was glad he was two hundred miles inland. "Where's the goddamned accountant?"

"Dead."

"Dead?"

"Uhu."

"Me?"

"Not this time. Natural causes. Sonofabitch was electrocuted by his new dishwasher."

"The one I gave him?"

"Right. He was installing it in his new house—"

"—the one I had built for him," said Escobar. He thought of unpaid Electrician's Union bribes. "Never mind."

The five men walked into the kitchen. Escobar looked around and took a mental inventory. He did this a lot. Everything in the kitchen had been imported from Europe. The plate rack hadn't arrived and there had been a mix-up over the taps, but it was still the only one of its kind in the country. He ran his fingers proudly over the oak-style veneer.

Escobar sat while Hipólito prepared coffee. The two hired hoods sat silently at the back of the kitchen, betraying no interest in the proceedings. Escobar knew they were waiting for their pay before disappearing. He would have Hipólito negotiate fees with them later. The stranger stood in the middle of the room, looking frail. He glanced nervously about him, seemingly terrified of everything he saw.

"Don't use too much coffee," Escobar told Hipólito, and then to the stranger: "Would you like coffee?"

"He doesn't speak Spanish," Hipólito interrupted. "I think he's an American."

Escobar switched into English.

"Would you like some coffee, my friend?"

The stranger's eyes widened. He shrank slightly and his gaze flicked between the two men. Escobar looked impatiently at Hipólito and asked in Spanish: *"Who is this? Why have you brought him here?"*

"He was at the factory," said Hipólito. *"In a fridge."*

Escobar shrugged. Hipólito had found people in stranger places.

"He was the only one there," continued Hipólito. *"I thought he might be able to explain a few things."*

"The only one? Are you telling me the place was empty?"

"Pretty much. It looked like they'd cleared out in a hurry. We found some equipment and a little bit of cocaine, but not the normal stuff. There was no coca paste. No ether. None of the normal manufacturing gear. But what we did find was lots of cans full of some kind of wax."

"Wax?"

"Yeah. Pink wax. I brought some back. It's in the car. We got rid of the rest. Burned it along with the whole goddamn factory."

Escobar absorbed this information for a few minutes and then turned to the stranger.

"Who are you?" he barked.

The stranger jumped out his skin, which was turning yellow. He was covered in an oily sweat and looked to Escobar like he might die at any second.

"Relax, my friend," said Escobar. "I don't mean to upset you. We would simply like some information. Why don't you sit down?"

The stranger looked at a nearby empty chair like it was a trap. Then he fell on it with obvious relief.

By this time the air was thick with the aroma of coffee. Hipólito distributed cups and, without asking, placed one in front of the stranger who eyed it suspiciously. Escobar raised his own cup, taking a few seconds to savour the smell before drinking. He closed his eyes and inhaled deeply, then drank with tiny, delicate sips. He sighed and a smile came to his lips. The clinking of coffee cups almost drowned a small voice that said: "Billy".

Escobar looked up, unsure if he had really heard anything. The stranger, seeing that he had everyone's attention, became suddenly more expansive.

"Billy Cook," he said.

Escobar smiled encouragingly. "Well, Billy Cook," he said, "tell me about yourself. What were you doing in the jungle?"

"Cook," mumbled Billy.

"Yes, I know your name —"

"— No, no, I was the cook. Not that I *can* cook. It's the name. Confuses people."

"I see," said Escobar, his patience thinning. "Who were you working for?"

"Díaz. Enrico Díaz."

Escobar flashed Hipólito a knowing look. He had been pretty sure his information was correct but it was good to get confirmation.

"And what were you doing there in the jungle?"

The American looked surprised, as if he couldn't understand why he'd been asked the question.

"I cooked," he said.

Escobar stood up. Billy grabbed his cup and raised it to his mouth, as though the act of drinking would somehow postpone any punishment. Strangely, it worked. Escobar sighed and sat down again.

"Billy. What I want to know is what Díaz was doing in the jungle. What were you making there?"

The American appeared reluctant to answer.

"Billy?"

"Look, I'm sorry, okay? I really can't tell you much." His voice rose in pitch as the terror crept back in. "It won't help you to . . . you know . . . *do* things to me. I really don't know anything."

"Relax Billy. Just tell us what you do know."

"I just cooked, you know? I didn't even cook very well." Billy's voice was getting uncomfortably close to soprano. "I didn't even like them."

"Why were you there?"

Billy seemed to be having trouble catching his breath.

"Breath deeply, Billy," Escobar told him. "Just calm down, drink your *tinto* and tell us your story."

* * *

Since his life with Rotsky had started, Vinnie had become used to being left in strange places. He tried to identify the locations from sounds and smells, and he was now pretty good at it. Bars were easy, of course, and he knew when he was in a strip joint from the added tang of the dancers' perfume. Hangars and aircraft presented no problem either: Vinnie loved the smells of oiled metal and avgas, and the roar of an aircraft engine was the nearest thing he had to a girlfriend. This time, however, he wasn't too sure.

It had started out easy enough. He knew they were walking across an airport. The breeze on his cheek felt like the constant wind that blows across the open expanse of airfields, and as confirmation there was the deep growl of a radial engine. He thought he'd picked up the scent of an aircraft, though the close proximity of Rotsky's cigar wasn't helping. Then there had been a short climb to a doorway. They were inside, in a small space with a sloping floor, and suddenly he wasn't sure anymore. There was a closeness to the atmosphere and the sound was muffled. And not even the cigar could cover the heady blend of perfume and incense.

A church? thought Vinnie. *No, can't be. Not with Rotsky.* Besides, he was half-convinced they were on an aircraft. Yet there was something distinctly erotic about the atmosphere.

He thought of asking Rotsky, but the big guy had been in a foul mood since the meeting with Shiny Shoes at the airport. Rotsky was convinced there was something sinister about it and had retreated into a paranoid sulk. After coming inside whatever place this was, Rotsky seemed to have disappeared. Vinnie was sure he was alone.

Moving slowly, Vinnie explored the space around him. The sloping floor made him giddy, so when he found a soft seat beneath his hand, he sat on it. It appeared to be some kind of overstuffed sofa, and unlike the floor it was level. Kicking off his shoes, Vinnie stretched out, closed his eyes and did his best to relax.

The next thing he knew was a soft hand brushing his forehead and a soft woman's voice saying: "Wake up, Vinnie. Wake up."

"Who's that?" His head was still stuffed with sleep.

"It's Lulu," said the voice. "You know who I am, right?"

"Uh . . . yeah. I think." Vinnie recalibrated, pulled data from his memory. "You're the one that phoned Rotsky." Vinnie knew something else about Lulu, a piece of information he'd picked up recently, but right at this moment he couldn't retrieve it. His entire consciousness was filled with Lulu's voice.

"That's right, hon. How are you feeling?"

"Like I've been run over by a truck," he lied. In fact, he was feeling better by the second. Lulu's voice was having a profoundly rejuvenating effect. It was like having your ears stroked with mink, he thought, though he was only guessing. Every syllable she uttered created tiny bursts of pleasure in unexpected parts of his body. The accent was vaguely southern but heavily modulated, as if worn smooth by many influences, as if it had been places and done things that Vinnie could only imagine.

"You stay right there, sweetheart. I'll get you a drink."

Vinnie wasn't about to argue. His mouth felt like an animal graveyard. A few seconds later he felt a glass being pressed into his hand, so he lifted it and took a deep swig. His chest burst and his throat caught fire. When he finished coughing and spluttering, he managed to croak: "What the hell is this?"

"It's Maker's Mark, honey. Don't y'all like bourbon?"

"Yeah, sure, no sweat," Vinnie gasped and wiped tears from his eyes. "It's just that I was expecting Gatorade. I thought that's what everybody drank down here."

"Not real people, hon. Now you drink that up and I'll get you some more."

Vinnie was starting to think that he was going to enjoy Florida. Rotsky rarely let him have more than the odd beer. A gentle wave of scent told Vinnie that Lulu was close again.

"Do you want to feel my face, hon," she purred. "Isn't that what blind people do?"

Vinnie thrust out his hand, palm vertical as though signalling someone to stop. The heel of his hand hit something hard, which yielded. There was a sharp cry, and when Lulu's voice came again, it was from slightly further away.

"Careful now, hon," she mumbled, her voice suggesting toothache. "You just keep your hand there and I'll come to you."

Vinnie felt fingers close around his and his hand was guided to skin that was smooth, cool and powdery. His fingertips traced cheekbones and lips while his mind built a picture of a face that owed more to signals from his loins than from his fingers. He was getting increasingly confused. If he didn't find a way to focus, he thought he might go under, or embarrass himself. With a huge effort, he let his hand drop.

"So. You and Rotsky are old friends?"

"Oh hell yes," said Lulu. "We go way back. Right back to the days of the OLC."

"OLC? Rotsky mentioned that. What is it?"

"The Outside Lomcovak Club. He hasn't he told you about that?"

"Not really. He's talked a bit about the old days — running dope and guns and all sorts of weird things. But since I've known him, Rotsky has been pretty straight, I think. Just hangar flying, I guess."

"Not all of it, believe me," said Lulu. "It's just that every now and then he needs to keep his head down, like we all do."

Vinnie felt suddenly apprehensive.

"He isn't here, is he?"

"No honey, he isn't here. You'd hear him if he was. When it comes to talking about Rotsky, nobody's better at it than Rotsky."

"Yeah, I've noticed. Still, I suppose he's got a lot to brag about."

"He has?"

"Well, he's a great pilot, right?"

"That's what he tells us," chuckled Lulu.

"So —"

"— I'm just having fun with you, sweetheart. I love the guy to death."

There was a tone in her voice now that made Vinnie oddly jealous.

"I've heard the Zulu story," said Vinnie.

"The what, honey?"

"How he got to be called Zulu."

"Right. Because he runs on Zulu time."

"On what?"

"Zulu time. Greenwich Mean Time. UTC. Whatever you want to call it. All flights are timed according to Zulu time. Gets a bit confusing when you're five hours from London, though."

"Zulu time?"

"Sure. You ask Rotsky the time. You'll find his watch is five hours faster than anyone else around here."

Vinnie was confused. "I thought it had something to do with alligators."

"Oh sweetheart, how could 'Zulu' have anything to do with alligators?"

Vinnie didn't have an answer for that. "So," he said, "how come everyone's so worried about this Walkaway guy? From what he says, Rotsky's had friends in trouble before, but he's never said anything about chasing around the country after them."

There was a pause, and it seemed to Vinnie like Lulu was considering her answer.

"Old times I guess," she said eventually. "Rotsky, Walkaway and me used to be real tight. There were a few others then, too. Don't know where most of them are any more. Rotsky got into some trouble and disappeared for a while. Walkaway . . . well, Walkaway carried on doing the same old thing, but it kinda lost its charm and we drifted apart. As for me — I made enough money not to worry for a while. I've worked on and off since, but the fun's kinda gone out of it. And anyway, I'm lazy."

"So what is it you do?"

"Oh, honey," cooed Lulu. "Rotsky really hasn't told you anything about me at all, has he?"

* * *

Quinn was thinking about writing a book on motels. He reckoned he'd seen just about every one and it would be a shame to let that depth of experience go to waste.

This one was about typical of the breed. It called itself the Rocket View Inn. On days when the Shuttle was launched, it held all-you-can-eat barbeques in the parking lot. It was next to the Bee Line, about an hour's drive from Cape Canaveral, though there was no way of getting to the motel straight from the Expressway. Quinn had had to go all the way to Rockledge and backtrack down a two-lane to find the place. When he'd arrived, the slow, half-asleep receptionist knew nothing of the special price Quinn had arranged on the phone.

Helluva place, thought Quinn as he flicked channels on the TV. He had to stand by the set to do this, because there was no remote control. There had been once, but a past guest had unscrewed it from the bedside cabinet and had taken it away, for whatever bizarre purpose. Every channel looked fuzzy to some degree, and most of them seemed to be running game shows, but eventually he found the weather channel he'd been seeking. He was going to be out following people all afternoon, and he wanted to know what to wear.

It was going to be hot, with the possibility of thunderstorms.

"Big fucking surprise," grunted Quinn. He smacked the TV. It spontaneously changed channel.

He walked to the bathroom and stared at his face through the crud on the mirror. His hand came up to wipe away the water stains and grease smudges but stopped before he touched the glass. The strip light above the mirror sank his eyes deep into his face and traced black lines across his skin.

Quinn sorted through the bottles, tubes and tubs ranged along the back of the sink — cleanser, toner, gel moisturizer with AHAs, firming mask. He unscrewed a tub of moisturizer and scooped out a generous portion of clear gel. There were blue flecks in it and he wondered if they would show on his face. He smeared it across his cheeks, into the grooves, around his mouth and the fans of furrows from his eyes, into the valleys of his brow and, hand cupped, up and into the folds of his chins. As he massaged the flesh, Quinn pressed hard, smoothing the ridges, pulling the skin back. And he narrowed his eyes, thinking that it gave a better impression of how others saw him.

With every last trace of the cream erased, Quinn walked back into the bedroom. He thought for a moment about doing a few push-ups, then remembered that he had a report to write, and he didn't want his hands to shake. He rested a hand on a pile of books on the bedside table. They were by a motley assortment of evangelists, people Quinn had seen on TV, in shopping malls, and even a couple of past clients for his personal protection services. He scanned the titles: *God: What He Really Thinks*, *The Truth the Bible Forgot to Tell You* and *Allah, the Unwritten Story*. There were several others along the same lines. Quinn considered making another attempt to understand them, but every time he tried he found himself more confused. They assaulted the basic principles that had so far held his life together — self-centredness and self-reliance, suppressing whatever was uncomfortable or alien, often through the use of deadly force.

Quinn lay on the bed that was mostly like a rock, apart from a spongy section in the centre, and looked at the TV, trying to make out what was being said above the rattle and hum of the air conditioner. Nothing made any sense. The information reaching him from the TV was so fractured that he couldn't even tell what kind of show it was.

He eased himself off the bed, already stiff, padded to the TV and picked up a splayed *TV Guide* from the top of the set. Underneath was a .38 detective special, one of many guns he owned and which he kept scattered here and there so that, in the unlikely event that anyone ever managed to surprise him, there was always ordnance within easy reach. The problem was that, lately, Quinn had been having trouble keeping track of the whereabouts of all the guns. This one, for example, he thought he'd stashed in his sock drawer.

He carried the gun to the armchair. He sat back and idly stroked the stubby barrel and whirred the full cylinder. He whiled away a few minutes in a happy fantasy about a burglar making the worst — and last — decision of his life by choosing that very moment to break into Quinn's room. He had re-run the final scene half a dozen times, each with different endings (all fatal for the burglar) when he realized that his bones and muscles had set, had taken on the shapes and angles of the chair, and Quinn shook with a rare instant of panic when the thought flashed through his mind that he might never rise again, that he would die in this chair like one of those old men discovered dead in their slippers, part-eaten by the dog, apparently indifferent to the chore of carrying on. Quinn struggled to his feet and cranked his arms around, flexed muscles and worked joints. There was a sharp *crack* deep in his right shoulder.

When the phone rang it took him by surprise. His nerves were jagged from long hours of surveillance and he hadn't got more than a few hours sleep in the past week. Even with the TV on and the air conditioning humming, the telephone seemed loud.

There was only one person who knew where Quinn was, so there was no need for preliminaries when he picked up the receiver.

"Speak," he grumbled.

"He's dead," said the voice.

"Who's dead?" asked Quinn, thinking that in his line of business it could be one of a long list.

"Our man in Colombia."

"Shit," Quinn said flatly. "Did he file a final report?"

"No. First thing we heard was about his body turning up."

"How'd he die?"

"That's the weird thing. It was natural causes. He was on an inflatable mattress, just off the beach when he got run down by a cruiser driven by some asshole from Miami."

"Spooky."

"Right."

"When did it happen?"

"Must've been a couple of weeks ago. And it took about a week to identify the body. They had to get hold of the dental records to be sure."

"So we've lost contact?"

"Yup, looks that way. Any ideas?"

Quinn thought about it for a moment. His first idea was to quit the job and take up stockbroking, or pig farming, or truck driving or anything that didn't involve strange people phoning him early in the morning to tell him that somebody had died. But he knew the money wouldn't be as good and the fringe benefits as irresistible.

"Yeah, I've got an idea. I think this Florida lead could amount to something. I'll let you know."

Quinn put down the phone without waiting for a reply. The TV was forgotten now. He was thinking that it was time he renewed some old acquaintances.

* * *

The coast wasn't being kind to Enrico Díaz. He was accustomed to the rare crispness of the mountains, and the sweet strangulation of the Caribbean air had ambushed him. It was just before the wet season and already the atmosphere was moist enough to touch.

Since they had arrived in Santa Marta, Díaz had spent most of his time in the back room of a café, trying not to die of the heat. In the jungle he had stayed inside the air-conditioned huts. The boat ride back from the convention had almost killed him, and then followed the nightmare journey to Santa Marta — a two-hour flight in a floatplane, six hours on the bus from hell, and thirty minutes trapped in a *colectivo* taxi — eight nearly suffocating people in a rat-trap Buick on a guided tour of the potholes of Santa Marta. And yet it wasn't the heat that bothered him most. It was the fact that he hadn't been met by a limo. That's going to change soon, he promised.

José and Jesus had followed on by truck bringing with them what Díaz liked to refer to as 'the merchandise'. They had passed the night in Santa Marta quite happily, sitting in the Papagayo café, drinking *aguardiente* and Aguila beer and playing *veinti una* with a couple of local musicians. The two hoods were losing heavily, but it was Díaz's money so they didn't mind.

They were almost disappointed when Díaz walked into the bar. Inevitably their eyes were drawn to his hands, and they exchanged furtive glances, stifling grins. Díaz kept his hands on the move, mostly down by his side or behind his back, hoping no-one would notice, but within seconds all eyes in the bar were on them. They were bright pink: indeed, a colour that went beyond pink, a preternatural cerise.

Díaz's accident with the pharmaceutical dye, while they were tearing apart the jungle factory, was the favourite topic of conversation between José and Jesus. Just about everyone who passed through the bar in the past few hours had heard the details, some of them accurate. In spite of their best efforts, both men broke out in broad smiles and a strangled titter bubbled up from José's throat.

Díaz wasn't in a laughing mood. He buried his hands in his pockets and glowered at his henchmen.

"What are you sitting around for?" he snapped. "We've got work to do."

He stomped outside and stopped in the dust-clogged street. He screwed up his eyes against the sun and concentrated hard on his breathing while he waited for the other two to join him. It took a while.

Díaz looked around at the whitewashed roughness of the buildings, the grubby, rampaging children and the windswept drifts of litter with an uncomfortable mixture of pride and embarrassment. He counted himself a Colombian, and where gringos might see poverty he saw honesty, an absence of affectation and a disdain for the self-deluding pretensions of northern civilization He despised those Colombians who embraced the attractions of gringo culture, who thought that wearing baseball caps and reading *Time* would make them cultured.

Díaz might have been born in Florida, but Colombia was his spiritual home. His grandfather had emigrated to the US long before the first Colombian flood, back in the days when Florida's first language was English. He'd got rich, got poor and then got dead when he failed to repay a loan from a gangster with no sense of humour. The wife and son he left behind continued the family tradition of starting, growing and destroying businesses, and it was the need to bail out an ailing kitty litter import company that had driven Díaz into the smuggler's trade. As with the other businesses, he was good at it for a while. Then, inexplicably but predictably, he got bad at it, though by that time it didn't matter. He was addicted — to the sense of danger, to the money, and to the endless opportunities for posing with high-class firearms.

"Work?" asked Jesus.

Díaz span around to face him. "What did you say?"

"Did you say work?" repeated Jesus. José's creased face posed the same question. "What kind of work?"

"We've got to get into the transport business," grumbled Díaz.

* * *

Phyllis put down her Diet Tab and closed *Dolphin-Friendly Diets* having read only about half a page. Normally she felt relaxed when lying on her steamer chair among the rampant greenery of her conservatory. She always went there when the aches got too much, or the lines staring back at her from the mirror drove her towards despair.

The conservatory had been the last good thing — and maybe the first good thing — her husband had done for her. He had done it by dying and leaving her something close enough to a fortune, which meant she could afford the surroundings she always thought she deserved.

The old bastard would have had a fit, she thought looking at the opulence of her surroundings. The image of her husband in apoplexy brought her a grain of comfort. During his life he had been frugal to the point where she had become convinced they were close to poverty. A massive thrombosis had liberated them both — him from a life of toil, and her from him — and she was astonished to discover that he had amassed minority holdings in nine companies, impressively full savings accounts with five banks, and no debts. The second the ink on the probate was dry, she sold the company shares, corralled the savings into one offshore account and started buying the life she wanted.

The conservatory, the pool, the Jacuzzi, the Pomeranians, the Porsche and a part-time butler had taken more out of the funds than she had anticipated, though, which was why she couldn't rest today, not until it was over.

For the millionth time she patted her hair. She liked to think of it as distinguished silver, the merest hint of blue giving it the chrome glint that so convincingly faked vitality. Just that morning, Antoine had worked his weekly miracle. He'd combed and snipped and teased and dyed, flattered and flapped, and the more he worked on her the younger she felt, right up to the point when he whispered in her ear: "I think I may have some business for you, sweetheart."

She knew what that meant and she knew she couldn't turn it down, but it would take days for her to feel comfortable with herself again.

Never in her wildest nightmares had Phyllis expected to have to work for a living. When her husband had been alive, she had stayed at home and complained of the meagreness of her existence. Since his death, her contribution to the world had been her very existence and her natural talents as a hostess, lunch date and confidante. From time to time she would organize fund-raising events for local, high-profile charities, but the idea of making that kind of effort simply to pay the bills left Phyllis with a sour taste in her mouth. That sort of thing was for other people, for those without conservatories and Porsches.

Then the finance company sent someone to take the Porsche away. It had taken every bit of her manipulative skills to persuade the stone-faced bailiff to give her an extra week, which she spent in frantic activity, hiring an accountant to get her affairs in order and raising loans to cover the debts.

She was stunned to find just how large those debts were. "This is how much you're going to have to raise, every month, to maintain your current lifestyle," the accountant had told her, pushing a piece of paper across his laminated chipboard desk. Phyllis had stared with disbelief at the figure and then looked up into the accountant's face for some sign that he had made a mistake. All she saw was a malevolent glee. Looking straight into her eyes, he'd said: "Why don't you kill the dogs?"

The Pomeranians had given Phyllis more joy in the past two years than her husband had in forty. She turned her anger at the accountant's remark into a determination to make money.

There was no way she could do it straight away, and so Phyllis had started another round of borrowing, this time going to people who didn't make her hit list the first time, including some she wouldn't normally have gone to even for a charity contribution.

Weeks went by, and still Phyllis couldn't think of a way of earning money. She simply didn't understand how people went about it. Was there somewhere you could *shop* for a job?

The debts mounted again, and some of the less sympathetic lenders were calling in their loans. It was one rainy morning, as Phyllis was explaining the privations of the penniless to twelve of her friends, serving them an embarrassingly impoverished snack of white truffle mousse and partridge vol-au-vents, that the doorbell rang and started her rise out of poverty and her descent into the criminal underworld.

The butler ushered in a young man who looked as at home among the gilded chintz of Phyllis' drawing room as a shark in a play pool. His leather jacket was old and worn, his jeans were faded by use rather than by fashion, and his gold jewellery was plated.

He scanned the room, not missing a single detail. Within thirty seconds he could have given a more accurate inventory of its contents than Phyllis herself — and a more accurate idea of the resale value. Finally, he turned his attention to the women, who by now were watching him silently, open-mouthed, with a damp, fearful awe.

"Hiya, Phil," he beamed, "how's it going?"

Phyllis bustled him from the room, demanding imperiously what the hell he thought he was playing at.

"Just after my money, Phil," he said, not losing his smile for a second. "I guess you don't have it, huh?"

Phyllis started to give him a lecture on patience and good manners, but the young man had cut her short. He complimented her on her house and on her obviously wealthy, aged friends. He said that seeing her place had given him an idea of how she might be able to repay him. And how that might mean he wouldn't have to come and rob her house and kill her dogs.

Outwardly, everything remained the same, though friends remarked how she never seemed to be worried about money any more. Indeed, although she hated what she did and what she was, Phyllis couldn't help but throw herself into it. Whatever she did, she did well. She could see no excuse for being second best.

From time to time the young man would get a message to her, through her hairdresser or beauty therapist, and later that day a man would turn up at her house. Within an hour it would be over, she would be richer, and she could concentrate on spending the money.

Today was one of those days. Phyllis couldn't rest, couldn't read, couldn't even enjoy petting the dogs. As usual, she'd given the butler the afternoon off, and as usual he had gone knowing exactly what she was up to.

When the doorbell rang, Phyllis flew off the steamer chair and was halfway to the front door before she caught herself. She paused, hitched her Montana leather pants into a slightly more advantageous position and, taking a deep breath, walked with as much grace as she could muster to the door.

The man on the other side wasn't quite what she expected. They never were. He had a well-travelled face that made it dangerous to guess his age, though she thought that it couldn't be far off her own sixty-odd years, and his body had a layer of fat over what had once been a trim frame.

He stared straight at her with no trace of friendliness, but then she thought she saw his resolve weaken.

"Is . . . is this the right place?" he asked.

"Depends what you're after, my dear," she replied, feeling more at ease now she could take charge. "Come inside and let's see what we can do for you."

She led him into the main drawing room. Its smothering wealth usually served to subdue anyone who wasn't accustomed to such opulence, but this man showed no reaction. He stared at Phyllis with a concentration that momentarily rocked her self-confidence.

"Can we get on with this?" the man said, pulling a thick wad of banknotes from his jacket pocket and dropped them on a reproduction Louis Quinze coffee table. "It's all there. Five thousand."

Phyllis smiled indulgently, trying to put the man at ease. She moved across the room to a door that led into her 'day room', a place she had designed herself as somewhere to escape the pressures of life. It was furnished with simple luxury, the silk-covered daybed half-hidden in satin drapes, the ever-closed velvet window curtains giving the room its rich red warmth. Pausing in the doorway, she looked back to see if the customer was following her, and was relieved to find that he wasn't.

Once in the room, it was a matter of a moment to find the package and retrieve it. Walking back into the drawing room she handed the cardboard box to the man. He opened it and stared inside with an uncertain expression.

"It's all there," Phyllis told him.

"It had better be," he said.

* * *

Vinnie's face had turned deep crimson and he was having trouble breathing.

"You're a wh-whore?" he stuttered, his voice cracked with ambivalence. His head and heart were outraged, his loins were intrigued.

"Well now, Vinnie honey, I like to think of myself as being more in the line of offering professional personal therapy of . . . ah, a physical nature," said Lulu with a smile in her voice. Then she thought for a moment and said: "But 'whore' will do fine, though I'm more on the management side of things, if you see what I mean. I mostly franchise these days. That's why we're in Florida, checking on the outlets. Making sure things are up to standard — customer service, value for money, that kind of thing."

"Best in the business," said Rotsky. He'd returned a few minutes before, just as Lulu was explaining the nature of her business. It had taken some time because she had been interrupted on several occasions by phone calls, though from what Vinnie could gather none of them had been about work.

Vinnie's head span with the possibilities. He wanted to ask all kinds of things, like 'how much?' and 'when?'. This new revelation just added danger to Lulu's list of alluring characteristics. He tried to remember where he'd put the video camera.

"So this is—?" Vinnie waved a hand in a manner that was meant to take in his surroundings.

"My office, yes," said Lulu. "It's a 1944 C-47, the military version of the DC-3. Last of my fleet." A wistfulness came into her voice. "Back in the good old days I used to have a DC-4, a Grumman Goose for the Canadian market, a beautiful Constellation and a Beech 18 for making house calls. We'd drop the girls off at the ranches and country homes all over the country. Our motto was: 'Anytime, anywhere, any size'. All that's over now." She sniffed. "Still, you know this business with Walkaway could turn out to be a lot of fun. Just like the old days. Live fast, eat well, die young."

"Die young?"

"Figure of speech, sweetheart."

Vinnie was left to think about this for a while, because Lulu was itching to tell Rotsky something.

"Listen, sweetheart," she said, "I just got through talking to a friend of mine, does crop dusting, charters, stuff like that, just north of Houston. Had an interesting story. See if this suggests the same thing to you it does to me."

"Try me."

"Well, this guy was in the FBO office at the airfield when a guy comes in looking to rent or charter a plane. Says he's a pilot and that he flew into a nearby private field the day before."

"So why didn't he fly out the same way?"

"Exactly, hon! That's what I was getting to. This guy says to the guy –"

"Whoa, wait a minute. Which guy says to which guy?"

"I'm sorry?"

"Which guy is doing the talking here."

"My guy."

"Your friend."

"Right."

"Okay. Just for the sake of clarity, let's call your friend Bob —"

"— his name's Harry —"

"— or Harry. And let's call the other guy . . . George, okay?"

"Right, Rotsky. Anything you say. Anyhow, Harry asks George how come he can't use his own plane. Something about the guy made him suspicious. I mean, the guy looked real nervous, he was shabby and he couldn't stand still."

"Okay, so your average pilot so far."

"Be serious. Anyway, this guy, sorry, I mean George, says his plane had a few problems and that it was grounded. So Harry says 'how come?' and this guy says that he had had a 'terrain separation failure' — those were his actual words — and that the plane needed what he called a 'major unscheduled overhaul'. Thing is, Harry saw the plane later that day and about all that was left was the data plate and a few wing ribs. Couldn't even tell if it was a single or a twin."

"Aha."

"What does 'aha' mean?" asked Vinnie.

"It means his name's not George. It's Walkaway."

* * *

Phyllis turned off the TV as soon as the doorbell rang. Then she cursed. My whole life is run by that damned bell, she thought.

She opened the front door and three seventies-something women in pastel jogging suits bounced in. It sounded to Phyllis as though they were having about a dozen conversations at once.

"You're early, dammit," she snapped.

"Shopping channel?" asked one of the women, dressed in pink, an eyebrow arched knowingly. "I'm sorry honey. We'd've waited if we'd realized Do you want to carry on."

"Too late now," said Phyllis in a more even tone. "They were just about to give out the details for some new high-fibre foods and a kind of calamine lotion that doubles as factor 100 sun cream."

"Ooh! Didn't you tape it? I always tape the good stuff."

"Do you have some Pepto-Bismol, sweetie?" asked a women in lime green. "I'm not sure that wheatgrass juice agreed with me. Or maybe it was the blue-green algae."

"Get some at the club," said Phyllis. "Let's go."

"Better take my Lincoln," said the third women, in baby blue. "Don't think we'll all get in the Porsche."

They piled into the Lincoln and drove the ten miles to their golf club. Phyllis said nothing the whole way, and was only vaguely aware of the storm of chatter blowing about her head. She fingered her cellphone thoughtfully.

At the club they were met by the manager, a weasly man with sweaty palms. He wore an expensive suit, but his frame was so bent and bony that it seemed he was wearing someone else's clothes. He looked about forty-five years old, but Phyllis had heard a rumour that his real age was thirty. Most of the theories about this centred around drugs, rare diseases and satanic rituals. Phyllis didn't care. She hated him anyway.

"Ladies! Delightful to see you again. It's been a while, hasn't it? How

- Lady Caine -

dare you stay away like that and deprive us so. Nothing wrong, I hope?"

"Just business," said Phyllis.

"Now what kind of business could possibly trouble four gorgeous ladies like you?"

Phyllis had a powerful urge to pull the .22 automatic from her purse and pump a few rounds into the man's head.

"If you'll excuse me," said Mrs Blue. "I have to make a call of nature." She walked across the reception hall to a door marked 'Colostomy Room'.

The manager didn't seem to notice her go. In fact, his eyes were glued to Phyllis.

"I just wanted to let you know about a few developments here," he said. "As part of our corporate mission to offer the best possible service to our golden-aged members, we've completed a major facility implementation programme. We've called this the Sunset Service. Included in this is a brand-new cardiac treatment facility in our health centre, complete with a full-time heart transplant surgeon, bringing us in line with our liver, kidney and lung facilities. All greens and bunkers now have emergency alarm buttons. All golf carts have been fitted with Zimmer racks. And in line with our members' oft-expressed wishes, we have a new Problem Resolution Manager whose job is to listen to your complaints, whatever they are, for as long as it takes. He's on call 24 hours a day. You'll generally find him in the bar. Finally —"

The manager took a deep breath, and his normally self satisfied expression turned up a notch. Phyllis opened her purse. "We—"

Phyllis almost fainted with relief when her cellphone rang. "Excuse me," she said to the manager, and walked away several paces. As she put the phone to her ear, she was aware that, in spite of expectant looks from the other two women, the manager hadn't resumed his speech.

"Yes?" said Phyllis into the phone.

"Just returning your call," said the man's voice. "This is a cellular phone, right? Be careful what you say."

"Our customer this morning," said Phyllis. "Is he really just a customer?"

"What do you mean?"

"There was something about him I didn't like, so I made a few calls. I hear he's been snooping around. His interest in our business seems more than just personal."

"Hmm. You could be right. I've been hearing all kinds of strange rumours, about people sticking their noses in."

75

"What should I do."

"Difficult customers we can do without. If he shows up again, introduce him to your silvery friend." Phyllis was now aware of the weight of the gun in her bag. "Make sure they get intimately acquainted."

* * *

"Holy dog-fuckin' mother of Satan," enthused Rotsky. "Quinn, you old shit-kicking piece of pond scum. What are you doing here?"

"Glad to see you too, Rotsky," grinned Quinn. He stepped up to the Shelby Mustang. "How's it hanging?"

"Be with you in a minute," said Rotsky. "I just got to order. You eating here?"

Rotsky's car was parked in the Drive-Thru lane of a McDonalds. It had been there for thirty minutes while Rotsky tried to make sense of the menu. Behind him was a queue of around twenty other cars whose occupants were apoplectic with rage but oddly silent. Once in a while a newcomer would storm out of a car and head for the Mustang. But one glimpse of Vinnie, sitting in the back seat happily cradling an M-16 with M-203 grenade launcher, and the frustrated diner would return meekly to the back of the queue, chewing over the concept that anticipation is often the best part of a meal, particularly in Florida.

"Having problems?" asked Quinn.

"I dunno, man," mused Rotsky. "Normally I don't have any trouble, you know? I walk into the place, order a burger and fries, sit down and eat. But a Drive-Thru is different. I mean, what *is* the appropriate meal for a *driver*?"

Quinn nodded sagely, as if he understood the dilemma. "Why don't you let me order?" he asked, discreetly scanning the street for any signs of approaching police cars. "I've got more experience with this sort of thing."

Rotsky smiled his appreciation, and a few moments later they were back on the road, heading for Tico. They ate as they drove. Vinnie was reluctant to put down the gun, so he was eating slower than the others. Rotsky had told him they were on private land and that it might be rough, so to hang on tight. That way, he knew Vinnie wouldn't worry about being seen with the gun.

From time to time, Rotsky put down his burger to aim the car between the traffic or ease it around a corner. Believing that momentum was his best friend, he kept his foot well clear of the brake pedal and firmly on the gas.

Between mouthfuls of food, he and Quinn filled in the details of the past few years. It didn't take long.

"Jeez, I thought it was just me," sighed Rotsky. "Looks like it's been a tough time all round. Everything's got so damn serious. No-one's got a sense of humour when it comes to drugs these days."

They shot a red light. Rotsky swerved around the front of a truck that had just pulled out of the side street. It had 'Gerry's Therapy Baths' painted on the side. Rotsky caught a brief glimpse of the grey-haired driver pushing himself back off the windscreen, mouthing oaths and reaching for something under the dash.

"Nice driving, Rotsky," said Quinn. "You in a hurry?"

"Just trying to lose the tail."

Quinn didn't bother to look backwards. "Sons of bitches," he muttered, then louder: "You eating them fries?"

"Help yourself."

Rotsky hauled the Mustang back into lane, cutting in front of an ancient Cadillac Eldorado convertible driven by a wrinkled man tanned to the colour of rich soil and wearing a Sanatogen baseball cap. Ahead, Rotsky saw flashing lights and heard the faint, wind-borne wail of a siren. He relaxed his accelerator foot. A horn blasted in his left ear and he span his head to see the Eldorado alongside, the driver snarling savagely.

"You young fucking punk," yelled the old man. "I'll teach you some goddamned manners." His right hand appeared holding a snub-nosed revolver. There was a *crack* and Rotsky felt, rather than heard, the whisper of the bullet just missing his cheek.

Quinn had leaned back over the seat — Rotsky assumed to get out of the line of fire — but now he fell back into the seat holding the M-16 he'd taken from Vinnie. He snapped back the bolt and aimed the gun at the old-timer. The man's tan faded a little. The Cadillac dropped back as the driver hit the brakes. The tyres squealed and he fishtailed uncontrollably across the road. Rotsky just had time to see the Eldorado plough through the window of a medical supplies shop before he was forced to concentrate on the road again. The turn to Tico was coming up.

They finished the food just as they swung through the gates of Tico airfield. Rotsky parked the Mustang under the nose of the *Divine Providence* and stepped out. He thought about raising the convertible's top, then realized that he didn't know for sure that it would rain.

As they stepped away from the car, Quinn turned and gave the Mustang an appraising look, as though he'd only just noticed it.

"Nice wheels. What is it? A sixty-eight?"

"Sixty-seven," said Rotsky. "Lulu's been taking care of it for me. Didn't seem right for Vegas somehow."

"Yeah? What'd you use up there?"

"Whatever was sitting around." Rotsky heard Vinnie cough and splutter. The boy had walked away from the car a few yards, now cradling the M-16 again and a large milk shake, some of which appeared to be dribbling down his chin.

A breeze picked up across the airfield. Rotsky thought again about putting the car's top up. He glanced at Quinn, who was now looking beyond the car, at the entrance to the airfield, as though expecting someone to come through it.

Without a word, the two men turned towards the aircraft. As Rotsky opened the rear door, he called to Vinnie and watched as the boy negotiated his way around the undercarriage.

Quinn was already inside the aircraft, and through the open door and the thin metal skin, Rotsky could hear the rumblings of affectionate greetings as Lulu and Quinn reacquainted themselves. Rotsky climbed the short ladder and, inside, saw Lulu pull back from the embrace, though Quinn seemed less ready to let it end.

"Hey, look at you," Lulu smiled at Quinn. "I guess we're none of us getting any younger."

Quinn recoiled at this. Rotsky half-expected him to make the sign of the cross.

"I'm doing fine," said Quinn, without conviction. "You got any booze on this damn crate?"

"Ain't you gonna tell me how good I'm looking for my age?" Lulu's raised eyebrow gave her the expression of a clever child.

Rotsky realized suddenly that Lulu *did* look *damned* good for her age. Her black hair, cut in a short bob, was glossy and thick, her figure lithe and supple, her skin fresh as a teenager. Professional pride, Rotsky assumed. He tried to work out how old Lulu was. Forty? Forty-five, maybe? Fifty? He knew she was born the same year as him, but he wasn't sure she'd aged at the same rate.

Lulu cracked open a bottle of Maker's Mark. As he breathed in, the smell of bourbon washed down into Rotsky's chest like a happy thought.

"I see you've had a refit," said Quinn. He moved to the front of the cabin.

For about the front quarter of the cabin length, either side of the gangway was partitioned, leaving just a narrow corridor to the cockpit. Curtains screened off the cubicles, reminding Rotsky of the train sleeper compartments in *Some Like it Hot*, and he thought wistfully of Marilyn Monroe and, strangely, of Tony Curtis. There were a few standard airline seats behind these, and the rest of the cabin was furnished with sofas and wing chairs mounted on adjustable platforms so that they could be levelled both in flight and when the aircraft sat tail-down on the ground. The walls were lined in dark-wine crushed velvet and there were reproduction oil lamps, powered by electricity. The overall effect was of a nineteenth-century frontier town bordello.

"You busy?" asked Quinn.

"We're kind of taking it easy at the moment," purred Lulu. She stretched herself along a sofa. "Had a parachuting school going in Charlotte County for a while, till we got shut down."

"How's that?"

"Hell honey, you know what it's like down there. Over half the county is retired. And they're the only ones with money. Dumb bastards kept forgetting to open their chutes. Even when we hooked 'em to static lines, about once a week one of the old buggers wouldn't make it all the way to the ground. We couldn't afford the insurance any more." Lulu sipped her drink. "How 'bout you? You work out that problem with the Vatican?"

"Oh sure. They paid up eventually." Quinn dropped into a chair. "You know, one day we're going to be those old buggers."

Lulu laughed. "Not us. We won't be *those* old buggers. We'll be other kinds of old buggers. Getting old isn't a problem, just the way you do it." Lulu brushed some invisible dust from the sofa back. She was a little more sombre now. "Some people just give up, you know? I don't mean they fall apart or go ga-ga or die or anything like that. That's stuff you can't help. I mean some people stop being themselves."

"You mean they become old people," said Rotsky.

"Right. There's nothing wrong with having a lot of years under your belt. That's a major achievement right there. But it's not enough by itself. That's what some of these people don't seem to get. It's like it's a competition to get the highest score regardless of how you fill each day." Lulu brightened. "Besides, sweetheart, you're as young as you feel."

Quinn stared morosely into his drink, like a man who had just heard bad news.

They talked for hours about old times. Lulu drew out of the two men memories they had failed to recapitulate in the car. Sometimes, Lulu and Quinn talked of times and events that meant nothing to Rotsky, though he was happy to lie back and imagine the scenes.

Vinnie sat quietly in an overstuffed armchair, sometimes slack-jawed and wide-eyed, sometimes with a cynical smile, but mostly he just slept.

Something clattered on to the top of the fuselage. It took a moment for Rotsky to realize it was rain. The frequency of the tapping sound rapidly increased. Distant thunder rumbled across the airfield and died against the side of the aircraft. Rotsky suddenly thought about the Mustang.

"Back in'mo," he blurted, then stood, swayed, and stumbled to the door. Outside, the cool rain helped him focus. He shut the aircraft door behind him, then realized that it had been his main source of light. Without it, he had trouble making out the shape of the car, but with the help of frequent lightning flashes and familiarity, he soon had the top raised and locked.

He re-entered the aircraft, closed the door and was smothered by the trapped Floridian air made thicker by bourbon fumes and cigar smoke. Lulu stood in the gangway, Quinn seated behind her, his eyes drooping, his head nodding, though his body was upright, supported by some inner tension.

Lulu turned to Rotsky. "Quinn was just asking me about Walkaway," she whispered. She threw Rotsky a quizzical look that he knew wasn't meant for Quinn's eyes. Rotsky stepped up close to Lulu and her perfume ran through him. He felt lighter, more awake, aware now of something else in the atmosphere.

"What's up?" he whispered. Over Lulu's shoulder he could see that Quinn's eyes were shut and his chin was on his chest. The hand holding his whiskey was still firmly tightened around the glass.

"I'm not sure, honey," Lulu whispered back. "It's just that Walkaway came into the conversation all of a sudden. Soon as you'd gone out the door."

"Did he ask about anyone else?"

Lulu frowned. "Like who?"

"You remember I told you about the feds at the airport?" Lulu nodded. "Well they said something about some broad, too. I think it might have something to do with Walkaway."

"Broad?"

"Yeah. English, I'd guess. Name of Lady Caine."

"Lady Caine?" Lulu's eyes widened. "Are you telling me that this

Walkaway business has something to do with Lady Caine?"

"Well, yeah, I guess," said Rotsky. "Maybe."

"Holy shit!" Lulu looked at the floor. She was quiet for a moment. Loud thunder boomed through the aircraft which rocked slightly. Quinn grunted and snuffled. "I should have known," whispered Lulu.

"So who is this Lady Caine anyhow?" asked Rotsky. Lulu cast him a withering stare.

Quinn coughed and hawked. His glass fell to the floor. "Shit!" he grunted. His eyes were wide open now. "Any chance of a refill?"

Lulu paid no attention. It seemed to Rotsky as though she had backed off from something, that she was being careful what she said. She laid a hand on Rotsky's arm.

"Rotsky, hon. You've been out of the drug business too long."

4:
Oh man, are those turnips?

Escobar was back in his vegetable patch. He shivered slightly in the early morning chill. His fingers were wet from stroking the dew off the cauliflower, which he could just make out in the pre-dawn gloaming. He hadn't been able to sleep. He was thinking over what Billy Cook had told them the previous day. True to his word, Billy hadn't had much to say, but the little he'd known had started alarm bells ringing in Escobar's head.

Billy said he'd heard the name 'Lady Caine' used a few times. He'd never seen any coca paste brought in, though there was always plenty of cocaine around. This was enough for Escobar to know that Díaz was up to more than a little coca cooking. Whatever scam Díaz was running, Escobar wanted it. If it turned out to be valuable, then it could be the saving of Escobar's career. At the very worst he could offer it to the Cali hotshots as a way of winning their favour. If it was a waste of time, he could simply squash Díaz without worrying about the consequences. The removal of such an irritant could also help Escobar score valuable points. Whatever happened, he couldn't lose.

The name 'Lady Caine' had pricked his interest, too. These were words he had heard uttered in hushed tones at the Corporation meeting. Escobar hadn't the faintest idea who she was, but he knew it was a subject much on the minds of the top guys in the organization. He decided to make it his business to find out more.

Escobar stood up and yelled for Hipólito. The hitman emerged from the house pushing Billy before him.

"What do we do with this guy, boss?" he asked, in a carefully neutral, business-like voice that still failed to mask eager anticipation. Several ideas ran part-formed through Escobar's imagination, but before he could make his choice, Billy interrupted.

"Oh man, are those turnips?" He gazed enthusiastically at a far corner of the garden.

"You know something about plants?" asked Escobar.

"Yeah, sure. Some. Specially vegetables. Love 'em."

"You want to be my head gardener?"

"Is it a steady job?"

"It's a lifetime's work."

"Cool!"

From behind a nearby hedge came a roar that would have been terrifying if it hadn't degenerated rapidly into an asthmatic wheeze.

"What's that?" asked Billy, wide-eyed.

"The zoo," said Escobar, sadly. "I'll want you to look after my animals, too. Treat them well. One day I will have the greatest zoo in all Latin America. And these bastards cost a shit-load of money." He turned to Hipólito. "Keep him here. Put him to work."

Hipólito jerked his thumb towards the house and Billy took the hint. He shuffled meekly back inside. Hipólito then turned back to his boss, expecting more.

"I've been thinking about what Billy told us," said Escobar.

"About vegetables?"

"About the pilot Díaz used."

"Walkaway," said Hipólito.

"Yeah. You know, I have a feeling that he might be more use to us than Díaz. He knows the product and where it has been going. Probably knows all of Díaz's stateside contacts. Díaz isn't going to tell us that stuff. He's stupid enough to want to die first."

"What you wanna do about it?"

"Find Walkaway. Find him alive and bring him to me."

"And Díaz?"

"I don't care much about Díaz."

Hipólito smiled.

"Though I do want to know what he's up to," Escobar continued. "He's abandoned the factory, which can only mean one thing . . ."

"He's on the move."

"Right. He's too small-scale to have his own transport so he'll be looking for some hired help. You know what that means?"

"Santa Marta."

"Right. Get down there and see what you can find out."

"If I find Díaz?"

"Use your initiative."

Hipólito's grin broadened.

"You know," said Escobar, "I have the feeling that we're about to go into a new line of business."

"Oh yeah?" said Hipólito. "What kind of business?"

"We'll know that when we find Walkaway."

* * *

This is Florida at its best, thought Rotsky. Early in the morning right after a thunderstorm. He drew the crisp atmosphere deep into his lungs.

Rotsky had put the Mustang's top down to make the most of it. Later in the journey it would prove a dangerous distraction, as he had a pilot's habit of watching every plane that flew over. But right now, with most of the state still waking up, they were safe enough. Rotsky shoved a cartridge into the eight-track and music scraped from worn-out speakers.

"Bar-bar-bar Barbara Ann . . ."

Sprawled across the back seat, Quinn tried to doze. Lulu was in the passenger seat putting on her make-up and putting Rotsky straight.

"Tell me Rotsky, when you look around Florida, what do you see?"

Rotsky thought carefully for a moment. It occurred to him that he saw a lot of stuff, not all of it easily classifiable, not all of it stuff he'd want to mention. He decided to compromise and muttered, "I dunno."

"No, come on. What do you see? What do we have lots of down here?"

"Ah, letsee. Beaches? Condos? Tourists?" Rotsky eased the car to the other side of the road to take them around a brand-new Lincoln convertible that was doing all of fifteen miles an hour. "Old folks."

"Right!"

"Old people? You mean including this Lady Caine, right?"

Lulu used her hand mirror to check on Quinn. He appeared to be fast asleep. "Wrong. Why do we have lots of old people?"

"Tell me," said Rotsky, reluctant to guess any more.

"Because these days folks are too greedy to die. They've got their retirement plans. They're loaded with money. They can afford the best medical treatment. So they decide they're gonna spend their sunset years in the sunshine. The only thing is, they're having the best time of their life and they don't want it to stop."

"That's only natural I suppose."

"Well maybe, but so is dying of old age. That's what scares them. They can deal with diseases and accidents. They're rich enough to be cosseted and cared for. But they can't stop getting older." Lulu checked on Quinn again. He snored loudly. "That's where Lady Caine comes in."

"So what does she do?"

"Not she, Rotsky. It. Lady Caine is a drug. To be precise, it's a drug that's supposed to slow down ageing."

Rotsky's eyes were wide with astonishment. "Does it work?"

"Who knows? The point is, the old biddies believe it works."

The Mustang flashed through some road works, past a sign that said *Ramp!* and hit a step in the surface. It left the road for a second then crashed back. Quinn sat upright and blinked.

Lulu showed no signs of having noticed. "It's like religion," she said. "If you're desperate enough, you'll believe any old shit."

Quinn winced at this, but kept quiet.

Rotsky was puzzled. "I still don't get it. Where does Walkaway fit? And why haven't I heard of this Lady Caine stuff?"

Lulu frowned at Rotsky and tilted her head slightly towards Quinn. Rotsky stared at her blankly. He knew that what she'd done was a signal, he just didn't know what it meant.

Lulu sighed. "Because it's illegal, honey, and you've been out of the action for too long. It was being made by some big pharmaceutical company, but the FDA wouldn't pass it. Rumour is that it's full of cocaine and that was enough for them to go apeshit and ban it. They were gonna call it Eternal Flame but they never got it to market."

"I see. But there's a demand so someone's supplying it, right?"

"Right. They're doing good business down here. It sells for about ninety-five bucks a pop and your average wrinkly is taking maybe four or five of them a day."

Rotsky whistled appreciatively. He ran these figures through his head. Then he did it again. He came up with two different totals, but they were in the same ballpark. "That's a hell of a habit," he said. "But it doesn't sound like your normal illicit drug clientele."

"Exactly," said Lulu. "That's what's got the authorities worried. There's a whole new bunch of people getting into the underground drugs market, and there's a lot of them — people who are rich enough to try it and close enough to death not to worry about the consequences."

"So you reckon Walkaway was smuggling this stuff?"

"You know as much as I do. I hear that Lady Caine is made right here, in the USA, but it's possible that some of it could be coming in from abroad."

There was a pause while Rotsky digested this new information. Lulu directed Rotsky down a side road, past the dazzling floodlights of a shuffleboard complex. A huge sign, brightly lit, said *24 hours, 7 days, 18 courts, no waiting.* Just beyond that were darkened bungalows hunched behind a high razor-wire fence. There were signs at regular intervals, also brightly lit, that read: *Autumn Joy Estate. Adults-only zone. Use of deadly force authorized.*

Rotsky asked a question that had been on his mind for some time.

"Where are we going?"

Lulu smiled at him indulgently. "I thought we should score some Lady Caine, so you know what we're talking about. I know just the place to do it. It's about a two-hour drive, so it should be open by the time we get there."

"What is it? A bar? Club?"

"No," said Lulu. "A beauty parlour."

* * *

If anyone asked, and most times even when they didn't, Horatio Jackson would tell people that the nearby city of Jacksonville was named after his forbears, who had bought the land from the Indians for a barrel of figs and had raised The First Church of the Blessed Mouse in Florida.

Horatio spent a lot of time by himself. With life passing so slowly at his backwoods, one-plane airstrip, dreaming up stories was the only thing he'd had to do since moving to Florida from his home in Pittsburgh.

Not that it was his airstrip exactly. The place belonged to a wealthy businessman who used it maybe once or twice a month, always at night and always without warning. And Horatio wasn't rushed off his feet even on those rare occasions that his boss showed up. He'd made it quite clear when he'd taken the job that he didn't work nights — never had, never would.

His days were spent in idle contemplation. Every once in a while a tourist or student would drop by in an airplane, to refuel or buy a sectional chart. Horatio let them pump the gas themselves, taking their word for how much they'd taken. And while he was counting their money, he'd give them one of his stories as a treat, something to remember him by. "Call back anytime you want to hear some more," he'd say. They never did.

It had been a slow day. Horatio hadn't even *heard* a plane and he'd spent the entire time in his rocking chair. The next thing he knew he was staring at an old codger in a chair who was staring straight back at him. The man was bald and wrinkled like a bloodhound, with myopic eyes straining to get the world in focus. Jesus, what a sad son of a bitch! thought Horatio, just a split second before he realized he was looking at his own reflection.

One whole wall of the airfield office consisted of glass panels and glass sliding doors. During the day they gave a great view of the single, three thousand foot runway, not thirty yards away. At night, with the uninhabited land outside pitched into total darkness and the office lit by the glow of the TV and the soda machine, the glass turned into a mirror.

He checked his watch and found that he'd slept through the night. Behind the glass, the sky showed the first signs of daylight, though greeting another dawn failed to instill Horatio with joy or gratitude. It was still dark enough for the skeeters to be out in force. Now he'd have to run the gauntlet to his car which was parked the other side of the field.

Horatio grabbed his keys and tottered to his feet. He moved to the door and eased it open gingerly, his skin tensing for the first bite. He edged through the doorway, slid the door slowly shut behind him and locked it, all the time making his movements as smooth and silent as possible, as though any sudden sound or motion would alert the insects.

He was just about to step down on to the field when he froze and a shiver ran up his back. From somewhere along the runway came the sound of voices, at least two people speaking low but clearly. Horatio's hearing was still good, and he recognized one of the voices as that of his boss. He wondered if he should make his presence known, but decided against it. He would probably have to admit to falling asleep on the job.

While he was trying to decide what to do next, Horatio's ears picked up another noise. It was the distant purr of an aeroplane that was getting closer.

Having been outside for a few minutes now, Horatio's eyes were adapting to the dark, and while the ground was still black, the sky now appeared as a rich blue, with just a few stars hanging on. Horatio squinted in the direction of the noise and after a while was rewarded with a faint, blurred shadow moving across the sky just above the black points of the trees.

He strained to identify the shape and the sound, and attempted to anticipate the direction of the plane, to guess its intentions. Dozens of new stars flared into life before him, dazzling in their brilliance, terrifyingly sudden in their appearance. It took a few moments for Horatio to appreciate that these stars weren't in the heavens but on the ground, that they were the runway lights which had been switched on by the approaching pilot. Like many smaller airfields, the lights at Horatio's strip could be activated by the pilot tuning his radio to the airport frequency and hitting his microphone button a few times.

Horatio patted every pocket, located his spectacles and hurried to put them on. There was now no doubt about where the plane was heading, and it was close enough for Horatio, with his long experience of watching planes land, to work out that it was a light twin, though even with the glasses, his rheumy eyes weren't quite up to the job of making out the details. All the same, Horatio felt that there was something distinctly odd about the aircraft.

The noise of the engines grew louder. The pilot was making a straight-in approach to the runway, not bothering with a circuit. It occurred to Horatio that he'd left the office Unicom radio switched on. The volume on the radio was usually turned high enough for him to hear it from outside, yet he hadn't heard the pilot make a single call.

The aircraft was now on short finals, and with a numb realization Horatio worked out what was wrong with the black shape, blurry as it was. *The aircraft had no wheels.*

There was too little time to unlock the office and get to the Unicom radio to warn the pilot. Horatio had no choice but to watch in fascinated horror as the aircraft sighed down towards the unyielding concrete of the runway.

At the threshold the plane was just feet above the deck. For a moment it levelled out, riding the cushion of air in ground effect. Then it eased down while the nose rose slowly. At the same time, the aircraft drifted sideways so that it was no longer above the concrete but was now heading towards the grass and — as far as Horatio could make out — the waiting people.

There was a deep rumble as the rear part of the fuselage stroked the ground, then a thump and a bang and the noise of the engines stopped suddenly, followed by the bellowing of tortured machinery. And then silence.

It had all been rather less dramatic than Horatio had expected and he felt disappointed, even cheated. Transfixed, he continued to stare in the direction of the most recent noises. Soon the silence was broken by the sound of a door opening, voices apparently strangled by barely-contained anger, a few shouts and then silence again.

Horatio heard men groaning and grunting. Car doors opened and

slammed. Again the blackness was pierced by bright new suns, but this time Horatio recognized them immediately as vehicle headlights. An engine started, the car moved off quickly and soon disappeared through the airfield gate.

By now, Horatio's night vision had disappeared completely, and he was back inside a dazzled blackness. He realized he'd been holding his body tense, so he took a deep breath, exhaled and relaxed. As he did so, he was dimly aware of a movement. Somewhere in the darkness was a blacker shadow that was closing in on him.

Seconds later, the shadow resolved itself into human form as a man moved into the dim illumination thrown through the windows by the office lights. Horatio was already working out how he would explain the experience to the cops — if he lived. Yet as the stranger got closer, Horatio was unnerved to find that he was unable to latch onto a single feature. If someone had asked him right then to describe the stranger, he couldn't have done it. All he could manage was a basic outline — a medium-size, medium-build man carrying a briefcase.

Horatio wanted to make sure he wasn't hallucinating, to prove to himself that this was a man and not some portent of his own deterioration. He decided to speak to it.

"Helluva landing fella," he said.

"Well, you know what they say," said the stranger distractedly. "Any landing you can walk away from . . ."

There was a moment of polite silence, then the stranger spoke again.

"Say, can you give me a lift into town? My airplane seems to have suffered an unfortunate landmass adjacency."

* * *

Lulu hadn't reckoned on Rotsky's driving and when they arrived at the beauty parlour it was still shut. The Mane Drag was a self-contained building that rose like an island in the huge, empty parking lot outside a mall. The walls were cerise and the roof had been replaced by a giant fibreglass wig, a Fifties-vintage blonde beehive decorated with a six-foot pink bow. To Rotsky it looked like a thatched cottage given away as a game show prize.

Rotsky thought they might be somewhere near Fort Lauderdale, but he wasn't too sure. In the air, he could pinpoint his position within a quarter of a mile at any time: on the ground he could get lost by getting out of bed.

Lulu wandered off to look for a take-out breakfast while Quinn made himself as comfortable as he could in the back of the Mustang. He closed his eyes, wrapped his arms tight and let his right hand sneak inside his jacket to touch the butt of the .45 automatic in his shoulder holster. The reassuring hardness of the gun helped him relax and he soon drifted off into a comfortable doze.

Rotsky gazed in wonderment at the Mane Drag's window display. It appeared that the shop did more than cut hair. It was a drug store, too, and one section of the window contained outsize women's underwear and a selection of studded leather harnesses. To pass the time, Rotsky attempted to identify the display objects, and he was battling with the purpose of wings on Girlie-Fresh Pantie Pads when he saw Lulu hurry back.

Quinn rose complainingly when Rotsky shook his ankle, but soon softened at the sight of steaming coffee cups and a box of fresh donuts.

Between sips of mocha latte, Rotsky asked Lulu: "Are all beauty parlours like this?"

"No Rotsky," chuckled Lulu. "This one's special."

As she said this, a 1957 turquoise-and-white Corvette hissed into the space next to the Mustang. Rotsky gazed transfixed as out of it stepped a six-foot blonde, with quarterback shoulders, stevedore hands and a silver skirt so short it could have qualified as a belt. It was a while before Rotsky looked up from her immensely long, elegantly-tapered legs to see the canary yellow fun-fur jacket and danger-red lips.

The blonde clacked on stilettos to the Mane Drag's front door, unlocked it and disappeared inside. Snapping out of his reverie, Rotsky said: "Looks like we're in business" and ditched his empty coffee cup in a garbage bin.

"Not yet," said Lulu. "Let's wait for a few customers to arrive. We'll be less conspicuous then."

Rotsky didn't see how they could be any more conspicuous, hanging around two classic sports cars in the middle of an otherwise deserted parking lot, but he'd learned to trust Lulu's judgment and said nothing.

It took about half an hour for the parlour to fill up. Several more statuesque women arrived, all sporting various shades of fake blonde, followed by a dozen or so elderly matrons, mostly in electric shades of blue or pink. Finally Lulu said, "Let's go" and headed for the door. Rotsky followed and Quinn trudged behind, looking around as if worried someone might see him.

Once inside, Rotsky was dazzled for a moment. The room was mirrored, lit by dozens of tiny spotlights and glittered with chrome and glossy nursery colours. Shelves packed with brightly-coloured hair products made the place look to Rotsky like an expensive toy store. He felt inexplicably happy. He was also smothered by countless artificial aromas that competed for his attention. Rotsky wondered if they had made the right decision in leaving Vinnie on the *Providence*. The boy would have loved it here.

Lulu picked out one of the blondes — the one they'd seen arrive first — and spoke to her in a voice that was too low for the others to hear. The blonde looked at Rotsky over Lulu's shoulder, nodded, whispered something back and then turned and walked away. Lulu followed and motioned for the others to do the same.

The four walked into a small back office that Rotsky found disappointingly ordinary: plain walls, a desk, filing cabinets and a computer but none of the cheerful clutter of the parlour. Quinn shut the door behind them. Out of habit, Rotsky checked the exits. There was another door and a window that was shut and barred.

"What exactly is it you want?" asked the blonde in a low voice that Rotsky found excitingly husky.

"You ever hear of a guy called Walkaway?" asked Lulu.

The blonde looked wary but not unfriendly.

"He in the beauty business?"

"Hardly, sweetheart. He's more in the line of what you might call pharmaceutical imports."

The woman scanned the strangers' faces.

"You're not cops, are you?" They all laughed. "I thought not. What's this to do with?"

"Lady Caine," said Lulu.

"You got some?" asked Quinn. Rotsky turned around and looked at Quinn. He had the expression of a man about to commit armed robbery. Rotsky shifted slightly to put himself between Quinn and the blonde and turned his attention back to the woman. Lulu and the woman were staring hard into each other's face, as though looking for clues. Lulu frowned hard.

"I really don't think I can tell you anything," said the woman.

"Excuse me, ma'am," said Rotsky, "We —"

"Please. Call me Nicola."

"*Or Nick*," muttered Quinn.

"Sure, Nicola," said Rotsky. "We not trying to make any trouble. We just want any information you might have that could help us out."

Nicola thought for a moment, staring at the ceiling, her lips pursed, her weight on one hip. Through the window, Rotsky saw a police cruiser rumble by. He thought of the Mustang. He'd had it so long he couldn't remember if it was bought or stolen.

The office door opened and a youngish woman with scary hair and neon-bright make-up stuck her head through the opening. "Nicola dear, we got another cold one."

Nicola tapped the desk in irritation. "She still in the chair?"

"Yep. Her hands are wrapped tight around the armrests. Can't move 'em. Eyes are shut. Looks like she's napping."

"Hair?"

"Frizzed and dried. We were about to do the final lacquer ... so to speak."

"Okay. Just keep teasing the hair slightly, like she's choosing a style for the next session. When you think it's safe, get her under a drier, but for god's sake don't turn it on. I'll be there as soon as I can."

The young woman grunted assent, backed out of the doorway and closed the door. Nicola looked like she was about to speak when there was a commotion in the parlour. The four of them moved quickly back into the shop to find it filling rapidly with men in black baseball caps and black jackets covered with large letters. Some of them said FBI, the others said DEA.

"Fuck me!" yelled Quinn. "It's a raid."

"*Get out quick!*" hissed Nicola. "This place is hot."

The feds had fanned out quickly and it would be only seconds before all the exits were covered. Rotsky was already moving back towards the office. Quinn was further inside the parlour and his path was blocked. The feds aimed their M-16s at him and yelled for him to stand still. In a flash Quinn had grabbed a portly and surprised-looking old lady. With one hand he held her in front of him as a shield and with the other he brandished a can of hairspray.

"Back off or the biddy gets it!" he snarled, though not with complete conviction. The diversion gave Rotsky and Lulu time to duck back into the office and try the other door. It led to a corridor piled with supplies and then to another door. This opened easily and Rotsky was outside, in the parking lot which was now half-full. He ran for a nearby truck, aware of someone behind him which he hoped was Lulu.

Rotsky ducked behind the truck and dropped to the ground. After a second, so did Lulu. Then, to Rotsky's surprise, so did an old woman. She was dressed in lemon chiffon and had lost the heel of one of her mules. Her silver-blue hair seemed to hover like a thin cloud around her head. Her face was thick with make-up that had cracked and flaked. What Rotsky could see of her real skin was red, deeply creased and sweating, and she was panting hard. She reached into a large, sequinned shoulder bag. Heart tablets, guessed Rotsky. She pulled out a chromed, pearl-handled .357 magnum. Seeing the surprise on Rotsky's face she said, "I'm carrying".

"Is that the Smith & Wesson seven-shooter?" asked Rotsky.

"Sure is, sweetie" said the old woman with pride. "Got it loaded with one-fifty-eight grain semi-jacketed hollow point. Pulls to the right a tad but at combat ranges it's a honey."

Lulu and Rotsky exchanged shrugs. In the distance they heard a squeal of tyres and the roar of a car engine. The Mustang screeched to a halt beside the truck and Quinn yelled, "Get in!"

As Quinn burned rubber getting out of the parking lot, Rotsky's last glimpse of the old lady was as she pulled a metal strip from her bag and broke into the truck. When they were about a mile from the mall, Lulu demanded to know what had happened back at the parlour and how come Quinn had got away.

"They had nothing to hold me on," said Quinn.

"What about threatening that old woman?" asked Rotsky.

"They thought it was a joke," Quinn said.

"You were out of there pretty damn fast," said Lulu.

"What the fuck is this?" asked Quinn with a real edge in his voice. "They weren't after me for fuck's sake. I just told them I was picking up my mother and they said to beat it."

Rotsky said nothing, but he had an uneasy feeling.

"And I'll tell you something else," said Quinn. "They made *him*." He cocked a thumb at Rotsky. "I heard one of the DEA guys mention his name."

"Fuck!" muttered Rotsky. "Sounds like it's time to move on again."

"Where to?" asked Lulu.

"Look," said Quinn. "Instead of us looking for Walkaway, why don't we let him come to us?"

Rotsky and Lulu said nothing, but waited for him to continue.

"This stuff involves cocaine, right? My guess is that the Colombians are involved somewhere down the line. And if the stuff is coming out of Colombia, and Walkaway is moving it, then there's one place he's bound to pitch up."

"Santa Marta," Rotsky said to Lulu. "Looks like we're going back to Locombia honey."

"Locombia?" asked Quinn.

"The mad country," answered Rotsky. "The question is, how are we going to get there? We could take a scheduled flight, but I'd like to have some private transport when we arrive. Can we take the *Providence*?"

"We could," said Lulu, "if we had a pilot."

"Yeah, I've been meaning to ask," said Rotsky. "Where *is* Sally?"

5:
Some are dead. Some have disappeared

Rotsky woke, panicked and tried to stand. Someone held him tightly around the waist. The floor pitched and rolled. His head span, lights flashed in his eyes, and his muscles rippled and twitched with a tender frailty. He gave up the struggle, relaxed back into his seat and, when his eyes stopped rolling, took in his surroundings.

He was on an aircraft, a biggish one, about half-way along the passenger cabin and in a right-side window seat, though the blind was shut. The cabin was decorated like a Victorian whorehouse, or an Indian restaurant, or a Turkish mosque, or . . . well, Rotsky couldn't quite put his finger on it, but he guessed this aircraft didn't belong to any of the better-known airlines.

There was a roaring noise, but strangely he couldn't identify it as either pistons or turbines. The bucking had stopped, so Rotsky assumed they'd come through some turbulence. There was another regular thudding, but he traced this to the inside of his skull.

Rotsky unbuckled the safety strap that had been holding him tight to the seat and allowed himself to slump. It was then he noticed the man in the seat across the aisle. There wasn't much to see — dirty jeans, scruffy leather flying jacket and a Stetson pulled low over his face — but Rotsky had a feeling this guy was looking at him and had watched his confused awakening. He felt the need to say something but struggled to know what. *Where am I?* was too corny and *Where are we going?* too embarrassing.

"How long have we been airborne?" was the best he could manage.

The guy in the Stetson grunted as if he'd been surprised in his sleep.

"Airborne?" he grumbled. "Whaddya mean airborne? We're still parked, bud."

Rotsky forced open the blind. Bright lights danced painfully in his eyes.

When his vision returned he discovered that the aircraft was indeed sitting on the ramp of a large airport. Low sunlight bounced from the wing's polished surface and brutally penetrated Rotsky's eyeballs. He shook his head to clear it and the roaring noise diminished. He shook it again and it faded some more, and this time he traced the hum to a generator truck sitting alongside the aircraft.

It was important to Rotsky to know what type of plane he was on. Fortunately, what he could see out of the window told him a lot. There were two engines on this wing, so four in all, and they were attached to tall props. At the wingtip was a long, elegantly curved blister. Rotsky knew of only one four-engined prop plane with wingtip fuel tanks — the Lockheed Constellation.

Slowly, parts of his memory dropped into place. After returning from the futile beauty parlour trip, Rotsky, Lulu and Quinn had gone in search of Sally, the *Divine Providence*'s pilot. She wasn't at her motel and her cellphone was switched off. Lulu had told her to make sure she was available and it wasn't like Sally to be unreliable, so they were getting worried.

Rotsky had offered to fly the DC-3 himself, but Lulu said she wasn't going anywhere until she knew that Sally was safe. That appeared to put an end to the Santa Marta mission for a while until Lulu said she had an idea. She put in some calls while Rotsky and Quinn made themselves busy with the *Providence*'s supply of Chivas.

An hour later, Lulu said it was all fixed. Transport was laid on, and they'd even have some help while they were down there. She'd called in some favours and offered some discounts, she said. And besides, the people who were offering the help wouldn't miss a caper like this. Most of them knew Walkaway too, and they were happy to help.

"Great," said Rotsky. "So what do we do now?"

"That's easy," said Lulu. "We party!"

The rest of the evening was progressively blurred in Rotsky's mind. He'd already missed one night's sleep, which he'd done often enough before but never without chemical assistance. Like most of the people he knew these days, Lulu was keeping straight because she had a hunch the feds were getting too close and she didn't want to give them any reasons to get tough. Quinn had mumbled excuses about "short notice" and "different lifestyle". The threesome found themselves uncomfortably drug-free.

It seemed to Rotsky that the instructions Lulu had been given on the phone weren't too precise. They picked up Vinnie from the *Providence* and tried six or seven bars — Rotsky wasn't quite sure how many — before she found their first contact. By that time, Rotsky and Quinn were already beginning to feel the effects of the high-speed bar crawl. And it didn't stop. There were more people to find, more bars to try.

They used Quinn's rented car, though Lulu insisted on driving. At some point in the night Rotsky had found a small bag of grass under one of the seats, which Quinn claimed to know nothing about but was happy to share. Rotsky had also discovered an automatic pistol, and had quietly replaced it without comment.

From then on, his memory was a kaleidoscope of images, some dizzyingly bright, some murky and sinister. He was convinced they'd reached Fort Lauderdale and had tried to ask someone about it. He wasn't sure he'd made himself understood because the reply made no sense to him. "This is where she is, man," the stranger had said. "*La Blanca*. This is where she is."

His memory made a jump cut to an old monk handing him some powder, for the *soroche*, he'd said . . . a woman holding him upright and screaming Spanish oaths in his ear . . . taking a piss in a parking lot with glaring spotlamps . . . three huge Hispanics with bad faces . . . a close-up view of gravel . . . a knife in his hand . . . a scream . . . a knife in his foot . . . a crowd of men, some with guns . . . flashing lights — red, white and green . . . deafening Salsa music and that woman again, smiling this time . . . and a close-up view of porcelain.

His final recollection, as he made himself comfortable on the hood of a car, was of a foul, black-toothed tramp with an expensive wristwatch rummaging through his pockets and whispering in Rotsky's ear: "See you in Santa Marta, motherfucker". It had all seemed perfectly normal at the time, but now he wished he'd asked questions.

Maybe he's on this plane, thought Rotsky. Gingerly he stood up and moved to the aisle. A memory returned and he looked at his feet. There was a neat, two-inch slash in the top of the right boot, but the knife seemed to have missed his toes. Rotsky offered a brief prayer of thanks and, as if in answer, the number one engine started. Rotsky thought about this, then wrote it off to coincidence. The cabin vibrated as the aircraft came to life and Rotsky paused to enjoy it. Then he looked around the cabin. Quinn was asleep, stretched across a row of seats. Vinnie was similarly unconscious on the row behind. Apart from the guy in the Stetson, there were three strangers in the front row. One of them stood up and came down the aisle.

"Good evening," he said, "or is it morning? How are you feeling?"

"Fine," Rotsky lied. "Who are you?"

The stranger laughed. "Yeah, it was quite a night, wasn't it? I'm Georgio Acidophilus. This is my aircraft."

As Rotsky shook the guy's hand, he dredged his memory for some details. "Greek, right?" he asked.

"That's right," said Georgio with only the faintest hint of an accent. He was expensively neat and had a body that glowed with health. He was heavily-built, dark-haired and had a tanned leather complexion. "We're about to take off. We don't insist, but you might want to get yourself strapped in."

Georgio and Rotsky took adjoining seats. While the other three engines were fired up and the aircraft taxied to the runway holding point, Georgio filled in some of the details. The Constellation had been restored by him as his private transport. He'd made his fortune by importing and exporting gynaecological creams, with a convenient sideline in high-grade cocaine for the rich housewife market. He'd then branched out into other areas of smuggling, specializing in weapons for no-hope political movements. "You get the money and then a week later you get the weapons back," he explained. But he'd always found himself drawn back to cocaine. "Nothing else gives you the same yield."

A year before, Georgio had retired and had been looking forward to a quiet life. Then the IRS had caught up with him and suddenly he was in need of serious cash. He'd been thinking about a trip to Colombia to renew some old business contacts when Lulu had phoned.

"Who are the other guys?" asked Rotsky.

Georgio nodded towards the two in the front seat and then to the man in the Stetson. "These are some business partners of mine. You needn't worry about them. They'll disappear once we get to Colombia. While we're down there, this aeroplane and the pilot are at your disposal."

"Thanks. Thanks a lot. But look, I don't want to seem ungrateful," said Rotsky, "but isn't arriving in something as big and as rare as a Connie bound to draw some attention?"

"I hope so," said Georgio. "If there's some major action going down, as Quinn seems to think, the locals will be expecting the major players to roll in. We want to make an entrance. In the meantime, we'll drop you off somewhere nice and quiet nearby. With your reputation you won't stay unnoticed for long, but it'll draw some of the heat from you to start with."

This kind of thinking impressed Rotsky. He thought about it while they took off. With so few passengers, the Connie was lightly loaded and the pilot pulled up into a screaming climb. Ten minutes later they levelled off, and Georgio asked Rotsky to follow him to the cockpit.

"We should be safe now," Georgio said.

"Whaddya mean 'safe'," asked Rotsky.

"We're high enough." As he said this Georgio and Rotsky arrived on the flight deck so there was no time for further explanations.

"Rotsky, I'd like you to meet our chief pilot. This is Squeaker. You've heard of him, right?"

The pilot turned around in his seat and beamed a huge, puppyish grin at Rotsky. He had one of those faces that appears young at first glance, until you notice the deep lines scored across it. He had a faint tan that looked like it had been there for twenty years, though the overall effect was still pale. His hair had receded in a perfect circle from the crown, leaving a ring of white locks streaked with either remnants of blond or nicotine stains. His face was round and a little jowly, with pale eyes protruding from beneath bushy white eyebrows. Rotsky had the feeling that he got this way from staying inside too much.

So this is the famous 'Squeaker' O'Leary, thought Rotsky. He was a man with a powerful reputation, named in admiration for his ability to land even the biggest aircraft with the minimum of fuss and noise — a useful asset in the drug trade.

Squeaker was the kind of human anachronism that the Peace Generation left littered around the world. His clock had stopped ticking around Nineteen-Sixty-Something. It was reflected in his attitude towards technology and aeroplanes. He was never really comfortable with jet turbines — if he couldn't look out of the window and actually see the engines turning how was he to know they were working? He also distrusted anything electronic. Anything that couldn't be fixed with a wrench and a hammer was an offence against nature. Squeaker put his trust in god, gears and push-rods.

Even with the biggest aircraft, Squeaker would make sure to kick the tyres before take-off, though apart from that his preflight checks consisted mainly of ensuring the bar was well-stocked and that he had enough music tapes to last the whole flight. As he hadn't flown anything but the Connie for many years, he could get it fired up and taxiing in less time than it takes most people to start their cars. All of this was fine with his clients, who knew nothing about aviating and were often in an undiscerning state of mind. However, Squeaker did have a few quirks that were liable to upset his customers — his habit of wandering back into the passenger cabin during the flight, the way he would open the door during the cruise to take a piss, and his penchant for using cocaine to combat altitude sickness. "Works for the Indians, man," he'd argue.

Like many craftsmen, Rotsky judged others by their workplace. He ran an expert eye around the cockpit, skimming the standard stuff and noting the modifications. He was particularly taken by the curtains, spread to cover all of the cockpit glazing. From what he could see, they appeared to be in an acid-coloured paisley pattern and gave the light in the cockpit a warm, candle-like softness. Apart from that, they reminded Rotsky of the anti-flash blinds carried by military jets to protect the crew against the glare of nuclear explosion. The Constellation wasn't renowned as an atomic bomber, though.

"Great drapes," Rotsky told him.

"Yeah! Neat, huh?" Squeaker beamed.

Rotsky had hoped for a little explanation, but Squeaker just sat and grinned proudly at the window dressing.

"So, I guess you don't like being blinded by the sun, right?"

Squeaker mulled this over for a few seconds.

"No, it's not that," he said, his brow furrowed. "It's distractions, man. All that shit going on outside the window. Can't deal with that."

"So, what? You pull 'em shut above the clouds?"

"No way, man! Too late by then. Nah, these suckers come down right before the . . . ah . . . you know . . ."

"Cruise?"

"Take-off."

"Before take-off?" Rotsky looked closer at the blinds. They appeared just the same as they had a minute ago. "So you fly on instruments the whole time?"

"How's that?"

"On instruments . . . ?"

"Yeah. Right. Instruments." Squeaker said this in the tone of one who recognizes the words but can't quite grasp their relevance. As he gazed at the instrument panel, his face lit up with uncomprehending fascination. Rotsky felt he was seeing some of the knobs and gauges for the first time.

"I love all this stuff, man. Looks real neat. All the dials and needles and stuff. I love to play with the dials and needles."

He sat in happy contemplation for a few minutes then spoke again with boyish enthusiasm.

"You wanna know why pilots crash?"

Rotsky felt this was going to be good. "Sure, Squeaker. Tell me."

"Looking out the window, man," he chirruped. "That's real dangerous. They should teach you about this stuff in flight school, but they don't. I mean this sucker travels at ... what ... a thousand miles an hour? Something like that. Your eyes can't keep up with that kind of speed. Light beams at a million miles an hour, an aircraft at a thousand, how you gonna keep track with that? You can't, man. The eyes ain't quick enough. The brain can't respond. Gets overloaded. You can't really see those trees and towers and hills and stuff. You have to sense them, feel them, know their presence by instinct and the deeper human powers that most people have lost. You know, every flight is a spiritual journey. I think Saint-Exupéry said that." His face was serious now. The mention of St-Ex brought a moment's reverential silence from both Squeaker and Rotsky. Squeaker's face creased. "Or was it Ernie Gann? Anyway, that's what I'm into. New Age Aviation, I call it. I navigate by feel, instinct, exploiting the darker powers of the soul to reach into the universe and really *know* it. Cocaine helps. You ever read *Dune*?"

* * *

Sally was having trouble with her head. It felt as though someone had built an interstate through it. It hurt. A lot.

She moved her head slowly, rotating the side of her face onto a cooler part of the pillow. And while she waited for the throbbing to subside, she tried to straighten out her thoughts.

She was in a private room in a hospital and she needed to leave, she was certain about that. No good could come of staying. Whoever the bum was — cop or crook, good guy or bad guy — his attempt to kill her implicated her in something — she wasn't sure what — that must be of interest to the cops. And Sally had a well-developed loathing of officialdom.

She gave herself a practised checkout, feeling for fractures and cautiously probing the bumps on her head. Nothing more than some bruising and maybe a slight concussion, she decided, but as far as the cops were concerned she was going to be unconscious. From time to time nurses popped in to check on her, but it was easy enough to fake it. She had come into the hospital with no ID, no cash, no credit cards and no evidence of medical insurance, so they weren't trying too hard.

Still, no-one is going to fall for this ruse forever, she thought. She was going to have to do something, and do it soon. Suddenly, Sally was convinced that people were coming to get her, that they might be walking up the corridor to her room at this very minute. In her agitation she forgot her bruises and her pains and slipped quickly from the bed. She swayed in ever-increasing arcs as she scanned the room. Finally, she had to hold the foot of the bed to steady herself. She realized she was dressed in a thin hospital gown that ran short of her knees. There was no sign of her own clothes.

Why would they take my clothes? she thought. What sort of people are they? Is this really a hospital?

Gingerly, she moved around the room, opening cupboards, looking under the bed. The search revealed nothing. The window was locked, and in any case she was thirteen or fourteen stories above the ground. The door wasn't locked, but when she peeked out, carefully and quietly in case the bum had turned up or *they* were waiting on the other side, she found herself guarded by a cop the size of Texas.

Now there are all kinds of reasons why a cop might be sitting outside your hospital room, thought Sally, but they all mean trouble.

Sally concentrated hard in an effort to form a plan, but her head span and she realized she was going to have to make it up as she went along. She decided to wait until the early hours of the morning, when everyone would be tired.

She slept for a while, fitfully and in ever-shorter doses as her nerves started to wind up. When she could wait no longer, she shuffled to the door, cracked it open a few inches, and in the croakiest voice she could manage, whispered to the guard: "Help me!"

Sally cursed inwardly when she saw it was the same guy. He turned slowly to look at her, with the expression of a man ready for trouble. As he moved closer, to hear her better, Sally stepped backwards. She wanted him inside the room where she could work undisturbed.

The guard seemed to only just squeeze through the door.

"Yes?" he asked cautiously. "Is there a problem?"

Sally sat heavily on the bed.

"I'm bleeding," she said. "Real bad."

"I know," said the guard unsympathetically, his granite face showing not a trace of compassion. "You hit your head."

"No, no. Not my head," explained Sally, staring him straight in the eye. "It's . . . you know . . . woman's trouble."

The guard took a second to take this in. Then he blushed.

"O-oh," he stammered. "Is it . . . well . . . that time?"

"No," whimpered Sally. "It can't be. You see, I'm pregnant. I think I might be losing the baby."

The cop shuffled nervously for a moment or two. Then, when Sally gasped "Please get help" he shot out of the door, throwing "I'll get a nurse" back over his shoulder. Sally went straight after him, into the empty corridor, and watched with something approaching sympathy as his huge bulk disappeared into the depths of the hospital.

* * *

Rotsky edged back into the passenger cabin. It might have been the Summer of Love on the flight deck, but back in the cabin it was pure 1990s smuggler's chic. These guys had read the books and the magazine articles and knew how to make an impression. The front half of the aircraft had the seats removed for whatever cargo the owners fancied carrying, though they'd taken up some of the room with a small kitchen and a bar. The back half was fitted with ex-Air France first class seats, tastefully re-upholstered in wine-red crushed velvet. The cabin was lined with Laura Ashley silk wall covering and subtly illuminated by reproduction Art Deco uplighters. The coat rack was heavy with Armani, Zegna and Valentino, the gun rack was all Uzis, HKs and Steyr AUGs and when Rotsky opened the fridge he found it stuffed with Perrier, quail's eggs and Dom Perignon.

"Like it?" asked Georgio proprietarily.

"Ah man, it's beautiful," Rotsky said. "But look, what did you mean before about it being 'safe', about us being high enough?"

Georgio gave Rotsky a comforting smile. "It's Squeaker," he explained. "He has this thing about bridges. He can't fly over them."

Rotsky was puzzled. "So what does he do? Go around?"

"Under."

"*Under*? You're telling me he always flies *under* bridges?"

"No, not always. Once he gets above three or four thousand feet he seems to be fine. Doesn't seem to notice them. But below that . . . well . . ."

Rotsky nodded. "I see." It seemed to him that, if that was how Squeaker flew, well ... that was how Squeaker flew. "So he does look out of the window sometimes?"

"Oh sure. We insist. Besides, you shouldn't take what he says too literally. Squeaker likes to think of himself as a kind of new age poet of the air. He's really full of it."

"Of what?"

"Shit," said Georgio slowly.

"Right. So he doesn't use the blinds?"

"Hardly ever."

Rotsky scratched his cheek and rubbed his throat. "I think I could do with a drink."

Georgio waved towards the fridge. Five minutes later Rotsky had constructed an unrepeatable cocktail and a plateful of smoked salmon with french toast. He took a seat and set about treating his hangover.

About an hour into the flight, Quinn woke, yawned, stretched and eased himself upright. Rotsky walked over to him with a full champagne glass and asked him how he was feeling.

"Great," said Quinn taking the glass. Rotsky hoped he was lying.

"You told Georgio that there's some major action going down?" asked Rotsky.

"That's right."

"In Santa Marta?"

"Yup."

"And he believed that?"

"I haven't the faintest idea, but it got us a ride, didn't it? Private plane an' all."

"So, what's our plan?"

"After we drop you off I'm going to look up some old contacts. I'll be gone for a few days. I'll meet you in Santa Marta."

"Where?"

"Oh, don't worry. I'll find you," said Quinn. He narrowed his eyes against the glare of Rotsky's flying suit. "You're hard to miss."

Rotsky couldn't think of anything to add. As usual, events were being organized around him. He settled down for the long flight, sometimes visiting the flight deck to check his impression of Squeaker, sometimes napping, or else reading Georgio's copious supply of magazines — mostly interior design glossies and gynaecological journals.

It seemed that Squeaker knew the location of the autopilot and most of the journey was uneventful, other than a few altitude excursions as he slumped senseless over the controls or, recovering from a micro-coma, used the yoke to pull himself upright.

When the aircraft descended, Rotsky strapped himself into the rearmost seat with every cushion he could find wedged between himself and the seatback in front. He was more than mildly surprised when they made a smooth landing, a real greaser, not even a hint of a bump, and almost perfectly parallel to the runway.

* * *

After she dropped the boys at the airfield, Lulu swung by the Mane Drag. She wasn't sure why, except that she had a hunch and had learned never to ignore such things.

It was edging towards light now, though dreary grey beneath early morning stratus. Lulu was cold. She was wearing the previous night's cocktail dress, a small black number in stretch Lycra. It followed her curves with a fidelity that inevitably made her new friends whenever she wore it, but it didn't do much to keep out the cold.

Lulu expected the beauty parlour to be shut tight and was surprised to see lights on and Nicola's Corvette sitting out front. Lulu parked the Mustang some distance from the building and settled down to wait.

She was woken by the clacking of Nicola's high heels. Lulu hauled herself up in the Mustang's reclined seat just enough to see over the hood. Her head swam from the effort. The day had brightened and she was dazzled by the light. It took her a few seconds to focus.

It wasn't hard to spot Nicola. The sky showed only the first hints of light, but even so she stood out. She wore a sunflower yellow patent leather biker's jacket, a gold lurex micro-mini skirt and scarlet hose. Her blonde hair was gathered in ratty bunches. Even across the expanse of the parking lot, the heels of her metallic pink stilettos sounded preternaturally loud.

Nicola squeezed herself into the Corvette and burned rubber. Lulu had to scrabble to get her seat upright and the Mustang started. She took off after Nicola, taking care not to get too close.

They drove for half-an-hour, out to an area of small suburban houses, each with a neat front lawn and ragged palm tree. Nicola pulled into a driveway. Lulu stopped twenty yards down the street. She reached into the glove compartment and pulled out a 9mm automatic. She checked the clip and looked up just in time to see Nicola unfold herself from the Corvette and head for the door. Lulu moved fast to catch up. The street was deserted and she held the gun in plain view.

Nicola had the door open and was about to step through when Lulu caught up with her. Nicola froze but didn't turn around.

"I had a feeling you'd be back," she said. "You by yourself?"

"My partner's taking a little vacation."

Nicola turned to face Lulu. She looked at the gun with apparent disinterest. "Quinn too?" she asked.

"You know Quinn?"

Nicola gave a throaty chuckle. "Oh sure. He's been sniffing around for weeks. Come on in. You look like you could use some coffee."

They walked through a hallway into the kitchen. Nicola made coffee without looking at Lulu, who sat on a tall stool by a breakfast bar and kept the gun in readiness. Finally, Nicola put a large cup of strong black coffee in front of her.

"I still need some information," said Lulu.

"I figured," said Nicola. She sat on a dining chair, leaned back and placed her feet on the edge of a table, knees bent, legs apart. Lulu looked up at the wall, at a calendar with a picture of a smiling alsatian. Nicola put her feet back on the floor and crossed her legs. "Sorry," she said. "I forget."

"I reckon you forget all kinds of things. Seems to me you knew more than you wanted to tell us. Are you going to talk to me now?"

"If I don't?" asked Nicola.

Lulu waved the gun in Nicola's direction.

"Shit," said Nicola. "Why doesn't anyone say it with flowers any more?"

"The only flowers you're likely to get are at your funeral."

"Oh honey. You've been in Florida *too* long. They don't even say stuff like that on *Miami Vice*. Now. Last time you were asking about some guy, before we were rudely interrupted."

"Yeah. Walkaway. He's a pilot. You know him?"

"Can't say I do. Maybe I've heard the name, but I really don't have any information. Sorry."

With her left hand, Nicola scratched the inside of her thigh, just under the hem of her mini-skirt. "Christ these pantyhose itch," she said.

Lulu looked around the kitchen. There were dishes piled in the sink. The cooker was spotless, but almost every other surface in the room seemed to be covered in dust or crumbs. The door of the microwave was open and there were encrusted food spills inside it.

"Look," said Nicola. "You said this guy's got something to do with Lady Caine, right?" Lulu nodded. "Well, why don't you ask Quinn. Caine seems to be his favourite subject these days."

Lulu arched an eyebrow.

"That surprise you?" asked Nicola. "Maybe you don't know the guy as well as you thought."

Lulu noticed a washer/dryer in the corner of the kitchen. It looked like it was full of clothes that had been through the cycle but not taken out again.

"Tell me what you know," she said.

Nicola narrowed her eyes for a moment, then shrugged. "The guy's a regular pain in the ass. He — you said you're not a cop, right?"

"Right."

"Because if you are and you're wired, this is entrapment."

Lulu stood. She ran a hand over her dress. "So tell me," she said. "Where would *you* put the wire?"

Nicola laughed. "Okay honey, sit down. I'll tell you what I can." She took a sip of coffee. "From what I hear, Quinn will work for anyone so long as the money's right."

"That's not news." Lulu waved the gun in encouragement.

"Yeah, but he's not working alone. A couple of weeks ago I heard he was looking to recruit some help — you know, some no-hopers to do the legwork for him."

Lulu picked up her coffee cup. She noticed cup rings in the surface of the breakfast bar. She sipped her coffee, then put the cup on a nearby coaster. "So what was he working on?"

"You want a lot."

"I want it all."

Nicola took a deep breath. "Well all I can tell you is what I know. He was always at the parlour, asking questions about Lady Caine — where it's coming from, who are the main dealers."

"Did you tell him anything?"

"I didn't, but some of the others around here might have done before I got to him. You know, we're pretty much Caine Central for Florida. It's hard to keep a lid on it sometimes. But I got the feeling that it wasn't all business."

"How do you mean?"

Nicola rubbed her chin thoughtfully with a thumb. "I think there was some personal angle in it. He got a bit weird, you know, a bit intense. I had to get rid of him."

"How'd you do that?"

"Well, I figured threatening him wouldn't do much good, so I came on to him, real strong. He was off like a scalded cat. Till that day the three of you turned up."

Lulu re-ran that day in her head. "How did he get away?"

"Didn't see for sure. I was busy being pinned down by three Special Agents. Was having myself quite a time. But I did hear him talking to the feds."

"Saying what?"

"Couldn't make out most of it. I was panting too hard. So were the Special Agents. But I did hear one of the feds ask him why he didn't draw his gun. You know, he threatened that old lady with a can of hairspray. Quinn said something about not wanting to get his head blown off. Then he was gone."

Lulu took a moment to process this information. "It's not enough," she said. She pulled back the pistol's slide. The *snack* as it snapped back into place seemed ill-mannered in someone else's kitchen. The gun shook in Lulu's outstretched hand. She wanted to put it down but something about Nicola was sending icy spasms through her chest. Something *familiar*.

"Oh for heaven's sake, sweetheart," said Nicola, "put it down will you? This kitchen cost a fortune. I've already had the place wrecked three times."

Lulu looked around. She couldn't see how anyone could have spent a fortune on *this* kitchen. She lowered the gun. "Wrecked?" she asked. "How come?"

"Two DEA raids and one bitchin' party. The party I didn't mind so much, but I'm getting sick of the raids. They've hit the parlour seven times. I tell ya, I've only been in the beauty business a year and already I'm thinking of getting out. You ready for a top up?"

Nicola stood, picked up the coffee jug and walked over to Lulu. Her hand shot forwards and Lulu thought: She's going to spill the coffee.

The coffee hit Lulu full in the face. It was already tepid but blinded her for a moment. Something smacked into her chest. She fell back but her right arm was trapped and she twisted. She hit the ground face down. Her right arm was bent back and Nicola's hand was tight around her wrist. For a second Lulu thought, she's trying to help me, and then realized that she was no longer holding the gun. Nicola let go of Lulu's arm. Lulu rolled on to her back and wiped the coffee from her eyes. She looked up to see Nicola standing a couple of yards away, smiling, pointing the gun at her.

"Where the hell did you learn to do that?" asked Lulu.

"In the Marine Corps. Recon."

Lulu coughed and sputtered. She wiped more coffee from her face. While her eyes were partially shielded she quickly searched for any potential weapons within arm's reach. She saw a knife that she must have knocked on to the floor as she went down. She shifted slightly towards it. "Yeah?" she said. She wanted to keep Nicola calm. "So how come you're not still a Marine?"

"I didn't like the uniform. I've always preferred silk."

Lulu was very still. A cold calm washed over her. The room seemed suddenly very light. "Nick?" she said. "Jesus Christ! *Nick?*"

* * *

"How's this?" asked Squeaker.

Georgio watched him cram the baseball cap on his head. It was glossy white and had 'I ♥ Santa Marta' in red on the front. Georgio thought it was the cheapest-looking thing he'd ever seen.

"It's like . . ." Squeaker struggled for the next word.

Georgio waited.

"Cool shit," said Squeaker. He looked at himself in a mirror, turned his head one way then the other and looked at his reflection from the corner of his eye. The cap was too small and wobbled on his bald crown as his head moved. He turned to the sales assistant. "You got this in a bigger size?"

"One size fits all, señor," said the assistant.

"Oh. Sure. That's right. It's like . . ."

"For fuck's sake," snapped Georgio. "We didn't come here to shop."

Squeaker looked around the shop, eyes wide. "Right," he said. "We came here to, like . . ."

Georgio waited. Squeaker said nothing. Finally Georgio picked the cap off Squeaker's head and threw it to the sales assistant. He shoved Squeaker towards the door.

They stumbled out on to the Avenida Rodrigo de Bastidas. Across the road was the beach. This side was a busy procession of restaurants, bars and tourist shops. The island of El Morro shimmered out in the bay. Georgio pulled his sunglasses from the top of his head and settled them on his nose.

Even so, he squinted.

The sunlight flared off awnings, flags, signs, umbrellas, tourist goods, cheap shirts and was reflected in a fluttering storm of primary colours. Georgio longed for the simple white and blue of his island home. He'd spent too many days in places like this. He was getting a headache.

The beach was busy. In the spaces between the people, Georgio saw empty plastic bottles and fast food wrappers. The sun scintillated off the pyrites in the sand, and the Caribbean surf was faintly brown. Georgio set off along the avenue in the hope of finding a pharmacy. Squeaker tagged along beside him, occasionally breaking his own stride with a skip or hop to match Georgio's pace.

"So this is where it's all happening?" Squeaker asked, gazing around with an expression that was probably meant to appear shrewdly appraising but actually looked uncomprehending.

"Where what's happening?" Asked Georgio.

"The deal. The action. The, you know . . ."

Georgio stared at Squeaker and considered the matter.

"Well," he said eventually, "that's what Quinn says."

Squeaker was surprised.

"You don't, like, you know, believe . . ."

"It's just odd, that's all. Quinn and Rotsky used to be big shots. But I haven't heard their names on the circuit for a while."

"But he's, like, famous or something. That's why you left him at the airstrip, right?"

"Wrong. I needed some time to do some research. Find out what the deal is."

Georgio stopped and looked carefully at Squeaker, who stared back with a look of sudden intensity. After a moment, Georgio realized that Squeaker was looking at his own reflection in Georgio's sunglasses. Georgio resumed walking.

"Quinn wanted to be in Santa Marta in a real hurry," he said. "He reckons there's something big going down but won't say what. So I decide to tag along, see what's happening. The thing is, the big deals never happen in rat holes like Santa Marta. Plenty of smuggling, sure, and small-time stuff, but the major action all takes place in the city."

"You mean Bogotá," nodded Squeaker, sagely.

"I mean Miami."

"So what do we do here?" asked Squeaker, enjoying the sudden vista of idleness that had appeared before him.

"I'm going to make a few contacts, have a good time, perhaps make a few deals of my own. You're going to stick with Rotsky and Quinn. From now on, you're their personal chauffeur. Take them wherever they want to go. But report back to me every day. I want to know where they go and who they meet. Got that?"

"Wow man, that's cool. It's like . . . you know . . ."

There was silence. Georgio watched him expectantly.

Squeaker's face brightened and he said: "Spy shit."

* * *

Rotsky sat on a rock and tried to remember why Georgio had dropped him here. He recalled something about avoiding attention, and it had seemed like a good plan when he was sitting in a comfortable seat sipping cocktails. Now he and Vinnie were alone at a deserted airstrip that was little more than a dirt runway and a pile of avgas barrels.

Before *La Blanca* had departed, Georgio had pointed in the direction of Santa Marta but hadn't said how far away it was. All Rotsky could see was countryside. It could be a one-mile walk or fifty.

Rotsky had strolled to the nearby road but couldn't see any signs or traffic. At the airstrip, Rotsky knew where he was — he was at the airstrip. But if he started walking, as soon as he lost sight of the field he would be lost. Under the circumstances Rotsky felt he had no option but to stay put.

Georgio had left behind a large hamper, so Rotsky and Vinnie had a picnic by the fuel drums. It smelled a bit, but the rest of the field was open ground and Rotsky felt that a picnic should be at a *place*.

"OLC Rule number 405," said Rotsky. "Always be *somewhere*."

"Why 'The Outside Lomcovak Club'," asked Vinnie.

Rotsky pulled open a plastic box. It contained caviar. He closed the box, dropped it and picked up another. "You know what a loop is?" he asked.

"Sure. You fly a big 'O' in the sky."

"Right. You know what an outside loop is?"

"Yep. You do the same thing with the aeroplane the other way up, pushing instead of pulling, nose going down instead of up, lots of negative g. Uncomfortable and difficult."

"Okay." Rotsky picked a chicken leg from the box, though it was smaller and darker than he would have expected a chicken leg to be. He chewed until his mouth was clear enough to speak. "Know what a lomcovak is?"

Vinnie thought about this for a second.

"Sort of. You go into a vertical climb, then kind of flick roll it, or spin it upwards. Tail spins round. Plane tumbles. Anyway, I'm told it looks totally out of control and crazy."

"Well, yeah, something like that. They say the word 'lomcovak' is Slovak for 'I have drunk too much plum brandy and my gyros have toppled'. Know what an outside lomcovak is?"

"Is it . . . well, sort of a . . . no, I guess not."

"It's impossible. Like the club. You heard of Groucho Marx? Well, maybe you haven't. You're not an American."

"Trust me, Rotsky. Word got out."

"Well, it's the same kinda thing. It's a club for people who wouldn't be members of a club. It's sort of a joke."

"Are there many rules?"

"Oh, we got lots of rules. All of them, in fact."

"All of them?"

"Yup. Any rule you can think of, we got it, from 'don't covet your neighbour's ass' to 'no spitting on the floor'. Having *every* rule means that every member has to bust a few of them from time to time. So no-one is in any position to judge anyone else."

"Are there many members?"

Rotsky started to count, then realized it was pointless. "Fewer and fewer all the time. Some are dead. Some have disappeared. Others just drifted away. Life has been hard on some of them, and they just forgot they were members."

"How do you join?" asked Vinnie.

Rotsky picked up a bottle of wine and checked the date. It said 1994. He wondered if that was a good year for whatever kind of wine this was. He scanned the hamper for a corkscrew. "Well, there's one important requirement — that you're not a member of anything else. We don't want golfers, cops, stockbrokers, masons, patriots, hippies, punks, mailmen, junkies, musicians, poets, painters, mechanics, soldiers, truck drivers, steel workers, miners, civil servants, politicians, sportsmen, drunks, journalists, gourmets —"

"Pilots?"

"Depends."

"On what?"

Rotsky put down the bottle. He'd failed to locate the corkscrew, though he felt certain there must be one.

"On how you use the word 'pilot'," he said. "If it describes what you are, then you're no good to us. If it just happens to be what you do, that's okay. Understand?"

"Not really."

"Well, that's okay too."

Vinnie tapped his fingers thoughtfully on his camcorder. Then he picked it up and switched it on, as though to record his thoughts. He shot about five seconds' worth of pictures of the fuel drums before there was a clunk, the whirring stopped and the camera emitted a high-pitch shriek. Vinnie turned off the camera and put it down. "Out of tape," he said. He searched the hamper and munched an ortolan sandwich. "Why is he called 'Walkaway'?" he asked.

"It's his name," said Rotsky.

"Not his real one, surely?"

"It's what people call him. Isn't that real enough?"

"But it's not the name he was born with."

"Oh, hell no."

"So ..." Vinnie took a deep breath. "Why do people call him Walkaway?"

"You ever hear the expression, 'a good landing is any one you can walk away from'?"

"No."

They finished the picnic in silence. Rotsky found some shade under trees at the edge of the field and they napped, on and off, most of the day. When it got dark, Rotsky lay back and looked at the stars. One day, he thought, I'm going to learn their names.

* * *

Sally hated hospitals. She knew for a fact that your chances of getting out of one alive were very slim. And it didn't help when there was someone actively trying to kill you.

Less than a minute after leaving her room, Sally spotted the bum. He had just opened the door to someone else's room and was peering in. He wore a large faded t-shirt loose over cut-off denims. Sally's trained eye quickly spotted the bulge in the back of his shirt, about where the waistband of his shorts would be. She backtracked and rounded a corner, the muscles of her back tensing in anticipation of a sudden blow. Somewhere, she knew, there had to be a storeroom full of clothes her size. It happened all the time in the movies. She tried door after door, but most of them were locked and the others were private rooms with sleeping patients. Finally, she found a nurses' changing room, lined with lockers. They were all securely padlocked, but there was a raincoat hanging on the back of the door.

Sally took off the gown. It had the name of the hospital stencilled on it. If she was to be stopped by the cops, Sally preferred to be arrested for indecent exposure rather than be returned to the hospital. She put on the coat.

It was tempting to stay in the changing room, to bolt the door and wait for the trouble outside to go away. Sooner or later, however, a nurse would need to use it, and then Sally would be trapped. Or the bum would try the door and, simply because it was locked, might guess that she was in there, with no other way out.

Making as little noise and as little movement as possible, Sally eased into the corridor. In each direction it ran some distance before meeting another corridor. There were no windows — no clue of how to get out. Sally found the lack of signs disturbing — and suspicious. She started slowly in one direction, then turned and went the other way, then stopped, started again, turned, stopped started and finally couldn't remember which direction she'd chosen in the first place. A wave of nausea washed through her and she had to steady herself against the wall. When it passed, Sally slapped the wall with the flat of her hand. *"Get a grip!"* she hissed to herself. She walked down the corridor, turned the corner and saw the bum again, some distance off, walking away. She reversed around the corner. "Dammit!" she breathed.

There was something almost supernatural about his ability to appear out of nowhere. Sally wondered if perhaps he was a figment of her imagination, the manifestation of some deep-seated guilt or warped desire. Then she knew for certain that he was nothing of the sort, that if this apparition had been conjured by dark forces, they were forces acting against her, not from within her. And that made her angry.

It was to prove a trying day. As Sally stalked the bum, so he must have imagined he was stalking her. Sally knew that the safest place was behind him, keeping him in sight. She followed him on his search of the hospital. She observed his consternation when he finally discovered her room number, only to find the room itself empty. She witnessed the mayhem when the police also learned that she had gone, and how the bum managed to stay invisible on the edge of the jabbering crowd. From time to time she lost him, when he made too many turns too fast, or when she was assaulted by sickness and paralyzing headaches. But she never panicked, knowing that the sinister forces at work here would ensure that their paths crossed again.

To keep herself going, she stole food and drink from carts left outside rooms. No-one paid much attention to the sight of a barefoot young woman in a raincoat padding around the corridors, even though she saw some doctors and nurses so often she learned to recognize them, and by the ends of their shifts was on nodding terms.

Sally didn't know how it might end. It occurred to her that, by staying behind him, she might prolong this search forever. Already the day had passed and they were well into another night. She watched the midnight shift change and thought about how they were into another day and that someone or something somewhere had her trapped in this hospital, bound to this obnoxious creature, and her anger welled up again. And that's when she lost him.

She walked quickly, faster and faster, sometimes breaking into a faltering trot, worried that the force of her anger had broken the link. Every few seconds, she threw a glance over her shoulder, aware that the change in circumstance meant that now he might be following her. And then once more, she nearly walked into him.

He was at the nurse's station with a bunch of flowers, talking to the duty sister. Sally couldn't hear what they were saying, but she guessed they were talking about her.

Sally walked to the nurse's station at a brisk pace. The bum was still talking to the nurse, leaning over the counter, and neither one paid Sally any attention until she was practically behind him. The bum finally turned his head towards her and his faced showed the first glimmer of recognition as Sally reached under his shirt and pulled out the automatic pistol. She cocked it, flipped off the safety and aimed the gun at the back of the bum's head, all in one fluid action.

He froze.

"Careful with that, would'ya," he said. "The trigger's a bit fucked."

"Won't be the only thing if you don't do what I say," said Sally. She saw the nurse staring at her with huge eyes. "Sorry miss, but me and this gent have something to discuss."

"No problem," stuttered the nurse. "Whatever."

Sally prodded the bum with the pistol. "Let's go." A wave of nausea hit her and she rocked forwards, her eyes closing. The bum span round and his hand came up towards the gun. Sally's eyes flicked open and her hand trembled. The gun went off. The sound slapped her around the face and her ears rang. The bum stepped back, hard against the counter. The nurse disappeared. A high, quivering voice came from beneath the counter.

"If you two want to talk, would you mind going outside?"

Sally pushed the bum ahead of her, walking fast, heading for where she thought a back entrance might be, working on instinct. They met only a few people along the way, all of them running fast towards the nurse's station, Sally kept the gun low, but in plain sight. No-one saw it.

They came out into a car park.

"Any of these cars yours?" Sally asked.

"No."

"Then steal one."

6:
Doesn't look like the kind of place that would have parts for a Mercedes

Hipólito drove to Santa Marta. There would be people at the airport who would recognize him and he wanted at least an hour or two in the town before word got around that he was there.

He'd taken Escobar's Mercedes. In fact, it was one of a dozen Mercs at the *finca* but the only one that still had a functioning suspension. This one had a broken air conditioner, so all four bullet-proof windows were wound down.

Escobar was much on Hipólito's mind. *Fucking cheapskate,* he thought. Hipólito would have left him a year ago, or was it two years ... anyway, about the time when Escobar lost direction and his ambitions began to outstrip his income. Hipólito had hesitated — he liked to think it was loyalty, but now he was beginning to suspect that he'd just screwed up. And now it was too late. To desert Escobar would look like cowardice, and though he could still jump ship and join another crew, he would never be fully trusted. He would never be put in a position of real power. He'd never have the same opportunities for hurting people.

Perhaps his future lay in killing Escobar. But he had to choose his moment, when he could grab what was left of the money and the drugs and offer these as a dowry to a new boss.

Hipólito slotted a cassette of his favourite Merino Brothers album into the tape deck. Lights flashed on the player and the rapid beat of a *caja* rattled from the speakers. It was joined by an accordion and *guacharaca* and soon the car was filled with the joyful pulsing of Vallenata music. A minute later, a sudden *thunk!* killed the sound. Hipólito smacked the tape player with the heel of his hand. Its lights went out.

About ten miles from town Hipólito passed an airstrip where, in past years, he had spent many hours loading planes making unscheduled flights to the States. He craned his neck to see if it was busy at the moment, but all he could see were occasional glimpses of fuel barrels.

When his attention came back to the road, he was amazed to see two men, both *gringos*, a tall one dressed in a multi-coloured flying suit and leather jacket, the other a scrawny kid in shades. The tall one had his arm outstretched, his thumb pointed skywards. Hipólito slowed. He had a nervous feeling he couldn't quite locate. Something was wrong here.

He stopped just beyond the two men. As they ran up to the car, Hipólito's left hand dropped into the map pocket of the door, where he'd left a .38 special. The tall guy popped his head through the window of the passenger door.

"Going anywhere near Santa Marta?" he asked in English.

"Far as I know, it's the only place on this road," said Hipólito in the same language. "Jump in."

"You haven't got any dogs in here, have you?"

"Do you see any dogs?"

"No," said the tall guy. "But then you don't always see them, not right away."

The big guy opened the rear door and let the skinny one get in. The boy looked somehow familiar. From the way he stumbled into the car, clambering across the back seat on all fours, Hipólito assumed he was either blind or simple-minded.

Blind! Hipólito felt like he'd had a slap to the face. Fuck me! It's the boy! His fingers closed around the .38.

The big guy climbed into the front passenger seat. Damn. This guy looks familiar too. Hipólito decided to bide his time. Finding the boy in Colombia had unsettled him. He thought there must be some purpose to it. He let go of the gun and put the car into gear.

As he drove off, he stole a look at the big man out of the corner of his eye. He was smiling back.

"The name's Hipólito."

"Really? I'm Rotsky. And that's Vinnie," said Rotsky. He frowned. "Have we met?"

Rotsky! Holy shit!

Hipólito got a sinking sensation in his stomach. Rotsky was a name he knew from the old days. If people like that were resurfacing then it could only be because of Díaz, or maybe Walkaway. Hipólito had the feeling that things might get out of hand. "No, I don't think so," he said.

The three men rode on in silence. Hipólito was reluctant to talk in case he gave something away. About five miles down the road, as the car hit the outskirts of a small village, there was a painful grinding noise from the engine and then silence. The car coasted to a halt.

"Fuck!" said Hipólito. He turned over the ignition. There was a brief cough from somewhere inside the hood and then nothing. He punched the steering wheel. "Piece o' shit!"

"Problem?" asked Rotsky.

An old peasant stood up from where he'd been sitting, on the veranda of a nearby building. He shuffled over to the Mercedes and patted the hood. "German," he said. "Nice car."

Fuck you, thought Hipólito, and then: "You got a mechanic in this goddamned place?"

"Mechanic? Here?" The old man chuckled. "We got no cars."

Hipólito sighed and stepped out of the Merc. He looked disconsolately at what he could see of the village. It wasn't much. "Isn't there anyone who can fix cars?"

"Oh sure," said the peasant. "My brother. You want I should get him?"

Rotsky got out of the car and looked around. "Doesn't look like the kind of place that would have parts for a Mercedes," he said.

Real fucking helpful, thought Hipólito. "Maybe he can just patch it," he said. He turned back to the peasant. "You get your brother. How long is all this going to take?"

"I don't think he can do it until tomorrow morning."

Hipólito stared at the man in horror. "Why the fuck not?"

"Well first we have to get him. His village is twenty kilometres away and we ain't got a car." He looked at the Mercedes with an arched eyebrow, as if presenting Exhibit A. "Then we got to get him drunk and talk him into it."

"Huh?"

"He doesn't like foreign cars. Can't get the parts." He gave Rotsky a complicitous look. "But once he's drunk, he's fine. You going to Santa Marta?"

"Where else?"

"He'll get you to Santa Marta. You can get it fixed properly there. But today I think you'd better stay at the hotel. And I suggest you get drunk too. It's not a very good hotel."

* * *

It took the bum about thirty seconds to get a Ford open and the engine started. Sally sat in the back, the muzzle of the gun pressed against the back of the driver's seat. The bum drove.

"Keep it legal," said Sally. They pulled out into the main road and left the hospital behind just as half-a-dozen squad cars screamed up, lights flashing.

Half-an-hour later they were in Sally's apartment. She tied the bum's hands behind his back and hobbled his feet, leaving just enough freedom so that he could walk, though very slowly. Then she ran more rope around his chest and upper arms.

"Nice tan," she said.

"Just got in from the south."

Sally stepped back and admired her work. Suddenly she was desperate for a shower. The bum's eyes nearly popped when she slid off the coat.

"Holy cow! Quinn was right about you."

Sally threw on a long t-shirt.

"Quinn? Quinn's paying you to kill me?"

Sally knew about Quinn by reputation only. She thought hard in an attempt to recall what she knew about him. It wasn't much. She didn't like the idea of being hunted by people she didn't know.

"I get paid by lots of people," said the bum. "Besides, I'm no assassin. I get paid to watch people."

"You tried to kill me."

"That was on my own time," he said. "Nothing personal. Just a hobby."

Sally walked up to him and tested the ropes.

"This is my hobby," she said. She tightened a knot, and as the rope bit into the bum's skin she saw his eyes slide shut. He raised his face and gave out a quiet "aah".

Sally tightened the rope some more and got a similar response. She slapped him across the face and the bum just looked up at her with a puppyish expression. Aha! thought Sally. She stood up and rummaged in a chest of drawers for a minute. When she returned to the bum she was carrying a sanitary pad and a roll of duct tape which she used to gag him.

"You stay there and be a good boy," she said. "I need to get dressed. She walked to the bathroom, showered quickly, then moved to the bedroom. In the corner was a trunk stencilled with the *Divine Providence's* nose art logo. She opened it and took out a selection of clothes.

When she walked back into the living room Sally was wearing thigh-high stiletto boots, a leather corset, long rubber gloves, and a rubber ball mask — all in black. In her right hand she carried a bullwhip.

The bum's eyes opened wide again. Muffled sounds came through the gag which Sally thought might be the words "Oh yes".

"Do you like to be teased?" purred Sally. The bum shook his head vigorously. "No? Well, do you like to be hurt?"

The bum nodded so hard Sally thought he might injure himself. "Whmmff! Umm whumff-whumff!" he said.

"Oh, this?" said Sally. She ran a hand down the curves of the corset. "It's just something I borrowed from the boss. Now, let's talk about your work."

* * *

Rosita Ortega dropped a little more parsley into the soup and stirred. She lifted the spoon, blew on the steaming liquid and sipped it. The second it registered on her taste buds, Rosita convulsed forward and sprayed soup on the kitchen floor, over the window and some of it back into the pan. "Mother of god!" she gasped. She stood erect and wiped the tears from her eyes. "Soup's off," she muttered.

She lifted the soup pan and carried it to the sink. As she poured the foaming liquid down the drain, her gaze drifted involuntarily through the window to the boats rising and falling gently at the quayside next to her café. "Thank you for those at least, Roberto," she sighed. She longed to be out on the ocean, an open bottle in her hand, the engine switched off, the wind and the sea taking her where they would. But now she had new responsibilities. At the age of forty-three, Rosita had just that morning become the owner of three boats and the harbour café.

She had discovered this from two policeman who had just left. They had come into the café with serious expressions. One was tall, morose-looking and fidgety. The other was small — so small that at first Rosita took him to be a child dressed-up. He quickly forgot to look serious and seemed to be in no rush to talk. He gazed around the café as though confirming something he'd been told. It wasn't until his partner nudged him that he remembered to give Rosita the news.

It wasn't a surprise to Rosita to learn that her husband, Roberto, had been found with another women. It had happened before, many times. Nor was it really a surprise to learn that he was dead, shot in a Bogotá motel room. The policeman said they thought drugs might be involved.

"Do you need me to identify the body?" Rosita asked.

"On no, we know it's him. He had a wallet, rings. There were eyewitnesses. Fingerprints. Besides, there isn't much to identify. They must have fired a thousand rounds into him and the girl."

"Yes, yes," Rosita nodded. "That's how I would have done it."

"It was a real mess." The policeman seemed to warm to the subject. "I ain't ever seen a room like that. Everything was smashed. The lights. The furniture. The little cartons of milk. And the blood . . ."

The taller policeman coughed. His partner looked at him questioningly, but when he got no answer, continued.

"Lots of blood. Covered everything. The ambulance crew couldn't tell which bit of body belonged to which victim, so they got a bunch of Ziploc bags and took them down to the city morgue that way." He reached into a pocket. "You wanna see some Polaroids?"

Rosita arched an eyebrow and leaned towards the proffered pictures, but without reaching out. "That's not necessary," she said.

"So I guess this place is yours now," said the policeman. "The boats too." He nodded in the direction of the quay. "I hear there's a couple of massage parlours in Bogotá as well, but there might be some problem about ownership there."

He resumed his examination of the café. Rosita followed his gaze and noticed for the first time just how shabby the place was. Paint peeled from the walls, and every surface was coated in grease. She discovered she didn't care much.

Outside, a large engine growled into life.

"Having that airfield right next door can't do much to help business," said the small cop.

"Goddamned airfield," grumbled Rosita. "When we bought this place, no-one said nothin' about no goddamned airfield." She spat on the floor. "The harbour, that's why we're here. The boats, señor, the boats were always mine. Roberto, he knew nothing about boats. I was the one who . . ." She looked into the frightened faces of the cops and realized she had been spitting out the words. She grabbed a can of goulash from the cupboard and attached a can opener to it. The tin gave a gentle hiss as the opener bit into the lid.

"I, er . . . I hear you do all the cooking here," said the small cop.

"That's right," said Rosita. She looked morosely into the can then threw it into a waste bin. "You want to stay for some food?"

"No no," spluttered both policeman.

"We ain't hungry," added the small one.

"That's a shame," said Rosita. "We don't get many customers these days. Not since our last chef . . . ah . . . left. Just a few regulars. Divorced men, mostly." She wiped her hands on her apron, which left a sticky residue on her fingers. "I eat out," she added.

After the policemen left, Rosita dropped into a strangely calm mood, unable to think about the future or what her change in circumstances might mean. The café was important to her: not as income — she had other, more enjoyable ways of making money — but as a stable base and a respectable front. All she could do for the moment was carry on as normal and wait for something to crop up that would determine her future course. It was, she realized happily, rather like drifting on the ocean.

The roar of a departing Lear Jet rattled the pots and plates, and without conscious thought Rosita moved swiftly to a lean-to shack outside the kitchen. There was a huge cage in which two dark, malevolent birds glowered at her. On the floor of the cage were the tattered remnants of several mice and a small dog. "Dear Ack-Ack," cooed Rosita. "Sweet Flak. Soon. Very soon."

A yell from the dining room reminded Rosita she had people to serve. She walked back into the kitchen and ladled stew from a huge pot onto two plates, careful to stay upwind of its sticky vapours. She ambled over to where three men waited silently and dropped the plates on the table.

"What's this?" snapped one of them. The man spoke in English. Rosita took this, as she took most things, as an insult.

"Food," she said.

"We ordered two steaks and a fried chicken. This looks like stew, fer chrissakes." The man used a fork to pick a piece of stringy meat from the food. "Just what the fuck is this?"

"Beef," she said. "Or chicken. Same thing."

The man glared at her and she glared back. There was something about him she hadn't liked from the start. It wasn't the cheap clothes or the scowling expression or the bad language. She was used to those. It was the pink hands.

"Well get us another one," the man snapped.

Rosita shuffled back to the kitchen. She had already forgotten about the pink-handed man and his food.

She leaned on the windowsill and gazed at her boats.

"Hey waitress!" bellowed a voice. "Where's our other meal?"

Rosita went back into the bar and straight up to the loud customer. "I want my steak!" he wailed. The other two men were silent. Their cheeks bulged with stew.

"Beef's off," said Rosita flatly.

"What? How can—"

An aircraft roared low above the café's roof. Rosita looked up as though expecting to see it. She hawked and spat copiously on the floor. "I hate planes," she snarled.

The pink-handed man withered under her stare. "For fucksakes," he muttered, then louder: "What about the chicken?"

"Chicken's off. Everything's off. We're closing."

"Closing? At lunchtime?"

"*Sí.*"

"Jesus H Christ. Get the boss. We need to speak to him."

"The boss?"

"Yeah, the boss. We were told that the person that runs this café also has some boats for hire: boats that a person might use for a little export operation."

"Ah. I see. You want to smuggle something to the States, no?"

"Shi—," the man's head span round to take in the other customers, but they were alone. "Fer chrissakes, keep it to yourself, will ya?"

"For your information, *señor*, you're talking to the boss. And my boats are busy . . . catching fish. I'll bring you the bill."

"Wait a minute. You don't understand. We need to move something, and soon."

"Then get yourself . . ." she snorted loudly, ". . . an aeroplane. I think somehow that is more your style."

Díaz turned to his colleagues.

"What the fuck are you doing? You just sit there eating. Persuade this *puta* that she should work for us."

Without looking up, José pulled an automatic pistol from inside his jacket, pulled back the slide, and pointed it in the general direction of Rosita.

"Work for us," he spluttered through a mouthful of stew. He shovelled in another forkful with his left hand and fired a couple of rounds with his right, to drive his point home.

Rosita didn't flinch, but she was aware of a sudden movement and noticed that one of the men had disappeared. There was a scuffling sound, and something that may have been a whimper, from under the table.

Rosita had had enough.

"Listen. I hear there's a pilot coming in today. He's bringing in one plane and taking out another. This is confidential information, you understand?"

Díaz nodded his head vigorously.

"Go to the airfield on the other side of town. The one on the other side, hear. Not this one." Her head nodded in the direction of her back yard and she spat viciously on to one of the plates. José put down his cutlery and pushed himself back from the table. "You talk to that pilot. Don't bother me again."

* * *

Rotsky reached forward and scratched his right ankle. He watched the margarita in his left hand carefully, not wanting to spill a drop. It had cost a small fortune.

From his wicker chair, on the veranda of the hotel, he could see the whole village. On the opposite side of the dusty road was the barn where they had pushed Hipólito's Mercedes. Its rotted wooden doors were shut, though the sounds of clanking metal and sloppy oaths travelled clearly to Rotsky. From time to time, a small, unidentifiable piece of car would sail through a gap in the doors' planking.

Hipólito was in the barn — had been there all day, reluctant to take his eyes off the vehicle. Rotsky had tried to sleep, but something in the atmosphere of the shabby room disturbed him and he had only napped fitfully.

There was no cantina in the village, and the hotel had no bar, so Rotsky took up residence on the veranda and simply yelled when he needed food or drink. He'd been doing this all day.

Vinnie passed the time exploring the village and the surrounding fields. Late in the afternoon he went to his room for a sleep. It was now early evening and Vinnie walked out on to the veranda, scratching his arms. "Rotsky?" he said. "Where you at?"

"At?"

Vinnie turned towards Rotsky. "Where are you?"

"Over here." Rotsky helped the boy into a chair. "You want a drink?"

"You bet. Sure. Whatever you're having."

"*Señor!*" yelled Rotsky.

A dusty, yellow man appeared at the door. "Sir?" he asked.

"A lemonade for the boy," said Rotsky.

They sat in silence with their drinks for a while. Every minute or so, one of them would scratch a part of his body. "That guy was right," said Rotsky eventually. "This isn't a very good hotel. Where's your video camera?"

"In the room. I didn't think there'd be much to video here."

Rotsky looked around, appraising the village in a new way. "You're right," he said.

The door of the barn creaked open and Hipólito walked out. He yawned and stretched his arms and cast a glance at Rotsky and the boy that Rotsky thought didn't seem altogether friendly.

"Are we getting anywhere?" asked Vinnie.

"Hard to say," said Rotsky. He watched Hipólito bend and tie a shoe lace. Rotsky was trying to remember where he'd seen the man before. Memory wasn't Rotsky's strong point, and what he had he didn't trust. But he knew for certain that he'd met Hipólito before.

"Do you think we might find out anything about King Zipa down here?"

At Vinnie's mention of 'Zipa', Hipólito shot upright again, his face betraying ... what? Rotsky couldn't decide if it was fear or merely recognition. Hipólito turned and disappeared back into the barn.

"I don't know if they have wrestling down here," said Rotsky, though his thoughts were still on Hipólito. "Maybe we should ask the big guy."

"Who?"

"Hipólito."

Vinnie faced Rotsky, his expression thoughtful. "Hipólito's big?"

7:
Too high, too fast

Vinnie was having trouble getting used to Colombia. The new language of sounds and smells and the incomprehensible voices made him feel like a lost tourist. It was only his faith in Rotsky that stopped him screaming for help.

He could feel from the air that it was early in the morning. Possibly very early. Rotsky had woken him half an hour ago and had steered him here, wherever here was, and left. Vinnie was still indoors, he knew that, and from the way his footsteps sounded, it was a small, bare room. There was a powerful stench of urine, but the whole hotel had smelled that way. And that was the extent of Vinnie's universe.

A door behind him opened and he sensed a man enter. Vinnie sniffed the air. Above the slum-stench there was now a top note of garlic. It was the same guy from the previous day, the driver of the Mercedes. Hipólito.

Vinnie wanted to call for Rotsky, but he didn't feel he could kick up a fuss just yet. This big man had a malevolent presence. The hairs on Vinnie's neck stood up and the room seemed suddenly much smaller.

"Have you finished?" asked Hipólito. "Do you mind if I . . .?"

Vinnie felt a hand on his arm. It pushed him gently to one side. He went with it. Vinnie heard Hipólito shuffle his feet, as if he was adopting a special position. There was a noise like a soft *burr* and then the sound of running water.

"Ah!" sighed Hipólito. "That's better."

Vinnie heard the *burr* and the shuffle of feet again. He had an urgent desire to speak, as if projecting himself into the void would somehow stop the room suffocating him.

"You on holiday too?" he asked. Vinnie instantly knew it had been a mistake to ask the man his business. The malignant aura cranked up a notch. Then, like a breaking wave, it peaked and faded.

Hipólito chuckled in a way that wasn't friendly. "Just looking up an old friend," he said. "Here. Let me help."

Vinnie allowed himself to be guided out of the room into one barely bigger. He guessed they were in the lobby of the hotel. Hipólito spoke again, but in Spanish. There was another voice, and then another. It sounded as though Hipólito was asking questions and not getting satisfactory answers. Vinnie was about to tune out the conversation when he picked up on a word he knew. Walkaway.

"Hey! You a friend of Walkaway?" asked Vinnie. "Is he here?"

There was silence. Then Hipólito spoke again. Vinnie thought there was caution in his voice. "No," he said. "He's not here. Do you know where he is?"

"No. We're looking for him. Rotsky seems to think he'll turn up in Santa Marta." Vinnie felt happier now that he had something in common with the big man. It made him friendlier, somehow.

"Rotsky knows Walkaway." It was a statement, not a question, spoken slowly, as though Hipólito had remembered something important. "Rotsky knows Walkaway."

* * *

Rotsky hoped the walk would ease his hangover. He had decided to drink himself to sleep. But it was hard to know exactly how much booze was required and he thought he might have overdone it.

He had just visited the rest room. Then it occurred to him that Vinnie might need to do the same, and as he didn't know how long Vinnie would take, being blind, he had left the boy there.

When Rotsky hit the street, the sun was very low and a breeze cleared the dust and made the air clean. He walked up the main street and then, because there was nowhere more definite to go, walked back down it again.

The Mercedes was right outside the hotel door. A pair of feet stuck out from a rear window. Rotsky looked inside the car and saw the mechanic stretched across the seat, hat over his head, apparently asleep. Rotsky grabbed a foot and shook it.

A deep voice grumbled and coughed. The mechanic sat up and glared at Rotsky. Then his eyes widened and he shot out of the car, disappearing back inside it for a second to retrieve his fallen hat, which he now held in front of his heart.

"I'm sorry *señor*," he said, then turned his face to take in the car. He swept his hand along its length as if selling it. "Is fixed. Good as new." The mechanic coughed again and put his hat on his head. "You have the money?"

"We paid you last night," said Rotsky.

"Ah yes. I had to be sure." The mechanic frowned and patted his pockets. He didn't seem to find anything.

Rotsky heard a door slam and turned to see Hipólito point Vinnie towards the Mercedes. The two men simply nodded at each other. Rotsky guided Vinnie into the rear seat of the car and then resumed his place in the front. Hipólito opened the driver's door but stopped and peered down the road. He seemed to come to some kind of decision and got into the car.

Hipólito inserted the key and turned it. The engine coughed and whined but didn't catch. The mechanic stroked the hood encouragingly.

The engine started on the ninth or tenth attempt. It rattled alarmingly, but as the mechanic had now disappeared there seemed little point in sticking around to complain.

They were out of the village before Hipólito broke the silence.

"You going to Santa Marta for business or pleasure?" he asked.

"Some of both," said Rotsky. "Same thing, really."

"Maybe I could help you. I have a lot of business colleagues in the town. I could put you in touch with the right people."

"Sounds good. Maybe I could help you too."

"Maybe you could," smiled Hipólito.

They hit Santa Marta pretty quickly.

"You got somewhere to stay?" asked Hipólito. Rotsky hadn't thought that far ahead, and said so.

"I'll drop you at the Malvado," said Hipólito. He cast a sideways look at Rotsky. "You'll fit right in. It's very popular with foreigners. No-one will notice another *gringo* there. Once you're settled, get a cab to the Hotel Yoshima. I have a suite there."

Hipólito stopped the car outside a shabby building. The front door was littered with young backpackers who looked like they had burst from the overstuffed hotel. Rotsky got out of the car, collected Vinnie and thanked Hipólito.

"Be careful in this street," said Hipólito. "This is Calle 10C. Much prostitution." He looked like he was about to spit out a bad taste. "Don't go that way." He pointed east. "And lock your door at all times. Have a nice stay."

The Mercedes squealed away. Rotsky pushed Vinnie ahead of him into the hotel foyer. Inside was even more densely festooned with backpackers, some sitting, some lying on the floors, several in hammocks, so that the room appeared to have been decorated in multi-colour nylon. A ceiling fan turned slowly, but its blades were largely rotted away. The walls were stained and it smelled of sweat, damp and dope. So this is where Woodstock went, thought Rotsky.

"Where the hell are we?" asked Vinnie.

Rotsky was about to answer when he heard his name called from the other side of the room. It was Squeaker, who now stumbled between supine bodies towards the new arrivals.

"Ain't this place great?" Squeaker burbled. "It's like . . . you know . . ."

"Woodstock?"

"Home."

Rotsky looked at Squeaker blankly for a moment. Something was bothering him. Then he realized what it was.

"What are you doing here," he asked.

Squeaker looked as though he didn't understand the question. "I'm staying here," he said. "Georgio's idea. Said I'd fit right in. Man, he was right. He's at the Yoshima."

Squeaker helped them check in, a process that took half an hour because the manager's Spanish appeared to be an entirely different brand from the one Rotsky knew. Their room was just big enough for its furniture and the three men to stand. It had two wooden cots with thin mattresses and ragged blankets. There was a small table with legs of different lengths, two equally rickety chairs, a table lamp and a ceiling fan. The previous occupant had left behind a bottle of tequila, quarter-full, and a shoe.

Man, this place has everything I need, thought Rotsky. Squeaker smiled constantly. Vinnie sniffed his way around the room and asked if there was anywhere nearby where they could buy air freshener.

Five minutes later they were outside the hotel, looking for a cab. A shot rang out from the east, there was a squeal of tyres and a cab hurtled down the street. Rotsky put out his hand and the cab screeched to a halt in front of them. "Get in, quick!" yelled the driver.

The three men piled into the back of the cab. It took off again at high speed. "What's the hurry?" asked Rotsky.

"Undercover cop's just been shot down there." The cabbie hooked a thumb over his shoulder.

"If he was undercover, how'd you know he was a cop?" asked Vinnie.

"I shot him," said the cabbie.

"All the same —"

"He's my cousin, okay?"

"So why the fuck did you stop for us?" asked Rotsky.

"Hey man, a fare's a fare, you know?"

The cabbie dropped them at the Yoshima, took a large banknote from Squeaker and screamed away without giving change. The three men walked into the hotel's foyer and immediately felt uneasy.

It was a large foyer, decorated in white and limed wood, with a parquet floor, potted palms and liveried bell hops. Even the air felt rich and Rotsky was afraid to breathe it.

Hipólito was waiting on a leather sofa. He stood and walked up to the men. He'd showered and changed since arriving and pushed an air of expensive cleanliness before him. Rotsky looked at Vinnie's clothes and then his own. They were shedding dust on the highly-polished floor.

"Perhaps we should go," said Hipólito. "I've got a Jeep outside. Who's this?" He nodded towards Squeaker.

"A friend," said Rotsky. "He's with us, I guess."

Hipólito nodded. His face showed no reaction.

Rotsky had several questions he wanted to ask. He decided to start with: "Jeep?"

"Yeah. The Moro didn't quite make it. I had to get a cab the last kilometre. I've hired a Jeep."

"Where are we going?"

Hipólito put his hands on the upper arms of Vinnie and Rotsky, shepherding them towards the door. "I've arranged a meeting with a business associate. Might prove useful."

"Hold on, man," said Squeaker. "I just gotta ... you know ..." He walked towards the reception desk. "Phone shit," he said over his shoulder.

Rotsky turned to Hipólito. "Would you excuse me?" he said. "While Squeaker's making his call, I think I'll just visit the little pilot's room."

* * *

Escobar's eyes streamed. He stared into four thousand watts of light aimed straight at his face. The rest of the room was pitch black. He didn't want to close his eyes because he was hungry for a glimpse of the man.

"Do you understand?" the voice said. The Spanish was perfect, but Escobar thought the accent might be Yankee.

"Yes, I understand," said Escobar. "Forget about Díaz. Leave him to you. Find Walkaway."

"We want him alive."

"Why's he so goddamned important?"

"He's not. What he's got is."

"Which is?"

"Never you mind. All you need to know is that the man is dangerous to us."

"He knows too much, huh?"

"He knows nothing. But he could be bad for business."

"Business? What business?"

"You ask too many questions."

Escobar squirmed in his seat. "Hey, I'm on your side. You're from the Corporation, right?"

"There you go again."

Escobar fought the impulse to scream. The impertinence of his interrogator was intolerable.

"I don't have to stand for this," he sneered. He straightened his back and held his head erect. "You know who I am, right?"

"Yes."

The flat simplicity of the answer deflated Escobar for a moment, but he soon puffed himself up again.

"I demand a little more respect. I must have the information I need to fulfil my mission."

"And your mission is?"

"I . . ." Escobar wiped the sweat from his eyes. "I cannot divulge that. I don't know who you are. All I know is that I received a message through a known Corporation contact saying I should come here." Escobar rotated his gaze as if to take in his surroundings. Against the glare of the lights, however, all was blackness. "I was good enough to grant you some of my valuable time." Even as he said this, Escobar knew he was losing ground. He'd effectively been kidnapped and had arrived blindfolded. "I demand . . . that you tell me . . ." He trailed off, unable to focus on what it was he wanted to know.

There was a sigh and the sound of a pen tapping on a table.

"Okay. This is what I can tell you. We were about to start a new line of business. Díaz tried to get in first, but that doesn't matter. He's small scale, just a minor irritant. But Walkaway has something that could put us out of business before we even get started. And that's all I'm going to tell you. Get down to Santa Marta—"

"—My man's already down there."

"Good. We've got someone working for us down there, too. We've set up a little operation that we think will bring Walkaway into town. It's just his sort of deal. I want you waiting for him when he arrives. There's a package on the table in front of you with photographs, so you'll know him when you see him."

"What if I miss him?"

"We'll be in touch."

* * *

Sally shifted down and hit the gas to overtake a Winnebago with *Catskills Groovers* and *Annoy Your Kids: Live Forever* bumper stickers.

"Where the hell are we going?" asked the bum. He was in the back seat. Sally had removed the gag shortly after the first crack of her whip. It had taken a while, but she'd got a lot out of him. Some stuff about Quinn and Lady Caine, and that the bum's name was Archibald. She'd really had to work hard for that. But most of the information meant nothing to her, just names and places. She wanted to run them by Lulu.

"Tico airport," said Sally.

"Gee. Wouldn't have anything to do with Lulu, would it?"

Sally pursed her lips. Maybe she'd already said too much. The bum made her nervous. He knew everything. She wondered how long he'd been watching her. Just what did he know? Did he know stuff she didn't?

Sally saw the yellow 'M' of a McDonalds loom up. She felt simultaneously hungry and nervous. She was very tired. She wanted to close her eyes. She cast a glance in the rear-view mirror. The bum was squirming. What the fuck is he up to? The turn-off for the restaurant went by. And then one for a Denny's, a Taco Bell, a KFC. Sally's stomach rumbled. She looked down, expecting to see something wrong with it.

Suddenly she was choking. Her head snapped back. Her vision blurred. Her hands weakened and she let go of the steering wheel. She hit the brake. The car veered and swerved, its movement oddly sensuous. It headed off the road into a parking lot. Oh shit! Here we go again, thought Sally. She was blacking out. Her hands flapped uselessly at the tight band around her neck. And then all she could think was: I wish I'd learned to tie better knots.

* * *

Walkaway scanned the aircraft instruments. They all appeared to be saying sensible things, but he wasn't all that familiar with this type, had had no opportunity to test the instruments and his vision was a little blurry.

He took hold of a jacket button and pulled it one way then the other. *Not a bad fit*, he thought. The man he'd stolen it from had looked a little small as he lay on the floor of the crew changing room. The cap fitted well, though.

He tapped the left breast pocket to reassure himself that the bag of cocaine was still there. It was much smaller now. Walkaway had been on the move for several days — he couldn't quite recall the exact number, didn't feel he had the right to be precise about it — and he was fighting fatigue. He knew that if he stopped, someone would find him, and it didn't feel like the right time for that. But the constant travel was taking its toll. He'd got a couple of legitimate ferrying jobs to start with, and had been paid in cocaine for both, but now he was having to dig into it in larger and larger doses just to keep moving. He knew he'd have to find somewhere safe, somewhere he could rest.

He'd lost count of how many aircraft he had stolen, but it must have been a few. Oddly, this airliner had been the easiest. The ground crew had been a bit surprised to hear that Walkaway was taking the plane without a co-pilot. But working for Caracas Universal Airlines they'd heard weirder things. And the Venezuela vs Panama match was about to start. They all wanted to get home.

Walkaway had the ADF navigation radio tuned to the match. It didn't make much sense to him because his Spanish — always patchy — seemed to have deteriorated under the effects of the drugs. He had no confidence in the veracity of the reported score — which was nil-nil — but he enjoyed the general sense of excitement.

A map lay on the co-pilot's seat. Walkaway hadn't looked at it in a while. The fine details and busy lines hurt his eyes. In any case, he knew where he was. This was familiar territory that he had mapped internally through years of experience and he was flying by instinct. He looked down at the sparkling coastline, and the shape of the waveline triggered an automatic reaction. Time to get down. He eased back the throttle levers.

* * *

Hmm, busy day, thought Rosita as four men came into her café. She considered closing for the day. Then she recognized the biggest one.

"Hipólito!" she called. He wasn't exactly a friend, but he was a good customer for her boats. They shook hands.

"I think we'll sit outside," said Hipólito and led the group out to the terrace. Rosita brought coffee. Sitting with Hipólito were three *gringos* — a tall man in a multicoloured flying suit, a small, balding man with a broad grin and a teenage boy who was pointing a video camera at the waste bin that blocked his view of the sea.

"Well, my friend," she said. "What brings you here?"

"We need some information," said Hipólito. "You seen any suspicious characters around recently?"

Rosita laughed. "Nothing but."

Hipólito smiled. "No. I mean anyone out of the ordinary."

Rosita considered her reply. In a place like Santa Marta it was wise to keep even casual contacts to yourself. However, if a man like Hipólito wanted information, it had to be a serious matter.

"Sure," said Rosita. "Some *puto* and a couple of two-bit gangsters. Wanted to use my boats. I told him to go away."

"Anything special about this guy?"

"Yeah. Pink hands. I hate people with pink hands."

Hipólito sipped his coffee. The other two older men followed suit. The boy videotaped them.

"You know where this guy is now?" asked Hipólito.

"No, but he might be at the old airstrip on the other side of town this afternoon."

"You got a map of the place?" asked Hipólito. He threw her a subtle wink and nodded his head almost imperceptibly towards the café.

"I think I've got one inside," said Rosita. "Why don't you help me look?"

Hipólito rose and walked with her into the café. Once out of sight of the others, he turned to her. "I don't need a map," he said. "I need to make use of your special skills."

Rosita smiled. "Guns or boats?"

"Guns." He cast a glance towards the entrance. "I think you'll enjoy it."

He opened his mouth to speak again, but there were cries from outside, quickly drowned by a thunderous roar. Hipólito and Rosita ran outside in time to see the sun blotted out by an airliner flying very low. The men instinctively ducked. The plane appeared to descend on them like a great, howling shadow. Only Rosita remained upright, shaking a fist at the aircraft, her shouts drowned by the noise of the engines.

"Seven-thirty-seven," yelled Rotsky. "Sonofabitch has still got its wheels up."

"Coming into that airfield," said Rosita. She nodded at her back yard and spat on the ground.

"No, too high and too fast," said Rotsky. "My guess is the other side of town. Something tells me we'd better find out where exactly." He got up and headed for the Jeep. Hipólito guided Vinnie through the maze of plastic chairs.

"I'll like, you know . . . catch you guys later," said Squeaker. He turned to Rosita. "Excuse me. Do you have a . . . like . . ."

"Menu?"

"Phone."

* * *

It took Lulu and her brother all night to catch up. They had twenty years to cover, more than half his life. From time to time they dozed on the couch only to get into it again as soon as they awoke. The morning passed swiftly and it was midday before they thought of eating. They moved to the kitchen and Nicola hunted down some eggs.

"You always said you were going to join the Air Force," said Lulu. She noticed the gun on the table. She picked it up, pulled the clip, ejected the chambered round and dropped the lot in her bag. Nicola made more coffee.

"I tried. You know they do psychological screening with pilot cadets? I flunked. They said the tests showed I'm a borderline paranoid schizophrenic and that maybe I'd be happier in the Marines."

"Were you?"

"You kidding? All that shouting and squirming around in mud. Ugh!"

Nicola handed Lulu a full cup. "Sorry about the coffee earlier."

Lulu just smiled and shrugged. "Like the old days. We always did fight a lot."

"You always won. You were angry with me a lot then."

"That's because I kept finding my underwear in your room. You know, somehow all this —" she nodded at Nicola, who had changed into a pink gown and peignoir "— kind of makes sense. But the Marines? Recon? That's an elite outfit. Real tough guys."

"You get to parachute in Recon. And, well, I thought it would be the only way I could get close to silk."

"They don't make parachutes out of silk any more."

"I found out. So I went AWOL. I became Nicola as a disguise at first, but I found that I was happier this way."

They sat in contented silence for a while, then started again, picking over the trivia of separate existences. There was something Lulu was desperate to ask, but she had to wait for the right moment. The sun streamed into kitchen by the time she got around to it. It was during another moment of silence, as they both fought sleep.

"Have you . . . err . . ." Lulu nodded towards Nicola's lower body.

"It's all present and correct," smiled Nicola. "For now. That's why I got into this business. To get the money together. I'm going to get the top Swiss surgeon and the very best in hormone treatments — luxury all the way."

"It's a shame mom isn't alive. She always did want another daughter."

"Tell me about it." Nicola picked up her cup and studied the dry coffee grounds in the bottom. "I heard she died." Her eyes moistened. Lulu searched in her bag, handed Nicola a tissue and dropped her bag back on the table. "Don't mind me," said Nicola. "It's the hormones."

After lunch, they shopped. Lulu was surprised at how normal it felt to shop for dresses with her brother. By the evening, she had put Nick away and had accepted the reality of Nicola.

That night they went to bed early, exhausted. They woke late the next morning. Lulu found Nicola in the kitchen. They each found jobs to do, washing up, tidying. Nothing was said. They had talked themselves out, and now faced the awkward decision of how to go forward. They both jumped as someone banged hard on the front door. "Get it, would you honey?" asked Nicola. "It's probably the milkman. I don't want him to see me like this. I think he's a bit sweet on me."

Lulu threw Nicola a wink and walked to the door. The guy the other side of it didn't look much like a milkman. He was short and dishevelled. He wore a dirty yellow Hawaiian shirt and grubby cut-offs. His face was badly bruised. A real bum, thought Lulu. Then she noticed the large, expensive watch on his right wrist. His eyes flashed when he saw Lulu.

"Nicola in?" asked the bum. He gave Lulu a deranged smile, then knocked her aside. Lulu followed him into the kitchen. Nicola stood quickly when she saw the bum. She looked pale.

"Get the fuck out of here," she hissed.

"Now that's what I call a warm southern welcome," he said. He looked at the cups on the table. "Is there any of that coffee left?"

Lulu hovered at the doorway to the kitchen, not sure if she should interfere. She watched Nicola walk to the window and stare out. She seemed to be shaking. When Lulu looked back at the bum, he was holding her gun and inserting the clip.

"Boy," he said, "People say that women carry everything in their bags. Now I believe it." He pulled back the slide. The noise seemed even louder this time. "This yours?" he asked Lulu. She nodded. "Thought so." He inclined his head towards Nicola. "Toots here never carries."

Lulu looked at Nicola again. She had turned round and was staring at the ground in front of the bum.

"If you and Quinn want more information, you can forget it," she said. "I've told you all I can."

"Oh, I don't want information, sweet pea."

Nicola looked cagey. "But I already told you I won't work for you. Not my scene."

"Yeah, I know. A real picky bitch. But that's cool too. I got what I came for, though I didn't think I was going to get it here. Must be my lucky day, I guess."

Nicola was plainly puzzled. "What? What did you get?"

The bum nodded at Lulu. "Her."

Lulu froze. She fell forward a step but the bum had already levelled the gun at her.

"Don't. I need you alive. For now. You bitches really are a pain in the ass. I've already had to take care of your cute little friend."

"Sally?"

"Yeah. She and I have got a thing about car crashes. In her case, it was terminal."

Lulu's head swam. She felt sick.

"Now you be a good girl. I have to talk to my friend here." He took Lulu on a tour of the house until he found an upstairs room with a lock on the door. It was a small bedroom, unused as far as she could tell. There was a bare bed, a chest of drawers and a wardrobe, both half-full of men's clothes, and an exercise machine covered in dust.

When the bum left, Lulu checked the lock and decided it wouldn't be too hard to break. She knew she could make the drop from the window, too, if she had to. But she was worried about Nicola and didn't want to leave her alone with the bum.

Lulu listened at the door and could hear the grumble of angry voices, but no distinct words. She lay on the bed and tried to formulate a plan. Then she was woken by the bum.

"Wakey-wakey honey buns. We're leaving."

"Where are we going?" asked Lulu.

"Home sweet home, sweetheart."

* * *

Díaz stared with dead eyes at the part-burned wreckage of the 737. It sat flat on the ground, its escape chutes spread like the legs of a dissected frog.

"This guy's a professional?" he said. "Where is he anyhow?"

"Nobody knows," said Jesus. "We asked around. He just disappeared. No-one knows why the plane's here either."

"Who are those people?" asked Díaz. He pointed to about twenty people milling around like escaped lunatics, their clothes disarrayed, all without shoes, some without teeth.

"The passengers," said José. "They thought they were going to Panama. I think they're pretty pissed."

"Hey, you!" Díaz pointed at a middle-aged businessman who was fully dressed in a three-piece pinstripe suit, unmarked except that both sleeves of the jacket had disappeared. He stared at the ground and clutched a large toy rabbit. Díaz walked up to him.

"What happened here?" he asked.

The man stared at Díaz with a blank expression. "Have you seen my rabbit?" he asked.

"What? Fuck the rabbit, I said what happened here?"

"My rabbit. Have you seen it? I think it's lost."

"What the fuck's that in your hand, an alligator?"

"Oh no," said the man. "This is my wife's rabbit. Have you seen *my* rabbit? Come to that, have you seen my wife?"

"Fuck your rabbit and fuck your wife. I wanna know what happened here."

The businessman's expression hardened. "What the fuck you think happened?" he said. "We crashed."

"No shit. I wanna know how come."

"Terrestrial convergence."

"Huh?"

"That's what the captain said. Least ways, I think that's what he said. Hard to tell. He was running so fast . . ."

"Oh shit," muttered Díaz and walked away. José and Jesus joined him as he strolled around the wreck. They had just passed the nose when a large shape loomed from the other direction. It was a man — two men in fact, both tall — but Díaz's attention was grabbed by the larger one.

"Mother of Christ," whispered Díaz. His stomach tightened. "I know that guy from somewhere. He's bad news, I know it."

He was within a few yards of the two men now. Díaz did his best to smile. "Quite a mess, huh?" he greeted them.

"Sure is," said the thinner one. "We were in a café in town when we saw it fly over. Had to come take a look. Know what happened?"

"The captain said it was terrestrial convergence."

"No kidding. Well, that makes sense . . ." The stranger was grinning now, apparently satisfied with the explanation.

Díaz's gaze shifted back to the bigger man. His gut flipped. The huge man said nothing but stared at Díaz with a predacious glower. The intensity of the man's scrutiny left Díaz feeling a little dizzy and desperate to run. He remembered that the smaller one had said they were at a café when they got the news and for some reason he felt relieved that the big man had already eaten.

José and Jesus picked up on the tension. They unbuttoned their jackets and let them flap open to give the strangers a glimpse of their guns. But Hipólito never stopped looking at Díaz and Rotsky stared bemusedly at the wreck. Then a third man strolled up, his attention also fixed on the aircraft. He whistled appreciatively.

"Nice work, Walkaway," said Squeaker.

* * *

As Lulu climbed aboard the *Divine Providence* she was uncomfortably aware of the bum's gun pointed at her back. She pulled her shoulders back, trying to make her shoulder blades meet, as if that would protect her.

Inside the aircraft, she turned and felt another shiver of disgust at the sight of the derelict. He grinned stupidly at her.

"Okay, *Señora*," he said. "Fly me to South America."

"Fuck you," said Lulu calmly.

The bum feigned shock. "This is no way to run a business." He waved the pistol at her.

"That won't do you any good," said Lulu. "We've got no pilot."

A glint came into the bum's eyes. "Oh, I think you know how to fly your own airplane, *doña* Lulu."

The use of her name made Lulu nervous. She ran through a fast mental inventory of the weapons stashed around the *Divine Providence*. Two automatic pistols under the instrument panel. A silenced mini-Uzi behind the pilot's seat. A pump-action 12-gauge under the bed. A flare pistol on the forward bulkhead. A hammerless .38 special in her underwear chest. And . . . she was sure there was another one. But where?

Just then there was a movement behind the bum. Sally stepped out of a small cubicle, a .44 magnum aimed at the bum's head. "Found this in the rest room, Lulu. You really should hide it better. As for you, *señor*, drop the gun and get on your knees."

The bum turned to look over his shoulder and turned white when he saw Sally. He dropped to his knees and the pistol fell from his limp hand. Lulu picked up the gun and tapped the barrel against the bum's cheek to get his attention. He turned to face her, his eyes still wide with shock.

"Just for the record, honey," said Lulu, "I ain't got the first goddamned idea how to fly this thing. You could say my skills lay elsewhere. Now keep your eyes shut and your hands behind your back."

The bum complied. Lulu turned her attention to Sally. The young woman's neck was bruised, and there was a dark purple patch over her left eye. Otherwise, there were no signs of injury.

"You look pretty good for a dead woman," purred Lulu. "How're you feeling?"

"Stupid," said Sally. "But better now that I've got this guy on his knees."

Sally put down her gun and rummaged in a drawer. She pulled out several lengths of thick silk cord with which she tied the bum's hands behind his back. "This is getting to be a habit," he said.

"What do you mean?" asked Sally. She picked up Sally's gun and stepped in front of the bum. He and Sally exchanged silent glares. Lulu felt like she was breaking up a fight between children.

"What are we going to do with him?" she asked.

"Take him with us, I guess," said Sally.

"Where are we going?"

"Santa Marta. Whoever is paying this asshole is planning something down there."

"He told you that?"

"Oh, he told me all kinds of stuff."

The bum looked sheepishly at the floor.

Lulu pursed her lips and brought the gun up to kiss the end of the barrel. "That's a coincidence. Rotsky and Quinn have gone down to Santa Marta."

Sally's eyes opened wide. "They were here?"

Lulu told her the story, including the part about how Georgio had been so keen to take them along.

"I don't like this," said Sally. She paced the cabin. It was small, so every few steps she had to spin around, and each time she did that her pace quickened. "Something stinks here. It feels like a set-up."

"You bet it is, sister," said the bum. "You all gonna die."

Sally was passing him at this moment. Without breaking stride she bent down and punched him in the face.

"That how you got the information out of him?" asked Lulu.

"Hell no," said Sally. "I used a bullwhip."

"You whipped him?"

"No, I *didn't* whip him. Drove him nuts."

* * *

Rotsky had left Vinnie at Rosita's café. He'd explained that he didn't know what was going to happen at the airfield and he wanted the boy safely out of it. Vinnie had said he didn't mind, that he needed to stay put for a while, to get his bearings. The truth was he wanted some time to himself. He was already over the first shock of coming to Colombia and was now beginning to enjoy himself. He had tamed the mêlée of sounds — the ebullient crowds, rapid Spanish, crashing waves, honking cars, screeching birds — that had so disoriented him at first. He had filtered and classified the noises, and could isolate those he enjoyed most — particularly the voluptuous mystery of Spanish from the mouths of young women. And he loved the feel of the sun on his skin, how his skin felt smooth and talcumed when he stroked it, how the warmth of the rays seemed like the closeness of another body.

He sat outside relishing the sound of the surf and Rosita's inventive oaths. He knew when she sat next to him more by the smell of fat than the noise, which was soft and heavy.

"You know any good cooks?" she asked him.

"No. Sorry. Don't you do the cooking yourself?"

Rosita hawked and spat. Vinnie ran a quick sensory check to make sure he hadn't been hit. "Sure I do," she said. "That's the problem. I can't cook for shit. No really. And if I don't get me a good cook real soon, and I mean *real* soon, I'm gonna be out of the restaurant business."

There was a minute's silence before Rosita disappeared again. Vinnie reached out to check that the camcorder was where he had left it, on the table. It was. He then put his feet on another chair and dozed. He wasn't sure how long he was asleep, but from the feel of the sun on his face he guessed it must have been some time. His head throbbed and his skin burned. He was working himself up into a fine state of self-pity when a voice made him forget all about it.

It was the voice of the man who had given them the lift — Hiposomething. Vinnie couldn't make out the words very easily and it took him a while to work out why. They were speaking Spanish. But a couple of words did make sense to him. They were 'Rotsky' and '*muerto*'.

* * *

Hipólito was right, thought Rosita. This was a job she would enjoy. There was a serendipity to Hipólito's proposal, or at least a synchronicity that Rosita found pleasing. One day she was confronted by one of life's irritations. The next day she had the means to eradicate it. And get paid into the bargain.

Choosing the location had involved some thought. She knew they would return to her, but the job couldn't be done too close to the café. There were many routes by which they could come — the mule track through the hills, the tourist track along the shore, a long taxi ride or a short drive if they had their own vehicle. It wasn't just instinct that had put Rosita in this newspaper stand, at the edge of the village square. They'll walk, she thought. He's too cheap to ride. And this is the shortest route from town to the café.

The newspaper stand was perfect. It was a small hut with a door to the rear for a fast exit. Opposite the door was an alley, and at the far end of that was Rosita's stolen car. The front of the stand had a full-length roller shutter that was now nearly shut, leaving just a slit that gave a full view of the square. Inside, there was a well-padded chair that put Rosita at just the right height. The owner of the stand knew her and had insisted on only a modest bribe to take the day off. The only factor left to Rosita's gut feeling was the timing.

She waited for about an hour. Either they're not so desperate as I believed, she thought, or they're even lazier. But even as she pondered these options she was alerted by movement on the far side of the square.

Rosita slid forward the bolt of the ancient Mauser and eased off the well-oiled safety. This was her favourite weapon for this kind of work. It had never let her down. She rested the front of the gun on a pile of *Newsweek*s and worked the butt snugly into her shoulder. She could hear them now, bickering. As the target walked, it also waved its arms. Rosita was momentarily distracted by a fluttering pinkness. She sighted along the immense barrel and breathed deeply. For a second, she held her breath. The old iron sight marked where the heart of the target would soon stopped beating. Then as she slowly exhaled, her finger tightened evenly on the trigger. The instant of the trigger passing the point of no return provoked, as it always did, a small sigh of ecstatic release. But this time Rosita followed it with a cry of anguish. At the very moment the rifle boomed and pressed tightly to her, the target had dropped to its knees. Where the heart had been, Rosita now saw an ear.

* * *

"Why the fuck are we walking?" asked Jesus.

"The exercise is good for you," snapped Díaz. He couldn't admit to them that his cash had almost run out. He had his emergency bribe fund, but he didn't want to start picking at that until absolutely necessary. However, it wasn't the lack of money that had put him in a foul mood: it was the way his bowels were burbling. He tried not to think about the previous night's seafood dinner.

"We going back to the mad woman?" asked Jesus.

"Yes," snapped Díaz.

"But she said talk to the pilot."

"You saw that plane, goddammit. You think I'd trust that asshole with my cargo?"

José's stomach gave a small flutter of relief.

"I don't like that woman," said Jesus. "I don't like her cooking. Besides, I been hearing things about her."

"Oh yeah. What things?"

"She's *loco*, they say. She's got these birds —"

"— birds?"

"Yeah. Real big fuckers. Eagles, or somethin'. Been training them, they say."

"Training?" Díaz tried to put a note of derision in his voice. "To do what? Tricks?"

Jesus glared sullenly at Díaz's back. By this time they were half-way across a small village square. Suddenly, Díaz was hit by an intense stomach cramp that sent him crumbling to the ground. Both knees fell heavily on a large rock buried in the soil. At the same time there was a loud *crack* in his left ear and a burning sensation across the side of his face.

Díaz stared stupidly at the earth, his brain numbed by the pain in his kneecaps, unable to grasp why that should cause blood to drip from his head. It was while he was probing the thick globules of blood in the soil that he heard a series of whizzes and cracks and then a wild animal tore his right ear from his head. With a feral howl he sprang backwards and tried to stand, twisted, collapsed, sat up and swivelled his head frantically, looking for what he knew had to be a tiger, all the while desperately trying to remember if there *were* tigers in South America.

* * *

The man in the seat next to Escobar belched and a shock wave of garlic fumes knocked Escobar's head against the aircraft window. For a moment, it smothered the enveloping aroma of stale sweat. Escobar tried not to breathe. He felt faint. To steady himself, his elbows went automatically to the armrests and, as had happened dozens of times during the two hours of the flight, he found the one to his right occupied by the rolling fat of his companion's gut.

Peasant class, for chrissakes, he hissed to himself. King Zipa in peasant class. I bet the Queen of England never sat next to this guy.

Escobar kicked up a fuss when the airline clerk explained that the aircraft only had one class. "I always travel first class," he bellowed. "I am . . ." He wanted to say 'royalty', but even in his head it sounded wrong. He compromised with " . . .an important man."

"All our customers are important to us, *señor*," said the young woman in a practised sing-song tone. "You could say that every seat is first class."

Escobar had actually bought this for a while — right up to the point where he'd had to climb over the fat man to squeeze into his seat. The next two hours were pure misery, and the second the wheels hit tarmac Escobar unbuckled and sprinted for the door.

Hipólito was in the arrivals hall. His implacable mass made him stand out from the babbling rabble screaming their welcomes at deplaning relatives. Escobar scanned the hall for bunting, balloons, flowers, maybe even a 'Welcome Your Highness' banner.

"Welcome to Santa Marta, boss," said Hipólito.

Escobar stared at Hipólito like one actor contemplating another actor who has just delivered the wrong line. "Let's get to work, dammit," he hissed. He handed Hipólito his suitcase and the two men walked to the car park where Hipólito's Jeep was waiting.

As they drove away from the airport, Escobar felt a sudden jolt go through him, and he looked at the Jeep as if he'd only just seen it.

"Where's the Merc?" he asked.

"Bust," said Hipólito.

"Just what the fuck do you mean by 'bust'?"

"Cylinder head gasket's gone —"

"— that's not too bad —"

"— and the cylinder head. Carb's fucked. Connecting rod broke —"

"Can fix all that —"

"Suspension gave out when I got to town. Crankshaft broke. Electrics gone. The tyres were bald. One of 'em burst. When I was calling for a cab, some sonofabitch bust a side window and tried to grab the hi-fi."

"What happened?"

"I put his head through the windscreen. I don't know why: the hi-fi didn't work anyway."

"So are you going to get it fixed?"

"No." Hipólito frowned as he took a tight bend. They turned into the street for the hotel and found their path blocked by a dozen playing kids. Hipólito didn't slow down or change course.

He's leaving it to the kids to get out of his way, thought Escobar. He smiled. Evolution in action.

"So why aren't you getting the car fixed?" he asked.

"It's been stolen," said Hipólito. He shrugged his shoulders. "It's Santa

Marta, you know? Besides, I've been busy. I've got some good leads on Díaz. Been following him for a while. You want me to kill him now?"

"I've had orders," Escobar said. "We're not to bother with Díaz. The big guys have their own plans for him. Walkaway's the problem, and they want him alive —"

Hipólito's face fell.

"— for now."

Hipólito smiled briefly, then pursed his lips sheepishly. Escobar noticed. "Something you want to tell me?" he said.

"Díaz. He had an accident."

"Fatal?"

"Oh no," said Hipólito reassuringly. "Just a slight hearing problem."

* * *

A man in blue overalls, blue cap and holding a clipboard stood before the door that Billy had just opened.

"This the Escobar Animal Research Centre?" he asked. He glanced around, one corner of his mouth lifted in a disparaging sneer.

"I guess it could be," said Billy. "Yes."

"Sign here." He handed Billy the clipboard.

Billy signed at the bottom of the paper, hoping it was the right place. The document was in Spanish. "What's it for?" he asked

"Consignment of fish." The man took back the clipboard and glanced at it. "Trigger fish, cow fish and clown fish. One dozen each. Where do you want 'em?"

Billy took the man through to the zoo. They passed several enclosures in which disconsolate animals slumped depressed, or possibly dead. Billy had buried a snow leopard just that morning. They entered a small wooden shack, dark inside until Billy threw a switch. A low-wattage bulb, hanging bare from the roof, revealed a row of half a dozen glass tanks, all empty, all smeared and stained faintly brown.

The delivery man walked along the row of tanks, touching them tentatively, his sneer increasing. "You're going to use these?"

Billy nodded. He couldn't see the problem. They were fish tanks, after all.

"There're no aerators, temperature regulators, gravel. No coral or little arches for 'em to swim through. No lights, goddammit. These are marine fish, you understand? They must have proper salt water. I can't let you keep 'em like this." He almost spat the last word.

Billy regarded the tanks with mounting embarrassment. He was very depressed. "You'll just have to take them back, then," he said.

The delivery man's eyes opened wide with shock. "Take them back? I can't . . ." He glanced at the clipboard as if for confirmation. "I can't take them back. Nowhere here does it say I can take them back."

"Then we're both screwed," said Billy. "And so are the fish."

A few minutes later, the delivery man pulled away in his truck leaving Billy with thirty-six brightly-coloured fish swimming innocently in plastic boxes. Billy spent an hour preparing the tanks. He scoured the glass, lined the bottoms with sand he found near a half-completed swimming pool, filled them with tap water and dropped half a bottle of table salt in each tank. "It's the best I can do fellas," he told the fish as he poured them carefully into the tanks. Within an hour they were all belly-up.

As he scooped the fish from the tanks, Billy ruminated mournfully on his short spell in charge of the *finca*. He was alone now. As soon as Escobar had departed for the coast, the few remaining staff had stolen what few valuables they could find, packed them into a van and left for Bogotá.

A close look at the vegetable garden told him that it was a lost cause. It was planted in thin mountain soil and the few plants that were hanging on to life would never yield anything edible. That just left the zoo.

Importing endangered species had been a short-lived sideline for Escobar. He gave it up because he didn't like the expense of contraband that you had to feed. Within a couple of weeks, though, he had collected for himself an impressive array of near-extinct species. It took just a few weeks to kill half of them by misfeeding, mishandling and mishaps involving drunken *contrabandistas* and large-calibre sidearms.

There were now just five animals left — well, actually four after the death of the snow leopard. There was a zebra which, to Billy's eyes, was starting to look more and more like a small pony with stripes painted on. He was sure the stripes had faded a little after the morning's brief rain shower. There was also a pair of gazelles — both males, as far as Billy could make out. And then there was the wolf.

The sight of these beautiful creatures dragging themselves morosely around their compounds or lying, panting in a corner, broke Billy's heart. "You are so beautiful," he'd tell them as he dished out their food. "Please get well." Every time he saw them, or stroked their heads, he was nearly overwhelmed by pity.

The exception was the Texan red wolf. It was the only one of the animals to live in a cage. Billy feared it, and he knew his terror arose from respect for the animal's deadly nature, which is why he loved it so intensely, too.

We're just the same, you and me, he told it. 'Cept you being a wolf, an' all.

Well, he didn't really tell it. He thought that talking to a wolf might be too weird. He used telepathy.

We're other people's playthings, he projected. People use us for their pleasure, then discard us when they're done. Billy paused. He was getting out of his depth. Well, not any more, buster. He had to pause again. Now was the moment for decisive action — if only he could think of something. He looked lovingly at the wolf. Its emaciated body looked frighteningly frail. He could see the outline of ribs through its thin, patchy fur. It's a damn shame, he thought.

He watched the wolf pant as it dragged slowly and incessantly from one end of the cage to the other, casting dark looks. There was something about its laboured breathing that seemed terribly familiar to Billy. Then it came to him.

It's the *soroche*! he thought. That's why they're all so unwell.

Billy was suddenly energized Altitude sickness was something he knew how to cure. He searched the house and grounds for coca leaves or plants. This is a drug baron's hideout, he thought, there have to be coca plants. He found none, but during his searching he discovered an impressive amount of cocaine, stashed into unlikely places and probably forgotten. He divided this into two piles, one for the animals and one for himself. I might need this for money, he thought.

By then it was time to feed the animals again. He prepared the bowls of oats for the zebra and the gazelles, poured in a generous quantity of cocaine and mixed thoroughly. For the wolf, he dusted a few defrosted steaks with the powder. This should perk 'em up.

He left the bowls in the open enclosures. The animals were at first indifferent, but as they started eating their enthusiasm for the new diet seemed to grow. As Billy walked away, towards the wolf, he thought he saw a change come over the animals. They look better already.

He took the steaks to the wolf's cage. Its yellow eyes tracked his approach as though calculating his trajectory. Billy threw the steaks through the bars. The wolf ignored them. I'll leave you alone, Billy transmitted.

Don't much like being watched when I eat either.

He returned to the gazelle enclosure to see how they were getting on. He was just in time to see them leap the low fence and run to freedom across a pasture, where they joined the zebra. Excellent, thought Billy. They're looking much better.

* * *

Horatio woke with a buzzing in his ear. He had trouble opening his eyes, which were glued together. He rubbed them and rolled hard grit-like sleep from his lids, blinked and tried to focus.

He was outside the office, lying in a steamer chair under a large patio umbrella. He struggled on to his feet and looked around. There was a paperback book on the ground next to him. He read the title, but couldn't remember ever having seen it before.

It was getting on for evening and he thought that he might as well pack up for the night. There were some documentaries on PBS that night that he didn't want to miss.

A roar overhead caused him to spin round and look up at the same time. Suddenly he was on his back again, lying across the chair, one leg twisted under him. He'd had time for only a brief, out-of-focus glimpse of the aircraft that had shot overhead, but it was enough.

Damned if that ain't a DC-3, he thought.

Horatio stumbled to his feet again. He rubbed his eyes once more to try to clear them. These guys might be customers, he thought. He rubbed his clothes as though to iron them, and tried to run his hand back over his hair, to straighten it. He found he didn't have any hair. When the fuck did that happen?

He found his spectacles and scanned the sky. Sure enough, it was a DC-3. It was circling the airfield and had its wheels down. Horatio watched happily as the aircraft made a curving descent towards the runway. Just over the threshold it touched down on its mainwheels with barely a squeak, then as it slowed, the tail dropped gracefully onto the tarmac.

The DC-3 turned off the runway onto the grass and taxied up close to the office. The engines rattled into silence and the propellers stopped. Horatio noticed that there was still a buzzing in his ear. I wonder if it's that damned stuff, he thought.

After a couple of minutes, two women dropped from the rear door of the aircraft. They were both beautiful, their hair cut short in a way that Horatio liked without knowing why. One was blonde the other a brunette. When they got closer, he worked out that the dark-haired one was probably older than the other.

"You got gas?" asked the blonde.

"You bet," said Horatio. He pulled himself erect. A pain shot through his hip, but he didn't let it show. "We got avgas 100LL and jet A1. I guess you'll be wanting avgas. How much ya need?"

"About seven hundred gallons, I guess."

Horatio knew his eyes were bulging, but couldn't do a damn thing about it.

"We've got a couple of long-range tanks fitted," said the younger woman, with a smile that made Horatio suddenly much more relaxed.

"You the pilot?" he asked.

"Yes," she said.

Horatio thought about what he was going to say, then said it anyway. "That was a damn fine landing, young lady." He chewed his lip for a second. "Not like the guy we had in here last." He nodded to a wreck on the far side of the field. "You see that twin over yonder?"

Sally looked, then nodded. "Uhu."

"That would've been a nice landing too, if the asshole had thought to put the wheels down. Premature arrival, he called it."

The two women swapped a look that Horatio didn't like. He couldn't make out what they were thinking, and that made him uneasy.

"Know where he is?" asked the younger one.

"He went away again," said Horatio.

"Damn," she muttered, "just my luck."

"But he came back. Last night. He's out back, sleeping it off."

"Sleeping what off?"

"Not too sure. Said something about a 737 and a 'real-estate interface', whatever that means."

The young woman smiled. She turned to the other, who was smiling too. "Walkaway," said the brunette. "Let's go wake him." The two women stepped forward, then the older one stopped and put a hand on the other's arm. "Better still," she said, "let me do this. After all this, maybe he deserves a treat."

The brunette sashayed through around the corner of the airfield office. Horatio watched until she disappeared.

"My name's Sally, in case you were wondering," said the younger woman.

Horatio turned to look at her, but couldn't think of anything to say, until finally he came up with, "Horatio."

"Well, Horatio, how about that gas?"

"Sure," he said, his head clearing now. "I'd better go check the fuel cocks."

"You know the DC-3?"

"Oh sure. You take the weight off. I won't be long."

Horatio walked over to the aircraft and stepped inside. Jeez, he thought, goddamn thing looks like a goddamned whorehouse. Those women oughta be careful flying around in something like this.

He made his way to the cockpit and checked the fuel cocks and gauges. As he was on his way out, he heard a muffled noise from inside a compartment. He opened the door. Inside was a small, dirty man bound with leather straps and silk cords. Horatio closed the door again. He jumped from the aircraft and hit the ground with a bump that sent a searing pain up his spine. As he walked back to the office he tried not to limp.

Sally was stretched out on the steamer chair.

"Do you . . ." Horatio couldn't speak. He realized that the pain had been making him hold his breath. He inhaled deeply and tried again. "Do you know there's a guy tied up in the back of your plane?" he gasped.

"Oh sure," said Sally. She smiled sweetly. "Is that a problem?"

Horatio stopped breathing again. Then he sighed and relaxed.

"Oh heck no," he said. "Happens here all the time."

* * *

"This time we don't take 'no' for an answer," said Díaz. He was unsteady on his feet, and blood flowed freely down both sides of his head. José idly wondered how much blood a man can lose before he passes out.

"And another thing," said Díaz. His face screwed up suddenly. "Get me something for these fucking ears."

Rosita said she had some bandages out back, and José followed her into the kitchen. There was something about the way she moved, about the way she did things, that made him nervous. Every action carried an air of competence and professionalism. He had trouble believing this was the same woman who had cooked their lunch the day before.

"What happened to his ears?" asked Rosita. She dropped to her knees and rummaged in the bottom drawer of an old wooden cabinet.

"Damnedest thing," said José. "They got hit by the same bullet. Weirdest ricochet I ever saw. Really amazing. Total fluke."

Rosita nodded without looking up. José felt he had just confirmed something for her. He didn't like not knowing what it was. He fished the gun from inside his jacket. "You know, you really are going to have to help us. We need your boat. Díaz is serious about this shit. He's really into something with this stuff. Something big. Something new."

Rosita stopped what she was doing and regarded him closely. "New?"

"You bet. Could be the start of a whole new life for me and Jesus. But we got to get to Florida. At least, we got to get out of Colombia or we won't have no life at all."

Rosita clambered to her feet and stared steadily at José. "I will get you out of Colombia," she said. As if to underline her promise, there came a weird, primeval *cawk* from outside. José went to the door to the lean-to, then froze. He stared rigidly at the two huge birds.

"Wow! Vultures. Cool."

"Eagles," said Rosita.

"No way. Those are vultures."

"Same thing," spat Rosita.

José didn't feel like pushing his luck. In any case, Rosita had disappeared back into the restaurant.

An hour later, a large van pulled up at the quayside close to Rosita's café. It was watched by Díaz, who sat on a large pile of nets, his hands in his pockets, stained bandages swaddling his head. José and Jesus stood at the back of a small fishing boat, *La Viuda Contenta*. Rosita moved busily about the boat, stowing supplies.

The van's engine wheezed to a stop and the vehicle settled onto its springs with a faint cracking sound. An old man stepped out of the cab. He was the owner of the 'Papagayo' café where Díaz and the others were staying. He scowled at Díaz, José and Jesus but said nothing. Instead he went to the back of the van, opened the doors and pulled out some large cardboard boxes.

José noticed Díaz looking at him and Jesus. They looked back. Díaz arched his eyebrows. They did the same. "Do you wanna give him a hand, for fucksake?" snapped Díaz.

The two men got slowly to their feet and shuffled over to the van. Within a few minutes there were around sixty boxes on the quayside.

Díaz smiled, walked over to the old man and took his hand. "Thank you, my friend," he said. "I will not forget this."

"Fuck you," snapped the old man. "I want my money."

"What?" said Díaz.

"I WANT MY MONEY."

Díaz's smile slipped a little. "In good time. I will be back with your money."

"*Cabrón*," spat the old man and walked back to his van. He started the engine, crashed the gears and came close to burning rubber as he drove away.

Díaz turned back to the others, his eyes on the stack of boxes, his smile gone. He closed his eyes and sighed. When he opened his eyes again he was looking at José and Jesus who looked back expectantly.

"I don't know," said Díaz. "Do you think it might be a good idea to get the merchandise on the boat?"

José and Jesus looked at each other with blank expressions, then turned back to Díaz.

"I think it might be," said Jesus.

8:
Don't get up

The pilot of the jet fighter pushed the throttle forward to climb through the clouds. From deep inside the single engine came a loud knocking that he could feel through his ass. Oh shit, he thought, not again.

He pulled the throttle back and let the aircraft descend to just below cloud level. Wave hopping all the way, he thought. Fucking great. What a piece of junk.

It didn't help that he was responsible. As chief pilot for the Corporation he'd been lobbying for years for them to buy some jet fighters. Too many planes were being lost to Customs and Coast Guard aircraft. He wanted some protection, some fighters of their own to fly top cover.

What he had in mind was a Phantom, maybe even an F-16. So he was excited when his bosses presented him with a bunch of crates, some of them very large.

Delight had turned to disappointment when he'd opened the crates. Inside he found two 1950s-vintage Sabre aircraft, not much better than scrap. They had been bought from US collectors and were ostensibly bound for a new museum in Cali dedicated to the Korean war. It hadn't occurred to anyone to question the Colombians' interest in Korea.

He'd managed to make one flyable aircraft out of the two collections of bits. Finding suitable guns had been surprisingly easy, finding spare parts depressingly difficult. Many of them were home-made and he never flew the Sabre without some kind of mechanical emergency.

The knocking had vanished but in any case his mind was now on other things. In the distance was a shadow, almost invisible on the green and silver speckled surface of the ocean. But his trained eyes saw it for what it was. A target.

* * *

For about the thousandth time that hour, Díaz's hand went involuntarily to his ear. He pulled it away again as soon as his fingertips met the sticky bandage that ran longitudinally from crown to jaw and latitudinally across his forehead. I look like a fucking cartoon victim, he thought bitterly, an opinion that was obviously shared by José and Jesus who had had trouble disguising their grins. He turned to see if they were still smiling but the sudden movement made his head wobble. The painkillers had kicked in, and with the gentle swell of the ocean Díaz was having trouble staying upright. It had been worse below decks, and though the sight of the water filled him with dread, Díaz had found the fishing boat's quarterdeck to be the place that made him least sick. They had slipped out of Santa Marta harbour just before dawn, As soon as it was light, Díaz had installed himself in a fishing chair and had Jesus bring him a constant supply of tequila and distalgesics. He had felt no pain for the past hour or so.

Díaz caught sight of an M-16 lying at his feet. He'd found it on the boat. It now lay on a bed of scattered shell cases. Díaz picked it up, pressed a button to let the empty magazine fall to the deck, reached into a fishing bag and inserted a full clip into the gun. He cocked the gun and flipped it into fully automatic mode.

His eyes roamed the nearby surface of the sea. He'd been doing this for some time now. Every now and then he'd see a shadow that he thought might be a dolphin. He'd raise the gun and fire a long burst into the water. "Treacherous bastards!" he'd mutter.

He saw another shadow now and pulled the trigger. After a couple of rounds the gun jammed. Díaz threw it at the shadow. "You stinkin' slimy sonofabitch," he snarled.

Díaz heard a muffled chattering. He swung round in the chair to see Rosita talking to him. "What?" he yelled. She raised her voice.

"I said I want you off this boat as soon as we hit Mexico, you hear? No bullshit."

José and Jesus shuffled closer, but not too close.

"Mexico? Whaddya mean, Mexico? This boat's going to Florida."

"Not Florida. Too much trouble. Mexico."

Díaz was stunned. He felt his life slip from his grasp. His hand fell on the bag. Jesus stared at the bag with a worried expression. "Hey boss! Mexico's not too bad. It's not the States, but it's next door. It's close, you know?"

Díaz knew there was a serious flaw in this argument but he was damned if he could think of it. "Give me your gun," he snapped at Jesus.

Jesus pitched forward and handed over his Uzi. Díaz rubbed his hand over it and sniffed the barrel. "This is yours?"

"Yes."

"It's really . . . *clean*."

"Never been fired," chuckled José. "The pussy's an Uzi virgin, you know?"

"Fuck you," muttered Jesus.

Díaz stared intently at the gun. It now seemed very strange to him. "Never been fired," he murmured. For a moment he wondered if it really was a gun, or just something that was gun-like. "Never been fired." He sat in silent bafflement for a moment, unable to get a grip on any single thought. When he looked up he saw the faces of his three companions swivel towards the west. Jesus pointed at something.

Díaz screwed up his eyes and saw it straight away — a black dot, just above the sea. A bird, he thought, and then a second later, a really big fucking bird and then a second after that, holy shit, look at the size of that fucking bird!

The dot turned rapidly into a plane. At the same moment that Díaz recognized it as a jet fighter the sea spat up plumes of spray that flew towards the boat. And when they hit it they changed to explosions of wood that Díaz felt as a rapid thumping in his chest. He realized he was lying on the deck. José and Jesus were prone next to him. There was a flash of silver and a crackling roar as the plane passed overhead.

"What the fuck was that all about?" whined Díaz.

The three men stood up cautiously. Díaz couldn't see Rosita but she soon reappeared from below, stumbling under the weight of two large boxes covered with cloth. She set them down on the deck and pulled off the covers.

Díaz was amazed to see they were cages that barely contained two huge birds. Looking up he saw Jesus with a 'told you so' look on his face.

"Holy shit!" yelled José. "The motherfucker's coming back." He pointed at the black speck in the distance. Sure enough it was getting bigger.

"*Ataca!*" screamed Rosita and Díaz turned just in time to see her throw one of the birds into the air. Quickly she scooped the other from its cage and launched it. The birds climbed lazily into the air and circled. From the distance came a chattering noise and once again fountains of spray came tripping towards the boat. Díaz, José and Jesus pressed themselves flat on the deck, but Rosita stood fast, her head tilted back and her eyes glued to the birds. Suddenly, one bird appeared to notice the approaching aircraft. It dipped down and, for such a large creature, alighted daintily on the roof of the boat's wheelhouse.

"Ack-Ack! *Hijueputa!*" screamed Rosita. "Coward!"

Her invective was cut short by the sight of the other bird turning towards the aircraft. Bullets were hitting the boat, tearing off huge chunks of wood that littered the air with lethal splinters. There was a *paf!* and a shower of feathers. Still Rosita stood her ground, watching the other bird as it headed directly for the plane.

"Yes Flak! Go Flak!" she yelled.

For a second, Díaz thought the bird and plane would collide nose-to-nose, but at the last moment the bird jinked and disappeared into the engine intake. As the jet screamed overhead, Díaz heard a muffled *whoomph* followed by the shriek of tortured metal. And then silence, until the aircraft disappeared in a huge geyser of disturbed ocean.

"Splash one!" screamed Rosita.

The three men raised themselves unwillingly, their eyes searching the skies for other attackers. Díaz realized that his right hand felt strange and looked down at it. The pills and tequila made counting difficult, but within a couple of minutes Díaz was sure. Two of his fingers were missing.

José had followed Díaz's gaze. "Jeez, boss," he said. "Must've been all that wood flying about." He seemed to think about this for a while. "Still," he said, with a placatory smile, "at least you don't have to worry no more about them being pink."

* * *

"What do you mean it's already happened?" Escobar slammed shut the door of the mini-bar. It swung open again. A small bottle of orange juice and a pack of dry-roast peanuts fell to the floor, next to a miniature bottle of mescal.

"Up at the old airfield," said Hipólito. He shifted slightly on the bed and sat upright. There was a can of beer in his hand. "He crashed a 737. I don't know how he got out again."

"I can tell you," snarled Escobar. "He flew out in the fucking Learjet that the Corporation put there. Only *we* were supposed to be on board. Do you think he noticed that he didn't have any fucking passengers?"

Escobar saw the open door of the mini-bar and slammed it shut. It swung open again and a chocolate bar joined the small pile on the floor. "Shit! The Corporation is going to have my nuts for this."

"I don't get it. How come the Corporation's involved?"

"I told you, I got my orders. Me! Orders!" Escobar raised himself to his full height. He was glad Hipólito was sitting. "Does a king take orders?"

Hipólito frowned and opened his mouth, but looked like he couldn't think of an answer.

"Now the fucking Corporation is gonna want to know where their Lear is and how come we weren't on it."

"Why were we supposed to be on it?"

"To get this goddamned Walkaway and whatever it is he's got, of course. The Corporation left the Lear at the airfield and put the word out that there was a job needed doing, knowing that Walkaway would hear of it. I guess it all just happened faster than they expected." Escobar picked up the pack of peanuts from the floor, yanked it open and tossed a handful of nuts into his mouth. "Is this the Royal Suite?" he mumbled through a shower of nut fragments.

Several people ran shouting down the corridor outside the room. A woman screamed and something thudded against the door.

"Presidential," said Hipólito.

Escobar walked around the room. He prodded the bed, ruffled the brushed-nylon eiderdown, ran his fingers over the leather-look furniture, felt the polyester curtains. "Nice," he said. He tapped a trouser press. "Have we got one of these?"

"What is it?"

"Just answer the question, goddammit."

"No. We haven't got one of those."

Escobar opened the drawer of the bedside cabinet and took out a Gideon's bible and a small revolver. "This yours?" he asked Hipólito, holding up the gun.

"No," said Hipólito. He took a sip of his beer. There was a loud bang from a few rooms down. Glass broke on the pavement outside the hotel. "So what do we do now?"

Escobar dropped the gun back into the drawer. "Fucked if I know. Any bright ideas?"

Hipólito got to his feet and checked the chains on the door, though he was obviously thinking of something else. "There's a guy called Rotsky in town," he said.

Escobar raised an eyebrow. "That name is familiar. Why?"

"He's from the old days. A pilot. Last I heard he got into some trouble in Mexico and disappeared. He's got this kid with him. Turns out he's the son of those English assholes I met up with in Chicago—"

"—who are now—"

"—no longer a problem. Yes." Out of habit, Hipólito threw his beer can at the window, expecting it to be open. It bounced off the glass and rattled on to the air conditioner. He took a full one from the mini-bar and slammed the door shut. It stayed shut. "They're hanging out with another pilot called Squeaker. He works for this Greek bigshot, Georgio Acidopholus, and I hear that he's in town too. And they're all looking for Walkaway."

"Jeez. It's turning into a fucking convention."

"Yeah, but these people could be useful. Díaz has taken his consignment out on a boat, but I got a feeling he's gonna be back."

"Maybe not," said Escobar. "We got your report about the boat. The Corporation has taken steps to make sure he never gets to the States. I don't think we'll be seeing Díaz again."

Hipólito thought about Rosita and sensed a hint of sadness. Then he thought about her again and knew she'd return.

"Well, maybe we will, maybe we won't, but if he does return, he's going to need some transport. And you need a plane as bait for Walkaway, right?" Escobar nodded. "The Greek guy has got a plane. We get Díaz to load his consignment on the plane, then waste him. Meanwhile, we put the word out again saying we need a pilot."

Escobar mulled this over for a minute. He was uncomfortable with the idea that Díaz and his goons would return. It hinted at weakness in the Corporation, a fallibility that made Escobar uneasy. On the other hand, Hipólito was rarely wrong in these matters.

There was a loud cheer from another room and something hit the pavement again, this time with a dull, wet thud that Escobar didn't like at all.

"You said the Greek guy has got a pilot," he said.

"I could always terminate his employment," smiled Hipólito.

"And this Rotsky's a pilot."

"Him too. We'll downsize the whole fucking Santa Marta pilot community if we have to."

"And the boy?"

"That's unfinished business. I lost him in Chicago. There was a riot in the bar." Hipólito finished his beer in one, long swig. "I won't make that mistake again."

* * *

Díaz could vaguely make out blurred white shapes against a solid wall of blue. The shapes never rested but scurried across his field of vision, first one way, then the other, back and forth. He heaved and turned his head away only to smack the side of his face against a wooden plank.

"You awake, boss?" said a voice.

I'm on my back, thought Díaz. It was the most sustained piece of thinking he'd managed in the past . . . what? Hour? Two hours? Four? Pain shot up his arm and embedded itself in the base of his brain and suddenly Díaz was upright, on his knees, gripping the rail and vomiting into the sea. When he finished, he stared at the water, his mouth hanging open, sweat in his eyes. He waited like that until his vision cleared because there was something bothering him. His eyes focused and he looked more closely at the water. It appeared to be unnecessarily close. Díaz turned to his companions.

"Is this boat getting smaller?" he asked.

"Don't be stupid," snarled Rosita.

"What?" said Díaz.

"*No!*"

"Well, something's happening," puzzled Díaz.

"Of course. We're taking on water."

"What?"

"*We're sinking!*"

* * *

When Escobar first saw Georgio, the Greek was lounging in an armchair in the reception of the Hotel Yoshima. He seemed to fill the chair and spill out of it at top and bottom.

"Don't get up," said Escobar quickly. He followed it with a smile and held out his hand. The Greek stood up anyway and Escobar was aware of the way his own head now tilted back. They shook hands.

Three *gringos* stood a little way off. They all wore sunglasses. There was a tall one in a multi-coloured flying suit and leather jacket. His shades were mirrored. There was a shortish bald one and a skinny kid. Escobar allowed himself to be introduced to them by Georgio, but he knew who they were from Hipólito's description.

Hipólito was there too. He stood a couple of yards behind Escobar, his hands by his side, tensed and watchful.

"Good morning gentlemen," said Escobar. He was about to say something about how glad he was to give them an audience this morning when a row broke out at the reception desk.

"What do you mean, 'refused'," screamed a middle-aged businessman in a grey suit. He held a piece of paper in his left hand. In his right was a Mac-10 machine pistol.

The hotel purser held up the man's credit card. "I'm sorry, *señor*," he said, with no trace of apology or fear. "They won't accept the transaction. Perhaps *señor* has another card? Or cash?"

The businessman stepped back, the gun levelled at the purser. "Try it again," he hissed.

Rotsky, Squeaker and the boy had disappeared. Georgio retreated slowly towards some potted palms, not taking his eye off the businessman. Escobar felt a tap on his shoulder and Hipólito's voice in his ear whispered "This way, boss." They joined Georgio behind the palms. Escobar saw that there were four more businessmen by the front door of the hotel. Bags were scattered around them. All four had guns in their hands. "Check what they're charging you for phone calls," yelled one of them to his colleague at reception.

"I think we should go," whispered Georgio. "Follow me."

Escobar, Hipólito and Georgio walked in a crouch around the outside of the reception area, keeping as much furniture and indoor greenery as possible between them and the businessman. They heard the businessman scream "I didn't order a full breakfast, for fucksakes. I had continental, do you understand? *Continental!*"

As they approached the front door Escobar saw that it was completely blocked by the other four men and their luggage. But Georgio didn't stop. The businessmen didn't seem to notice them as they approached. Georgio uttered a polite "Excuse me" and one of the men turned to face him. The stranger's face was lined with concentration, but then he seemed to focus on Georgio and his expression softened.

"Oh, I'm sorry," he said and stooped to pull some of the baggage out of the way.

As Georgio, Escobar and Hipólito slipped through the front door there was a single shot, then a brief burst of automatic fire from the direction of the reception desk. The three men ran along the street until they reached the corner.

They stopped. Escobar straightened up, brushed down his jacket and turned to Georgio.

"How about some breakfast?" he asked.

* * *

"Hey, this isn't Mexico," said Jesus. He stared slack-jawed at the quayside. "We're back in Santa Marta, for fucksakes. We're supposed to be in Mexico."

"Same thing," said Rosita.

"What?"

The woman scowled and jumped ashore.

Jesus moved back along the boat to where José was trying to revive Díaz. It had been quite a relief when he'd fainted. His mounting hysteria as the boat had settled lower and lower into the water had worn raw the nerves of his fellow passengers.

Díaz opened his eyes.

"I know who's behind this," he snarled. "I've remembered where I've seen him before. That guy at the wreck. The big one. He's Escobar's man, Hippo-fucking-something. Fucking *cabrón*. I'm going to kill that sonofabitch."

"This isn't Mexico," Jesus told his colleagues. He always enjoyed being the first with any news. They appeared not to hear.

"What you want us to do, boss?" asked José. Díaz said nothing. His eyes were shut again and his head rolled limply.

Jesus prodded José's arm. "You hear what I said? I said this ain't Mexico."

José span round to face Jesus. "I don't give a shit where this is," he snarled. "You heard what the boss said. Escobar's man is on to us. This is bad fucking news."

"*What!?*" screamed Díaz. He had raised his head a little. His eyelashes fluttered and his eyes rolled, almost disappearing under the lids. "What you say about Escobar?"

"Nothing, boss," said José.

Díaz's eyes opened wide. "You said something about Escobar," he yelled. "Why won't you tell me what you said?" There was a squeak in his voice. "Tell me what you said!"

"*I* said this ain't Mexico," said Jesus. He cast a scathing look at José, like someone assuming a superior rank.

"Fuck Mexico," whined Díaz. "Who gives a shit about Mexico? What are you saying about Escobar? Is he here?" Díaz's eyes were so wide and flickering so fast, Jesus thought they might actually come out of his head.

José put his hand on Díaz's forehead. "No, boss. He ain't here. Don't worry."

Díaz let his eyes close and his head sink back on to the deck.

"Well, *I* give a shit about Mexico," sniffed Jesus. He stomped along the deck and climbed a ladder to the quay. He turned back to the boat and tried to think of a devastating parting line. "I'm going to get a drink," he said.

* * *

Rotsky's ears were still ringing when he pulled himself from under the sofa. He looked around the hotel reception area in amazement. It hardly seemed possible that it was the same place he'd been staring at a few minutes before.

The reception desk had been extensively remodelled by the disgruntled customer's Mac-10. Rotsky had counted four clips' worth of ammo which the businessman had used in his attempt to have his bill reduced. There was now a wide breach in the wooden counter and what was left was liberally sprinkled with holes.

Rotsky wasn't sure who had used the grenades, but they had certainly left their mark. One had taken out a ceiling fan which was now embedded in a chaise longue, between the thighs of a young, smartly-dressed man who appeared unhurt, and who stared at the fan with wide, unblinking eyes. He was praying. There was a crater in the centre of the reception area, and a mangled cigarette machine in a corner. Cigarette packets littered the room. Rotsky noticed one at his feet that just happened to be his brand. He picked it up.

"Rotsky?"

He turned and saw Vinnie roll from under the sofa.

"Over here," said Rotsky.

"Rotsky?"

He realized Vinnie couldn't hear him. Rotsky took Vinnie by the arm and helped him stand. He put his mouth to the boy's ear and yelled: "*Right here!*"

Vinnie jackknifed away. "Sodding hell! There's no need to shout."

Squeaker appeared from behind a palm. He had his arms clasped across his chest, supporting a large pile of cigarette packs.

There were no other signs of life. Or death. Rotsky was surprised at the lack of corpses. Faintly disappointed, in fact.

"I think we should find Hipólito," said Rotsky. "I've got a feeling something is about to start happening."

"Good idea," said Squeaker. "Smoke anyone?"

* * *

Hipólito walked back to the table where Escobar and Georgio waited with their drinks. Otherwise, the bar was empty. Georgio had watched Hipólito make the phone call with mounting curiosity. He felt that finally something interesting might be about to happen.

"It's definite," said Hipólito. "They're back. I called Rosita's café and she was there. Seems they ran into a bit of trouble."

Hipólito and Escobar exchanged smiles.

"So," said Georgio, "if I help you rip off this Díaz guy, I get exclusive distribution rights for the merchandise. Is that it?"

"Right," said Escobar.

"And you don't want any payment up front?"

"Nope."

"And I can pay you when I off-load the consignment?"

"You got it."

Georgio sipped his beer and looked happily around the bar. It was a small place, a half-dozen tables inside. Hipólito had chosen it because he said it looked quiet.

Escobar hadn't said what kind of merchandise Díaz was trying to move, but Georgio didn't care too much. He wasn't going to go home empty-handed. And if he could get rid of Escobar and his gorilla en route, so much the better. He didn't like the idea of sharing the profit.

"What about this Rotsky character?" said Georgio.

Hipólito turned to Escobar and smiled. "You said you want him dead, right?"

"Dead is fine," said Escobar.

Georgio's attention was caught by a flash of sunlight reflected off the suit of a man standing in the doorway. He was squinting into the bar, his eyes not yet adapted to the gloom. Hipólito had seen the newcomer too. "One of Díaz's goons," he whispered to Georgio, then leaned towards Escobar, nudged him, nodded at the door and uttered a discreet "Boss". Escobar and Hipólito stood and disappeared through the back door of the café just as the man at the door entered.

He sat at the bar and ordered an *aguardiente*. Georgio moved over and sat next to him. "Hello my friend," he said to the stranger. "Let me introduce myself."

* * *

Díaz's head tilted back and swivelled as he sniffed. "Can you smell that?" he asked. It was as though the smell was coming from somewhere close, but he couldn't quite track it down. It seemed to move away from him. A solid wave of pain battered him about the head. Evil things with sharp teeth bored into his head and tore at his hand. Díaz fell off his chair.

He felt himself being lifted and put back on the seat. Someone moved from behind him. The pain washed away. Díaz saw that it was José. Well, it looks like José, he thought. Can't be too certain. Must be careful. They come in all guises.

The man he thought might be José stared at the side of Díaz's head and wrinkled his nose.

"*Escobar!*" yelled Díaz. Shouting exhausted him and he slumped in the chair, tears in his eyes. "Escobar sent that fucking eagle."

The José-like man's lips moved, but no sound came from his mouth. Díaz's stomach turned to ice at this manifestation of evil. Struck dumb! he thought. Poor bastard. Maybe the eagle had got his tongue.

Díaz closed his eyes, inhaled deeply, exhaled slowly and opened his eyes. He raised his hand and found a bandage wrapped around his head like a bandanna. He tugged at it and it fell loosely around his neck. He pulled at it repeatedly until it unfurled and he held it up before him like a dead snake. Attached to the bandage were two thick wads of gauze, stained red and yellow and coated in places with thick dark pus. He raised his other hand to examine the bandage but found that it was also swaddled in gauze and sticking plaster making it appear horribly stump-like.

"I said, what eagle?" said José.

Díaz looked at him blankly. "Eagle? What eagle?"

"For hours you've been yelling about some eagle that attacked you."

The door banged. Díaz looked towards it and saw a moving shape. He squinted. It looked like Jesus.

"Hey boss, I got us some transport," said the shape of Jesus. His voice was muted and indistinct.

"What?" said Díaz.

"Some transport. I got."

"What?"

"A plane," said Jesus.

"Oh, fucking great," muttered José darkly. "A plane."

"*What?*"

"*A plane!*" yelled Jesus. "*I got us a plane!*"

"Where the fuck did you get a plane?" asked José.

"I got talking to this Greek guy in the bar. Told him we were looking for some transport. Says he's got a plane up at the airport. Took me to see it. It's a big sucker. Four engines."

José looked a little happier about that.

"Yeah. Got these amazingly long propellers."

"Propellers?" José reached for his drink.

* * *

Georgio surveyed the wreck of the 737 and shook his head sadly. What a waste, he thought. Think how much dope we could have moved with that.

The jet had been bulldozed to the edge of the airfield and then set on fire. But the fire had been badly set and only the cockpit had been damaged. Georgio turned to his own aircraft, *La Blanca*, standing tall and proud on its slim undercarriage. Georgio had had Squeaker fly it to the strip earlier that day. A thoroughbred, he thought proudly. He couldn't help smiling.

Just then he heard a vehicle approach. A taxi pulled up. Georgio could make out the driver and three other men, including the stupid one he had spoken to in the bar, the one who called himself Jesus. Georgio was happy to call him Jesus even though he knew it couldn't be his real name. Nobody used real names in this business, no-one was *that* stupid. But names meant nothing to Georgio and Jesus was as good as any other.

There seemed to be some kind of argument going on inside the taxi. There was a burst of muffled bangs and a group of ragged holes appeared in the top of the car. Jesus yanked a door open and half-fell, half-leapt from the vehicle, eyes staring madly. He scurried away from the taxi on all fours for about ten yards before collapsing on the tarmac. He covered his ears with his hands and let out a hoarse scream.

Another young man, dressed similarly to Jesus, stepped calmly from the taxi. He held an Uzi in his right hand. The barrel smoked. "Hi," he said to Georgio. He shifted the Uzi to his left hand and held his right hand out to shake Georgio's. "My name's José. I guess you're the Greek."

Georgio regarded José carefully. He took in the ponytail, the receding hairline, the weight around the stomach. No threat, he thought. "Call me Georgio," he said. He nodded at the taxi. "That's the man with the merchandise, I presume."

José span around to look as though he had forgotten all about the taxi and it's contents. He reached inside, retrieved two bags, a couple more Uzis, then took the arm of the third man and helped him out of the car. "This is our boss, Enrico Díaz," he said over his shoulder. Díaz fell to his knees. The second he was out of the car, without waiting for anyone to close the door, the taxi driver hit the gas and burned rubber across the airfield. He'd disappeared by the time José had pulled Díaz upright.

Georgio examined Díaz with a growing sense of distaste. He took in the filthy clothes, the yellowed and bloody bandage around his head, the equally disgusting bandage on the stump of one hand. His stood with his head low, his shoulders hunched, and his bloodshot eyes constantly scanned the sky.

If I wasn't about to rip him off, I'd be worried about this man, thought Georgio. He looked at Jesus, now upright and brushing down his clothes. At José, stroking his Uzi. At the cowering Díaz. A smile broke on his lips. This is going to be easy.

Georgio reached out his hand to Díaz. "Pleased to meet you, *Señor* Díaz."

Díaz's hands stayed limply at his side. He appeared to see Georgio for the first time and recoiled slightly. "Eagles!" he rasped. "Have you seen the eagles?"

Georgio let his hand drop and scanned the sky. "No eagles here," he said.

Díaz seemed to relax a little. He pointed with his stump at the Constellation. "This your plane? Are you ready?"

"I've sent word to my pilot. He'll be here soon. Where's the cargo?"

Díaz's eyes narrowed. "Why do you want to know?" he hissed.

For a moment, Georgio wasn't sure how to respond to this. He decided it must be a joke. He chuckled. Díaz wandered off, muttering.

"The goods will be here soon," said José. "Excuse the boss. He's had a hard few days."

Díaz's voice came screeching across the aerodrome. "Ask him what he knows about Escobar and the eagles." Then Díaz slumped down by a pile of oil drums.

"What's this about eagles?" asked Georgio.

"We got shot up by a jet," said José. "The boss thinks it was sent by Escobar. You know him?"

"Pablo Escobar? Isn't he dead?"

"Yeah. I mean the other one."

Georgio shook his head. He wondered what part Raúl Escobar played in all this.

"Anyway," sighed José. "Like I said, we got shot up. There were these birds. It was all a real fucking mess. You don't wanna hear about it."

In fact, Georgio was quite interested. Still, in a few minutes it'll be irrelevant anyway, he thought. By this time, Jesus had joined them. He collected his Uzi, dropped the other into one of the bags and carried them to where Díaz sat muttering by the oil drum. Then he rejoined Georgio and José. The three men stood in silent contemplation, staring at their feet, until they picked up the sound of another approaching engine.

An ancient van with 'Papagayo' painted on the side drove towards them. It stopped about thirty yards away, as though the driver was trying to come to a decision, then came closer. The engine died.

An old man stepped from the cab and spoke directly to José.

"Where's my money?" he said.

José fired a burst from his Uzi into bushes at the edge of the field. Georgio was surprised to see Jesus lying flat on the ground again. In the distance, Díaz was on his feet. In his good hand was a pistol which he pointed at the sky. "I'm ready for you, you sons of bitches!" he screamed.

The old man shrugged his shoulders and walked to the back of the van. He opened the doors and pulled out boxes. José went to help him. "Are you just gonna lie there or are you gonna help?" he yelled at Jesus.

Jesus was on his feet once more, brushing down his suit again. "This is the second fucking suit you've ruined," he whined.

"*I* ruined?" spluttered José. "What the fuck d'ya mean *I* ruined?"

"You always got to fire that fucking gun? You couldn't just threaten people like a normal person?"

"If I wanna fire my gun I'm gonna fire my fucking gun. I'm a hoodlum, fer fucksakes. It's what I do."

"Bullshit."

"Bullshit yourself."

Jesus pulled a box from the van and walked with it towards the Constellation. Holy shit, thought Georgio. These guys deserve to get robbed.

* * *

Squeaker appeared to be having trouble with his Jeep. He sat in the driver's seat, key in hand, his head bobbing as he hunted for the ignition.

Rotsky approached the vehicle and stood alongside Squeaker. "You got your own Jeep?"

Squeaker's head span round, eyes wide. "Ugh . . . right." He stared at the Jeep as though considering whether to deny its existence. "Got it for, you know . . . like . . ."

"Personal transport."

"Right."

Rotsky nodded. "You could have used ours. Hipólito's. But I guess it's good to have your own."

Squeaker was hunting again and merely nodded his head. He found the ignition, turned the key and the engine rumbled into life. "See ya," he said, then drove cautiously away, like a man unwilling to commit himself to a specific direction.

Hipólito arrived at Rotsky's side. "Where's Squeaker going?" he asked.

"Didn't think to ask," said Rotsky. "He made a phone call, then said he had to leave. Do you think they're connected?"

"Could be," said Hipólito. "My Jeep's here. Maybe we should tail him."

Rotsky looked and saw that Escobar was already in the back of the Jeep. He pouted as he prodded the upholstery. "A Mercedes it ain't," he grumbled.

Rotsky helped Vinnie into the other back seat. "I'll drive," he said to Hipólito.

"Why?"

"Because I'm a driver."

The two men climbed into the Jeep. Rotsky started the engine and put it into gear before he noticed that Squeaker had stopped a short distance away.

"What's he doing," asked Escobar.

"I think he's looking at a map," explained Hipólito. Suddenly,

Squeaker's Jeep roared out of the parking lot. Rotsky hit the gas, let out the clutch, stalled, restarted the engine and followed.

Squeaker swung left into the main road and Rotsky followed, hanging back a little to avoid suspicion. "This is the way to the airfield," he said. About a mile down the road, Squeaker turned left. "Well, it ain't the airfield," said Rotsky. He hauled the Jeep into the same turning. Coming back up the road towards them was Squeaker. Rotsky stepped hard on the brake. "Get down," he yelled. The four men did their best to hide in the open-top Jeep. As Squeaker drove by they heard his voice shout "Hi Guys!"

Rotsky waited thirty seconds before tentatively straightening up and looking around. Squeaker's Jeep was behind them, at the road junction. There was a map in Squeaker's hands. He threw this on the floor of the vehicle and took off, turning right into the main road.

Rotsky followed, hanging back a little further this time. Squeaker drove back through town, out the other side and after four or five miles hung a sharp right. Rotsky slowed before the junction and took it slowly this time. Squeaker's Jeep was stopped just around the corner. Then it started again, moving fast. Rotsky still kept well back. Squeaker's Jeep slowed again, got slower and slower. There was no other traffic on the road. Rotsky stopped. Squeaker accelerated then hauled the Jeep round in a hundred and eighty degree turn, straight towards them. Rotsky shifted into reverse, hit the gas, let out the clutch and stalled. Squeaker came to a scrambling, swaying, dusty stop beside them. "Guess you guy's are lost too, huh?" he asked. "Any idea of the way to the airfield?"

* * *

Sally tapped the fuel gauge again. It didn't move from the empty mark, where it had been for the past half-hour. She moved the switch to select the right main tank. The needle twitched slightly.

"Are we okay, sweetheart?"

Sally turned to see Lulu standing in the short passage behind the cockpit. Behind her, Sally could just make out the bum, bound tight on the bed.

"Sure," she said. "We're nearly there. We just passed over Santa Marta itself and we should find the target any second."

"What exactly is the target?"

"It's the old smuggler's strip, remember? We used it a few times in the old days. Get Walkaway up here. I could do with another set of eyes."

Thinking about the fuel reminded Sally of something. At their last refuelling stop, in Nicaragua, the lineman at the tiny, backwoods FBO hadn't been able to accept Lulu's fake Diner's Club card. They had got the fuel, what there was of it, by Sally promising to return for an 'overnight stay' on the way back.

Sally climbed the aircraft to five hundred feet for safety. She took out a school atlas that she kept tucked into a pocket on the back of the pilot's seat. She turned to the right page and, with a fat felt-tip pen, put a large red dot on the airfield's location. It was one more place to which she would never return. She looked at the map. It appeared to have a bad case of measles. She put the atlas away and brought the aircraft back down to treetop level, where they had been for the entire journey. Sally had a natural aversion to showing up on radar.

Walkaway sat in the right seat.

"We're pretty close now," said Sally. "Keep an eye open for the strip. And let me know if you see anything that indicates wind direction."

"For the landing?"

"For the approach. OLC rule four-sixteen: don't let the bastards hear you coming."

She scanned the ground. In the distance, a thin column of smoke staggered into the air, drifting sluggishly to the east. *It ain't much*, thought Sally, *but it'll do*. Then she saw the airstrip and immediately set up an approach to come at it from downwind. She pushed the aircraft still lower and heard a *thwack!* as the starboard prop took off the top few inches of a tree. She reduced power, set the props to fully fine, eased back on the control column and trimmed for the lower speed. Her hand moved automatically to the mixture knobs, to select fully rich, but the sight of the fuel gauge made her pause. The engines were running hot, but she needed every bit of juice. She moved the levers but left the mixture leaned out slightly.

Her attention shifted to the strip. At the closest edge she saw a burned-out wreck. Maybe the bastards who did that are still down there, she thought, though she knew that it wasn't an unusual sight at the kinds of strips she habitually used. The runway and ramp were littered with vehicles, oil drums and a huge white aircraft. Sally's eyes widened.

"Fuck me," she said. "That's a Constellation!"

9:
Don't kill me! Please god don't kill me!

Díaz swooned. The pain killers and tequila had stopped doing their job some hours before, in spite of increasing the dose. He had got José to score some cocaine for him, which he had rubbed on his wounds. He snorted some, too, and rubbed it into his gums. Now he throbbed all over, but in a dull, pleasant sort of way. Yet even as he enjoyed the sensation, Díaz knew it would soon wear off. He contemplated sampling some of his own merchandise, but couldn't see anywhere private where he could do it.

A sudden movement behind him made Díaz jump. A short, balding man hurried past. *"Got to get the engines warmed up!"* he yelled and disappeared inside the plane. Georgio followed him inside.

Díaz looked around in confusion. Everything around him took on new colours that changed and pulsated as he watched. He winced as the first of the Constellation's engines burst into life, soon followed by the other three.

A Jeep pulled up and stopped some distance away. Díaz was dismayed to see Hipólito in the car. Escobar was with him, that guy Díaz saw at the crash site, and the skinny kid with sunglasses.

With his right hand, Díaz reached into the bag at his feet and bumped against something hard. The pain that shot up his arm was so intense that for a moment everything snapped back into focus. He used his left hand to pull the Uzi from the bag. He held it by his side, hidden from the others by a fuel drum.

Suddenly Díaz's world went dark. A huge, black eagle swooped around his head and he knew that any second its vicious talons would tear into his skin. He threw himself to the ground and screamed. "Don't kill me! Please god don't kill me!"

*　*　*

José was taking a rest when the Jeep pulled up. Jesus lounged on the ground, a hand held to his forehead. They had loaded about a quarter of the merchandise on to the plane, but with every box they had to climb a ladder to reach the doorway. Every minute or so José looked up at the plane's propellers and muttered a quiet but heartfelt curse. He felt ill.

It was Jesus who saw the Jeep first. José grabbed his Uzi straight away and checked the magazine. He looked over at Jesus to make sure he was doing the same, but Jesus was backing towards some nearby bushes, his gun hanging uselessly from his shoulder. José was about to say something when he was distracted by the sudden arrival of another plane.

*　*　*

Rotsky watched the *Divine Providence* swoop low across the airfield with a full heart. Beautiful, he thought. Great approach. Must be Sally.

The aircraft had run in to the field from directly behind the guy with the bandaged head, who didn't seem to have heard it coming. He was getting to his feet again now.

"Recognize that guy?" asked Hipólito.

"Nope," said Rotsky. "I don't know anyone with bandages."

Squeaker appeared from *La Blanca*, and dropped to the runway, his head craned upwards, and watched the DC-3 with an expression of professional curiosity. The aircraft banked steeply and turned in for its final approach. It touched down with hardly a sound, taxied up and stopped some distance from the Jeep. The two aircraft and the Jeep now formed the points of a large triangle with sides of perhaps fifty yards.

"Come on Vinnie," said Rotsky. "Let's go say hi to the guys."

By the time Rotsky and Vinnie reached the *Providence*, the engines had shut down. The rear door opened and Lulu, Walkaway and Sally jumped out. Sally looked around, got back on board the *Providence* and reappeared a moment later with a pump-action shotgun.

Rotsky kissed Lulu and Sally hello. By this time Squeaker had joined them, and he did the same.

Rotsky turned to Walkaway. "There's a lot of people want to talk to you, man," he said.

"Oh, they don't want me," said Walkaway. "They want this." He tapped the briefcase under his arm.

"The case?" This appeared to be news to Lulu.

"What's in it?" Rotsky took the briefcase.

Walkaway looked at the case as though he had never seen it before. "I don't know," he said. "I was waiting for the right time to open it — you know, the moment when it *should* be opened."

The clarity of Walkaway's logic stunned Rotsky. He handed back the case.

"Oh man. It really is a Constellation," said Walkaway, and walked trance-like towards *La Blanca*.

* * *

Hipólito watched Walkaway hungrily. That's him, he thought, and his trigger finger twitched involuntarily. He glanced to his right and saw that Escobar's gaze was similarly fixed.

Oblivious of the attention, Walkaway strolled across to the Constellation, its engines still grumbling, its huge props turning lazily. He stared up at it admiringly.

Hipólito's gaze continued across to Díaz who stared straight back at him. Díaz's left hand was hidden by an oil drum, but Hipólito could see he was holding something heavy. José and Jesus were a little way behind him. José cradled an Uzi. Jesus slowly backed away towards some bushes.

Hipólito reached into the Jeep and took hold of his MP5 machine gun. He saw Escobar reach into a bag in the back of the Jeep and pull out the Sten gun, the silenced one Hipólito had bought for him. Hipólito flushed with pride.

He scanned the scene again. In spite of the growl of the Constellation's engines, there was an eerie calm hanging over the airstrip.

Hipólito tightened his grip on the gun.

* * *

Díaz tried hard to concentrate on Hipólito. His vision blurred, and the throbbing in his ears and hand now had a sharp edge. He turned his head to see where José and Jesus were, but the world swam so fast around him that he couldn't make them out. He brought his left hand up, still clutching the Uzi, and rested it on the oil drum to steady himself.

Someone moved. Díaz thought it might be Hipólito, but then saw that it was someone from the other group, near the new plane. It was a skinny kid with sunglasses, walking with his hands held out before him, walking straight towards a pile of rusting fuel tins.

Is he blind or something? thought Díaz. Unnerved by this new development, he tightened his grip on the Uzi.

* * *

Sally slowly swung the barrel of the pump-action shotgun between the Jeep and Díaz. Lulu had told her to be ready for trouble but she didn't need telling. She'd been expecting trouble since they'd taken off from Florida. Suddenly there was a voice by her right ear.

"Think I left my jacket in the Jeep."

It was Vinnie. Before Sally realized what was happening, he was already out of arm's reach. None of the others had heard him speak because of the noise from *La Blanca*. By the time they noticed him, he was too far away to be reached easily. No-one wanted to make any sudden movements.

Sally watched in fascinated horror as he headed towards some fuel cans. She pumped a shell into the shotgun's chamber, checked that the safety was off, and tightened her grip on the stock.

* * *

Quinn took a long sip of his cocktail and gazed out from the café terrace. The flat sea shimmered brilliantly in the unshielded sun and he found it hard to focus on the horizon.

He was in a subdued mood. That morning, in the shower, as he finished rinsing the shampoo from his head, he found his hand thickly laced with hair. He felt weary, and when he looked hard at himself in the mirror that morning, he was sure the lines across his face had multiplied overnight.

Damn stuff ain't working, he snarled to himself, then shifted uncomfortably in his seat. He noticed a discolouration of the skin on the back of his hand, the one holding the cocktail glass, and he made a note to buy stronger sun cream.

A little way along the street the late afternoon sun brilliantly illuminated an old adobe church. Quinn thought about going inside, but he wasn't sure how to use a church — when to go there, what to do there, what it could do for him. He suspected that a single visit would not yield whatever benefits lay behind its doors, that more might be expected of him.

A waiter bustled from the interior of the cafe.

"*Señor*, your telephone call."

Quinn stood up stiffly. His muscles ached. His bones ached. Must get some more exercise, he thought. He gathered himself erect and marched with as much confidence as he could muster into the cafe. The telephone handset was lying on the far end of the deserted bar. Quinn picked it up and growled "Quinn" into the mouthpiece.

"How's it going?" replied the voice. Quinn thought he heard an echo on the word 'going' but it might have been an effect of the long-distance call. "Is everything going according to plan?"

"What goddamned plan?" Quinn hitched himself up on to a bar stool. "And no, nothing's going according to plan because nothing's happening. Zilch. Zero."

"Have you flushed out Walkaway yet? Our client is getting impatient."

"Seen hide nor hair of him," said Quinn.

"How's Escobar working out? Is he doing what he's told?"

"Sure, sure. The Medellín boys were right though."

"How so?"

"The guy's got about as much class as a forty-second street hooker."

"You're keeping an eye on the others, right?"

"Oh sure. Never outta my sight."

"So . . . they're with you now?"

"Not exactly," said Quinn. "But they're around. Like I said, nothing's happening."

* * *

Another bullet whizzed past Rotsky's head and hit the *Providence* with a dull *ding*. A ferocious crackling in the distance told Rotsky that the man with the head wound was firing again. From another direction came the muffled tap of Escobar's Sten and the hammering of Hipólito's MP5.

Shee-it! Thought Rotsky. That was close.

He was taking what shelter he could behind the undercarriage of the DC-3, and was acutely aware of the hundreds of gallons of aviation gas he imagined in the wing tanks above his head.

There was a loud *bang* close to his left ear as Sally loosed off another round from her shotgun. She was firing wildly, making sure that the others kept their heads down and couldn't get a properly-aimed shot.

When Vinnie had tripped over the fuel cans, the sound of them hitting the ground was surprisingly loud. The tinny crashes carried above the Constellation's engines and several trigger fingers spontaneously twitched. Over the next few minutes the shooting became progressively more sporadic and ill-aimed, but there was enough of it to keep everyone under cover.

* * *

Hipólito carefully raised his head above the hood of the Jeep, which was now creased and pitted with bullet scars. All four tyres had been punctured and the windshield was heavily starred. Hipólito heard only the occasional shot now: there was the bang of the shotgun from over by the DC-3, but Hipólito instinctively knew it wasn't aimed at him. Then there was a whimpering sound at his feet.

Escobar lay on the ground, his arms around his Sten gun, his cheek against the metal. The Sten had taken a direct hit. The bullet had torn up the leather and ripped a hole in the metal, bending the barrel back like a bird's broken neck.

"My Sten," whimpered Escobar. "My beautiful Sten."

"The bastards!" snapped Hipólito. He knew it couldn't have been a shotgun that did the damage, so the bullet that hit the Sten must have come from Díaz or one of his goons. Hipólito felt his muscles ripple with righteous anger. His brain raced with vicious plots of revenge, but then came a noise that made him go cold — a noise that changed everything.

"Son of a bitch!" yelled Hipólito as he ran across the airstrip, shooting from the hip.

* * *

Díaz was on his knees behind the oil drum, his hands scrabbling frantically in the bag. He brought out a plastic bag containing white powder. With the trembling fingertips of his left hand he shovelled the powder into his nose, sniffed hard, forgot to breath, coughed. The powder plastered his sweating face. His eyes closed tight as the pain from his right hand shot through his body. His shoulders shook. His head rocked back and forth.

He reached into the bag again and drew out a fresh clip for the Uzi. He stood, rocking and twisting, his head falling side to side. Fumbling and cursing, he managed to get the new clip into the gun, which he cocked and held before him, like a crucifix against evil.

In the bag was a half-full bottle of tequila. Díaz picked it up with his shattered right hand and had almost finished it before it slipped from his grasp and shattered on the ground. The world was a stuttering blur. His head thrummed, and the ground dipped and swayed. He tried to walk forward, hit the drum and staggered sideways for several steps.

Then the world roared, a heart-chilling bellow of evil. Soft, tenacious demons whirled around Díaz's body, pulling it this way and that. They tugged at his clothes, and dragged him back towards a doom that his pain-wracked eyes could no longer see, but which his destroyed mind could fearfully imagine. Díaz opened his mouth and howled. He flung his arms out in supplication, his heart bursting with terror. And in one desperate act of defiance, he blindly pulled the trigger of his Uzi.

* * *

To Rotsky, everything seemed to happen at once. The Constellation's engines revved into life and the aircraft moved ponderously towards the threshold of the runway. Rotsky thought he heard a yell from the Jeep, and saw Hipólito running towards the plane, firing his MP5. But the most unexpected sight was the man with the bandaged head who appeared from behind an oil drum, his face ghostly white. He staggered in the slipstream of the Constellation, his arms outstretched, his head back and mouth open, a baying beast engaged in a strange, ritual dance. His left arm jerked violently as he fired his Uzi. Within a second or two the gun was empty, but not before Hipólito lay motionless on the ground.

The Constellation roared louder still, and Rotsky watched with professional fascination as the big bird accelerated down the runway and lifted from the ground. Rotsky was oblivious to any danger now. His entire attention was captivated by the beautiful machine as it clawed its way into the sky, its skinny legs disappearing into the wings and fuselage to make it a soaring beast of inestimable elegance.

The noise of the aircraft soon dimmed to a distant murmur. Rotsky felt a great calm descend on him. No-one was shooting now. He looked around the airfield. To his right, Escobar stood over the inert figure of Hipólito. To his left, Díaz banged his Uzi on an oil drum and muttered something that sounded like "you treacherous bastard". José walked towards him, no magazine in his gun, a hand held out, ready to either comfort a distressed man or fend off a madman. The bushes behind Díaz suddenly shook into life and Jesus appeared, his suit dirty and crumpled.

Rotsky heard a noise behind him and turned to see Lulu, who reappeared from a ditch at the edge of the airstrip.

Rotsky smiled serenely at her, as two people who had just shared something beautiful. "Looks like everyone ran out of ammo," he said.

Lulu's brow was creased. Less than five yards away was Squeaker, still watching the Constellation, now just a dot in the sky. Lulu's gaze switched between the dot and Squeaker, and back again. Then she turned to Rotsky.

"Have you seen Walkaway?" she asked.

* * *

Escobar stood astride the still body of Hipólito. He rocked gently back and forth. He wanted to reach down, to touch the face of his dead friend and bodyguard, but he wasn't sure his legs would support him and he was worried about never getting up again. Now I understand, he thought. Now I know that I am alone. This is what they wanted all along. To bring me here. To surround me with my enemies. To leave me alone with my only friend dead.

The word 'dead' reverberated around his head. He sobbed.

"Dead is fine," he whimpered. "Dead is fine."

* * *

Billy's bowels clenched uncomfortably as he opened the cage door.

All day the word *shame* had reverberated through his mind. He saw Escobar's behaviour to the animals and himself as one and the same thing. And as he repeated the word to himself, an idea had gradually formed.

Shame! That's what I'll do. I'll shame Escobar into . . . into . . . doing something. As a scheme, Billy knew it was a tad vague, but it was the best one he had. He would track down Escobar, wherever he was, and confront him publicly with the wolf's shabby condition. Billy felt fairly sure he could come up with the rest of the plan later. And if that doesn't work, he thought, I'll find the poor bugger a decent home.

Billy wanted the wolf to be relaxed and so scoured Escobar's drug reserves for a suitable sedative. It took a long time. Escobar had plentiful supplies of uppers and screamers but not much in the way of downers. The best he could manage was some old cold remedy that, he seemed to remember, made him sleepy as a child. And a handful of Quaaludes.

He marinated a steak in the cough mixture and topped it with crushed Quaaludes. He wasn't sure how long a cough mixture marinade should take, but half-an-hour seemed like it might do. He took the breakfast out to the cage.

The wolf lurked sullenly in the far corner. If I didn't know better, thought Billy, I'd swear that wolf has a hangover. He opened the door, threw in the steak and closed the door quickly. The wolf showed no signs of having noticed his existence. Eat it, willed Billy. Please!

Eventually the wolf loped over to the meat and sniffed it suspiciously. It took a tentative nibble, then another, then devoured the steak in a rage of teeth and slavering growls that sent Billy running back to the house.

He left it an hour, then took a slow walk back to the cage. The wolf lay in the centre of the floor. It looked dead. Billy checked for signs of breathing but saw none. He picked up a stick to prod the wolf through the bars, but it was too short. He found a longer stick.

It took him a while to convince himself that the wolf was deep asleep. It took him a lot longer to haul it into the cage on the back of the pickup truck.

He had heard Escobar and Hipólito mention Santa Marta, and he found a tourist map of Colombia's beaches in the house. Billy wasn't too sure where he was starting out from, but reckoned that if he headed north he'd finally hit somewhere marked on the map. He would work it out from there.

In fact, he drove straight to Santa Marta, by accident. It took several hours and one wheel change, during which odd gurgling noises came from the still-supine wolf. At first he thought he'd arrived in Atlántico, until he realized that the sign he was staring at pointed left down another major road and was mounted beneath another that said 'Welcome to Santa Marta' in four languages.

He drove through the town, trying to work to a system so that he would try every street at least once. He wasn't too sure what he was looking for — he just thought there might be some kind of sign pointing to Escobar's whereabouts. Surely someone as important as Escobar couldn't be in town without it showing in some way.

It had just got dark when he decided to give up for the day. He was outside Santa Marta proper, in a small suburban village on the seashore. He parked the pickup on the quay and got out to check on the wolf. It was awake now, its head resting between its paws. It flinched at sudden sounds. Billy threw a tarpaulin over the cage. Sleep well, he transmitted.

"Nice doggie," said a voice behind him.

Billy turned. It was an old man dressed the way Billy would expect a fisherman to dress.

"It's not a . . . nice doggie," Billy hedged. "Damn thing'd bite ya head off, man." He didn't want anyone messing with the wolf. It then occurred to Billy that the man had spoken English to him. "You from around here?" he asked.

The old man chuckled drunkenly. "From over there." He nodded towards a bollard.

"Over there?"

"Sure. That's where I was just now. It's where I usually am."

An idea crept into Billy's head.

"You ever heard of Escobar?"

"Oh sure, man. Everyone heard of Escobar. Big man."

"Know where he is?"

"You bet. In the ground."

"In the ground? You mean —"

"Sure man. He dead. Been dead for years."

"Raúl Escobar?"

"Raúl? Who's Raúl?"

Billy felt a headache coming on. "I'm looking for Raúl Escobar. The *contrabandista*."

A finger flew to the old man's lips. "Shhh!" He looked around cautiously. "Don't use words like that around here." He moved closer. Billy could smell the old man now. He took a step back.

"I never heard of any Raúl Escobar," said the old man. "But there has been a lot of shit happening around here. Lots of people coming and going, you know what I mean?"

"Yes," lied Billy. "Do you know where these people are now?"

"They've gone!" yelled the old man. "Gone. To Florida is my guess. Where else?"

Billy slumped. This was something he hadn't foreseen. He was very tired all of a sudden. He needed time to think. He faced the old man again. "Anywhere around here I can get something to eat?"

"Depends. How hungry are you?"

* * *

Rotsky liked to watch Lulu work. Her movements had a lazy elegance, he thought, a sexy languor, so that every sweep of her hands was like a caress. He admired the way she wrapped the bandage around Sally's arm and then fixed it with duct tape.

"It ain't pretty, but it'll work," said Lulu.

Sally's wound was superficial, not much more than a crease, but painful. "I'm not sure I can fly with this," she told Lulu. "My arm aches and I don't feel like I've got much strength in it."

"Don't you worry, sweetie. One thing we ain't short of round here is pilots."

Rotsky looked around the interior of the *Divine Providence*. There was a dishevelled man bound and gagged on the bed. Vinnie sat in a wing chair looking shell-shocked. Squeaker was in the cockpit, familiarizing himself with the controls.

"What exactly did Walkaway say?" said Rotsky. "Why is he so popular?"

"Hard to say, hon," said Lulu. "You know Walkaway. The way he talks. 'Information' is what he said. I guess he knows something they don't want him to know. Or don't want someone else to know. Or maybe he knows something they don't."

"Or all of the above," said Rotsky automatically. He thought about what Walkaway had said about the briefcase. He was about to remind Lulu of it when there was a clattering and two men in ruined suits climbed into the aircraft. They pulled after them an older man whose head and right hand were swaddled in filthy bandages. He fell against the aft bulkhead and slid to the floor, leaving a smear of blood on the wall. He murmured something that sounded like "never been fired", chuckled in a deranged, semi-conscious way then passed out, his head nodding on to his chest. His colleagues look at him dispassionately, then turned to the others.

"He got shot in the ass," explained José. He then waved an Uzi. "We need to talk to you people. You might call it a business proposition."

"And you are?" asked Lulu.

Good question, thought Rotsky. Damned good question.

"José. This is Jesus. That's our boss, Enrico Díaz. And this here's *Señor Uzi* who says that you should listen to what we've got to say."

Díaz's head nodded up, his eyes still closed. "Never been fired," he mumbled. Bubbles formed on his lips. He slid back into unconsciousness.

José looked briefly at the tied-up bum on the bed but showed no surprise or interest.

"Well my guess, honey, is that *Señor* Uzi is feeling a tad *empty* right now," said Lulu, "so why don't you just get the hell off our goddamn airplane." She turned to Sally. "Sweetheart, could you go outside and see if any of those fuel drums have fuel in them. Otherwise we ain't going anywhere. And just make a final check that nothing essential got hit during that firefight."

"Sure, boss." Sally walked down the aircraft, past José and Jesus who watched her intently. After she'd dropped from the doorway their gaze remained locked outside, as if they'd forgotten why they were there. Díaz moaned.

"You got any drugs?" asked José. He nodded at Díaz. "They're for him."

"I think we've got some aspirin somewhere," said Lulu. "Maybe some paracetamol in the medical kit."

José shook his head irritably. "No, no. I said *drugs*. Like cocaine."

"Cocaine? No, no cocaine."

"Smack?"

"No smack either."

"Some speed, maybe. Or ether."

"I'm real sorry, honey lamb," cooed Lulu.

José's voice got louder. "Grass, for fucksakes, you gotta have some grass!"

Lulu looked at the floor and shrugged. "The last time we had stuff like that on this aircraft it was cargo, you know? And that was a while back now."

José looked at them, disbelievingly. "You can't be serious. You telling me that between a bunch of people like you there ain't one scrap of narcotic?"

"You know, he's right," said Rotsky. "Weird, isn't it?"

"But you do got some booze, right?" snarled José.

Lulu opened the drinks cabinet, poured a large bourbon and handed it to José. He drank it and handed back the empty glass. "It's empty," he said. Lulu refilled the glass and this time offered it to Díaz. He recoiled in horror. Drool dropped from his slack mouth. José stepped forward and took the glass. He downed the drink.

Sally's voice carried from outside. "Hey Lulu! I found some fuel and a hand-pump. I need someone to help me with this."

"I'll go," said Vinnie. He shot out of his chair and stumbled back down the plane. José and Jesus had to jump out of his way. A second after he disappeared from the doorway there was a sickening *crump* and a frail voice that called: "I'm okay."

Lulu poured herself a drink. "Now what did you boys have in mind?"

José dropped the Uzi onto Vinnie's vacated chair and refilled his glass. "We've got some merchandise that we need to move. It's turned out to be more difficult than we thought. That bastard in the other plane —" he spat on the floor "— took some of it. But there's more. We want to use your plane."

I wonder what kind of merchandise it is, thought Rotsky.

"What kind of merchandise is it?" asked Lulu.

Another good question, thought Rotsky.

José looked at Jesus as though he needed help with a decision. Jesus was looking at the bourbon bottle and missed it.

"Lady Caine," José told Lulu. "Good shit, too. Real fresh. Real pure."

"Excuse me a moment, would you?" said Lulu. She took Rotsky by the arm and led him to the short passage between the cabin and the cockpit.

"I think it might be a good idea, hon," she whispered. "Whatever Walkaway is involved in, it's got something to do with Lady Caine. If we stick close to this cargo we might find what this is all about, and find Walkaway. It might even help get *Delicious Tricia* back."

This all made sense to Rotsky. José's use of the words 'Lady Caine' had been like a code word. Rotsky was already convinced that their fate lay with these strange men. He told Lulu to do whatever she thought was right.

"You've got a deal," Lulu called to José as she walked back down the cabin. "We take twenty-five per cent of the merchandise for shipping costs. We'll take you and the cargo to Florida — I assume that's where you want to go —" José nodded enthusiastically. "You disappear when we get there. End of deal."

José kept nodding.

"Ten per cent," said Jesus. Lulu and José looked at him as if he was a dangerous drunk who'd just wandered in from the street.

"Bullshit, ten per cent," said José.

"Bullshit yourself. Ten per cent is standard."

"What the fuck would you know about what's standard. This here's the only plane we're likely to get. So it's twenty-five."

José and Jesus glowered at each other for a while.

"Getting the stuff on board might be a good first step," said Lulu soothingly.

The two hoods exchanged malicious stares and shuffled to the door. José nudged Jesus out of the way to drop to the tarmac. "I think I'll lend a hand," said Rotsky and followed them out. Sally was on the port wing, holding a hose that disappeared into the fuel tank. Vinnie was on the ground at the other end of the hose, working the handle of a pump that was clamped to a fuel drum.

Rotsky and the hoods took twenty minutes or so ferrying cardboard boxes from the other side of the field to the *Providence*. Rotsky was inside the aircraft, with José, when Jesus brought the last one on board. It had been hit by a stray bullet, and as Jesus dropped it on to the pile of other boxes, it split wide open. A number of small pink pellets spilled on to the floor.

Rotsky picked one up. It was bullet-shaped, about the size of an ear plug and waxy. "What is this thing?" he asked. "How do you use it?"

"It's a suppository, Rotsky," explained Lulu.

Rotsky looked at her blankly. "A what?"

Lulu gave Rotsky a brief but graphic explanation of what a suppository is and how to use one. Rotsky listened open-mouthed and wide-eyed. He failed to grasp the reason for such a bizarre method of drug-taking, but was impressed by the image of thousands of geriatrics across the country, their sweatpants around their ankles and their knees bent, pushing small pink pellets up their asses. For the first time, Rotsky felt he understood the true extent of their desperation.

A pair of hands pushed Vinnie back inside the aircraft. Sally followed close behind. "All set," she said. "We ain't exactly fat with fuel, but there's enough to get us to Honduras. I know somewhere there where we can pick up more without attracting too much attention. That's if they're still alive, and the feds haven't got there first, and—"

"That'll be fine, sweetie," said Lulu.

Sally walked through to the flight deck from where she yelled: "Get strapped in folks. This flight's about to leave."

Lulu walked to the rear door, to shut it. But she stopped short and reversed down the gangway. Through the door came Escobar. He cradled a damaged machine gun in his left arm. In his right hand was an entirely undamaged Heckler & Koch. "In case you're wondering," he said, "I found some ammo in the Jeep."

* * *

Billy felt a little apprehensive when the woman marched up to him. She didn't look happy.

"A salad for me and a steak for the wolf," he said.

"Wolf?"

"Out front. In the truck."

"How does it want the steak?"

"Very rare."

The woman cast a wary look at the door, then turned and went back into the kitchen. She was back in a couple of minutes. "Salad's off," she said. "We got beef or chicken."

Just at that moment, Billy caught a hint of sea salt on the breeze and realized what he really wanted. "I could really go for some fish."

"No fish. Beef or chicken."

Billy stared at the table top. "Chicken, please." The woman walked away.

"And—"

She turned. "Yes?"

Billy's stomach was tight. He lost his appetite. "Do you know anything about . . . you know . . . smuggling." He winced as though expecting a blow. Since learning about Escobar's departure for Florida he had been asking around, trying to find a way to get the wolf to the States. He was also still very hungry. When someone had told him to ask the woman who owned the cafe, he'd known that fate was taking a hand.

The woman's expression didn't change. "The wolf?" she asked.

"The wolf," he nodded. "I hear you've got boats. I love boats. Boats are cool."

The woman arched an eyebrow. The corners of her mouth twitched in faint intimation of a smile. "It would be quicker by air," she said.

"Oh man, I hate planes," said Billy. "Too noisy. Too fast. All that pollution, you know? Ozone and stuff."

The woman broke out in a smile that nearly knocked Billy off his chair. My god, he thought, she's beautiful. He had never been more afraid.

"I'll be back," she said and marched away. Billy knew his fate went with her. His future was out of his control now. It made him a little more relaxed.

The woman returned a few minutes later with a bowl of steaming stew and threw it on the table in front of Billy. He scooped up a spoonful and tasted it. "This is chicken?" he asked the hovering woman.

"Yes," she said. "You have a problem?"

"No way," he enthused genuinely. "This is great!" He ate quickly and soon finished the bowl. "Is there more?"

He was rewarded with that smile again. The woman took the bowl to the kitchen and came back with it full. She dropped it on the table. "I can move your wolf for you," she said.

"You've got a boat?"

"I've got two." A cloud crossed her face. "I used to have three." She spat on the floor. "But we only need one." She stepped closer and reached out her hand. Billy recoiled, but couldn't go far because of the wall. She got closer still and stroked his hair. "You like boats. You like my food. You can call me Rosita."

* * *

Walkaway felt he should look out of the window, maybe get a grip on his situation. The coke was still hitting his nerves hard. His eyes fluttered and bounced from the sides of his orbits and it seemed to him that the aircraft might be coming apart.

I wonder where the ground is, he thought.

There was a massive blow to his spine that pushed him deep into the seat. Outside, the gear that he'd left down for just such an emergency buckled like straw. It snapped and screeched under the immense g-load. The aircraft bounced slightly then came down heavily on the tarmac, its belly skin ripped open with a terrifying shriek until, finally, it came to rest in a storm of angry dust.

Ah! There it is!

* * *

Hipólito rolled on to his back and groaned. There was a sharp pain in his gut and his head throbbed. Jesus! he thought, you'da thought I'd been shot.

He put a hand to his waist and pressed. A pain scorched through his body. He couldn't breathe. Fuck!

His shirt was wet. He raised his hand in front of his face and saw that it was bloody. Sonofabitch! That scum-sucking fucker Díaz. The motherfucker shot me!

He rolled again, brought his knees up, managed to sit upright. It hurt, but he knew he could manage the pain. Something else was running through his system now. He was charged with anger and that gave him the energy to stand. I'm gonna kill that fucker. I'm gonna tear the motherfucker's head off and . . . another wave of pain shot through him.

Hipólito looked around. There was no-one to be seen. The big white plane had gone. The other one was still there, but even through pain-blurred eyes he could see holes in it. Fucked, he thought, like me.

He considered his predicament. He knew he needed help, that if he didn't get patched up he would die before he got the chance to kill anyone else. Gut shot, he thought. Could kill me now. Could kill me tomorrow. Must get to a doc.

He took a few tentative steps. They hurt like hell. It felt like his guts might spill on to the ground any second. Bastards! They're not gonna kill me. I won't let them kill me.

He saw a jacket in the Jeep, took it, tore it into strips. He wrapped these tightly around his waist, tied them as tight as he dare and watched them soak with blood. He took a deep breath and started the long walk into town.

* * *

Georgio Acidopholus dropped from the passenger door of the Constellation. It wasn't a long drop, but Georgio's legs were weak and he hit the sun-baked earth in a crumpled heap. The air was thick with the smell of aviation fuel from the aircraft's ruptured tanks.

Georgio felt a thump on the ground next to him and looked up to see the pilot, apparently unshaken, now wearing the airline captain's jacket and peaked cap that he'd removed at the beginning of the flight. Tucked into one armpit was a battered briefcase.

"You son of a bitch!" yelled Georgio. He was on his feet in a flash, his hands around the pilot's throat, pushing him back, repeatedly smacking his head against the skin of the aircraft. "My beautiful plane! Look what you've done to my plane. You crashed my fucking plane!"

The pilot's own hands tried ineffectually to loosen the Greek's grip. He made a gurgling noise through which came: "That . . . ugh . . . wasn't . . . a . . . crash . . . ugh . . . controlled . . . flight . . . ugh . . . into . . . ugh . . . terrain".

From the far side of the plane came a *whoomph!* and a flash of light.

Georgio let go of the pilot and dropped back a couple of paces. His legs gave way and he sank to his knees. The pilot started to walk away. "What the fuck was that?" yelled Georgio after him.

"Fire," said the pilot calmly over his shoulder. "Or something that sounds very much like it."

"Holy mother of god!" gasped Georgio. "The merchandise!" He rose unsteadily, tottered to the door of the plane and climbed inside.

* * *

Billy really liked the boat. It had all the wooden charm of an old fishing smack, planks and rails worn smooth and dark by generations of sailors, brass portholes, and lots of fishing boat-type stuff that Billy couldn't name.

"This one's special," explained Rosita. "It ain't my favourite." Her head tilted and Billy assumed she was indicating the noise of the engines. "But business is business." She appeared lost in thought for a second, then added: "I only use this boat for customers I really like." And she smiled in a way that, not for the first time, sent a shock through Billy's nervous system. He couldn't decide whether it was fear or excitement.

Colombia had already dropped below the horizon. They were travelling faster than Billy had ever moved on water, running without lights in the slowly dying dusk. The boat was designed so that, from a distance of a mile or so, it might be taken for an ordinary trawler. Up close, the illusion soon disappeared. Then you would see the two slim hulls. The wood and brass that Billy liked so much was wafer-thin. Beneath it was a featherlight body of aluminium and plastic. The deep roar from within the boat's bowels, that grumbled through the hissing of their wake, came from two jet engines that Rosita's family had stolen from the airport. Their shafts were coupled directly to water turbines that could put the craft on its standing wave in the blink of an eye. In another blink, the boat would be up on its hydroplanes. It could outrun almost anything except a jet fighter.

Billy watched Rosita work, tying stuff down, putting stuff away. Man, she really knows what she's doing, he thought, awe-struck.

"You like animals?" Billy asked.

"Oh sure," smiled Rosita. "You like women?"

"Oh . . . uh . . . like, you bet," guessed Billy. "I think I'll feed the wolf."

Billy went below to the galley. He took some raw meat from the cold store. They had laid in a large stock, though no food for themselves. "I can't pilot the boat and cook," Rosita had explained. She'd looked at Billy with an arched eyebrow, as if expecting a response. He'd felt the need to say something. "Right," he'd said.

Back on deck, he approached the wolf's cage with more trepidation than ever. It was awake now, and bad-tempered. Billy didn't want to give it any more drugs unless absolutely necessary.

Billy threw the meat into the cage. The wolf bared its yellow teeth, snarled and snapped its jaws. Billy turned and ran, almost colliding with Rosita. She smiled. He backed towards the cage.

"Don't worry," she grinned. "It won't be long now."

Billy wasn't sure what she meant.

* * *

Walkaway turned and looked at the wreck with a mixture of pride and expectation. For a moment his face wore a concerned frown, but a second muffled *whoomph* from under the port wing brought a satisfied smile. Blue flames licked around the engines.

From inside the aircraft came the barely audible cries of the Greek. "The merchandise! The merchandise!"

The flames grew higher. A box flew from the open doorway of the Constellation. Flames ran along the fuselage, and there were more stifled explosions. Another box appeared. There was a louder, sharper bang. The aircraft broke apart, and Walkaway could hear the fire now, crackling and roaring. The flames flicked high into the air, turning the rose pink of a winter sunset, sputtering like a giant candle.

A voice from behind made Walkaway spin around. "Not your best landing young fella." It was the old guy who ran the airstrip. "You got something against wheels?"

"No," said Walkaway. He frowned. "I don't think so. You got a phone?"

"Local call?"

"Sure."

"In the office."

* * *

Escobar rubbed a pink pellet between his fingers. "What is this? Wax?" He sniffed it, then looked around the cabin. He glanced at the tied-up man on the bed without comment. "What's that goddamned smell?" Finally his eyes settled on Díaz, and he snarled. "Goddamned bum," he muttered. He waved the Heckler & Koch in the general direction of Díaz.

Rotsky felt a warm glow of satisfaction from his new-found knowledge and he looked around the aircraft to make sure there was a good enough audience for his triumph. Díaz lay face-down on a sofa, murmuring and wheezing, occasionally breaking into a faint, high-pitched song for a bar or two, then sighing back into his stupor. His trousers were around his ankles and bandages were taped across his backside. During his final pirouette on the tarmac he had caught a blast from Sally's shotgun, and was lucky it was only birdshot. Lulu had patched him up.

José and Jesus were crouched by the fridge, arguing about whether Scotch should be chilled. From time to time one of them would cast a surreptitious glance at Lulu who was now sleeping on a chaise longue. Vinnie was in the wing chair, headphones on, Walkman turned up high, tapping his toes to Sheryl Crow's 'Strong Enough', rocking a little and occasionally letting out an off-pitch caterwaul that sounded vaguely like singing but which contained no identifiable words.

Squeaker and Sally were out of sight, in the cockpit going through aircraft systems and handling characteristics of the plane. Every now and then, Rotsky heard Squeaker's voice say "wow" or "cool".

Now Rotsky found Escobar looking straight at him.

"What is this thing? An earplug?"

"It's Lady Caine," said Rotsky.

"You mean this is a drug?"

"A suppository."

"A what?"

"It's a kind of pill you take by jamming it up the kazoo."

Escobar dropped the pellet.

"Don't worry," beamed Rotsky, "these are fresh ones, hardly used at all."

"Don't fuck with me!" growled Escobar.

Díaz opened his eyes, which seemed more focused than they had been recently. An expression of horrified recognition passed across his face.

"Escobar!" he hissed. José and Jesus stopped their bickering and stared at Díaz. Then their gaze shifted to Escobar.

"The Corporation," said Díaz. "The Corporation sent you. They sent you to kill me!" His voice got louder, higher pitched. He rolled onto his back and sat up. He grimaced like a man with a bad case of piles. "You've come for me," he hissed through clenched jaws.

Escobar was unsteady on his feet. He looked like a lost man, his expression weary. "Yes," he said distantly. "And yet . . ." He looked uncertainly around the aircraft. "I don't know. Maybe . . ."

There was a rumble and then a roar from outside.

"What the fuck's that?" screamed Escobar, his eyes wide and flicking wildly.

"Engine," said Rotsky. "There'll be another one along any time. Better check that door is shut properly."

"Are we leaving?" whimpered Escobar.

There was another clattering and the intensity of the roar increased.

"Any second now," said Rotsky. "Now would be a good time to take your seat and fasten your seatbelt."

"You won't get me!" screamed Díaz. His head wobbled as the plane rolled forward.

"Get seated, Rotsky," said Lulu. She had moved from the chaise longue to one of the standard aircraft seats near the front of the cabin. Vinnie strapped himself into the wing chair. The aircraft hit a bump in the tarmac.

"They're taking me away!" yelled Díaz. He lurched to his feet, fell forward out of control and careened into Escobar, who staggered backwards. He hit the door, the door swung open and Escobar disappeared from the aircraft.

"Guess it wasn't shut properly after all," murmured Rotsky. He walked back down the aircraft, slammed the door shut and locked it, then returned to the front of the cabin to take the seat next to Lulu. She craned her head around to look back down the plane. "What happened to our new friend?"

Rotsky buckled his seat belt. "He changed his mind."

10:
What the fuck happened here?

The airfield was deathly quiet when Quinn arrived. It was early morning and Quinn had spent a restless night wondering where everyone had got to. He stepped out of the taxi and paid-off the driver. They call this an airfield? he thought. The only aircraft in sight was the burned hulk of a Boeing that had been bulldozed to the edge of the field. On the ramp was a Jeep, its tyres flat, its windshield starred with bullet holes, its body holed like a cheese grater. In it sat Escobar, his lands limp in his lap, head hanging, his chin on his chest. There were blood stains on the ground nearby. When Quinn got close enough, he could hear Escobar muttering, "Dead is fine. Dead is fine".

"What the fuck happened here?" asked Quinn. The sight of the scattered cartridge cases made him queasy. He fingered the holes in the Jeep's bodywork and thought about the fragility of softer tissues. His hip ached.

Escobar didn't bother turning to look at Quinn. "They told me to get Díaz," he said. "But they didn't tell me why. Then I found all these other people here, and I know that something bigger is going on. And it's got something to do with someone called Walkaway. And everyone else is after Walkaway. And it's got something to do with Lady Caine. And I don't know why I'm taking instructions from people I can't even see."

"Really," said Quinn, without much interest.

"And now they've all gone without me," sobbed Escobar. "Why does no-one pay me any respect? Why am I the last to know what's going on?"

Quinn was afraid that Escobar might break down completely. "Did you see Walkaway?" he asked. "Was he here?"

"Yes . . . No . . . Maybe . . . Who can tell?"

"Try."

Escobar brought his head erect and breathed deeply. It seemed to steady him. "Yes. I think it was him. I'm pretty sure. Hipólito would have known for sure. He had the description and the photographs that . . ." Escobar threw a suddenly suspicious look at Quinn. "That we'd been given. He arrived in a plane with some other people. They seemed to be friends of your friends. They've gone now."

"With Walkaway?"

"No. Walkaway went in the other plane, I think. It was a mess. Everyone was shooting. It was horrible."

"Where's Hipólito?"

Escobar's face creased. Tears flooded his eyes. "Dead."

"Dead? Holy cow. How?"

"That bastard Díaz. I tell you, that man is also dead. I will kill them all. Díaz. His goons. Even those friends of yours, *señor*. I don't care what orders I'm given. Now it is simply a matter of honour and revenge. I will kill them as soon as I work out where the fuck they are. Everyone must die!"

Quinn worked his shoulder and winced. He flexed the fingers of his right hand several times. "I know where they're going," he said. "At least, I reckon. It's got to be Florida. I suggest we go there ourselves."

"How?" asked Escobar. "We don' have no plane."

"I can arrange transport," said Quinn. He checked his wallet for credit cards.

* * *

José's eyes were dry and sore. He hadn't blinked for the past hour or so. His head remained rigid as he stared through the *Providence*'s tiny windscreen. The aircraft was so low that the sea seemed to rush straight at them. His entire body was rigid as he anticipated the inevitable crash. His hands took an even firmer grip on the seat cushion.

For the first leg of the flight, José had kept his nerves under control with huge amounts of alcohol. And flying during the night didn't seem so bad. There was nothing to see out of the windows. The stop in Honduras had taken several hours because there were some problems with the aircraft — José preferred not to know what they were. They had set off again just before dawn. When daylight had first peeked through the windows it had woken Díaz. "Go to the cockpit," he whispered to José. "Keep an eye on the pilot. I don't trust them. When we get to Florida, kill them. Kill Escobar too. Kill everyone!"

José didn't much like being in the cockpit. He couldn't escape the fact that he was on a plane. The thought of flying on *La Blanca* had been bad enough, but this plane had half as many engines and was being flown by a half-crazed hippie who, every now and then, would spend fifteen minutes running his hand over the instrument panel looking for the hi-fi before he remembered that this plane didn't have one. They made three more stops, and each time José prayed that it was Florida, and each time it was harder to get back on the plane for the next stage. The sun was up now and José was terrifyingly aware of the remoteness of the ground.

The sight of the instruments and levers and buttons terrified José. He was certain that no-one could understand them all. The entire cockpit looked as though it had been salvaged from a wreck. Every piece of paintwork was worn and scratched. Bright, eroded metal showed on the moving parts. There was rust on the static parts. There were holes where instruments and switches had been removed. To make it worse, the pilot wouldn't stop babbling.

"Oh yeah, man, I know every, like, *inch* of this coast, you know? I mean, they got all kinds of radar now — airborne radar, marine radar, sonar. And they're all out there, man . . ." Squeaker swept an arm across the top of the glareshield. "Customs. Coast Guard. FBI. ATF." Squeaker's hand dropped and he sighed, as though disappointed in the way the world had turned out.

"Uh-huh," croaked José. His throat was so dry and constricted he thought it might have closed off altogether.

"But you see, these are government men. They work to rules and schedules. And they knock-off on time and go home to their families. And I know all their schedules, all the holes in the radar cover, all the planned downtime. Man, I could fly a fucking formation of DC-3s through here and the poor fuckers'd never see 'em."

"Uh-huh."

"Still, pays to be safe." Squeaker eased forward the control yoke. José felt his body lighten a smidgen. The sea came closer still. He looked at the altimeter which Squeaker had pointed out to him. It dropped slightly below the zero mark.

José tried to say "Uh-huh" again, but couldn't get it past the knot in his throat.

Squeaker ran a tender finger over one of the instruments. "I wonder what this is?" he said.

José went light headed. He felt himself slipping. His grip on the seat cushion was no longer enough to keep him upright. His strength drained out of him. But then something appeared in front of them that gave him a tiny shot of energy. It was no more than an indistinct smudge on the horizon, but it was hope. He pointed at the land and squeaked.

"The Keys," said Squeaker. "We'll be over land in about a minute. Then we'll climb, as if we've just taken off from the airport."

José found enough reserves to tense his body again and remain upright. He was surprised at how much he liked the idea of being higher. Heights terrified him, but this wave-top flying was worse.

A beach flashed beneath them. Squeaker rolled the plane on to its right wing tip. José's heart nearly burst and he felt his bowels being crushed in ice. He put a hand against the side window to stop himself falling through it. He stared wildly, his vision blurred with fright, at the ground directly beneath his window. Then the aircraft fell back, wings level.

"Slight course correction," said Squeaker.

"Uh-huh."

José's eyes rolled uncontrollably. He shut them tight. When he opened them again, he saw a small airfield straight ahead, littered with the tiny white crosses of light aircraft. Soon they were over it. Squeaker pushed forward the two throttle levers, made some other adjustments, then pulled back on the yoke. The plane stuck its nose into the air and climbed. With every foot of height they gained, José felt his guts loosen and his chest relax. He started to feel annoyed.

Squeaker squinted through the windscreen at the clear blue sky that now filled it. "Great day for flying, huh?" he asked.

"Fuck you," growled José. Squeaker didn't seem to hear.

At five thousand feet, Squeaker levelled the plane. He set the aircraft's transponder to seven thousand. "On radar we'll look like any other pleasure flight," he explained.

José didn't have the slightest idea what he was talking about. He didn't care. He was pleased to be far above the surface.

"I love Florida, man," said Squeaker. "It's so goddamned *flat*, you know? Ain't nothing much above sea level 'cept condos and a few NASA rockets. You can fly like this, if you want." He let go of the controls, closed his eyes tight, and waved his hands in front of him, in imitation of a blind man.

Fear gripped José's stomach once more and he grabbed the yoke with both hands, knowing that the plane was about to tumble to its doom. The aircraft wobbled slightly.

Squeaker opened his eyes and frowned at José. "What you doing, man? Don't do that—" He slapped José's hands away from the controls. "You don't need to do that. This plane is trimmed right and flies like a dream. This is a real hot ship. She'll fly for hours like this. She don't need your help."

"I've got to do something," said José. He didn't like the begging tone that appeared in his voice, but he couldn't help it. "Give me something to do."

Squeaker grinned. "Sure thing. Now you're talking." He reached into a pocket behind his seat. "How about some navigating?" He handed José a dirty and tattered Rand McNally road atlas of the USA. "I think you'll find we're on page thirteen."

José took the atlas. His hand shook so much that the pages fluttered as if caught by a strong breeze. With some trouble he found page thirteen. He stared at the map uncomprehendingly, unable to divine any correlation between its lines and shades and names and his present situation. Finally, a single name in large type filtered up into his consciousness. "Milwaukee," he said. "Is Milwaukee any good?"

"Shit," said Squeaker. He leaned over and riffled through the atlas until he found the page showing southern Florida. "There ya go," he said. "We're, like . . . um . . . there!" He pointed.

Now José could make the connection between the map and the ground beneath them. For some reason, this made him feel better.

They flew on for some time in silence. José watched Florida unroll beneath them. Gradually, his fear of heights reasserted itself. He gazed at the fields and cities longingly, and his chest ached with the desire to feel solid earth beneath his feet. A vision of the Pope kissing the ground flashed through his head.

"Must be nearly there," said Squeaker.

A list of movie titles rolled through José's head like closing credits. *Airport. Airport 75. Airport 77. Airplane!*

"You, like, know where we are, man?" asked Squeaker.

Mayday at 40,000ft. Alive. Die Hard II.

"Ahem . . . you wanna help me out a little here, buster?"

Flying Down to Rio. José came to with a snap. "What is it?" he asked. "What do you want?"

"Where's the . . . you know . . . like, airfield."

José ran a trembling finger over the map. He tried to calm his fears by concentrating on the map-reading, but he had trouble finding the airport from Sally's description. He turned to another page in the road atlas. "Ain't you got no proper pilot's maps?" he snarled.

"No use," said Squeaker. "They don't show the . . . you know . . . like, monuments, recreation areas, points of interest . . . tourist shit."

Just then, José's finger crossed a tiny aircraft symbol on the map.

"Got it!" he said. His attention shifted between the view outside and the map a few times as he related the real world to the two-dimensional version on his lap. "It's over there," he pointed. "Just past the bridge."

Squeaker's head snapped up, his eyes suddenly alert.

"Did you say bridge?"

* * *

There was something about the doctor's surgery that Hipólito didn't like. This man's a fake, he thought.

The walls were lined with sets of books, their spines uncreased and shiny. There were certificates from unlikely universities. The wood panelling on the desk, walls and door looked like wood-effect paper. And the more he looked at the large bust of Simón Bolívar, the less it looked like marble. He decided eventually that it was cement.

Hipólito lay on an examination couch. His head was still woozy from the anaesthetic. His left side hurt like a bastard. He was pissed off.

The door opened. A tall, thin man in a cheap pinstripe suit came in. "Ah, awake I see," he said. Hipólito growled. "Would you like the good news or the bad news?" asked the doctor with a sadistic smile.

"Give me both right now, without bullshitting me, or I will tear out your liver and feed it to the village dogs."

The doctor's expression only faintly registered the threat. "You shouldn't get too excited," he said. "It could be bad for you. Fatal, in fact."

Hipólito stood up. The doctor backed away, then appeared to think better of it and stepped closer to Hipólito again. He had to crane his neck back to look Hipólito in the face. He adopted a superior expression. "You have a serious problem." He clasped his hands behind his back and rocked up on to the balls of his feet, then back on to his heels. "I'm afraid I couldn't get to the bullet. Not without more invasive surgery than I would care to conduct in this surgery, without access to blood transfusions and sterile conditions. I don't think anything very serious has been damaged, and I have largely stopped the bleeding."

"It hurts like a bitch," grumbled Hipólito.

"Well, I am, after all, a TB specialist." The doctor coughed to clear his throat, as though delivering a calling card. "Actually, I'm rather pleased with my stitching." He held out a hand towards Hipólito's bandaged waist, as if to examine his handiwork. Hipólito growled and the doctor's hand shot back. "Anyway, the bullet is still in there. If it's any consolation, I don't think it was a properly aimed shot. You were just unlucky. From the x-ray, the bullet looks pretty mangled and I'd guess it was a ricochet. Still, it really shouldn't be left in there. You must have it removed soon, before it moves and does heaven knows what other damage."

He arched his eyebrows as if in anticipation of a flood of gratitude. "You've done all you can?" asked Hipólito.

"Yes. No doctor could have done more."

Hipólito turned, picked up his jacket from where it lay on an armchair and put it on.

"Now. About my fees . . ." said the doctor.

Hipólito reached inside his jacket. The doctor backed off, like a dog surprised by a snake. "No guns," he said. "I don't allow guns. The neighbours . . ."

Hipólito drew out his bolas and whipped it around his head a few times. It leapt from his hand and smacked against the bust. Bolívar's severed head thudded heavily to the floor.

"That'll be fine," said the doctor. "Would you like some drugs to go?"

* * *

Rotsky pinched his nose and blew hard into it. The rapid descent had left his ears blocked and buzzing. Behind him, Díaz screamed in agony and terror. Lulu had already suggested dropping him out of the door and Jesus had said nothing to contradict her.

"I'm gonna find out what the fuck's going on," said Rotsky, and headed for the cockpit. When he got there he made a fast scan of the instruments and looked out of the windscreen to judge their height. He noticed that José, in the right seat, was unconscious.

"So, what's our height, about fifty feet?" asked Rotsky.

"That'd be about right," said Squeaker.

Something in the distance caught Rotsky's eye. The aircraft was over the middle of a river headed directly for a bridge. "There's a bridge coming up," he said.

"You bet," said Squeaker.

Rotsky looked at him.

"Hey. Squeaker, you've got your eyes shut, man."

"Yes, Rotsky. I know."

"Is that a good idea?"

"Can you think of a better one?"

He's got a point, thought Rotsky and closed his own eyes. He was aware of a faint *whoosh* above the noise of the engines. He opened his eyes and the bridge had gone. "We're through," he said.

"Thanks, man," said Squeaker. He opened his eyes and calmly pulled the aircraft into a gentle climb, rolling it slightly to the left. "Airfield should be here somewhere . . . yep, there it is. You'd better sit down."

Rotsky moved back to the cabin, sat down and strapped in. Díaz had stopped screaming. "I won't be sorry to see that guy go," muttered Lulu.

Moments later they were on the ground. The landing was so smooth that Rotsky wasn't sure exactly when it had happened. He noticed, however, that they had landed on the grass, not the runway.

Squeaker craned round in the cockpit and yelled back at them. "Here we are, guys. Looks like they had a goddamned . . . you, know . . ."

"What?" shouted Lulu.

"Air raid."

Rotsky peered out of the window. He saw a light twin with its belly to the ground and its props bent. And there were the still-smoking remains of something much larger occupying the end of the runway. The sight of damaged aircraft made him a little nauseous. Something deep inside his skull went cold and hard. He drew the curtain closed.

The *Providence* rolled up close to the airfield office. The engines clattered into silence and Rotsky rubbed his ears with relief. "Where is this?" he asked.

"Home," smiled Lulu.

Rotsky thought about that. "Where's that?" he asked.

Lulu patted Rotsky's hand. "Florida, sweetie. Home of the brave, land of the free, and where the rest of us go heavily armed. At least here we might get some answers."

"Right," grunted Rotsky. He scratched his balls, rubbed his face and stretched, then turned again to Lulu. "What's the question?"

Lulu opened her mouth, then frowned. "Something to do with Walkaway, I guess. And Lady Caine. And I think we should be asking a few questions about Quinn. There's something about him that I don't trust anymore. And then there are those other guys we met down there. Maybe we can find out something about them . . ."

"That's going to be a lot of questions," yawned Rotsky. "I'd be happy if I could just have a talk with Walkaway, find out what the hell's going on and get those feds off my back. Where do we start?"

"I don't know," said Lulu, then dropped her voice to a mutter. "But I know who to ask."

"Can we start on this tomorrow?" said Rotsky. "I got, maybe . . ." he looked at his watch, "you know, not much sleep. I'm beat."

"Me too, honey. But I'm real worried about Walkaway. There seem to be a lot of unhappy people tied up in this thing. Besides, you want to get *Delicious Tricia* back, don't you?"

Rotsky rubbed his temple. "Yeah. You bet. You know, I've been thinking about that . . ." He walked back down the aircraft, opened the door and dropped to the ground. Standing by the office was an old man putting on his glasses. "Hi!" he called. "My name's Rotsky. Anywhere round here we can hire some transport?"

The old man walked towards Rotsky, hand outstretched. They shook. "Name's Jackson. Horatio Jackson. You can rent my pickup, if you like. How long you need it?"

"Couple of days."

"No problem. Fifty bucks a day. Payable in advance."

Rotsky scanned the field. "You got any dogs."

"Nope, sorry. No dogs. You want dogs you'll haveta go into Jacksonville, I guess."

"Good," said Rotsky.

By now Lulu and Sally had joined them. The women nodded to the old man in recognition. He stared at them blankly. "I'll get the truck," he said.

Sally looked worried. "We've still got a few problems with the aircraft," she said. "Mag drop on the left engine. The right's running hot and we're getting through more fuel than we should."

"We'd better get that stuff fixed right away," said Lulu. "I want to be sure we can run if we need to. See what's available here." She glanced around the airfield and pursed her lips. "Get on the phone for whatever else you need. But let's get it fixed today."

"Right." Sally headed for the office.

Jesus dropped from the plane. He turned round and pulled Díaz out. Díaz staggered for a moment, then collapsed on the grass. "Where are we?" he asked, then stretched out unconscious without waiting for an answer.

A rusty pickup truck, mostly white except for the doors, which were red and didn't fit well, rattled across the grass and stopped near the door of the aircraft. Jesus and Horatio got to work moving the cardboard boxes from aircraft to truck. Half-way between the two, a box in his arms, Horatio stopped and stared across the airfield. Rotsky followed his gaze and saw three people, all at least as old as Horatio, dressed in vividly-coloured jogging suits. They were close to the burned wreck. Seeing the dead plane again gave Rotsky a jolt and took his mind off the old people for a moment. It took him a little while, but he finally recognized the faint outlines of a Constellation. He turned to Lulu. "That's *La Blanca*, Lulu. That's the one Walkaway flew out on."

"Sure does look like one of Walkaway's landings," said Lulu.

Suddenly Horatio was shouting at the old people and waving his arms. "Hey you! Get outta here!"

Rotsky saw that two of the old biddies were kneeling by a large pink pool of solidified wax, chipping away chunks. The other walked a little way towards Horatio. Rotsky heard the *snick-snick* as the old guy chambered a round into his pump-action shotgun. "You got a problem, buddy?" he yelled. Horatio went back to loading the boxes. "Goddamned junkies," he muttered.

Half-an-hour later, the boxes were all loaded on to the pickup. Jesus helped Díaz into the vehicle, then went on board the *Providence*. He appeared a moment later with José, who looked groggy. José fell to the ground and kissed it.

"What the fuck you doing?" snarled Jesus.

"What the fuck does it look like?" hissed José, getting to his feet. "Kissing the ground."

"You think you the fucking Pope or somethin'?"

"Fuck you."

"Fuck you."

They glared at each other, then started, as if suddenly noticing their audience.

"We're leaving," said Jesus.

"Ain't you forgetting something, honey?" asked Lulu. "Our commission."

"Fuck your commission," snarled José. He lifted his Uzi. "And you're wrong. Mr Uzi ain't empty."

Jesus looked at the gun nervously. "Is that my Uzi?" he asked.

A chuckle came from within the pickup truck. "Never been fired," muttered Díaz.

Jesus climbed into the truck. José backed to the other door. He waited until Jesus had started the engine, then jumped in. The truck screeched away across the airfield.

Squeaker appeared at the door of the aircraft. "No manners, some people," he said. "But they missed a box. Must've slid under the bed."

Rotsky looked at Lulu. "What now?"

"Back to Tico, I guess, and start again, once we've got the *Providence* fixed up."

Horatio tapped Rotsky on the arm. "Are those young fellas gonna bring that truck back?" he asked.

Rotsky thought about this for a moment. "Shouldn't think so," he said.

"Goddamn it!" swore Horatio. "What's the goddamned world coming to?" He should his head. "I've had enough. I'm getting outta here."

"Can we give you a lift anywhere?" asked Lulu. She indicated the *Providence*.

"No, thank you ma'am," said Horatio. "I'm getting the Greyhound to my sister's place in New York. They're crazy there too, but not this bad."

11:
You still don't get it, do you?

Quinn and Escobar walked out into the arrivals hall at Miami airport. They carried no luggage. Their clothes were creased and they each wore stubble and tired frowns. Escobar was especially exhausted because for the past two hours he had been forced to listen to Quinn complain about his aches and pains. All the same, the flight had been useful time. He had calmed down. He was no longer driven by a confused passion for revenge. He simply wanted to kill everyone he'd met in the past few days. That included Quinn.

He needed a drink.

Escobar saw that Quinn was craning his neck, looking around. "You expecting someone?" Escobar asked.

"Yeah," said Quinn. "I called ahead from Bogotá. There they are." Quinn lifted his head and tilted it back in a beckoning motion. Escobar picked out the two men he had signalled. They both wore sober suits. Escobar noticed that one of them had amazingly shiny shoes. The other wore sneakers.

The men shook hands with Quinn. "How's it going?" asked Shiny Shoes.

"—going," said Sneakers, staring at the ground.

"It's a total fuck-up," said Quinn. From their expressions, Escobar guessed that the men in suits didn't like this reply. "But let's not talk about this here. You got a car?"

Shiny Shoes nodded and led them towards the door. He noticed that Quinn was limping. "What the fuck's wrong with you?"

"Damned hip," said Quinn. "Seems to be getting worse. And the sciatica's playing up again. And I think I'm getting these veins in my leg—"

"—Is that the car?" They were outside now. Escobar had indicated a large, black Buick. Shiny Shoes nodded. So did Sneakers. In fact, it looked for a while as though Sneakers wouldn't stop nodding. They piled into the car, the suits in the front, Quinn and Escobar in the back. Escobar was dismayed to see that Sneakers had got behind the wheel. He didn't trust this man. He added him to the execution list.

They sat in silence for a moment. Sneakers stared at the wheel. "Key," said Shiny Shoes softly. Sneakers nodded as though suddenly awakened, pulled a key from his jacket pocket and started the engine. He put his hands on the wheel and fell back into his reverie. "Parking brake," said Shiny Shoes. "Select drive." He then turned to the back-seat passengers. "Don't worry. He's fine when he gets going."

The car pulled out and headed for the Interstate. Shiny Shoes twisted round in his seat to talk to Quinn and Escobar. From time to time he reached across, grabbed the wheel, and made small steering corrections.

Escobar liked the car, and he liked being in the back. It was nearly a limo, he felt. The car was appropriate to his station. People would look and think that the other three men were his bodyguards.

"Did Walkaway turn up?" asked Shiny Shoes.

"Well..." Quinn threw a look at Escobar. "We think so."

"Was he carrying the briefcase?"

"I don't know," said Quinn.

"Yes! Yes!" interrupted Escobar. "He had a briefcase. Yes."

Quinn looked at him quizzically. "Last time we talked about this you weren't even sure it was Walkaway. Now you remember the briefcase?"

Escobar felt a fire build inside him. "You doubt my word? I say he had a briefcase. So, he had a briefcase."

"Well... whatever," said Quinn warily.

Shiny Shoes lifted his leg, as though he was about to climb into the back of the car. Instead he reached his foot across and stabbed it briefly on the brake pedal. He collapsed back into his own seat with a grunt.

"So I guess you have no idea of his whereabouts now. Is that right?"

Quinn nodded.

There was something going on here that Escobar didn't like. "I don't get it," he said to Shiny Shoes. "You look like feds to me."

"So what don't you get?"

"Why I'm not under arrest. Hell, I'm the bad guy. You're the good guys. What's the deal?"

"You'd be surprised how much we've got in common."

"Well if you want that scumbag Díaz offed as well, then you're right."

"Díaz isn't important."

"Seems like I heard that before," said Escobar cautiously. "But to me, he is important. It's a matter of honour."

"You still don't get it, do you?" snapped Quinn. He switched into Spanish. *"Who the fuck do you think gave you your orders?"*

"The Corporation," said Escobar uncertainly. He shifted on the seat and glanced around him, as though the whole world had suddenly become dangerously foreign.

"Fuck the corporation. They were never part of this. Oh sure, they've got their own interest in Lady Caine. It's a new market for them. And they want what Walkaway's got too. It'll wipe out that market. But they're way behind us in this."

Recognition hit Escobar like a bullet. It was Quinn's accent — the almost perfect Spanish with a hint of Yankee. Escobar's body took on the density of lead and sagged deep into the seat. He was very tired. He got that cold knot in his stomach that he knew was fear, but he preferred to call excitement. "I'm excited," he whispered to himself. His bottom lip trembled and an eyelid flickered. "I've been working for you all this time?" Escobar felt more comfortable in English for reasons he didn't want to examine. "But you're Corporation. The things you said to me. The orders. The photos. The lights. You were working for the Corporation, I know it."

"So?"

Escobar stared at Shiny Shoes. "But you're feds." He looked back at Quinn with an accusatory sneer — a lawyer about to deliver damning evidence. "And I never saw you before a day or two ago." He ransacked his memory and was alarmed at how vague and confused it was. "You were with Hipólito. He knew you because you knew Rotsky and the blind kid. He gave them a lift. He told me all this. This is all coincidence that we are together here."

"Coincidence my ass," snarled Quinn. "I admit that this isn't exactly how I planned things, but you go with the flow, right? We had you targeted from the beginning. We knew that Díaz was involved in Lady Caine in some way. We had two agents down there. One died in a freak motorboat accident. The other one . . ." He quizzed Shiny Shoes with his eyebrows.

"The other one is missing," said Shiny Shoes. "We gave him the job of making sure that Rotsky and his friends didn't go anywhere. We didn't want them confusing things in Colombia. We wanted them looking for Walkaway here, in the States. I don't know what happened."

"Fucking great," growled Quinn. "Anyway. We wanted to use you to get to Díaz. The more noise you two made, the more likely Walkaway would be to hear of it and get his ass down there. You were the bait."

Escobar rubbed his forehead. "Me? Bait?" He looked around the car. He felt like a prisoner being taken to jail. "And what is so important about Walkaway and this briefcase?"

"You'd have to ask my bosses."

"And who are your bosses?"

"Them." Quinn nodded at the two suits.

Escobar wanted to ask the two men in suits who they were. But he was no longer in control and the realization made him uneasy. He felt very naked and tender without a gun. He looked out of the window in an attempt to orient himself, to gain a fix on his situation, but the scene outside was a hot blur of sun-scorched highways and dusty buildings.

"So why am I here?" he squeaked.

"Maybe you've still got your uses," grumbled Quinn. He turned to stare out of the window, then said, more distantly, "and maybe not."

"Where are we going?" Escobar croaked.

"North," said Shiny Shoes. "Somewhere quiet where people won't notice us."

Escobar had an urgent desire to slide down into the crack at the back of the seat.

"What do you want from me?" he whispered.

* * *

Rotsky was jolted awake when the *Divine Providence*'s wheels hit the ground at Tico. He blinked and brought Lulu into focus.

"How long've I been asleep?"

"About a minute, sweetie."

"Goddammit, I'm tired. You sure we've got to do this today?"

"No time to lose, hon."

They had spent the previous day, all night and most of the morning getting the *Providence* back into shape. There hadn't been time for sleep.

As soon as the aircraft was stopped and shut down, Lulu began making arrangements. She told Sally and Squeaker to stay on board and watch the prisoner. "Try and get some rest," she said, "but Sally, sweetheart, we're gonna need some fuel and supplies, if you get a second."

Lulu went to the bathroom at the back of the plane to freshen up. Rotsky fell into a wing chair and Vinnie shuffled over to him, a worried frown on his face.

"What about me?" Vinnie whispered to Rotsky.

"You better stay here with Sally. She'll look after ya."

"She's got a great voice," said Vinnie. "Really smooth and like ... chocolate, or velvet, or something." He appeared to think about this for a moment. "What's she like?"

"Real hot."

"Oh-oh."

Lulu came back into the cabin wearing jeans, four-inch stilettos and a t-shirt that read: *GET A GRIP, Tampa Church of the Virgin Christ Celibacy Tour '95*. Squeaker's lips moved as he read the words. His eyes wandered up and down as they tracked the letters like contours across Lulu's topography. "Gift from a satisfied customer," she explained, then raised her voice for a general announcement. "If we're not back by twenty-one hundred tomorrow, you guys make yourself scarce."

"Better synchronize watches," said Rotsky. "What've you got?"

"Thirteen fourteen," said Sally.

"One o'clock," said Squeaker.

"Lunch time," said Vinnie.

"Zero eight one four," said Rotsky, "Zulu. Okay."

Squeaker kept staring at his watch. "Man, is that really the time? What date is it?" The others looked at each other and shrugged their shoulders. "It's just that it feels kinda late, you know?" Squeaker stared out of the window at the burnt remains of *La Blanca*. "Guess I'm out of a job, too."

Lulu walked over to him and rested a hand on his shoulder. "You can always stick around with us for a while, hon."

"Oh no," sighed Squeaker. "You know, all the best jobs have gone now. The South Americans have got all corporate and heavy. There's no fun in that shit any more. South Africa's, like, legal and respectable, so a lot of that work's disappeared. Same goes for Russia. Eastern Europe's broke, and besides they've got all these ex-Soviet Air Force pilots flooding the market. Forget Africa, man — bunch o' fucking loonies with RPGs and AK-47s." Squeaker seemed to retreat inside himself for a moment, as if scouring a mental globe. "Asia. Now Asia might be worth a try. How long does it take to fly to, like . . . name me somewhere in Asia."

"Thailand?" ventured Sally.

"Yeah. Thailand."

Sally shrugged. "I guess you could be there tomorrow."

Squeaker's face brightened. "That's it, then. When you guys take off, could you drop me at an airport?"

"Talking of which, hon," Lulu said to Rotsky. "It's time to hit the beauty parlour."

"You think that Nicola broad is going to tell us anything?"

"Oh yes. I think she's going to tell us everything."

Rotsky raised a hand and let it fall again. He closed his eyes. "I could really do with a pick-me-up."

Lulu shrugged. "We've been through this, sweetheart. I could maybe rustle up some strong coffee."

Rotsky threw her a pained expression. Then his eyes fell on a box on the floor. "What about the Lady Caine? Doesn't that have cocaine in it?"

Lulu looked at the box too. "Well . . . yes, I guess it does. I've heard the buzz can last up to eight hours. It's slow-release, you see." Lulu popped open the box and pulled out a couple of pink pellets. "I guess it's worth a try. You do know how to take one of these, don't you?"

"I reckon I can work it out," said Rotsky. "There can't be too many ways to get it wrong."

Lulu turned to the others. "Would you people please mind turning the other way?"

Squeaker walked to the cockpit. Sally put a hand over her eyes, the bum stared at his feet and Vinnie, for reasons known only to himself, closed his eyes. Lulu unbuttoned her jeans. Rotsky watched her do this, suddenly unable to move or think of anything else. She slid her long fingers, hands flat, inside the waistband of the jeans, as though stroking her hips. She started to push the jeans down, then paused. "You too, Rotsky," she said.

Rotsky came around sharply. He unbuckled his belt and dropped his pants. Lulu handed him a pellet and they both squatted, hands disappearing between their legs.

"You know, the Incas believed that if you died with the taste of coca in your mouth, you went to heaven," said Rotsky. "I wonder if this counts."

* * *

Escobar's face had turned bright red and sweat lay over his features like a thick varnish. His arms and legs twitched but remained firmly locked. "I'm not moving until you tell me!" he screamed.

Quinn pulled harder, but Escobar had braced himself solidly against the walls of the toilet stall. "This is Burger King, for fucksakes!" Quinn hissed.

"You want to get us all arrested?"

"You must tell me! Tell me! Tell me!"

"Tell you what for chrissakes?" Quinn let go of Escobar's coat and staggered backwards. A wash basin caught him in the kidneys and we winced. He put a hand down to steady himself. As his fingers met the porcelain they slid across the surface on a layer of grease. Quinn felt nauseous. He looked for a towel to wipe his hand but there was only a hot air blower. He turned to the sink, pumped soap on to his fingers and ran water. It was lukewarm and slightly brown in a way that suggested traces of unstrained sewage. Quinn felt sick again. As he washed, he called over his shoulder. "What is it you want to know?"

There was a thud as Escobar let go of the stall and his feet fell to the floor. "Are you going to kill me?"

Quinn turned to the hot air blower, and threw a glance at Escobar. He was slumped on the toilet, head between his hands.

"I can honestly say," said Quinn, "that killing you forms no part of our current plans." He hit the button. The machine whirred and barely warm air flowed around his outstretched hands. He imagined all manner of germs breeding in the tepid current. With all the noise, he nearly missed Escobar's next comment. "What's that?" shouted Quinn.

"I said, I demand to know what's going on. What happens now?"

The blower stopped so suddenly that it felt to Quinn like a signal to reach for his gun. His hands didn't move, however. He looked at them. Thick ropey veins ran along their backs. There were dark spots in the skin. The joints ached. And his fingers were still wet. He turned and walked towards Escobar, who shrank back in the stall. Quinn leaned on the doorframe.

"Laying human bait hasn't worked," he said. "Now it's time to use what we should've used in the first place."

"What's that?"

"Money. We'll put up a reward for the briefcase."

"But we'll have every weirdo in Florida banging on our door. And there's a lot of them."

"I'm not talking about announcing it on the eleven o'clock news. We just need to get the word out to a few interested parties — dealers, importers, maybe even Rotsky's crew. Walkaway will hear about it soon enough. We'll start with Phyllis."

"Phyllis?"

"She's a big-time dealer. I've met her. I guarantee that anything we say to her will be out on the streets within minutes." Quinn tapped on the doorframe. "It's going to take a while to raise the dough. I'd better get the Tweedle brothers out there on to it straight away." He moved back from the doorway. "Was there anything else?"

"Yes," said Escobar. He pulled himself erect on the toilet seat, chin up. "I want more respect. I want you to treat me properly. Like a . . ."

"—like a what?"

"Just properly."

"Fine. Is that it?"

"And I want the biggest burger they do. No pickle."

Quinn harrumphed and turned towards the exit. Escobar stood and hurriedly pulled up his trousers. He buckled up as he stumbled after Quinn.

"Just one more thing. What if the reward doesn't work?"

Quinn paused in the doorway and smiled at him. "Then we start shooting people."

* * *

Rotsky tried unsuccessfully to stop his eyeballs bouncing around in their sockets. It was getting difficult to focus and he had a feeling that the Mustang's speed had crept past ninety again.

"Lane!" chirped Lulu. Rotsky concentrated hard and managed to get the car back between the blurred white lines. He let his foot off the gas a little.

"Holy shit, this stuff's good," he said. "Are we there yet?"

"Couple of minutes. Turn right."

Rotsky span the wheel. The car lurched and screeched and Rotsky was thrown against the door. *"Straighten up!"* yelled Lulu. Rotsky turned the wheel back and bounced upright again. The Lady Caine had kicked in about five minutes after they dropped off Squeaker at Orlando airport. That had been twenty minutes ago and Rotsky was wondering how long the initial rush would last.

"Shit," he said, "this is almost as much fun as flying *Delicious Tricia*." An ache suddenly flowered inside him. "Jeez, I have *got* to get her back."

"Have you any idea where she is?"

"No, they didn't say."

"What did they say, exactly."

"That they'd impounded the aircraft because of unpaid debts, and that unless I helped them find Walkaway, I'd never see her again. And some stuff about jail and maybe killing me."

"You know, these don't sound like regular feds. You did check that they had actually taken her, didn't you?"

"Why? They said they had."

"And you just believed them?"

"Sure. They ... they were ... they were wearing suits." A billboard flashed by. It said *Repent!* in huge letters. Rotsky didn't have time to read the rest. He read the next one instead. *Snap Up the Fun at Gatorworld!* it instructed. "You know, Lulu, I think it's time to make some calls."

* * *

Hipólito was so busy making his list that at first he didn't hear the stewardess. The list was important. The list defined the entire purpose of his life at that moment.

"Chicken or fish?" asked the stewardess for the fourth time. Hipólito looked at up her. His eyes focused slowly. Her face was round, almost white. He thought she might be made of plastic.

"What?" he said. The stewardess backed away, as far as the narrow aisle would let her. The tray in her hand shook slightly. "Chicken or fish?" she repeated with the hint of a shiver.

Hipólito couldn't get a grip on what she was saying. He couldn't grasp the meaning of chicken or fish, not now, not at a time when his very existence was turning to a new heading, when the momentum of his life was being channelled into a single and terrible purpose.

He ignored her and turned back to his list. He smiled. He liked its terseness, its completeness. The list told the entire story of his future. It was headed 'People to Kill'. He underlined this three times. Underneath, the list itself consisted of two lines:

1. Díaz.
2. The blind kid.

Something intruded into his meditation. It was the voice of the stewardess. He raised his head and smiled at her. She backed away again. There was no tray in her hand now. Instead, she pointed at the vicinity of Hipólito's seat beat.

"Excuse me, sir," she said. "You appear to be bleeding."

* * *

- Lady Caine -

The Mane Drag was heaving when Lulu and Rotsky walked through the door. The smell of unguents and lacquers nearly pushed Rotsky outside again. The sharp scent forced its way through his nose and deep into his skull. Above the chattering voices, Rotsky made out the sound of Mantovani on the hi-fi. His eyes were settling down now, but he still had trouble focusing. All he could make out was a nebulous haze of pastel colours. Finally he identified it as hair. It scintillated and buzzed and chattered. Nicola appeared suddenly through the tinted cloud.

"Busy day," said Lulu. She hugged Nicola in a way that made Rotsky vaguely jealous.

"Anybody would think you two were sisters," he said.

"You could say that," said Nicola.

"Have you got a minute?" asked Lulu. She nodded her head to indicate the melee.

"Sure," said Nicola. "It's been like this since the bust. Made us famous. Plus, it's our last day before the film crew arrives."

"Film crew?"

"Yeah, we're being used as a location for *Miami PD*. Can you believe that? It's supposed to be a hangout for drug dealers. Come into the office."

The chattering noise was clipped to silence as soon as the office door was shut behind them. They all sat. Nicola and Lulu smiled at each other and appeared in no hurry to start a conversation. Rotsky wondered when it would be okay to speak. He took a chance.

"We need some information."

"Seems like we've been through this movie before," said Nicola.

Lulu chuckled. "Yes, but at least you know we're the good guys now."

"What is it you need to know?"

"We need to unload some Lady Caine." Lulu paused. She thought something over. "Actually, that's just the cover. We're still trying to locate Walkaway. It's all wrapped up with Lady Caine, and I figure we need to get to a major dealer. Ask some questions."

Nicola stroked imaginary dust off the surface of the desk beside her. "It's a question I get asked a lot." She looked up and locked eyes with Lulu. "Sure. Why not?" Nicola found a pen and paper and wrote. "This is the name and address of the biggest dealer around here. Phyllis. She's your best bet."

"Thanks sweetheart." Lulu stood, leaned forward and kissed Nicola on the cheek. She stroked Nicola's hair. To Rotsky it seemed to move slightly.

"Something making you nervous, honey?" asked Lulu.

"I'm a bit worried about these film people," said Nicola. "In my situation it doesn't always pay to hang around weird people."

"You can always come up to Tico," said Lulu. "Be with normal people for a while." She waved the piece of paper. "I guess we'll get started with this contact tomorrow morning. You could come with us, or just hang out on the *Providence*."

The mention of the aircraft prodded Rotsky's memory. "Can I use your phone?" he asked.

Nicola just pointed to a handset. She and Lulu seemed to be lost in each other.

Rotsky called six numbers from memory. Three didn't work. One got an answering machine for a massage parlour in Reno. The fifth was busy. Finally he got through to the maintenance company at Stead. He had the information he needed within a couple of minutes.

"They lied," he told Lulu. There was disappointment in his voice. "Nothing's happened to *Delicious Tricia*. I've asked them to deliver. She'll be at Tico tomorrow morning."

"What about the debts?"

"They're putting it on the tab. Told 'em I needed the aircraft to shoot some feds."

* * *

It was early evening, with the heat just abating when Hipólito eased himself from the cab. His bolas fell to the floor. By the time he'd picked it up the cab had already screeched away, leaving behind it a shimmering dust cloud. That'll teach the fucker to hustle for a tip, thought Hipólito.

He stumbled around the airfield, one foot dragging slightly, head rolling. The tarmac beneath him gave up the day's accumulated heat, and Hipólito sweated profusely. His skin was raw and infected. It wasn't doing much for his mood.

Sonofabitch has got to be here somewhere, he thought. This was the third airfield he'd tried. The guy at the last one had told him of a shitbox DC-3 with a gorgeous pilot that hung around Tico. There can't be two, Hipólito reasoned. He took a whiskey bottle from his pocket and knocked back a long slug. It made him dizzier, but it eased the pain a little.

Hipólito rounded the corner of a hangar and there it was. The shabby plane. The one that drove Díaz into a frenzy. The one he'd thought was shot-up and grounded in Colombia, until he'd gone back to look at it and it had vanished. The one with the blind kid.

Hipólito fumbled in a jacket pocket and pulled out the list. The paper was thin and holed along the crease where he had constantly folded and unfolded it. He checked it every few minutes, just to be sure he hadn't forgotten anything. He patted down the jacket and smiled at the reassuring bumps caused by the bolas. He thought briefly about barging his way on to the plane and taking out the kid right now. Maybe Díaz was on board too. He frowned and looked again at the list. Díaz's name was first. A melancholy knot formed in his stomach as he realized that he had no idea where Díaz was. He'd disappeared after the firefight, and Hipólito had assumed he'd flown out on this plane. But even if that was true, there was no guaranteeing he was on it now. And he was first on the list. The kid would have to wait his turn.

Hipólito sat on the ground, against the hangar wall, hidden by some oil drums. He'd decided to wait and see what happened with the aircraft. It was the only plan he could think of. He reached for the bottle and tried not to let his eyes shut.

12:
It might get a tad messy

José and Jesus thought Díaz was joking when he told them to check out local beauty parlours. "No fucking way, man," said José. "You don't get me in those places." Jesus nodded agreement behind José's back.

Díaz was propped up on a motel bed littered with empty whiskey bottles and boxes of pain killers. A syringe was duct-taped to the back of his left hand. From it, a tube ran to a needle buried in his forearm. He was in one his sporadic lucid moments. "You want the fucking money?" he asked.

Jesus moved forward and punched José on the arm. "Yeah, you want the fucking money?" José threw him a look he hoped was both dismissive and threatening. Jesus didn't seem to notice.

"Fuck this," muttered José. He picked up the keys of the rental car and scowled at Jesus. "You coming?"

"Hey!" yelled Díaz. He tapped the syringe on his hand. "Get some more of this."

The first four parlours were a wash-out. The women recoiled in terror when José snapped at them: "You bitches wanna buy some drugs?" At the fifth try, Jesus stayed in the car, sulking. José walked in to find a middle-aged guy in skin-tight Lycra pants, gold chains and a buccaneer's shirt fluffing up an old lady's hair with his fingertips. Otherwise the place was deserted. He turned to face José, taking him in with a fast up-and-down glance. "Anything I can do for you?"

José took a deep breath, took out his pistol and asked: "You need any drugs?"

There was a flash of jewellery. The gun was knocked from José's hand, he was dragged into a back room and pinned against the wall.

"You come in here again, scaring my clients, and I'll rip off your balls and feed them to the sharks at Sea World," hissed the hairdresser.

"Jeez," said José, not the least flustered. "You wouldn't think it was so hard to get rid of a bit of Lady Caine, not in a town like this."

The hairdresser's grip loosened a little. "How many pellets?" he asked.

"About three thousand," said José. "Give or take."

The hairdresser dropped his gaze. He let go of José and backed off. "Too much for me," he said. He rearranged some cans of lacquer on a shelf, without really looking at them. Then he looked at José again, as though weighing him up. "Try the Mane Drag," he said, and gave directions. "They have a bigger customer base. And while you're there . . ." he reached out and tousled José's hair " . . . see if you can get yourself a hot oil treatment."

José picked up his gun on the way out. The old lady was still staring at herself in the mirror, turning her head first one way then the other. "I don't know," she whinnied. "I just don't know."

José said nothing to Jesus when he got back in the car. He followed the hairdresser's instructions to the letter, and wound up back at the same place. He tried again, with the same result. At the third try it worked.

As they pulled into the mall's car park they could only just see the thatch-like roof of the salon above a milling mass of people and vehicles. Fuck, it's a raid, thought José. Then something caught his eye.

"It's a fucking raid," said Jesus.

"Bullshit it's a raid," sneered José. "How many raids you seen use lights." He stabbed a finger at some large floodlights on stands. "Or cameras." He pointed at a video camera on a crane. "Or catering trucks." His finger jabbed again. "This is a fucking movie set."

He parked some distance from the buzzing crowd around the Mane Drag.

They ambled around the edges of the crowd, ignored by the crew. Finally, around the back of the salon, José saw an open door and headed for it. A voice cried "hey you" and José turned to see a thick-set man in a filthy baseball cap, moth-eaten bomber jacket, shades and three-day growth. He headed towards them. In his right hand, held casually by his side, was a Mac-10.

José pulled his pistol and fired a couple of warning rounds into the air then aimed at the man. The surrounding buzz died. Faces turned to stare at him. Then the buzz grew back and José was ignored again by everyone except the man in the bomber jacket. He stood absolutely still. Then he smiled and walked up to José.

Jesus crawled out from behind an upended trash can.

"Hey, you've got those moves down pretty good," said the bomber jacket man. "You guys ever done any acting?"

* * *

Quinn dropped the coins into the slot and pulled the newspaper from under the cover. He raised it before him but only glanced at it. Out of habit he scanned the scene around him, analyzing, trying to commit details to memory. It was an unremarkable small-town street. A few shops. The black Buick was parked in front of a laundrette and Quinn could make out the shape of Escobar slumped in the back. He checked the license plate. Something was wrong. Quinn squinted but still couldn't read the characters on the plate. He rubbed his eyes. Must be more tired than I thought. He looked at the paper. He had to hold it at arm's length before he could read the smaller headlines.

Shiny Shoes emerged from the laundrette carrying a heavy canvas bag. Sneakers followed him, both heading for the car. Quinn dropped the paper in a litter bin and joined them.

"How much?" snapped Quinn once they were inside.

"Hundred grand," said Shiny Shoes.

"—grand," said Sneakers.

"It's all the department would authorize," said Shiny Shoes. "If you want any more it'll take an Act of fucking Congress."

"I guess it'll have to do," grumbled Quinn.

"And we want it back. All of it."

"I'll take care of it," promised Quinn. "The last bit of bait didn't work too well. Maybe this will be a bit tastier." He noticed Escobar pouting. "What's your problem?"

"I don't seem to have been consulted about any of this."

"Consulted?"

"Yes. I would expect to be consulted on all such matters. A man of my position."

"Which is?"

Escobar struggled to find the right word. He failed.

* * *

The noon sun bounced hard off *Delicious Tricia*'s bare metal skin. Rotsky squinted into the glare and searched for his shades, until he realized he was wearing them. The aircraft had just arrived and its cooling engine ticked an irregular beat. She sat nose high as though taking pleasure from scented air. Mechanics had already displaced a few panels on the wings and fuselage, giving her an exhausted, dishevelled appearance.

My god, she's beautiful, thought Rotsky. He hadn't seen her for several months. The P-51 had been hired out to a film company before being flown to Stead for the maintenance. The code letters of a fictitious squadron still adorned her empennage.

A mechanic walked up beside Rotsky. "That yours? She's a babe. Mind if I take a look?"

Rotsky put out an arm to stop him. He couldn't stand the thought of another man touching her, not right now, not when she was still warm. The mechanic studied Rotsky's face and gently took hold of the outstretched arm. "It's just a plane," he whispered.

Rotsky sniffed. "Yeah. You're right. Help me check her over, would you?"

They climbed up the wing-root walkways, either side of the cockpit. The mechanic whistled when he saw the instrument panel. "Jeez, this thing's got everything. VOR. GPS. What's that . . ."

"Police band scanner and radar detector. I like to fly low sometimes."

The mechanic dropped onto all fours and shuffled along the wing to an open gun well.

"Gee, I see you still got the guns fitted. Howd'y'a deactivate them?"

"Deactivate?"

"Yeah, you know. Decommission 'em."

Rotsky looked blankly at the mechanic.

"You know," said the mechanic, "fix 'em so they can't fire."

"What's the point of guns that can't fire?" asked Rotsky. He felt suddenly anxious and moved to the nearest open gun well. He reached inside to touch the gun. It was solid against his fingertips. He relaxed. "That reminds me. Know anywhere around here I can get .50-cal belt ammo?"

The mechanic stared at Rotsky. "Uh . . . no. Besides, you'd have trouble firing these puppies. There's something in the gun ports. Guess the film people must've put 'em there. They're wired to the cockpit, I think."

Rotsky was distracted by a clacking noise behind him. He turned to see Nicola walking across the ramp. She wore a short wrap-around skirt of metallic scarlet that reminded Rotsky of a customized T-bird he'd had back in the seventies.

"Hiya," she yelled and flipped a pastiche of a military salute. "Nice plane." She stopped by the nose, reached up and patted the spinner. "Lulu around?"

Rotsky pointed at the *Providence*. "That's her bird there. I think she's in."

"Thanks. See ya around." Nicola clacked off towards the DC-3.

"Oh man," groaned the mechanic. "She *is* gorgeous." He was on the ground now, in front of the wing, his hand running along the engine cowling. Rotsky watched Nicola approach the *Providence*, then turned to the mechanic again.

"Do me a favour, would you? Check the fluids and gas her up. Wing tanks only. I want the fuselage tank empty."

"Yeah? Why's that?"

"I may need to do some aerobatics. I'll be back in a minute."

As Rotsky reached the *Providence*, Lulu and Nicola were coming out. Rotsky noticed how they constantly touched each other while they were talking. He looked back briefly at *Delicious Tricia*.

"We're going to check out this Phyllis contact," said Lulu. "You coming?"

"No," said Rotsky. "I want to get *Tricia* sorted, maybe make a test flight."

"Okay honey. Here, take this." She handed Rotsky a heavy slab of plastic.

"What the hell's this?"

"It's Sally's phone."

"Phone? There's no wires. How do I plug it in?"

"It's a cellphone Rotsky. Where *have* you been?"

"Somewhere else, apparently."

"Yes, well, anyway . . . I'll call you on it if we find out anything useful."

Rotsky hefted the phone. "Call me anyway," he said.

* * *

Hipólito watched the two women walk to their car, then glanced back at his list. He'd seen the one with the short black hair somewhere before.

A pain stabbed him in the side and he swallowed the last of the distalgesics he had taken from the doctor in Colombia. And the pain reminded him. It had been at the airstrip. This woman had arrived on the plane, the one that had driven Díaz crazy, the one . . .

Anger burned in Hipólito's chest. That someone should shoot *him*. His anger and his shame would not be appeased until those responsible were dead. He read the list again. There was no mention of any women. Hipólito pulled a pencil from his jacket and thought about adding the two women to it. But he didn't know their names, and the two names already on the list seemed to shout at him. Díaz! The blind kid! They must die first.

The women climbed into the old Mustang. Maybe they knew where Díaz was. Or the blind kid.

Hipólito stumbled to his feet, fighting down the pain and nausea. I must follow them, he thought. I must . . .

He couldn't finish the thought, but it didn't matter. Things were happening. He half-ran, half-staggered to a nearby car and pulled a man from the driver's seat. He was vaguely aware of the man screaming. The Mustang moved off. A wave of blinding redness smacked Hipólito around the head. He shook it off, climbed into the car and put it in gear.

* * *

The creature was on his chest again, rock-hard talons digging with deadly purpose between his ribs, huge leathery wings encompassing his head, drawing him into a void of total darkness save for the bloody glow through the thin parched skin of the wings and the sulphurous goat-like eyes boring their evil with dagger pains to the back of his skull and the depths of his soul. As it breathed in it sucked the life from his lungs. As it exhaled it drowned him in the hot stench of despair and decay. Its bat-twisted face loomed closer to his, yellow fangs bared, dripping with unholy poisons.

Boss! it hissed.

He was too weak to resist. A mournful craving for release welled up from his soul and flooded into every part of his being. He gave himself up to the creature. But it didn't move except once more to test his ribs with its claws. Behind the creature, Díaz could make out the monstrous slavering of a satanic hound. It too hissed *Boss!*

Something snatched at his left hand, tugged and clawed, and in an explosion of light, bliss burst from his arm and flooded his body. The shadow lifted and claws withdrew and the creature was gone. A face drifted into Díaz's line of vision. It was José who said, to some unseen presence beside him: "Do you think I gave him enough?"

Díaz found he could move. He looked around. He was back in the motel room, back on the bed. Memories returned. He groaned.

"What happened?" he said. "Did you find out anything?"

"Yeah lots," said José. "We got perfect profiles."

"What?"

"Yeah. Me and him are naturals." José nodded at Jesus, who grinned broadly.

"What the fuck are you talking about?"

"What I'm talking about is that we're handing in our notice, as of this minute. We're going into show business."

Díaz felt himself sink into the mattress as the fugitive strength loaned to him by the drug began to fade. "Have you been sampling the goods?"

"No way. We're clean now. We gotta think of our image. You betta have these." José dropped an Uzi and a pistol on to Díaz's bed.

Díaz's head swam. He wondered if he was really awake.

"Did you find the beauty parlour?" he asked. His eyes fell on the Uzi. He reached out and stroked it. "Never been fired," he muttered in awe.

"Oh sure. Here's what you wanted." José handed Díaz a slip of paper. "That's the name and address of the main dealer. If you like, we'll drop you off there on the way to the location."

"What location?"

"*The* location. As in 'location shoot'."

"What's with all the show biz shit?"

"We been discovered. There was this TV crew there, you know? They was filming *Miami PD*. Shit, I can't believe it. That's my favourite show. This guy — I thought he was an undercover cop, or mafia or something. Jeez, I nearly shot the sonofabitch. Anyway, he says that these actor guys hadn't turned up. They'd gone on a bender down on the Keys and had made a raft and sailed it to Cuba. Some sorta political thing. So this guy — the director — was short two extras. And we got the job. He said we were perfect."

Díaz's eyes opened wider and wider. He thought he might faint. He cast a nervous glance around the room for the return of the creature or its dog.

"So," said José, "we're like these two vice cops. Jesus is the sensitive one and I'm the . . ." he turned to Jesus. "What did he say?"

"The gun-happy paranoid with personal problems."

"Yeah, that's right. Anyway, they're just bit parts but it pays two-fifty a day, the food's free and we get to hang out with some real cool babes."

"But you can't do it. You can't just become actors."

"Oh there was a problem with some guy from the union, but we just took him aside and made him see our point of view. He's happy now. We'll send him flowers and grapes and shit."

* * *

Rotsky was in the *Providence*'s rest room when he heard the voice from outside. "Any chance of a drink?" it called. "If you have one. If you think a drink is appropriate."

Rotsky shook, zipped, yanked the door open and squinted into the light coming through the *Providence*'s main doorway. Part of it was blocked by a slight, hesitant figure. Rotsky was immediately lifted with joy. "Where the fuck have you been?" he said.

Walkaway climbed into the cabin. "Here and there. Hard to say." He moved towards the drinks cabinet but Rotsky intercepted and threw his arms around him. "You fuckwit," said Rotsky. "You've been a real pain in the ass."

"I have?" grinned Walkaway. "Really?"

Rotsky wasn't sure how long he should keep hugging Walkaway, so he let go and opened the drinks cabinet. As he poured the whiskeys he pointed at Vinnie and the tightly-bound bum as though simply reminding Walkaway of their existence. "Sally's out getting supplies," he said. "You missed Lulu and Nicola."

"Nicola?"

"Yes." Rotsky felt suddenly unsure. "Yes . . . I think . . . yes, Nicola. Anyway, they've gone to talk to someone. This whole Lady Caine crap is driving me nuts. You know . . ." A realization flickered across Rotsky's head like a jumping spark. "Wait a minute. You . . ."

"Well, about time." Sally struggled up into the cabin, two large paper bags in her arms. She dumped them on the floor. "Where the hell have you been?"

"Like I said . . ."

"Do you know what a complete pain in the ass you've been?"

"Yes."

That stopped Sally in mid-tirade. She poured herself a drink.

"Could someone please tell me what's going on?" asked Vinnie. He had just taken off his Walkman headphones.

"Walkaway's here," said Rotsky.

"Great!" cried Vinnie. He groped around for his video camera, found it and switched it on. It was pointed at Sally. The tape whirred. After two seconds the red light went out and the machine stopped. "Bloody batteries," mumbled Vinnie. He fiddled with the camera, apparently having lost interest in anything else.

The three adults sat down and sipped whiskey in silence for a while. Then Rotsky noticed the briefcase. "What's that?"

"A briefcase."

"Uh-huh. Same one?"

"Yup."

They drank some more whiskey.

"You know," said Walkaway eventually, "I've watched you all running around, looking for me, looking for this." He tapped the briefcase. Rotsky looked at it again, knowing there was something significant in what Walkaway had just said, that somehow it had shifted the ground a little. "I've been busy too, here and there, but I've spent a lot of time just watching. I saw you in Santa Marta, and at Jackson's strip — times when you didn't know I was there. I've watched Quinn and those other guys, people I don't know and who don't know me, not personally, not as anything but the keeper of this." He tapped the briefcase again, then stroked the plastic, but without apparent pleasure. Rotsky looked hard at the briefcase now, aware that it, not Walkaway, was the cause of everything. "I thought, when I took this briefcase, that it would make something happen," continued Walkaway, "something simple, a straightforward act of retribution or desire or even greed, but something obvious and human that I could participate in, be one of the team, get involved." He took a slug of the whiskey. "Maybe it was too human. I wanted to witness great acts of detection and feats of logic. Instead it was chaotic and random and dangerous." He looked at his feet. "Do you think it's the right time to stop now? How do you know when it has gone on long enough?"

"It's all fucked up and there's nothing you can do about it." All eyes turned to the bum. The gag lay around his neck like a filthy cravat. "That's how you know. You let me go, you never see me again. I'm outta this."

"Is that what we do?" asked Rotsky. "Throw away the briefcase and forget about it? Walkaway's safe. I've got *Delicious Tricia*. What else is there?"

"A lot of ugly people with bad manners and dangerous notions," said Sally. "Lulu and Nicola are still out there among them. Besides, that briefcase intrigues me."

Rotsky picked up the briefcase and turned it over and around, studied it minutely from every angle.

"What are you doing, Rotsky?" asked Sally.

"Just trying to work out what's so special about this briefcase that someone is ready to kill for it."

"Maybe it's got something to do with the *contents*, Rotsky."

Rotsky handed the case to Sally. She pressed the buttons and the catches snicked open. "Unlocked," she said and looked at Walkaway. "What's in here?"

"Not too sure," he said. "I knew it was important from the way that my ex-employers talked about it."

"And they were?"

He shrugged. "Just people. But they took themselves very seriously and they took that briefcase very seriously. Enough to send me a couple of thousand miles with it. I had orders to hand it to one person and one person only."

"Who?" asked three voices at once.

"Quinn."

Sally looked stunned by the use of that name. To Rotsky, it made as much sense as anything else.

"And you never looked inside?" she asked.

"It never seemed like the right moment," shrugged Walkaway.

Sally opened the case, drew out a thick bundle of documents and scanned through them.

"So?" said Rotsky.

Sally didn't answer at first. She frowned, leafed through the documents some more and frowned harder. She looked up at Rotsky and arched her eyebrows.

"Means nothing to me. It's all scientific — tables of figures, graphs, equations and stuff. But look here —" She pointed to the cover page. "This is an FDA report."

"FDA?" asked Vinnie.

"Food and Drug Administration. They do things like approving medicines. Do you think this is anything to do with Lady Caine?"

"Of course it is," sniggered the bum. "Everything is."

Rotsky took the empty case and turned it upside down. "But there's nothing in here." He dropped it and took the papers from Sally. "No drugs, no money, no gold coins. Just . . ." He flicked through the pages, his face registering mounting consternation. "Information."

They handed the documents, one to the other, each leafing through them without a flicker of comprehension.

"What now?" said Rotsky.

"I say we get out of here," said Sally. "The feds are involved in this one way or another. Let's go somewhere quiet, chill out for a few months and see what happens." She walked to the flight deck and came back with the school atlas. She turned page after red-dotted page. "Hmm, tricky. Ah!" She poked at a map of central America. "I've got some friends in Nicaragua." She snapped the atlas shut. "We're fat with fuel and provisions are on board. How about it?"

"I guess we'll wait for Lulu to get back."

"Better still," said Sally, "I'll go get her. She told me where they were heading."

Walkaway volunteered to go with her. "Time to do something positive, I guess."

"And I'll get the P-51 ready," said Rotsky. "I'll fill the long-range tanks and take her too. Might be some work for her down there."

Walkaway picked up the papers, put them back in the briefcase and closed it. "I'll take this," he said. "Maybe it's not over yet."

"What about this guy?" Sally was retying the bum's gag.

"Soon as Lulu and Nicola are back, we'll let him go. Until then " Rotsky looked from one person to the next, counting. "Vinnie, you'd better guard this guy."

"Yeah," said Vinnie. "Right."

* * *

"You know, we sell a lot of these," grinned the salesman. He patted the door of the Winnebago as though it were a faithful dog. "In fact, this'un's the last one I got. Real popular round these parts. You need to stop for any reason — need a sudden nap in the afternoon, or gotta take your medicines — you just pull over and your whole house is right there with you. You got a bed, bathroom . . ."

"No kennel, though," said Billy.

"Kennel?"

"Yeah. We've got a . . . big dog." He threw a conspiratorial look at

Rosita who stood by the door of the used car lot office. She winked and blew him a kiss. "I'm afraid it might get a tad messy. You got anything more . . ." Billy craned his neck to peer around the lot, ". . . practical?" His eyes settled on a medium-size truck with a box-like body. "That looks interesting."

Billy and the salesman walked over to it.

"You bet this is interesting," said the salesman. "We don't sell many of these. That makes it special."

Billy read the words on the side of the truck. 'Attenborough Specialty Meats. High-class abattoir. If it flies, walks or swims, we kill it.'

"Yeah, real nice." The salesman sounded distracted. He was reading the price stuck to the truck's windshield and didn't seem to like what he saw. He turned back to Billy, whose words then filtered through. "Oh yeah, that's right. They went bust. Someone found they were selling meat that didn't agree with folks' ethics."

"Endangered species?"

"English beef. You know there's a lot of retired Texans hereabouts."

Billy opened the back door and patted the side wall. "Thick."

"Yeah, it was refrigerated. Cooling unit's bust, but with those insulated walls stuff'll still stay cool." The salesman narrowed his eyes. "Soundproof, too," he said, taking a chance that he might be making a shrewd comment. "You keep a dog in there, though, and you'll have to open the door at regular intervals to let some air in."

Billy looked back at Rosita who was still smiling. She played with her hair. Billy found this unsettling and astonishingly arousing at the same time. "We'll take it," he said.

The two men walked backed to the office to rejoin Rosita. Inside, she hefted a bag on to the desk and drew out a thick roll of banknotes.

"You take cash?" she asked.

"Lady," said the salesman, his face brighter now, "round here nobody pays with anything else."

A few minutes later, Rosita was at the wheel of the truck, Billy beside her, heading back to the dock to collect the wolf. "Where you gonna start looking?" she asked.

Billy thought this over for a minute. "I know Escobar was looking for Díaz," he said. "And we know that Díaz was trying to bring in Lady Caine. I guess I should start at all the major Caine outlets."

Rosita nodded. "I have many business acquaintances around here. I'll give you a list. They will help you." She looked over at him and broke into a smile that had Billy edging towards the door. "You take care of yourself," she said.

Billy was surprised by the warm flood of gratitude he felt at this remark. He settled back into his seat.

"You come back to me when you're done," said Rosita. "Then we talk about the rest of our lives."

Billy felt cold again.

* * *

Lulu downshifted for the corner, a dab of brake then power on for the curve, never letting the Mustang drop below sixty-five.

"Your mind on something else?" asked Nicola. "You seem to be slowing down."

"Just wondering if we're doing the right thing," said Lulu. "If we should be doing anything at all." She let her foot off the gas and slowed right down. "Isn't your place around here somewhere?" Nicola nodded. "How about we think about this over a cup of coffee?"

They were at Nicola's house in five minutes. As Nicola searched her bag for the door keys, Lulu watched a car draw up. It stopped, lurched and stalled. From it emerged a huge man, his clothes filthy and tattered, blood on his shirt, a scowl on his sweaty face. Lulu recognized him from the airstrip outside Santa Marta. That time, he'd been shooting at her.

"Check your six," she muttered to Nicola.

Nicola turned around and watched as the man approached. He drew what looked like a short skipping rope from inside his jacket. He whirled it like a lasso. It gave out an eerie moan.

"Get the fucking door open and get inside," he hissed.

"How come no-one waits for an invitation these days?" snapped Nicola.

Hipólito shoved them inside, into the kitchen, all the time keeping the hand holding the bolas away from them, keeping the weapon in motion. Lulu noticed how every few seconds his eyes closed as if in pain. Then he would shake his head, his eyes would roll and slowly refocus.

Nicola's heels clacked loudly as she paced to and fro. "Feels like the place is hardly my own any more. People busting in—"

"—save it, *puta*," growled Hipólito. He stumbled forward a step, put a hand out to steady himself. It landed on a mandoline on the breakfast bar. Hipólito screamed and raised the bleeding hand in front of him, staring at it in disbelief. Nicola took a few purposeful steps forward, but Hipólito caught the movement and the bolas flicked out. There was a dull thump and Nicola stumbled backwards, her hands to her head. Hipólito still held the bolas, but now it was limp in his hand. His head wobbled as his gaze roamed the kitchen. His entire face frowned. Something appeared to be confusing him.

"Kitchen," he murmured. "Same."

"What's that, honey?" asked Lulu. She attempted a soothing tone, hoping it would calm down the big man.

"Kitchen. Same. Same as Escobar's." He rubbed a hand over the work surface. "Same as Escobar's. European."

Nicola's voice came from somewhere behind Lulu. "European my ass," she snarled. "It's Le Parisienne. Made in Taiwan."

Hipólito's scowl suggested he didn't like Nicola's negative attitude. He straightened up. "Where's *el loquito* Díaz?" he snapped.

"Long gone," said Lulu. "He took his cargo and left. I don't think we'll see him again."

Hipólito face fell. His eyes sagged. Lulu thought for a second that he might burst into tears. He picked a piece of paper from his pocket and studied it. "The boy," he said. "The blind boy. Where's he?"

His hand shook violently. The bolas flicked and waved like a live snake.

"Why do you ask?" said Lulu. She cast a quick glance at Nicola who stood well back now, one hand still to her head, another against the wall to steady herself. Her eyes were shut tight, her shoulders hunched and a trickle of blood ran down in front of her left ear.

Hipólito looked at the paper again, then at Lulu with a surprised expression, as though the answer to her question was almost too obvious to need stating.

"Because I have to kill him," he said.

"That's what you think, big fella." Nicola pulled herself erect and sashayed towards Hipólito, just the faintest wince betraying her injury. He stared at her with a puzzled frown and span the bolas again, though its arc was erratic. Nicola tore the skirt from around her waist. Hipólito's jaw dropped as his eyes settled on her crotch. Nicola seemed to give a little curtsy, half-turned and span in a blur. Her foot kicked high and the stiletto heel plunged into Hipólito's temple. The bolas whipped out of his hand and he fell back, crunched against the wall, slid down and sat on the floor. His eyes stared straight ahead, unblinking, slightly crossed as though in irritation, past the shoe embedded in his head, into the eternal distance.

Lulu turned to Nicola. "I bet you didn't learn that in the Marines."

"No honey. I picked it up on a Geraldo special on self-defence." Nicola stumbled backwards. Another drop of blood rolled from her temple. "The nasty shit really gave me a crack with that rope thing." She gingerly put a hand to her head. "Dammit."

Nicola hobbled over to Hipólito and tried to pull the shoe from his head. "Damn thing's stuck fast," she grumbled. "Wait here. I'll have to get another pair."

She returned a few seconds later wearing new shoes and with a field dressing pressed to her head. "I'd better get this sorted out," she said. "It's worse than I thought."

"I'll take you to the ER," said Lulu.

"Oh no, honey. I know people who can take care of this stuff privately. People like me aren't always welcome at hospitals."

"You mean drug dealers?"

Nicola looked shocked and hurt.

"No sweetie. I mean ex-Marines in drag." Nicola smoothed down her clothes. "I'll get a cab. You go on ahead. And honey . . ." She touched Lulu gently on the cheek. "Be careful."

* * *

Díaz stared at the door, unable to recall for the moment where he was or why he was there. He remembered José and Jesus pushing him out of the car, but couldn't say for sure if that had been a few seconds ago or a few weeks. A sharp pain shot up his arms. His head span and buzzed and a savage fear tore at his heart as he sensed the shadow of the beast fall over him from behind. He wanted to turn and confront it, look into the face of doom, but before he could twist around his bowels gave out. The septic stench from his hands and ears was now overlaid by a more wretched reek.

He gave the syringe taped to his arm a gentle nudge. Warmth and contentment surged through him. His knees buckled but he remained upright. The world brightened. He regarded the door again. A word floated into his mind, as though whispered by an invisible companion. Phyllis.

"Yes?"

Díaz realized he'd said the word out loud at the same time he realized that the door was now open and a middle-aged woman in a faux leopard-skin sweat suit stood before him. Her nose wrinkled spasmodically and she had already started to back into the house by the time he lifted the Uzi. Jesus' Uzi. He looked at it fondly. Never been fired, he thought, and chuckled. He put the gun's barrel to his nose and sniffed. Never been fired. No. Never been fired. No. Never been fired.

The air around him darkened a tad, and Díaz knew the demons and the blackness and the pain would return soon. He saw a box on the ground beside him and remembered. He stared at the woman.

"Excuse me, madam. Can I interest you in some drugs?"

* * *

José tapped the side of the truck. "An' I'm telling ya man, I heard this fucker growl." He saw Jesus' lips moving and followed his gaze to the words painted on the side of the truck.

"Some kinda meat thing," said Jesus.

A small man walked around the truck towards José and Jesus. He regarded them quizzically, as though trying to place their faces. José felt there was something familiar about him too.

"Hi," said the man. "Do you know where I can find someone called Nicola?"

José jerked his head at the Mane Drag. "She owns that joint, but I don't think she's there." He pulled back his shoulders and raised his chin. "We're making a TV show."

Billy stared at the beauty parlour. "That's a shame," he muttered, then flinched as a serious of loud bangs came from nearby.

"Don't worry about them," said José. "They're blanks. We're doing an action scene."

Jesus was flat on the floor. As he stood he stabbed a finger at the man. "Don' I know you from somewhere?"

Billy stared at him blankly. Then smiled. "Colombia," he said. "The name's Billy Cook."

"Yeah! That's right," chirped José. "From the jungle. The cook who couldn't fucking cook. How ya doin'?"

Jesus seemed less happy to see Billy. "What you got in the truck? My colleague here says he heard growling."

"I'll show you," said Billy. He led them to the back of the truck and threw open the door. Inside was a vicious-looking beast with long, slavering jowls and yellow teeth. Its eyes radiated pain and hate. It paced furiously, back and forth, each time to the limit of the chain that tethered it to the far end of the truck interior.

"Shit!" said José. Instinctively he pointed his gun at the animal. He had been given the automatic pistol just a few minutes earlier by a props man and had been enjoying the familiar feel of it. Now he raised it as a talisman against the evil he felt emanating from the beast.

"Would you mind watching him for a minute?" asked Billy. "I need to leave the door open a while for him to get some air. I won't be long. I just need to ask inside about Nicola."

Without waiting for an answer, he walked off. José and Jesus turned their attention back to the animal.

"It's a tiger," said Jesus.

"Bullshit it's a tiger. That's a hyena, man. Crazy fuckers. Tear your head right off."

"Not with that chain around its neck it won't."

José peered into the truck. "It's kinda dark in there. I want to take a closer look."

The top-heavy truck shook a little as they climbed inside. The beast eyed them malevolently and growled. José thought about getting out.

"I think we should get out," said Jesus.

"You fucking pussy." José took a nervous step forward. The animal shot forward, snarling and drooling. José leaned back. His foot slipped on the saliva-slick floor and he fell heavily. Suddenly his world darkened as the truck's door slammed shut. The murmuring of the animal seemed to come from deep within the blackness, but José could feel the warmth of its corrupt breath. He cocked the pistol.

There was a dazzling flare as Jesus held up a lit match. The beast shrieked and surged forward again. Jesus screamed. José aimed the gun as though holding a cross before a vampire. He fired. The crash stabbed his ears. He fired again, his fear mitigated by his belief in the power of firearms. The animal howled, snapped its jaws and pounced once more. José shook. He fired and fired and the beast lunged and lunged and above its deafening roar José heard the distinct *snack!* of a breaking chain.

* * *

Escobar examined his surroundings. The room contained all the things he'd meant to order from the high-class catalogues he'd stolen from his lawyers' offices. This broad's got money, he thought, then remembered the contents of the canvas bag in his hand. But then, so have I.

Díaz stood holding on to a sideboard, rocking from side to side. There was an Uzi in his other hand, but it hung limply by his side. His eyes roamed randomly around the room. He drooled. Occasionally he threw a spastic glance over his shoulder like a man pursued by hounds.

On a glass-topped coffee table near him lay a cardboard box, opened to reveal scores of small pink pellets.

Phyllis stood a few yards away. One hand squeezed the fingers of the other. She seemed perpetually on the threshold of saying something.

"I came here to set up a deal," said Escobar. He nodded at the box. "But I guess you were already making one." His mind raced. He knew there had to be a way of getting away and keeping the money. His problem lay outside the room. Quinn and the two weird guys were in a car watching the house.

He thought about shooting Díaz and the woman and making a run for it. But he hadn't had a chance to check if the gun Quinn had given him was actually loaded. In any case, the noise would bring them running.

A rat-like scurrying noise turned Escobar's attention to a doorway. Two Pomeranians pattered into the room and made straight for Díaz. To Escobar's amazement, Díaz screamed and staggered backwards. "The hounds!" he howled. "The hounds!" He backed up against a fake Georgian armoire. His hands scrabbled at its surface and finally found a door handle. In a second, Díaz was inside with the door shut. Escobar heard him sob, then sigh and there was silence.

Phyllis' mouth opened and closed and she looked like she might be on the verge of apologizing for her guest's behaviour. The dogs scrabbled at the door of the armoire. Then a noise that Escobar wasn't expecting. The door chime.

He raised his pistol and pulled back the slide. Through the ejection hole he could see that the gun was indeed empty. He held down a small lever on the side of the gun so that the slide snapped all the way back, making it look as though the gun were loaded. "Answer it," he said.

Phyllis took a few tentative steps, never taking her eyes off Escobar, as though testing whether she had heard correctly. He followed her to the front door. She opened it and, without a word, stepped back to let the new arrivals enter.

Sally and Walkaway stepped inside and their eyes fell immediately on Escobar's gun. "Please join us," he said. "Getting to be quite a party." He motioned them towards the living room.

The sight of Walkaway filled Escobar with delight. Now he had everything. The money and the man. All he had to do now was think of what to do with them.

The four of them stood around like early guests at a party trying to think of something to say. A whimpering noise came from the armoire and Sally looked at it. A muffled voice muttered incomprehensibly. The only clear word was "never".

"Have you got a car?" Escobar asked Phyllis. She opened her mouth and nodded yes. "Can I get to it without going out the front?" She nodded again. "Show me. And I'll take our friend along with me." He waved the gun at Walkaway. Then he noticed the briefcase in Walkaway's hand. Maybe it contained more money. Or drugs. "Bring that with you," he said.

Phyllis led them through the house into the garage. She pointed to a bright pink Porsche. "Keys?" asked Escobar. Phyllis pointed to the Porsche again. "Thanks for everything," said Escobar. "It's been nice talking with you." He turned to Walkaway. "You drive."

* * *

The Porsche came straight at her. Lulu swerved and the painfully pink car flashed past. Lulu got only a blurred glimpse of the occupants, but even that was enough to give her an instinctive sense of foreboding about what she would find at Phyllis' place.

Lulu parked the Mustang and locked it. She had already spotted Quinn in another parked car with the two suits. She tried to remember how long it had been since they first approached her. Was it days or weeks? She decided to show no sign of having noticed them.

She was surprised when Sally answered the door and ushered her in.

"Where the hell did you get to?" asked Sally.

"I stopped off for coffee," said Lulu. "What's happened."

Sally quickly filled her in, but Lulu couldn't help being distracted by a strange whimpering noise coming from a large, tasteless armoire. Two ugly dogs were scratching at its door. She made out the words "never" and "fired".

"So what do you think we should do?" asked Sally.

"What? Oh. Ah . . . let's call Rotsky. Maybe he'll think of a way to intercept them, or at least find out where Escobar is headed."

Lulu scanned the room but couldn't see a phone. She turned to a woman with fluffy hair who stood in a corner of the room, shaking. "Phyllis?" The woman nodded. "Phone?" The woman pointed to a large doll dressed in some kind of east European peasant costume. Lulu lifted it to find a gold-coloured cordless phone beneath. "A phone cosy?" The woman nodded.

Lulu sighed and tapped out the number for Sally's cellphone. Rotsky's voice said "yes?" in a way that suggested he was querying his own response more than the caller.

Lulu told him about Escobar kidnapping Walkaway. She got Sally to describe the Porsche and asked Rotsky what they should do. "I'll go looking," he said. "What are you going to do?"

"We'll get back to the *Providence* and fly it down to Jackson's strip. We'll meet you there. I've just got one problem."

"Oh yeah?"

"Quinn's in a car outside with two men in suits."

"That's a problem?"

"It could be. But we'll—"

"—Did you say 'suits'?"

"Yeah."

"Shit." They were silent for a moment. "By the way," asked Rotsky, "what's that whimpering noise?"

* * *

Quinn was napping when the Porsche screeched from the drive, bucked into the road and roared into the distance.

"Sonofabitch! That's Walkaway," screamed Shiny Shoes. "Get after him. We don't want to lose him."

Quinn was having trouble waking up. His head felt like it was stuffed with foam rubber. Everything seemed darker. He had a headache coming. There was a weird echo in the car. He squinted down the road. "Where?" he asked.

Shiny Shoes punched the dashboard. "Shit! The fucker got away again."

Quinn squirmed upright in the seat. His joints creaked and complained. He ran his tongue around his mouth. Some of his teeth wobbled. He ran his hand over his head to smooth his hair and large clumps of it came away in his fingers. He couldn't focus on anything. His ass itched. He reached into a pocket and found it empty. He couldn't remember what he'd been looking for. When he took his hand out again, it trembled badly. "Where are we?" he said.

"Staking out the dealer, for fucksakes."

Quinn remembered then. They had sent Escobar in with the money. He was supposed to show it to Phyllis and tell her it was available to the first person to bring Walkaway in. Then Walkaway had turned up anyway, with Sally. Now Lulu was there, and Walkaway was gone. Quinn's headache got worse.

"Was Walkaway driving?" he asked.

"Yeah."

"—yeah."

"Then he ain't going far. Was he alone?"

"It all happened too fast," said Shiny Shoes. "Didn't see anyone with him."

Quinn stared down the street, as though the Porsche might have deposited a clue to its purpose in the dust eddies it left behind. Then he looked at the house. "I wonder what's going on in there."

"Haven't heard any shooting."

"—shooting."

"Then let's go in," said Quinn. He popped open the car door and swung his legs around. "Can someone please help me get out of the car, goddammit."

* * *

Díaz could hear the beasts at the door, the monsters with the heads of lions and the bodies of giant poodles. Their talons clawed through the wood. Soon they would be on him. A wave of unutterable pain convulsed his body. He jabbed at the syringe but it wouldn't move. Now the hounds redoubled their rabid scratching. Díaz sucked on the metal tube in his mouth, taking comfort from the clean, oiled, virgin taste. "Never been fired," he muttered, then said it louder, knowing somehow there was a link between the Uzi and his salvation. "Gotta fire. Never been fired." The pain rocked him again. "*Gotta fire!*" he screamed. "*Never been fired!*"

* * *

Where's that fucking greaseball got to? thought the props man. He'd given the extra the gun because he had whined so much about wanting one, but now he needed it back. The light was fading already and they were securing the set for the day. He needed the gun back so that he could quit work and start making his moves on the new makeup girl.

His stomach rumbled. Goddamn cheapskate productions. He was a vegetarian, but the catering truck served only burgers and hot dogs and there was a limit to how many Snickers bars he could eat in one day. He needed food. He needed a drink. He needed to find that gun.

He stomped around to the back of the beauty parlour. There was no sign of the extra, nothing but a shitty-looking meat truck. He opened the rear door. It was pretty dark inside so he had to look hard. Suddenly he realized what he was looking at. Man, look at all that raw meat. He was knocked back by a wave of nausea, but his stomach rumbled treasonably. He left the door open. Serves 'em right if it goes off, he thought. As he walked away, he thought he heard something growl.

* * *

Lulu was glad she'd thought to bring a gun. She'd said a silent prayer of thanks the second that Quinn and the two suits had walked through the door. She had used the gun to encourage them to talk. A quick frisk by Sally revealed one weapon on Quinn and none on the suits.

Lulu was shocked at how much Quinn had changed in the brief time since Colombia. He stooped badly now. His face was deeply creased and he walked with a pronounced limp. His rheumy eyes seemed unable to focus.

Sally picked up the box of Lady Caine pellets.

"Give me that," snapped Quinn. "I've got to have it." He grabbed the box. After a brief tussle, it fell to the floor and pellets scattered across the carpet. Quinn fell to his knees and feverishly gathered a couple of handfuls.

"You used the last lot already?" said Phyllis. A cup of camomile tea, made by Sally, had restored her equilibrium. There was a small, shiny gun in her hand, aimed steadily at Quinn. He appeared not to notice. "Fella, you got it bad," she told him.

"You taking this shit?" asked Shiny Shoes. "You a Caine junky?"

"What's it to you?"

"What the fuck for?"

"Because I want to live forever, okay?"

"But your life's shit."

"I know, but it's the only one I got."

Quinn remained on his knees. He stared at the pellets in his hands as though he'd forgotten why he wanted them.

Lulu aimed her gun squarely at Shiny Shoes. "Where do you guys fit into all of this? You friends of Quinn? If so, how come you're not armed."

"We don't generally carry guns in our line of business. That's why we hire people like Quinn."

"—Quinn," said Sneakers.

Shiny Shoes turned and threw Sneakers a warning glare. He nodded towards a sofa. Sneakers sat in it and stared sullenly at his shoes.

"And your line of business would be . . .?" asked Lulu.

Shiny Shoes threw Lulu a mute smile. One corner of his mouth twitched slightly. There was sweat on his forehead and he rubbed the palms of his hands against his thighs. His gaze was locked on Lulu's gun.

Lulu moved closer and pressed the barrel of the gun against Shiny Shoes' chest.

"Please don't do that," he said.

"Are you gentlemen operating in some kind of official capacity?" asked Lulu. Shiny Shoes nodded. "And this would have something to do with Lady Caine?" Another nod. "You some kind of expert?"

Shiny Shoes inhaled deeply as though gathering his courage. He raised his chin. "Maybe," he said.

Lulu tapped the gun on his chest. "So tell me, how does this stuff slow down ageing," she asked.

Shiny Shoes shook. The strength he'd just summoned flooded out of him. "If I tell you, will you stop pointing that gun at me?"

Lulu stepped back and let the gun drop to her side. "Sure," she said.

Shiny Shoes wiped his brow. "Thank you. That really wasn't very pleasant."

"So, tell me—"

"—the answer is that it doesn't," he said. He spoke in a flat monotone, the voice of a tired and defeated man. "That's what it says in the papers that Walkaway took it upon himself to borrow. The one that we've spent all this time and money trying to get back." He surveyed the room, as though to confirm that Walkaway, the report and the money were all absent. "It's the FDA report on Lady Caine."

"So it doesn't work at all?" asked Lulu. There was the glimmer of realization at the back of her mind.

"Oh sure, up to a point," Shiny Shoes continued. "In low doses it slows down oxidation of the cells, stops you wrinkling so fast. But once the dose goes up — and with Caine junkies the dose always does go up, 'cause the older they get the more scared they are of dying — you soon build up a tolerance. Once you're over the threshold the side-effects kick in and flood the body with free radicals. At the kind of doses most of these junkies are using, they're ageing about seven years for every year they take the drug. In some cases it's worse, and deterioration in some areas can be very rapid."

"Oh my god," coughed Quinn. "I think I'm gonna puke." He rushed from the room.

There was a silence as Shiny Shoes played contemplatively with one of the pellets. "You know, there's a theory that we're all pre-programmed to live to a certain age. That from the moment we're born, we're destined to die at sixty-five or sixty-seven or ninety-two or whatever, providing nothing gets in the way, like cancer or a runaway truck, and that once you get to the preset age, that's it. An alarm clock goes off inside you and everything stops working. Lady Caine doesn't change that. It just gets you there quicker."

"Is that why you guys are trying to put a lid on this stuff?" asked Lulu.

"What do you mean by 'you guys'?" asked Shiny Shoes.

"Feds," said Lulu. "You're feds of some kind."

"I really don't think—"

The shot made everyone jump. A scream came from the armoire, then quickly faded to a whimper and finally silence. Shiny Shoes was on his knees. The bullet had only just missed his head. Lulu stepped forward and pressed the smoking gun to his temple. "I'm sorry about that, honey, but I'm kinda running out of patience. Now you were about to tell us that you're FBI agents, or CIA?"

"Wr-Wrong." Shiny Shoes sat back on his heels, his head slumped forward, his head in his hands. Then he looked at Lulu, his face creased with resignation. He stood tiredly, walked to an armchair and slumped into it. "We're FDA," he said. "I'm a biochemist. My friend here —" he nodded his head at Sneakers, who grinned broadly and bobbed up and down on his chair, "— is a toxicologist. One of the best. Usually. And no. We're not trying to put a lid on it." He cackled derisively. "Jeez, the government loves this stuff. Did you know the average age of the population in this country will be 60 by the year 2005?"

Lulu didn't.

"Hell, by 2010 the working population will be outnumbered by mossbacks. Already the over-eighties are the fastest-growing section of the population. Do you know how much the retired population costs this country every year?"

Lulu tried to think of a figure, and decided it was pointless.

"A third of the federal budget," continued Shiny Shoes. "Just wait until the baby boomers are all retired. There's a lot of them, a whole chunk of 'em already addled by drugs. Imagine looking after an eighty year-old with no teeth, no bowel control and who reminisces endlessly about an acid trip in sixty-seven, getting laid at Woodstock and how you can't get decent Thai sticks today. Do you really want to change that person's diaper? Besides, old people are a nuisance. The sons of bitches actually vote. Proportionally twice as many of them compared to the general population. So you can't get the old bastards legally. They'll stop any law they don't like. You remember the 1988 Medicare Catastrophic Coverage Act?"

Lulu shook her head.

"Would've—"

There was an incomprehensible yell from the armoire. Shiny Shoes seemed on the point of mentioning it, but chose to continue.

"Would've made the wrinkly SOBs pay towards their health bills. But they crushed it. They got organized and motivated in ways that your commie or union activist can only dream about. Hell, the government doesn't want people to stop taking Lady Caine, they want more people to do it. They just want them to do it illegally. That way there's no comeback, no recriminations about lack of federal oversight or drug approval. No work for the lawyers. That's why it's being made top of the agenda in the War on Drugs. Top of the priority list for military logistics. Something like ninety per cent of the CIA's cocaine production is going into Lady Caine this year. And then, if someone's granny dies and they complain, Washington just shrugs its shoulders and says 'hey, we made it illegal, what more can we do?' It's perfect. We don't have to get rid of the old bastards. They're getting rid of themselves."

Sally came into the room with more tea. Lulu sipped hers as she took in the new information. There were bangs from inside the armoire and the sound of demented muttering. The Pomeranians became more frantic in their attempts to get inside.

"So you need to crush this report," said Lulu, "because it might deter people from taking the drug."

"Right."

"And I guess the drug cartels want the same thing, because their business is at stake. So you've been working with the drug barons."

Shiny Shoes laughed. "I have no knowledge of any such relationship."

Lulu gave him a sarcastic smile, then sipped her tea. She thought about threatening him with the gun again, but decided he was beyond that. And besides, she really didn't care about the answer.

"Just as a matter of interest," said Shiny Shoes, "do you have any intention of actually shooting us?" He nodded at the pistol in Lulu's hand.

"No," she said.

"Then I think we'll be leaving. We have to catch up with that Porsche." He stood, took his colleague by the arm and moved towards the front door. Then he paused, as though he'd forgotten something. "Any idea where Quinn got to?" Lulu shook her head. "No matter. We've no further use for him. He's on his own now."

Shiny Shoes walked to the door with Sneakers bobbing alongside him. Lulu turned to Sally. "Let's get back to the *Providence*."

* * *

Rotsky spotted the Porsche on Highway One. The sun was low now, throwing long shadows across the flat landscape. He'd started the search at several thousand feet, up where the sun was still shining brightly, but he couldn't make out one car from another and so had drifted down to two thousand. He had just rolled the P-51 inverted to get a clearer view of the ground and there it was. Doing about ninety, I'd say, he thought. He rolled *Delicious Tricia* upright and pulled into a climbing turn. He needed the altitude to plan his approach. The aircraft bucked underneath him, sensitive to the slightest touch.

Rotsky climbed to five thousand, away from the highway, then rolled back and put the Mustang into a wide descending turn, aiming to approach the Porsche head-on. The aircraft quickly picked up speed and Rotsky felt through the stick and his backside how the machine had started to punch right through the turbulent Florida atmosphere. He pulled back some of the power but still it got faster. He was through four thousand feet, then three thousand. Now the nose was lined-up with the highway. Rotsky nudged the stick to straighten up. Two thousand and the controls were heavier, the aircraft rock solid. Rotsky flicked the safety off the gun trigger. One thousand and he was picking up ground details. He saw flashing lights around two Winnebagos mashed together at a junction, hearses backed-up at a funeral parlour, a crowded golf course.

Ground level. Rotsky hopped the aircraft over street cables, flying by instinct. A gigantic billboard for haemorrhoid cream flashed past one wingtip, a massive pair of dentures atop a fifty-foot pole past the other.

Rotsky made gentle S-turns, to see beyond the long nose of the P-51. He picked out a small pink dot in the distance. He made minor adjustments to height and direction. His attention was now focused entirely on the pink dot, which grew rapidly.

He wasn't sure exactly what he could achieve, other than to create a diversion, to give Walkaway an opportunity to take control, or get out, or do something. Whatever was about to happen, Rotsky knew Walkaway would survive it. He was, after all, Walkaway.

At this speed, the thoroughbred's friskiness was gone and the aircraft locked onto its target with a terrible certainty. The pink Porsche floated into the crosshairs of the gunsight. Rotsky pulled the trigger. High-intensity strobe lights in the leading edges of the wings flashed brilliantly in perfect mimicry of gunfire. Rotsky felt it a shame there were no cameras rolling.

The Porsche flashed beneath the aircraft and Rotsky pulled up into a steep climb. "Got ya!" he cried.

* * *

Walkaway knew something was out there. He had an instinct for such things. He squinted into the sun, knowing that that was the most likely direction from which death would come. He saw nothing, but when he turned back to the road, brightly coloured dots danced before his eyes.

"Watch what you're doing for fucksakes," yelled Escobar. He sat hunched on the passenger seat clutching the canvas bag and the briefcase.

The Porsche bounced off the kerb and shot a red light. Walkaway was dimly aware of other vehicles but assumed they would take care of themselves. He had enough responsibility with the Porsche.

A distant movement caught Walkaway's eye. A tiny black speck seemed to drop from the sky ahead and hide in the clutter of the buildings and advertising signs. A second later he made out the sharp shape of a fighter heading straight for them. Lights danced along its wings. Escobar had seen it too.

"The sonofabitch is shooting at us!" He ducked down into his seat. The aircraft zoomed over their heads and the Porsche rocked in its wake. Walkaway craned his neck to see if he could follow the plane, but the view from the car was too poor.

"*Look out!*" screamed Escobar. The car mounted the pavement, sideswiped a fire hydrant, ploughed through a hedge, hurtled across a lawn bowls court, into a parking lot, bounced off a Mercedes, a BMW and two Lincoln Continentals, smacked into a ten-foot Pepto-Bismol bottle and hit the wall of a pharmacy. Walkaway sat and listened to the creak of collapsing auto glass and the groan of twisted metal. He felt the trickle of what might be blood on his forehead.

Escobar was slumped in his seat, eyes closed, but with no apparent damage. Walkaway noticed he was breathing.

Walkaway had to force the door open. He stepped from the car, then turned and retrieved the canvas bag and the briefcase. He was aware of other noises now — sirens and shouts. He walked around the far side of the Pepto-Bismol bottle. There was a small door that the crash had popped open. He crawled inside. It was crowded with boxes of drug company leaflets but there was just enough room for him to crouch down. He pulled the door to and listened.

The sirens got suddenly closer and he heard the sound of squealing brakes and tyres. There were shouts of "*Freeze!*" and "*Spread 'em!*". He thought he could hear Escobar's voice, then everything was drowned by the *thudda-thudda* of a helicopter. It landed somewhere near and its engines whined down to silence. A new voice barked "FDA!" and something soft thudded against the side of Walkaway's hiding place. Now he could hear Escobar's voice distinctly, if a little muted by the thick plastic of the bottle. "What's the charge?" he snarled, with what sounded to Walkaway like pride. "Reckless endangerment," said the new voice.

* * *

Phyllis opened the bathroom door. The shiny .22 was still in her hand. She thought of her instructions from Antoine, her hairdresser and supplier, but she'd never killed anyone and didn't like the idea of starting in her own house. She put the gun in her purse. Inside the bathroom, Quinn lay on the floor, drooling, mumbling, eyes rolling wildly. Incontinence had obviously struck suddenly and he hadn't made it to the toilet, though his trousers were around his ankles. Pink pellets were scattered everywhere. He made an attempt to stand, but slipped on the slick floor. He rolled onto hands and knees. His arms collapsed, leaving his ass high in the air. Phyllis noticed another pink pellet, half-inserted. Quinn was still and Phyllis thought she could hear snoring. She shut the toilet door.

Back in the drawing room she paced the carpet while she tried to come to a decision. The Pomeranians were quiet now, exhausted, though muttering still came from the armoire. One of the dogs got up, somewhat dispiritedly and made a half-hearted attempt to paw the door. There was a scream that stabbed Phyllis' nerves, and the voice cried "*Never been fired. Gotta fire. Never been fired. Gotta fire*". Another scream and then the deafening *blatter-blat* of gunfire. Wood splinters cascaded from the top of the armoire. The ceiling shattered in a boiling cloud of bloody plaster.

Phyllis staggered backwards and collapsed into an armchair. She sat still for a while, her head in her hands, while the storm inside her head subsided. Then she drew a deep breath, stood, collected her purse and a wrap. By the front door she paused, drew the small silver gun from her bag and dropped it into a jardiniere. Then she turned to the interior of the house.

"Fuck you all!" she yelled. "I'm going shopping."

* * *

To pass some time, Walkaway clicked open the briefcase. It was very bright inside the Pepto-Bismol bottle. A few moments before, a lamp set into the top had come on. It flashed on and off at about two-second intervals. Walkaway considered for a while that it might be a code, or a warning, but when it didn't stop, and when the duration of each flash didn't vary, he concluded that no-one would go to that much trouble to say so little.

He didn't mind looking inside the briefcase now. It had already been done, so there was little point in reticence. He leafed through the pages during the illuminated spells, idly processing individual words and phrases but reluctant to read properly. Unsure of the provenance of the documents, he was afraid of being told lies.

Walkaway couldn't discern any significance, either from the form of the briefcase's contents or the words. For the first time, he doubted the power of the briefcase. He felt now that he must have been mistaken, that at some time he had misread the signals, that the briefcase was some kind of imposter, that it had all been for nothing.

He waited a couple of hours, until he was sure that the cops had gone. By the time he squirmed out of the bottle it was dark. He walked into the night, leaving the briefcase in the bottle, now convinced of its worthlessness.

* * *

Rotsky rolled the P-51 onto its side and peered down at the ground. At two thousand feet he still enjoyed the final glimmerings of the sun, but the ground was in complete darkness. Nevertheless, he felt he could work out the position of the airstrip from the arrangement of black shapes beneath him.

He got *Delicious Tricia* slowed down, dropped the wheels and flaps, prop into fine pitch, fuel mixture rich and set up for a curving approach to where he thought the strip should be. He made out the dull gleam from Jackson's office window. Within a minute the wheels of the P-51 squeaked gently and Rotsky taxied towards the light. Now he could make out the curved silhouette of the *Divine Providence*. He shut down, climbed out and walked to the DC-3.

Lulu swung open the door as he approached. "How'd it go?" she asked. Rotsky climbed aboard and fixed a drink. He looked around. Sally was asleep on a sofa. Vinnie waved hello from a wing chair, his headphones leaking a rhythmic hiss. There was no sign of the bum.

Lulu had followed his gaze. "He got away," she said. "Just wasn't here when we got back. Sally reckons he could've done it any time. I guess he finally got bored of being tied up." She put ice in Rotsky's drink and stroked his cheek. She looked into his eyes, her brow creased. "Sweetheart, did you find Walkaway?"

"Sure," said Rotsky. "Found him, buzzed him, crashed him."

"Crashed?"

"Yeah, but he's okay. I saw him get out. I guess he'll turn up if he wants to. He knows this place. He'll know where to look for us. The cops got Escobar."

Lulu smiled. "I think we could all do with some sleep."

13:
As good as it gets

In the morning, Sally busied herself preparing the *Providence* for the flight to Nicaragua. Rotsky did the same with Delicious Tricia. They'd planned a dawn departure, but kept finding reasons to delay. At about ten o'clock a taxi pulled up at the office and Walkaway stepped out carrying a canvas bag. Sally and Lulu hugged him as the cab pulled away.

They all sat on the grass and basked silently in the sunshine for a few minutes.

"What happened to the briefcase?" Sally asked.

"It isn't important," said Walkaway. "Didn't think I needed it any more."

"What's in the bag?"

"Money. About a hundred grand."

"Why do you have a bag full of money?"

Walkaway shrugged. "I've no idea. Do you think I shouldn't have it? Is there someone else who should have it?"

An idea occurred to Rotsky. "Yes," he said and nodded at Vinnie. "There's someone who needs it."

Walkaway stood and handed the bag to Vinnie. "Enjoy," he said.

Vinnie stroked the bag.

"There you go, Vinnie," said Rotsky. "A hundred grand. How much did you need to get the family homestead back?"

"About two million," said Vinnie. "Sterling. But never mind. This'll get me a nice little studio flat in Kilburn, some satin sheets, a decent hi-fi, maybe the services of some professional ladies for a while."

"Whatever," said Rotsky. He tugged at some grass. "I guess you're headed back then."

"I suppose."

"Where's your video camera?"

Vinnie poked around on the ground. "Shit. I don't know. Must've left it somewhere."

"So that's it," said Lulu. "Not a bad adventure for these sorry days."

"Adventure?" Rotsky wasn't convinced this was the right word. "All we did was go to Colombia and come back again."

"Honey, that's as good as it gets now."

"I guess." Rotsky nodded. "And you know the best thing?" Rotsky looked around. "No dogs."

Lulu stood, followed by Sally and Walkaway. "We're out of here," said Lulu.

"Sure," said Rotsky. "I'll get Vinnie down to the airport, then follow you in *Tricia*."

Walkaway stalked off purposefully towards the *Providence*. Sally caught up with him and took his arm. "I'll drive," she said.

* * *

Billy dropped on to the deck of the boat. He smiled when Rosita emerged from the wheelhouse.

"Did you find him?" asked Rosita.

"No," said Billy, sheepishly. "And I lost the wolf. I left José and Jesus looking after it and the next thing I saw was the bugger running across the car park. I chased it for a while, but it was getting dark. It'll be fine, though. Probably head down to Miami. No-one'll notice it there. At least it was well-fed. Someone had given it some meat. Quite a lot, really. I stayed in a motel last night and tried the rest of the places on the list this morning, but no luck. Oh yeah, I got your money back for the truck."

He handed her a thick pile of notes.

"Are you coming back to Colombia?" Rosita asked.

"I thought I would. If that's okay?"

Rosita smiled and turned away. She picked up a couple of empty cages and threw them on to the quayside.

"Will you marry me?" spurted Billy.

Rosita turned back. She was still smiling. She reached out and brushed her fingertips across Billy's cheek.

"Sure," she said. "On one condition." Her expression turned serious. "Can you cook?"

www.ingramcontent.com/pod-product-compliance
Ingram Content Group UK Ltd.
Pitfield, Milton Keynes, MK11 3LW, UK
UKHW041257180426
11947UKWH00008B/540